SCATTERLINGS OF AFRICA

by

Peter Davies

Literally Publishing Limited

Scatterlings of Africa

by

Peter Davies

Published by Literally Publishing Limited
www.literallypublishing.com

ISBN(10)   0-9554409-0-4

ISBN(13)   978-0-9554409-0-8

Literally Publishing Ltd
The Covert
Main Street
Claydon
Oxfordshire
OX17 1EU
England

For Lynn

Historical Background

The African continent has a turbulent past... and present. The events in this novel take place during a period when a small, vicious war was being waged over the control of an African country. The country was first formed by white settlers during the 1890s when the new British colony was named Rhodesia. Ninety years later it was renamed Zimbabwe. The country is located in southern Africa, surrounded by South Africa, Mozambique, Zambia and Botswana. The 1960/70s war is often misrepresented as being between black and white; it was more complicated than that. But why were white people there in the first place? Historically, surely only black people occupied Africa?

The first recorded 'European' settlement in South Africa was in 1652, just 32 years after the Pilgrim Fathers' Mayflower arrived in what is now Massachusetts, USA. The South African settlement became Cape Town, and white settlers of Dutch, French and German origin drove far inland over the next 200 years. In 1652, there were no black Africans in the Cape or its hinterland. The native inhabitants were copper coloured Khoikhoi (Hottentot) people, and a few hunter-gatherer San (Bushman) people. While the white settlers were moving east, and inland from the Southern African coast, black 'Bantu' settlers were slowly migrating south and east from their place of origin, some 3,000 miles away in west central Africa. There was no written language in southern or central Africa before Europeans arrived. There were no horses, and no wheels – even the plough was unknown in this vast trackless wilderness. It was called 'the dark continent'.

By 1800, the warrior Bantu Zulu nation occupied the coastal area in the far north-eastern corner of present day South Africa. They began to expand their territorial claims and ruthlessly drove other, less organised black tribes south and west. Refugees from the Zulu Mfecane (the crushing) encountered white settlers in what is now the Eastern Cape Province of South Africa, along the Great Fish River. By 1820 this river, 800 miles from Cape Town, had become the border between black and white settlers, the original Khoikhoi and San inhabitants having been driven by both black and white invaders into the arid areas of the north-west.

Shortly before 1800, the British had taken over the original Dutch administration in Cape Town, a move not welcomed by the descendants of the original European settlers, who by now were called Boers (farmers). The Boers moved further inland to escape British rule, creating two Boer nations. Towards the end of the 1800s, these nations fought two wars of independence against the British. They lost the second Boer War (1899 to 1902), and Britain incorporated the Boer republics into South Africa, with borders that have lasted into the 21st century (including the former Zululand, defeated in battle by the British in 1879).

Meanwhile, British missionaries were exploring the interior, and in 1855, Dr David Livingstone was the first white man to see the mighty Victoria Falls (one of the seven 'natural wonders of the world') on the Zambezi River, which now forms the border between Zimbabwe and Zambia. Even here, the devastation wreaked by the Zulus had taken its toll, and the population in the interior was sparse. As well as marauding south and west into the Cape, the warriors penetrated 1,000 miles north into areas previously occupied by other Bantu tribes. The Zulus took cattle and, if convenient, young women, but slaughtered everyone else during the Mfecane.

The first permanent white settlement in what became Rhodesia was in 1859 – a mission station in the 'Matabeleland' half of the country, which had been occupied a few years earlier by one of several breakaway Zulu factions. This Zulu splinter group called themselves Matabele, and they dominated the weaker neighbouring Shona tribe who lived in the northern half of the country, in an area known as 'Mashonaland'. The Matabele raided there regularly; destroying villages, capturing cattle... and women (as slaves and concubines), and killing the Shona men and children.

In 1890 white settlers (financed by Cecil Rhodes, then Prime Minister of the British Cape Colony) arrived in Mashonaland, and built a fort they named Salisbury in the virgin bush. It became the capital city of Rhodesia. In 1896, the Matabele, alarmed at the prospect of their country becoming overrun by white invaders, revolted. While the white settlers were engaged in fighting the Matabele, the Shona, having prospered under benign white rule, took the opportunity to rebel, slaughtering many isolated white settler families on their newly built farms and mines. The settlers, supported by a small British force, quickly crushed both uprisings and took over the administration of Matabeleland. These rebellions were named the First Chimurenga (war of freedom) by black African Nationalists in the 1960s.

By the 1960s, the white population of Rhodesia was around 250,000, while the black population, Shona and Matabele combined, had mushroomed to some 4 million. During this period, several moderate African political parties had their bases in Rhodesia itself, and were working to increase black political representation in the country's Parliament.

But there were two, more radical (and rival) African Nationalist Organisations, both committed to Marxist principles. They soon fell foul of the law in Rhodesia and moved out of the country. Their support among Rhodesian blacks at the time was limited and, by and large, split tribally. The Matabele supported radicals were backed by the Russian Soviet Union and its allies, and moved to newly independent Zambia (north-west of Rhodesia). The Shona supported radicals were backed by Mao's Communist China, and made their headquarters in newly independent Tanzania (north-east of Rhodesia). Insurgent terrorists from both these groups began attacking Rhodesia in the 1960s. These attacks intensified after Rhodesia made its Unilateral Declaration of Independence from Great Britain in 1965, which was modelled on the 1776 United States Declaration of Independence. Rhodesia's UDI was followed by United Nations sanctions in 1966.

* * *

It is December 1972; Rhodesia stands alone, shunned by the rest of the world. Cracks are starting to appear, the lives of both black and white people are affected as sanctions bite, and terrorism takes its toll...

RHODESIA
MAIN MAP
APPROXIMATE SCALE

0   50   100   150   200
Kilometres

AFRICA

Equator

ZAMBIA

Zambezi River

Chifombo

Chirundu

Mukumbura

Escarpment

Sipolilo

Umvukwes

Mt. Darwin

Mazoe

Salisbury

Victoria Falls

Umtali

BOTSWANA

Bulawayo

Fort Victoria

Plumtree

MOZAMBIQUE

Beitbridge

SOUTH
AFRICA

GLOSSARY

AK 47 "Avtomat Kalashnikova 1947"	Soviet automatic assault rifle
ANC "African National Congress"	South Africa's ruling party (Mandela)
Bantu	Black 'people'
Boer	Descendant of Dutch or Huguenot settlers in South Africa (usually farmer)
Braai	Barbeque
Brew	Mug of tea
Bush	Uncultivated, sparsely settled wilderness
Dagga	Cannabis
Donga	Gulch, wash-away, gully
FN "Fabrique Nationale" (Belgian made)	Semi-automatic assault rifle used by 1970s European and UK troops
Gandanga	Bad person, usually referring to terrorist, or bandit
Ishe	Respectful salutation, equivalent of "Sir"
Jesse bush (*L. Combretum*)	Tough, often impenetrable vine-like thickets up to ten feet tall and twenty feet in circumference – also known as savannah bush-willow
Kilometre	1 mile equals 1.61 kilometres (approx)
Knobkerrie, kerrie	Club formed of hardwood
Kopje	Rocky hillock
Kraal	African village, or a secure holding pen for livestock
Lapa	Literally translates as "there" but means an open, walled courtyard in the context

Madala	Old
Madoda	Adult man or men
Metre	1 metre equals 3.28 feet (approx)
MAG "Mitrailleuse d'Appui General"	FN's 'universal' machine gun (belt fed)
Mboro	Penis
Mukiwa	White 'people'
Musikana	Young girl, approaching puberty
N'ganga	Witch doctor
Recce	Reconnaissance
RLI "Rhodesia Light Infantry"	Crack commando regiment
RPD "Ruchnoy Pulemet Degtyarova"	Light Machine Gun, of Russian or (copied) Chinese origin (drum fed)
Rupert	Nickname for any army officer
Sangoma	Spirit medium (see also Swikwiro below)
Sitrep	Situation report
Skellum	Disreputable looking; Rascal
Skokiaan	Distilled alcohol, used to fortify beer
Swikwiro	Spirit medium (highly influential in African tribal society)
Takkies	Trainers
Terr	Abbreviation for "terrorist"
TTL "Tribal Trust Land"	Equivalent to US Indian Reservation
Tsotsi	Smart ass and con-man/thief
Tula	"Shut up", "Be quiet", "silence"
Veldt	Prairie-like open spaces
ZANLA	Zimbabwe African National Liberation Army (Military arm of ZANU)
ZANU	Zimbabwe African National Union (Mugabe's party)
ZAPU	Zimbabwe African People's Union

x

Chapter 1

Zambezi Valley, December 1972

"Contact... Contact... Contact..." the radio crackled into life; it was the dawn patrol. Lieutenant Ron Cartwright could hear the suppressed excitement in the corporal's voice as he made his report. After nearly two weeks of nothing, this sounded too good to be true. "We've picked up a whole bunch of terrorist tracks... and 'Big Feet' is with them."

Ron scrambled to his feet, spilling his coffee in the process, and rushed closer to hear more. Shit, if it really was that bastard, Big Feet...

Within minutes he was on a chopper, leading seven picked men from his platoon. The terrs would be on their way to infiltrate the land above the Zambezi Valley, for sure. The area behind the escarpment was occupied by African peasant farmers, where terrorists would rapidly blend in among the country folk and become difficult to find. After several years of intimidation up there, the poor bastards were now too afraid to report the presence of gandangas to the authorities.

Half an hour later, they jumped from the two hovering Alouettes onto the tracks. Ron made a last check before raising his thumb, signalling to the pilot that all his men were safely deployed on the ground. No time was wasted – dust and dry vegetation flew as rotor blades bit into the air, and Ron got his fighting patrol going. The chase was on.

They'd been on the go for hours when Ron stopped suddenly, dropped onto one knee in a single fluid movement and froze. Rifle ready in the firing position at his waist, he signalled the rest of the patrol to halt and melt into the bush.

He studied the veldt ahead and to each side of his position, using the sweeping eye-patrol system; the best way to catch real movement, separating it from the mirages that danced before his eyes in the shimmering summer heat. The slightest motion would be detected. Ron knew each of his men would be doing the same, and that the two rearmost soldiers would cover the area behind them. All their lives depended on this.

Confident that his zone was clear, Ron stayed vigilant but his tense muscles eased. At least he'd not led his men into an ambush. Herbie, their leading scout, must have seen something up ahead. There were no birds about, but this was not unusual. They kept to the cooler, green forest during the worst heat of the day. In any event, they would keep clear of human activity in the bush. The background noise of the Valley was still there – a steady screech of insects. Ron allowed his eyes to focus closer in from the middle distance, and saw how the dust lay thick on the small grey leaves of the nearest jesse vine. Shit, but it was a long time since these bushes had felt rain.

The still heat forced more sweat from Ron's forehead below his jungle cap. It mingled with dust, and he could feel rivulets of mud trickle onto his cheeks and running down to form droplets on his chin. Some found their way into his mouth; his teeth were gritty. More sweat dripped from the end of his nose. He wiped it away with his left forearm, still keeping his rifle ready for instant use in his right hand. Hell, they needed the bloody rains to start, especially up there on the Highveld farms.

He sensed, rather than heard heavy movement through the bush nearby and shrank back into the jesse. Then he caught sight of an enormous black shape moving though the scrub. More followed. The rank smell of game assailed his nostrils. They were in the middle of a herd of Cape buffalo, some of the most dangerous animals in Africa.

Tsetse fly came in swarms with the buffalo and settled, easily biting through clothing, especially on Ron's back. No point swatting them. Apart from the danger of alerting the buffalo with the noise, he knew from experience that mere swatting would not shift them. He endured the painful bites stoically.

Suddenly, a buffalo caught the scent of the patrol and stopped. Ron saw the head and horns of a massive bull as it sniffed the air suspiciously a few metres away, moisture darkening the black nostrils, and frothy saliva drooling from its mouth. What a magnificent beast. The damn thing must be eight feet high. Two tons of violent muscle and bone. Ron knew it could move that huge bulk with explosive speed. Shit, he hoped the vicious old bastard wouldn't take it into its head to attack. His FN would be unlikely to stop a charge – just not heavy enough. The rest of the herd all seemed to have stopped, probably waiting for the old bull's signal. That tingling feeling you get when facing imminent and overwhelming physical danger crept over Ron's body and his buttocks tensed. But the old bull snorted, tossed his massive boss, lifted his tail and trotted away, evacuating his bowels noisily as he went. Bloody nearly did the same myself, Ron mused ruefully.

Despite being aware of the human intruders, the herd chose to ignore them as they continued passing through, heading for water or shade. Ron relaxed. It must have been the buffalo that caused Herbie to stop the patrol. Unfortunately, many of the tsetse remained behind to plague them. Easier meat than buffalo.

Moments later, Herbert Zimunya, the patrol's best tracker materialised from the bush a few metres ahead of Ron. His white teeth blazed into a grin which split his black, sweat covered face. "Buffalo all gone, Ishe."

"OK, Herbie." Ron glanced at his watch. "Let's get moving." He saw the corporal struggle with the urge to argue – no doubt pressured by weariness and the fierce heat of the Valley. But they could not afford to relax while the trail was so fresh.

Anticipation of the fight to come twisted Ron's stomach into a tight knot. The terrorist they were after was the biggest game of all; Gadziwa, a notorious leader nicknamed Gumbarishumba by his communist comrades, had outmanoeuvred Ron in previous skirmishes. This time, Ron was determined to finish the bastard. The name translated as 'Lion's Paw', but the Rhodesian soldiers called him Big Feet for obvious reasons. There were 22 terrs including Big Feet, but Ron was confident his fighting patrol could deal with them. He could call for support in the form of helicopter gunships, and more troops could be choppered in if necessary.

* * *

Simeon feared greatly for his life. He'd never been in wild country like this before. He was used to his comfortable home village far away from this place. Here, the soldiers were sure to catch them… and he'd never wanted to take part in the Chimurenga war of freedom against white people anyway. What had the mukiwa ever done to harm him or his family? By contrast, these so-called sons of the soil had kidnapped him and three of his siblings, along with many others, and taken them far from their homes. Simeon cooperated with them because he had no other choice. They'd been force-marched for many days out of Rhodesia, to a distant place across the border in Mozambique, where he'd been trained how to use a gun. But he soon found that his real role was to carry arms and explosives back across the border to Rhodesia – Zimbabwe as they called it. He knew the soldiers would treat him as a terrorist if they caught him with a gun and these people. He was thirsty and tired.

"Hurry up, you!" his section commander shouted at him. "Do you want the soldiers to catch you?" Simeon adjusted his heavy load of land-mines, and forced himself to keep up with the others. Although they'd trained together for a few weeks, his 'comrades' were like strangers to him and came from different parts of the country. They'd already made a long march after completing a frightening night crossing of the wide Zambezi River in small, overloaded dugout canoes. Their objective was the distant escarpment, still many hours away. Simeon could hear the aeroplanes and helicopters of the soldiers constantly flying around, seeking them out. He did not want to die.

They came to a dry riverbed with shady trees and their leader, a famous but cruel man called Gumbarishumba ordered a stop. This was the very man who had beaten Simeon's parents, and taken him away to an existence that seemed to him no better than slavery. Now as they settled down for their rest, they were each given a small ration of water and everyone in sight dozed off. There had been no point in trying to escape while they'd been in a foreign country, but now they were back in Rhodesia...

Simeon slipped away as soon as he dared, leaving his heavy load. He considered throwing his AK47 assault rifle away, but there were many wild animals here and he might need it. He'd try to find someone – a policeman rather than a soldier – to surrender to as quickly as possible. Better still; find a settlement by the River, throw the gun away and no one need ever know he'd been a gandanga. His father and mother would be ashamed of him. How could he explain to them that he feared for the safety of his younger brother and sisters, who were probably still in Mozambique? They had become separated on arrival at the big training camp. He'd heard terrible stories of how girls were used as sex slaves by the gandangas. He did not know where his siblings were. Would his mother and father understand that he'd been powerless to help? After all, he had seen only 16 summers.

Aaaiii… He almost blundered into a herd of buffalo. He fell to the ground and shut his eyes, shaking with fear. Powerful as guns were, he knew he could not defend himself against a whole herd of these terrible animals. And he knew he was not good at using the gun anyway. He sent a silent prayer to his ancestors for protection.

A few minutes later his prayers were answered and the huge creatures moved away, unaware of his fearful presence. It took many more minutes before he could find the courage to move again. But his fear of the comrades coming after him was even greater so he set off, running this time. Home… Mama would welcome him, and Baba would forgive him.

Movement flickered ahead, and a powerful force struck Simeon. He felt no pain, but was surprised to see before him his grandfather and grandmother. They came towards him with their arms open… But how could this be? His grandparents were dead.

* * *

Ron's squad had barely moved away from their buffalo stop, when a black man ran from the bush a few metres in front of him. He came from the side of the tracks they were following. In an instant, Ron saw he was carrying a Kalashnikov carbine – the ubiquitous AK47 of communist armed forces throughout the world.

Crack…Crack… Ron fired from the hip. His favourite method – classic double-tap shooting.

The first of Ron's 762 longs struck the terrorist in the centre of his abdomen. He saw exactly where it hit because there was a puff of dust on the terr's denim jacket at the entry point. It must have struck bone because it stopped the terr in his tracks… even made him stagger backwards slightly. Ron forced the barrel of his rifle down with his left hand the instant before he fired the second time, countering the lift of the weapon from the recoil. Even so, it struck slightly higher than the first, but it finished the job the first round had started. Impact threw the terr down flat, and Ron saw blood spray onto the dusty bush behind him, just before the body hit the ground. The AK flew from the dead man's hands into the jesse behind him. The terr had not even had time to raise it from the position he'd been carrying it in.

Ron dived for cover… Typical terrorist lack of discipline; still, he was relieved that the terr had been carrying the carbine carelessly, making it difficult to fire. But it was likely that more terrorists would follow. "Get down!" His command was superfluous. His men had gone to ground as soon as the first shot was fired, automatically facing out in all directions with their weapons at the ready. Until they knew exactly where the danger lay, they would maintain all round defence.

The sound of his two shots echoed round the bush, ending with the familiar 'whoosh' that seemed to come all the way back from the heights of the escarpment, nine or ten kilometres away. The deep booming whip-crack of the FN was easy to distinguish from the lighter crackling sound of an AK47, so his boys would know which weapon had been fired.

Ron spent the next few seconds waiting... but when nothing happened, his anger got the better of him. "What the fuck are you up to, Zimunya?" His use of Herbie's family name exposed his irritation with the scout. "What kind of shit tracker are you that you can't see a terr running through the bush like a fucking herd of mad elephants?"

"No way that gandanga came from the tracks *I've* been following," Herbie snapped back from the jesse a few metres ahead. "No fucking way," Herbie hardly ever used bad language, "...Ishe." The delayed salutation was another sign of his indignation.

"OK, Herbie, so where the hell did he come from then?" Ron gave him the benefit of the doubt.

"I'm going to take a look around, Ishe." Ron heard Herbie stand up.

"Wait. Stand still... Blignaut, get over here and join Herbie and me on a recce."

"On my way, sir." The soldier directly behind Ron came quickly up the path.

"We're doing a three-sixty, boys," Ron addressed the rest of the squad. "Look out for us, and keep your fingers off the trigger." He wanted everyone to know that the glimpse of an armed man through the bush might be one of their own. He was not anxious to be shot by his own men. "Acknowledge my instruction, each of you."

As soon as he heard Sergeant Njube make the last response from his position at the back of the patrol, Ron quietly ordered his small group to move. Herbie led them along the dead terrorist's tracks, back about 100 metres from where he'd run into their line of march. Then they turned, and went on to complete the full circle round the patrol, crossing the main enemy trail, and back over their own to the lone terr's tracks. It soon became clear that the dead terr had been running on his own.

But Herbie said he'd originally been part of the same gang they were following. "He must have left them earlier this morning to get back here," the tracker surmised thoughtfully. "But why would he come back at all... unless he was running away, to escape from them?"

The way Herbie skilfully separated the terrorist's trail from both game and human markings, and was able to identify individual tracks, reminded Ron of the specialist skills he brought to the platoon. He felt somewhat embarrassed at his earlier outburst but said nothing. Instead, he went to have a look at the dead terrorist and squatted beside him in the dust, turning the body so he could see the face.

Ron considered himself a bit of a hard man, but this threw him. Poor sod was just a teenager. He clenched his fists. Shit... it was always the little guys who suffered most. This poor kid had almost certainly been forced into joining the terrorists. He'd heard reports of gangs abducting young peasants from their homes, and taking them to terrorist training camps in Mozambique and Tanzania. A nagging feeling of remorse struck, but Ron knew he had no alternative other than to kill anyone carrying a weapon down here – it was a case of kill or be killed. Shoot first and ask questions after. A moment's hesitation by him could cost the life of one of his own men. Not something he was prepared to risk.

"Contact... Contact... Contact..." Ron radioed base camp to report the incident and agreed they should waste no more time at the scene. They took the terrorist's weapon and ammunition with them, leaving the body to be recovered later by a support patrol.

The tracks led them to a dry tributary, marked by green riverine bush and a canopy of trees. It was a typical resting place where terrs might set an ambush. They approached cautiously.

There was no ambush, but Herbie confirmed Ron's fears. "This is where they stopped, Ishe." He stood up and moved around the area, before he knelt again where the tracks consolidated on the way out from the sheltered place. "They left in a big hurry, and from the tracks leading out of here, I think they were less than an hour ahead when that fool ran into us."

"Shit!" Ron gave voice to his frustration. There was no doubt in his mind that his earlier shots had caused the hurried departure. "We might have caught the bastards here. Now they know we're right behind them… Damn sure they didn't know before, or the one we killed wouldn't have run straight back into us."

He was about to order them to get going again when Sergeant Mike Njube intervened quietly. "The men are tired, sir."

Ron fought the urge to keep going after the terrorists, now they were hot on the trail. But his men had been on the go almost non-stop for six or seven hours, and would need energy when the fighting started… and Herbie said the terrs were heavily loaded, so they still ought to be able to catch them. "OK, you're right sarge… but keep 'em well spread out in pairs. We'll take a five minute smoke break here in the shade."

Mike went off to have a smoke with the troopies and Ron settled himself comfortably, resting the bulky patrol radio he carried against a convenient tree trunk. The tsetse had gone, but were replaced by mopane flies that swarmed round his eyes, nose and mouth – no longer kept at bay by the motion of his fast walk. He was resigned to the fact that because he was a non-smoker, they targeted him more than the others. He tried to ignore them. These 'flies' were actually minute stingless bees and pretty harmless. Even so, they could drive a man to distraction with their persistent and invasive search for moisture, seeking every orifice in the human body.

Pests like these were just one of the many problems they had to face. But Ron was happy doing what he did best… in the place he loved best. Combining part-time soldiering with civilian life was tricky, and Ron accepted that he was unusual among his fellow Territorials. He looked forward to his stints in the bush. He'd volunteered this time, and felt satisfied that this was his third tour of duty in less than 12 months. There'd been a hell of a fuss at home when he finally got round to telling the wife though.

"Ronnie, this really isn't fair on me or the children." Angela had raised her voice; all the telltale signs of her anger were there. "Especially as there's no need for you to go so often." She'd objected before, but this time she really went for it.

He found her attitude both baffling and irritating, but he'd kept his cool. It was difficult for Ron to explain himself. He always told her it was his duty, but secretly acknowledged to himself there was more to it than that. For one thing, he had this love–hate relationship with the Zambezi Valley. It filled him with both excitement and fear. Here in the Valley, the law of the jungle still held sway. In the early days of the war, he'd been more afraid of wild animals than terrorists. This time even his mother had voiced her concerns, supporting Angela. He shifted uncomfortably. Why couldn't they see that the more often people were out fighting terrorists, the sooner this bloody war would be over?

Ah, well... no time to think about family now, and there was little hope of celebrating the coming New Year – not even a bush celebration, as Christmas had been. Ron glanced at his watch and stood up. "OK, Mike," he signalled Sergeant Njube to get himself and the men ready to move, while he radioed base for a sitrep.

Their company commander, Major Swain came on the radio himself. "We're moving stop groups at the base of the escarpment into your line of march, Ronnie." He'd obviously been busy back at HQ... "And we have fixed wing support – a Trog – on standby for when you need it." Ron took note of his CO's emphasis on the air support being a Trojan. He was making sure Ron didn't expect much from the noisy old piston-engined aeroplane. Well, he hadn't expected one of Rhodesia's few Hawker Hunters... but a Trog?

Not even a Provost, Ron grumbled to himself. But there was no point in calling for air support or reconnaissance yet anyway. The terrorists would not be visible to any aircraft until they emerged from the thick bush.

He settled the radio pack on his back and turned to his soldiers. "Let's go for it, men, it's no good relying on a Trog. We've got to catch 'em ourselves first." The tracks led out of the sparse shade, heading straight through the thick jesse towards the escarpment. That bastard Gadziwa seemed to lead a charmed life. But Jesus H Christ, he couldn't allow the fucker to get away... not again.

Chapter 2

Mark le Roux couldn't help smiling to himself as he drove through Salisbury's light evening traffic. The day's meetings had gone better than he'd expected. New contracts signed and hard US dollar payments arranged. He was going to be pretty busy over the next few months, and his trips to Rhodesia would have to be stepped up. His mother would be pleased...

Leaving the city behind, he headed for the northern suburbs. Yes, on the surface it was hard to see that United Nations sanctions had been in force for six years. Even now, only the absence of new cars and imported luxuries were apparent to him.

He slowed, and turned into the Grevilles' driveway. Subtle outdoor lighting enhanced smooth green lawns, and he glimpsed a tennis court through the trees. Parking the car, he walked to the front of the house. Light from behind amber coloured glass on each side of the door flooded down the curved steps. Loaded down with flowers, chocolates and a couple of bottles of wine, he pressed the doorbell clumsily.

"Hello, Mark." The young woman smiling up at him as she opened the door took him completely by surprise. He'd expected his mother or his aunt.

"Oh, hello..." He paused awkwardly. She obviously knew him, but who the hell was she? "...Long time no see." Bloody weak but just might conceal his confusion. Christ, but she was good looking too. His mind raced.

"You don't know who I am..." she challenged him with a mischievous look in her eyes, clear and sparkling bright.

Yes, there was something about her face... but he still couldn't place her. Damn, she was enjoying his discomfort... it took the edge off his complacent, successful day. "I hate it when a lady has me at a disadvantage," he said lamely. His usual sharp wit had deserted him, and he felt gauche... a disagreeable sensation.

"Oh dear; we can't have that." She raised her eyebrows in mock concern, but softened the gesture with a smile. "I'm Angie. Just spending a few days over the Christmas holidays with my parents. But I'm not surprised you don't recognise me... you didn't take much notice of me when we were children either."

Ah, memories stirred. "I was pretty stupid as a kid..." Of course, Angela was his Uncle John's eldest daughter. "But I've improved with age." He felt his confidence returning. Deliberately holding her eyes with his, he appraised her frankly. "Where on earth have you been all these years?" She must be older than she looked; he tried to remember, probably three or four years younger than him.

She ignored his teasing question, and opened the door wider. "I've just put my children to bed, and was passing the door when you rang."

"I suppose we cousins should greet each other properly?" He stooped down smoothly, but she turned her face slightly and his lips brushed her cheek. She smelled clean and fresh, with the slightest hint of... was it perfume? No – baby powder.

"Your mother's really looking forward to seeing you." She pushed the door closed behind him. "Come, I'll lead the way." He noticed how straight she kept her back – one of those small women who 'walk tall'. She moved gracefully too, and he supposed she must have trained in ballet or gymnastics at some stage.

"How many children do you have?" he asked, his curiosity aroused.

"Three girls; six, four... and three." She looked over her shoulder as she spoke.

Hmmm... His little cousin had become a really attractive woman. The wall lights lit up her short blond hair. "Keeping up the all-girl tradition, hey? You should have a son."

"Three's quite enough," she laughed. "And anyway, I might have another girl."

"Harriet, Mark's arrived," she called out as they reached the sitting room. He greeted his mother affectionately, but his mind was on Angela... or Angie as she called herself. Interest had replaced his earlier irritation. He had a feeling they'd get on rather well.

* * *

Angie sat opposite Mark at the dinner table and studied him covertly. As a schoolgirl she'd had a crush on him; he'd been good looking then and it was no surprise that he'd grown into a handsome man. She'd been looking forward to seeing him again and had momentarily enjoyed his confusion at the front door. As a boy he'd always been so sure of himself and it was rather refreshing to be the one in control. Not for long though – he'd recovered almost immediately and even started teasing her back – no change there then...

At the first opportunity, she asked Mark about himself. He seemed to travel a great deal. Besides visiting London and New York, he also mentioned Europe, North Africa and the Middle East. But although he spoke casually about London and New York, he seemed guarded about the other places. He concentrated on the travel aspects, keeping them laughing with his anecdotes of the peculiarities of foreign customs.

She soon realised that he avoided saying anything about what he did in any of these places. In fact he hadn't mentioned his career at all and, when she asked about it, he dismissed it as "trading", and then smoothly changed the subject.

"It's been a long time since I saw you and your sisters," he said. "What are they doing now?"

Angie smiled; this was beginning to intrigue her. "Mum's the family correspondent, so I'll pass you over to her for that one. She's more up to date with my sisters' news."

Her mother chuckled. "Well, someone has to keep track of you all," she touched the side of her head, "and these grey hairs are testimony."

She was a good storyteller, and Harriet embellished with enthusiasm. Judging by his reactions, Mark was enjoying it all, asking the occasional question to fill in any gaps.

Angie was surprised that he seemed to know so little about them. She knew that her aunt occasionally travelled down to Cape Town to visit him, and she must have mentioned something to him. Perhaps he'd forgotten? But then, most men weren't very good at that sort of thing. And to be fair, she couldn't recall much about him either. Unusually for Harriet, she'd always been rather uncommunicative when she came back from her visits to the Cape. Besides, Angie's own life was too full to think about a cousin she hadn't seen since she was a child. Still, she *could* have made an effort to look up that side of the family during her student years at Cape Town University. She wondered what his wife was like; Harriet never seemed to mention her anymore, and was there still only one child?

"What about *your* family, Mark?" Angie asked.

"They're fine thanks."

"We've seen photos of course." She wasn't going to let him off the hook that easily. "How old is Jack now?" She'd remembered his name at the last minute.

"Seven. It was his birthday a few weeks ago," he smiled. "Twenty small boys running riot – I'm still recovering. Are girls just as manic?"

As she replied, Angie realised that once again he'd turned the conversation around; he was definitely keeping something back.

Her mother asked after Uncle Anton, Mark's father.

"He's very well, thank you." Mark offered the iced water around before topping up his own glass. "Still running the farm at Stellenbosch of course…"

While he carried on talking, Angie glanced over at her aunt to see how she was reacting to the conversation. Her divorce from Mark's father had been pretty traumatic, but that was a long time ago. She wondered how Harriet felt now; it must have been very hard at first, losing both her husband and her son.

Of course, Angie had been too young at the time to understand everything, but she'd finally managed to get the story out of her mother, soon after her 16th birthday.

Mark's father, finding Harriet in what her mother described as a 'compromising situation' with her RAF lover in the 1950s, had flown into a rage – almost killing the young officer. Angie, remembering her uncle as a large and powerful man, could well believe that. But he didn't harm Harriet, in fact he'd arranged for her to divorce him on grounds of 'desertion', rather than publicly accuse her of infidelity. Back in the 50s that would have been very hard on her. However, the price for the arrangement had been that Mark went to live with his father. Harriet had moved into the cottage behind her brother's house, and her nieces had grown up regarding her more as a 'big sister' than an aunt and her little place had become like a second home to them.

Looking across the table, Angie realised that Mark did look a lot like his father, but without the black beard, thank goodness. As a child she had found her uncle quite intimidating, but then she'd only been nine or ten when she'd last seen him.

"How is the banking business, Uncle John?" Mark asked her father during a pause, drawing him into the conversation. Her father was being unusually laconic, quite out of character, and she was puzzled.

"With the rains being so late, the farmers are having a hard time of it. And you know as well as I do the problems with foreign currency and sanctions." Her father paused to sip the wine that Mark had brought from South Africa. "But we get by. This is an excellent wine; Neederberg was always a good estate." He examined the label. "I applaud your taste, Mark. I presume the sanctions-busting business is good?"

The question caught everyone's attention; you could hear a pin drop. So that was why Mark was so careful when talking about his activities. Angie knew her father well enough to detect some disapproval in his voice, either of Mark, or his line of business. She leaned forward to listen.

"We do our best, sir, but it's not easy. As you know, the whole western world is against us." She sensed that Mark had restrained himself from a more aggressive reply, but his tone suggested he didn't want to say more.

There was an uncomfortable gap in the conversation so Angie, surprised by her father's brusque manner, took it upon herself to change the subject. "Would you like to come out to my in-laws' farm for their New Year party, Mark?" She knew her mother-in-law was worried about not having enough men for the event, because so many were away on military service. In fact, she'd mentioned it again on the phone only a few days ago.

"Oh yes, Mark, you must come," Harriet enthused. "It's not far and it's a lovely farm. You'll really like it."

He paused and looked thoughtfully at Angie before replying. "I'd have to change my plans. Are you sure your in-laws won't mind?"

"Not at all. There's plenty of room." Angie was confident. "Besides, we're short of men this year with so many being in the bush. My husband Ronnie has been in the Army since before Christmas."

"Surely he'll be back for New Year though?" Mark arched his eyebrows.

"No. There's no way he'll be able to come," Angie said firmly, "he's only halfway through a four-week call-up."

"That's hard on him... and the family," Mark sympathised.

Recalling her arguments with Ronnie on the subject, Angie doubted that he would be missing her or the children. But she concealed her irritation. "If you come out with the family on Friday afternoon, we'll put you up in a room of your own until New Year's Eve. After that, I'm afraid you'll have to share, because there'll be quite a few people staying over." Mark's work in sanctions busting sounded exciting; he was cosmopolitan and in touch with the outside world, so she was sure he'd be a popular addition to the guests. "Oh, I forgot; do you have enough petrol coupons?"

"I've a full tank; will that be enough to get there and back? The car hire people said I could get extra coupons if needed."

"Lucky you. I wish I could." Rationing was such a pain. "But a full tank is plenty. The farm is out in the Umvukwes district, only about 90 kilometres past Mazoe. It's an easy drive – main roads all the way."

Her father, seemingly making up for his earlier terse attitude, outlined their plans to travel to the farm after lunch on Friday and invited Mark to follow them, so there'd be no problems finding the way. Angie heaved a sigh of relief; the cheerful atmosphere at the dinner table was restored, and she impatiently brushed aside the slightest notion that any residue of her childhood infatuation might have influenced her decision to issue the invitation in the first place.

* * *

Mark was puzzled by Angie's invitation. What motive could she have? Was it as simple as she'd said? Would he be welcome... and did he really want the hassle of changing all his arrangements? He wasn't sure he wanted to spend a whole weekend with a bunch of people he'd never met – especially not New Year.

But as the evening wore on, his interest in her increased. The repartee between Angie and her father revealed sharp minds and mutual affection; she was a polite, sympathetic listener, but not afraid to say what she thought. She displayed a determined and open nature; he couldn't think of any other woman he knew who was quite like this. An intriguing contradiction; a petite, feminine woman, yet full of tomboyish vigour, and certainly no shrinking violet. He recalled the way she'd teased him when he arrived. By the end of the evening, he'd made up his mind.

He already had several invitations lined up for the New Year weekend back in Cape Town, including a big New Year's Eve celebration with some of the City elite. But with a bit of effort, he reckoned he could make his excuses with no harm done.

* * *

"Well, I've had a wonderful time..." Angie listened while Mark thanked her mother and father for their hospitality. He really was quite a charmer, and she could hardly restrain a smile when she saw mother flush with pleasure at his praise for the meal. Harriet said she'd walk with him to his car on the way back to her cottage.

He turned to Angie. "I really will do my best to take you up on your invitation for New Year," he said, taking her hands in his. "I'm almost certain I can make the necessary changes."

"That's great; we'll see you there then."

He looked towards her father. "I'll phone tomorrow if I can't make it, Uncle John; otherwise I'll be here on Friday as planned." When her father acknowledged the arrangement, Mark bent and kissed Angie lightly, keeping his lips against hers a fraction too long, while pressing her hands firmly before he released them. "Until Friday, then."

Angie was amused, and a little embarrassed to find herself blushing; she could just see other women falling for his deep voice and old-fashioned manners. Well, she wasn't about to join his list of conquests. He'd be a perfect match for Charlie though... if he came to the party that is. Her best friend would have no qualms about playing games with him. It was going to be an interesting weekend.

Chapter 3

"Remember it is Big Feet, Ishe," Herbie said diffidently when Ron came alongside. Herbie was dragging his feet, which was why Ron had caught up with him; but he was right to worry. Gadziwa was known to be utterly ruthless, the murderer of scores of his own people; a skilled and cunning military opponent, he was also responsible for the death of at least four soldiers caught in ambush.

Ron didn't break stride, considering his options as he reflected on these unpleasant facts. He could hear Herbie breathing as he kept pace by his shoulder. "I don't think the bastard will try anything down here in the Valley, Herbie, he'll wait until he gets up in the TTLs."

"He is *very* dangerous, Ishe." Herbie rolled his eyes, revealing the whites. His persistence was irritating; Ron knew he was hinting at the ambush they ran into last year, when they'd both narrowly escaped death. The shit had really hit the fan that time, and the memory of it still sent shivers down Ron's spine. He restrained his quick anger. After all, as tracker, it was Herbie who would be the first to run into any ambush.

"He won't try it, Herbie. There's nowhere for him to hide down here." But Ron could still see wariness in his subordinate's eyes and relented. "OK... I'll run in front with you." The terrorists were not trying to cover their tracks now, the trail would be easier to follow, and Ron knew it would reassure Herbie if he were up front with him. Otherwise the little soldier, plucky though he was, would keep slowing down, fearing an ambush at every likely spot – and there were a hell of a lot of those around.

Their chase took them quite abruptly out of the thick bush, as they came closer to the escarpment. "Bravo One to Sunray." Ron delayed the chase long enough for him to call his CO on the radio again.

"This is Sunray. Go, Bravo One." The immediate radio response showed that Swain had been waiting for the call.

"It might be worth trying that air support now, sir. We're out of the jesse."

"OK, it's standing by. Give me your current position. In the meantime, I'll get him airborne."

Ron opened his map case to prepare a grid reference for the Rhodesian Air Force. He could read the country around him like a book, automatically sensing the contours of the land. Features like rivers, streams, hills and valleys, no matter how small, and bone dry at this time of the year, all registered with him as he passed across or within sight of them. They formed a picture in his mind, making it easy for him to translate his surroundings onto a detailed map. In less than a minute, he'd made an accurate fix on their position and passed it back to base.

"OK, you should have fixed-wing overhead within 20 minutes, Ronnie. A chopper has already gone in above the escarpment, to place a stop group along your line of march. There's another one standing by, ready for when you get onto your terrs."

Ron looked at his watch; 20 minutes would give him time to get closer to the enemy.

"They're not heading straight for the escarpment, sir. Running parallel, more like. I reckon they don't want us to know where their bolthole is, up among the locals." Ron started marching again as he spoke. Being in the middle of a hot follow-up gave him radio priority. It was important to keep the gap between him and the terrs as small as possible. Adrenaline would work on the patrol now, keeping exhaustion at bay as they maintained their killing pace after the terrorist gang.

"I can hear the Trog approaching now, sir. Tell him to fly as low as possible. I don't want the terrs to hear, or see him coming until the last possible moment."

"Try him on channel seven yourself if you like." One of the worst things about sanctions was that much of Rhodesia's military equipment was obsolete. Ron could maintain contact with either his company commander, or with the approaching aircraft – not both. 'Talking in' the aircraft had priority. He switched channels.

"Hello, Cyclone Four, this is Bravo One." Ron used the Trojan callsign.

"Got you, Bravo One. Where are you?" The pilot answered immediately, and Ron gave a new grid reference over the air.

"I think the terrs are about four or five Ks ahead of us, probably still just outside the jesse line; see if you can sneak up and give them a blast. I must have them slowed down, or they'll get clean away." There was little chance that the old, single engine aeroplane could 'sneak up' on anyone, much less an opponent as wily as Big Feet, but it was worth a try.

"Shit hot!" Ron was impressed as the pilot flew overhead, the wheels of the aircraft barely clearing the tops of the four-metre high bushes. There was just a chance. The sound of aircraft had been present in the Valley – on and off – all day, and Big Feet might not realise this particular one was close enough to pose a direct threat.

"I've got the bastards visual." The pilot's voice came back almost instantly, betraying his excitement. "I'm going to strafe them as I go in, and I'll drop napalm if I get a chance. At least it'll mark their position for you."

Ron heard the chug-bang, chug-bang sound of the slow firing cannon a second later. The terrs were closer than he thought. He increased the patrol's pace from a fast march to a lope.

Judging by the sound of the aircraft, he guessed that it was only 2,000 metres ahead. Like Herbie had said, the terrorists must be very heavily loaded, really slowing them down. He heard two more short bursts of cannon fire. But even 20-millimetre cannons were too heavy for the Trojan, and Ron could visualise how their recoil would slow the airspeed of the light plane down to almost stalling speed. He waited to hear the 'whump' – and to see the smoke from the napalm bombs.

* * *

Gadziwa cursed when he heard the aeroplane, moments before it came up behind them. They were 50 metres from the nearest jesse, so they had no cover. Shells from the aircraft's cannon exploded as they churned up the dirt around them. He dived to the ground, and in a few seconds the immediate danger was past when the slow, clumsy plane flew over them.

Then he saw the cans, spiralling lazily to the ground. "Bombs!" Gadziwa yelled and rolled away as the first hit the ground, barely three metres from him.

It burst open but failed to ignite. The stink of petrol hung in the air around them. "Run for the bush," Gadziwa sprang up, and looked around to make sure his boys were heading towards cover.

* * *

The pilot's voice burst over Ron's radio. "Shit, shit, shit! ...Napalm's failed to ignite, and the bastards have ducked back into the jesse." He sounded bloody angry.

Stupid bugger must have forgot to arm them, Ron guessed. He knew that for safety reasons, ground crew had to load napalm unarmed; the pilot was supposed to arm the dangerous bombs himself. Well, he hadn't expected much from the Trog but shit, this was a major fuck up... Ron felt pissed off; big time.

* * *

Gadziwa saw Commissar Weiner spit dry dirt and leaves from his mouth, and shake his head as if to clear it. A trickle of blood ran down the side of the man's face, and flies gathered. The half-breed got groggily to his feet and stumbled towards the bushes. Gadziwa made sure that he was last, before he followed them into cover.

"Help," Weiner yelled in panic, "Where is everyone?"

"Come here!" Gadziwa's harsh command was aimed at reaching the entire group and steadying them. He turned back to Weiner. "We must get the boys together quickly. The white dogs will be onto us soon."

"What happened? ... How did they find us?" the commissar demanded.

"You're lucky to be alive; their aeroplane caught us in the open with cannon fire, and it dropped napalm bombs on us." He watched warily as the plane turned slowly in the distance. "But the aeroplane is so old it can't strafe us without falling out of the sky. And their bombs failed to detonate – can't you smell the petrol? If they had worked, we'd be in flames. As it is, I don't think even one of the boys is injured." He signalled the section leaders to collect their men together.

"*I've* been injured." Weiner touched his face gingerly, and his hand came away covered in blood. "Aaah, I'm bleeding heavily!"

Gadziwa stooped to look. "It was a close thing comrade, but your injury is not serious; the dust from an exploding shell has covered your face with black spots, and broken the small veins at the surface. You will be able to wash away the black marks." Gadziwa lost interest. "Unless you want to pretend to be a *real* black man, instead of half-white," he added maliciously, dismissing Weiner from his mind. He had more important things to attend to.

It took him less than a minute to gather his shaken group together and take them deeper back into the bush. Meanwhile he took grim satisfaction at the frustrated pilot flying about overhead, looking fruitlessly for them, and all the while getting further away from his target. He'd outwitted him all right. Now all he had to do was get his men past the soldiers...

Gadziwa quickly decided to double back. That was hazardous, actually taking his demoralised boys towards the enemy soldiers and danger. But he was now desperate, and willing to face a confrontation if it came to it. They were running 500 metres inside the protection of the bush line, and the soldiers would not expect his freedom fighters to be heading towards them. The element of surprise would be on his side.

Chapter 4

Angie left for the farm the day after the dinner party. Her old car ran smoothly, and she felt as if she was on holiday. She loved her children, but it was nice to have this short break without them, and she was glad her mother had persuaded her to leave them behind for an extra day. Despite the wind messing up her hair, she kept the windows wide open; it was just too hot to even think about closing them.

The bush on each side of the road was parched; even the leaves on the trees looked dusty, and the massive bare granite boulders on the kopjes shimmered in the heat. Some farms were irrigated and their lush, green fields made a welcome contrast against the brown bushveld. It was quiet, and there were hardly any other cars on the road. She drove through the few small settlements; dusty little places, each with a corrugated iron roofed store, with a petrol pump in front. Near one, a group of African women – the younger ones with babies wrapped comfortably on their backs – were sitting in the shade of a large tree that served as a bus shelter. The older children interrupted their play, shrieking with joy and energy as they danced and waved excitedly at her approaching car; Angie laughed at their antics and returned their enthusiastic waving. Mazoe even boasted its own café, and there were a few cars parked outside. She'd never seen the water in the dam so low.

An elderly African man in collar and tie was pushing his bicycle up a hill; he paused to raise his hat, and she waved politely to return his dignified country greeting. Slowing down, she turned off the main road and crossed the cattle grid that marked the entrance to Sapphire Blue. Ron's grandmother, inspired by the deep blue colours of the distant Umvukwes Hills, had named the farm, and Angie thought it perfect. Just five more minutes along the sandy gravel road to reach the homestead.

Acres of cultivated land stretched behind the big old blue-gum trees lining the road. Before Britain's Government called for United Nations sanctions against Rhodesia, the main crop had been tobacco.

Now it was maize. The unreliable rainfall was supplemented by an irrigation system. It left a haze of water droplets in the surrounding air, which made the farm feel cooler and moister than the surrounding bush. Angie cared more for the farm than Ronnie did. He was just not interested. She knew that his folks now nourished the hope that her affection for it would, some day, persuade him to come back and gradually take it over from his father.

She'd hoped that too when they were first married. But as time went by, with Ron becoming so preoccupied with the Army, she knew it wouldn't work. She imagined herself stuck in the farmhouse as she got older, the girls going off to boarding school, and Ron away with the Army most of the time. His parents wouldn't be around forever. Besides, farming was a partnership. She'd seen how Ron's parents worked together, in good times and in bad. It wouldn't be like that for her; she'd be left to handle it all on her own. At least in town she had her own family and friends for company.

She slowed again to negotiate the second cattle grid, which protected the two acres of homestead gardens from grazing cattle, and from the wild buck that still roamed the area. This was Kate's domain. Huge leafy trees and shrubs marked the boundary of the long gravel driveway, which led round to the farmhouse. Close-cropped lawns, massed flowerbeds and smaller, flowering trees and shrubs came into view. There were vegetable gardens and orchards round the back, but these weren't visible from the driveway.

She heard deep barking before she saw the two Rhodesian Ridgebacks; big and courageous enough to hunt lion, they had been called 'Lion Dogs' in the old days. It took all Angie's willpower not to bring the car to a halt for fear of running into them as they bounded up, seemingly right in front of the bonnet and against the wheels.

"*Don't* stop for them, Angela, you'll never get anywhere if you do. And they shouldn't chase the damn car anyway," Ron always told her. "Ignore them and they'll keep out of your way." But it was hard to follow his advice, and she felt as if he was here now, impatiently criticising her again. It was not just what he said, but the way he spoke to her; the last time they'd visited the farm together and she was driving, he'd ended by snapping "Stop buggering about, woman."

She'd told him not to speak to her as if she was one of his soldiers and, as usual, there'd been a row. Darn it, he didn't talk like that when her parents, or his for that matter, were around. Just thinking about it made her angry and it spoiled her mood.

"Get down, Ben, get down, Sheba," she shouted crossly at them, but managed to keep the car moving until she reached the front of the house. As soon as she stopped, both dogs jumped up to greet her through the car's open window – their laughing jaws on a level with her face. She tried to push Ben's head out of the window to stop him slobbering all over her clothes, but her hand slipped into his open mouth and became covered with saliva.

"Yeugh, you messy dogs," she complained, but their exuberant greeting took her mind off her problems, and helped restore her happy mood. Old Joseph the head-gardener materialised and grabbed the dogs, while Angie used the tissues she kept in the glove compartment to clean up. One of the longest serving of the Cartwright employees, Joseph had worked for Ronnie's grandfather, his 'Nkosi', even before Ronnie's father had been born; he'd travelled up from South Africa's Eastern Cape with the old folk by train, ox-wagon and horse-cart back in 1910.

"Welcome, missus." His almost toothless smile and cheery greeting made her feel at home again. He hauled on their collars and the dogs allowed him to pull them back further, so she could open the car door easily.

Angie replied in the Shona language, which she practised whenever she was with him. "Thank you, Joseph. How are you?" She got out of the car and fussed with the dogs to ease the strain on the old man. That unique scent, given off by well-watered plants growing within an intensely dry climate, greeted her like another old friend. All so well remembered in this peaceful and prosperous place.

"I am old but still strong, missus." Joseph clearly enjoyed speaking his own language with her, and corrected her grammar when necessary. "Baas Ronnie still in the bush?" he asked, while one of his assistants came to carry her luggage to the top of the verandah steps.

"Yes, but I'm expecting him back in about two weeks. How did Connie do with her finals?" Joseph's granddaughter was studying at the University of Rhodesia, and the old man told Angie he was confident that she would pass. Ronnie's father encouraged all his employees to send their children to school at a nearby farm, and he sponsored anyone who showed sufficient aptitude through higher education.

The dogs calmed down enough for Joseph to release their collars, but it took another minute of Angie's attention to settle them. Finally satisfied, they went to flop down in the dappled shade of nearby frangipani trees, the dog's long pink tongues hanging out as they panted in the heat. Joseph said his farewells, and peace was restored. Angie revelled in the comparative silence, but the background screech of the cicadas soon returned, seeming to increase in volume until it dominated everything.

She paused by the steps leading up to the verandah, which ran right around the building. This was her favourite house, and without the children being there to distract her, she took the opportunity to appreciate it again. To anyone not used to the old colonial style home, it looked as if the deep thatched roof had been made much too large for the building... but the overhang played a role in keeping the place cool, and storm-water off the foundations. Solid granite block pillars, which stood at intervals along the verandah, gave the house a sturdy appearance. Like most Rhodesian homes, it was a single storey dwelling.

A splendid wisteria grew along one side; it carried pendulous blossoms in the short September spring. But now in midsummer, the purple blooms had gone and it was heavy with green leaf instead, creating deep shade. The other side of the front verandah was covered in a prolific mass of bougainvillea, sporting a riot of colour in their full summer glory. The two varieties met in the middle by the front entrance.

At this time of day, the heat seemed at its most intense. Heavy black thunderclouds built up and by mid-afternoon, the unfulfilled promise of a tropical storm left the air humid and oppressive. Old-fashioned though it might look, Ronnie's father had known what he was about when he'd rebuilt the farmhouse, endowing it with the deep verandahs of years gone by. Angie picked up her luggage and, shoving the outer gauze door back onto its hinges, passed through the wide-open front door.

Typically, there was no one to be seen in the front part of the home. Ron's mother, Sam the family cook, and the other staff of the Cartwright household would probably be in the kitchen at the back. She paused while her eyes adjusted from the bright outdoors to the dark interior. The polished stone floor of the hall added to the cool feel of the place; the dark hardwood panelling of the walls did nothing to lighten the gloom, but it was beautifully fitted and matched the rich substance of the home. The ceiling was high above her head. Deciding to drop off her luggage before she went to look for Katherine Cartwright, she turned towards the bedroom area where she and the children usually slept. Miriam, the Cartwright's only female servant, must have heard her coming down the steps and came bustling out from one of the bedrooms.

"Mees Eeengie!" the housemaid squealed with delight the moment she saw her.

"Miriam, it's lovely to see you again." She placed her bags on the floor, and was engulfed by the African woman's ample embrace.

"I've just finished making your room ready, Mees, and the picannin misses' room is ready too." Miriam released her, her smile displaying perfect white teeth. "Where are the children?" Her face changed to a look of surprised concern, and she peered behind Angie as if they might be hidden there.

"The girls will be coming out with my parents tomorrow," Angie said reassuringly, and Miriam's cheerful countenance returned. She commandeered the luggage and disappeared towards the bedrooms, while Angie popped into a bathroom to freshen up before making her way to the kitchen.

As usual, it was busy. Kate came in from the scullery and saw her. "Hello, my girl, how nice to see you again." She came over wiping her hands on her apron, and hugged Angie. "You've made good time. Put the kettle on, Sam and make us a pot of tea." A slim, energetic woman, Kate still managed to be motherly in a rather stern sort of way. Angie had been a little intimidated by the older woman when they'd first met, but had eventually grown to understand her. Now, there was an unstated, quiet bond of mutual affection and respect between them.

Moving across to the main table, Kate reached up to take a biscuit tin from the dresser. "Now, tell me about the girls – is Joanne looking forward to starting school?"

Angie sat down opposite Kate, happy to pass on her family news. As always, Kate's face lit up as Angie spoke. She adored her three granddaughters and never seemed to tire of hearing about them.

A short while later there was a break in the conversation when Sam placed the tea tray on the table and went out the back, leaving them alone in the main kitchen. Kate busied herself with the cups and, without looking up, took Angie by surprise. "And how about you and Ronnie?" She paused and looked up. "You know…"

Angie had sensed her mother-in-law was worried about their relationship, but she'd never actually said anything before. She wasn't sure how to handle this; Kate and Ron were very close. Ron was her only child, and Angie felt uncomfortable discussing their problems with anyone, never mind Kate. She was his mother, after all. "We're OK thanks, just the usual disagreement about his…" she nearly said 'obsession' "… involvement with the Army."

"Yes… he can get very wrapped up in what he's doing, very enthusiastic…" Angie could see Kate was searching for the right words; obviously embarrassed.

Taking advantage of the pause, Angie changed the subject. "What about Granny and Granddad?" Peter's elderly parents still lived on the farm, in a cottage not far from the main house.

"They're very well, considering their age. And looking forward to seeing you of course."

"I'll go there later today or first thing tomorrow morning, but now I'm ready to help with your preparations for the weekend – and the celebrations. Who's coming?" Angie stirred her tea as Kate went to fetch her notebook. "Do you remember I asked if my cousin Mark could come with my folks tomorrow?"

"He'll be more than welcome, Angie, and I'm looking forward to meeting him. I'm sure Harriet will be pleased to have him around for a little longer."

They were soon deep in discussion over the logistics of the coming New Year's Eve party. The Cartwrights hosted around 40 guests, family and friends, for this event each year. Only Angie's family were planning to arrive on Friday. Most of the other guests would not be joining them until Sunday, so they concentrated on the party itself and the accommodation.

"Are you sure everything is all right between you and Ron, dear?" Kate's return to the subject caught Angie off guard again. She must be very worried to be so direct.

"Oh, fine thank you." Of course Kate and Peter must suspect she and Ronnie were having problems, especially over the Army. There were other things too… His obsessive hatred of the terrorists he was fighting was taking over his life… their lives. He could be so single-minded; how could she say what she really felt, would his mother understand?

Kate carried on. "You must feel free to talk to me if you want to. I know Ronnie can be difficult... but he's a good man at heart."

"He seems to want to spend all his time in the bush with the Army, Kate..."

"He loves the bush. He's very like my brother, Edward." Ron's Uncle Ted was a bachelor, who lived on his own on a remote farm near the border area.

"But if Ronnie loves the bush so much, why isn't he interested in the farm?"

Kate took a few moments to reply. "You know how he quarrels with his father whenever they're together for too long," she sighed. "Two strong but very different characters, I'm afraid." She reached across the table and pressed Angie's hand reassuringly.

Angie knew which strong character she preferred. She didn't want to think about it now, but she knew her relationship with Ronnie couldn't carry on this way for much longer. They would have to sort it out... and soon.

Chapter 5

The risk paid off, so at dusk, about half an hour after the aircraft attack, Gadziwa was able to leave the majority of his group resting. They were gasping with exhaustion, but well hidden under cover of the bush. With just enough light to see by, he signalled a scout to move with him to the edge of the jesse line to select an escape route.

They saw the tracks of the soldiers close to the edge of the jesse, and judged them to have passed not more than 40 minutes earlier. Sending the scout back to fetch the others, Gadziwa kept watch from the edge of the bush. Darkness was approaching quickly and he was in a hurry, the last of the light fading just as his boys arrived. He gave them no rest, aware that the soldiers must see that he'd doubled back and turn in their own tracks to catch them. Marching rapidly, they cut diagonally over several kilometres to the edge of the escarpment.

The stars were covered by the thick black thunderclouds that Gadziwa had seen building up all afternoon. He called silently to his ancestors for rain, so their tracks would be washed away. There was sure to be a break in the weather soon. If rain fell tonight, he could be certain that his ancestors were looking upon him with favour.

They came up under the loom of the escarpment, and Gadziwa allowed another rest break. He knew the men were fatigued, more with fear and the after-effect of adrenaline, than from physical work. He rounded them up, making sure they were close together, before allowing them to drop down in the broken ground just inside the opening to a re-entry. "Make sure you watch the new boys well... no more must escape," he muttered darkly to the section commanders. Although he had been furious when the loss of one of the new comrades had been discovered, he now grudgingly admitted to himself that those shots ringing out over the Valley had alerted him just in time to the soldiers' approach.

Instead of collapsing with the rest, the coloured commissar came over and interrupted Gadziwa's train of thought. "Surely it's too dark for them to find us now, comrade." Gadziwa could tell that the man had framed the question as a statement, to conceal his fear.

"They will not find us tonight, Weiner – unless they have been very lucky and set an ambush in *this* re-entry, which we are going to use to climb out of the Valley." He indicated the darkest patch in the escarpment face above them, marking the lush bush of the deep watercourse, against the lighter and drier scrub that covered the rest of the escarpment.

"But there's small chance of that. We are far from where they first sighted us, and there are too many places for them to watch." Gadziwa relaxed as he analysed their situation after so much danger that day. "We will move off in half an hour and climb the escarpment, which will take us four hours in the dark." A tough challenge for his boys; it was a 400-metre climb, and very steep in places. "We must be with our people before dawn. It will be easier for the white men to find us up there, unless we are hidden among our people."

The commissar relaxed, and started rolling himself a dagga joint. "Don't light that, unless you want to bring the soldiers here," Gadziwa warned. There was a dull flash of lightning in the clouds far away over the escarpment, across to the south and east. Gadziwa waited for the roll of thunder. It came, but faintly after a very long time. The rains were on their way, and Gadziwa felt his heart sing with pleasure and satisfaction. He offered thanks up to his ancestors. Yes, he knew it would rain that night. The white men would not find them tomorrow.

"Do you hear my ancestors speak, Weiner?"

"The thunder?"

Of course the thunder, what else did the fool think he was talking about? "They are pleased with me and will protect us as we move out of the Valley."

On the way up, Gadziwa carefully checked for signs of recent human presence along the escape route, and was satisfied that no soldiers had passed this way. Not even the best of the enemy troops, with all their anti-tracking techniques, could have concealed their passing from his skilled eyes and sixth sense. He boasted with good reason that he could *smell* danger. He knew it was more than expert bushcraft – his abilities were near enough supernatural, and all his subordinates feared him accordingly. They didn't suspect him of being an n'ganga for nothing; he scoffed at the very idea, though being thought of as a witchdoctor had some advantages…

* * *

"We're OK, but many farmers are beginning to get into financial difficulty because of this drought, Angie." Peter went over to the mahogany sideboard as he spoke that evening. "Anyone for wine?" He raised one eyebrow at Kate, who nodded.

"Yes please, Peter," Angie smiled back at him. "When do you think it will break?" She was always pleasantly surprised how much Ronnie's father looked like an older version of Ron. Tall, lean and bronzed by the sun, but with his hair greying and receding steadily as the years passed. If Ronnie still looked like him when he was the same age, he'd be lucky. Pity he hadn't inherited his father's courteous manners and thoughtfulness.

"I think we'll have some rain tonight but then it will clear up for a while. The main rains will probably come within a week or two though. At least I hope they will; we'll all be in trouble if we don't have steady rain to fill our rivers and dams soon." Moses, the elderly black butler came quietly into the room, and deposited a hot plate with a roast beef joint in front of Peter's place at the head of the table. "But I'm more anxious about the security situation."

Angie was also worried; Ronnie seemed to think he could win this war on his own with his few soldiers. The fact that other people were getting fed up with all the Army call-ups and sanctions didn't seem to worry him at all.

"You mean the terrorists coming into the tribal trust lands and threatening the people?" Kate asked.

"Yes, the tribespeople are being tortured and even killed if they don't support the African Nationalist cause, so of course they're afraid. After all, they're unarmed and the terrorists have modern weapons; anyone would be intimidated." He paused while he began carving. "So the country people are confused and scared, especially those to the north of us, near the borders with Zambia and Mozambique. But what really concerns me is that it won't be too long before the terrorists get into the towns."

"The towns?" This was disturbing news to Angie. "What about farms then, do you think the terrorists might attack a farm like they did before?" When was it... back in '68? She shuddered at the thought.

"Hopefully we'll have plenty of warning before that happens," Peter said rather too smoothly. "The police say they have good information on terrorist activities in the tribal trust lands near white farming areas."

Angie sensed that he didn't quite trust the police reassurances.

"We should also be concerned about the effect they're having on the African people. If we don't protect them, we'll lose their loyalty." He served a portion of beef onto Kate's plate.

"What more can we do to stop it?" Angie could see no solution. "Our men are spending so much time in the bush as it is."

"We're working with the authorities to find a way."

But Angie didn't believe he had an answer to the problem either. She watched while he served thin slices of rare beef onto her plate. He always remembered her preferences.

"Do you know what part of the country Ron is in?"

"He told me he'd be in the Zambezi Valley, somewhere between Mana Pools and Kanyemba," she replied. Being reminded of Mana Pools had brought back memories of the peaceful days before the war, when she and Ron had taken long weekend breaks in the remote, unspoiled game reservation on the banks of the Zambezi River. It had been a more peaceful time in their marriage too.

How exactly had they drifted so far apart? She didn't really know for sure but since Helen, their youngest had been born and the war began to 'hot up', it had got worse, with him spending more and more time in the Army. But it had started long before that... from the time Emma was born, actually. Then of course, the others had followed fairly soon after; there was a houseful of little ones, and the inevitable chaos that went with that. Was it the babies or was it the war? He seemed to have little interest in her or the children...

Peter was still talking. "He'll get the rain soon after us then. It's coming in from the east."

* * *

Angie lay in bed, feeling hot and uncomfortable. Kate's mention of Uncle Ted's bachelor existence had struck a chord with her. Was that the problem? Would Ronnie have been happier single? They'd married young... too young perhaps. But they'd been so sure about it all. Was Ron regretting it now? Did he feel tied down? Angie tossed the bedcovers aside. But what about her... what about their children? He couldn't just pretend they didn't exist. She'd tried so hard to get through to him, but Ron just clammed up and walked away. In the last year, even when he wasn't away on call-up, he'd taken to driving off to spend hours in the Officers' Mess with his fellow soldiers. She was getting so weary of it all...

* * *

A particularly heavy rumble of thunder woke her. Angie watched the flickering lightning through her bedroom window for a while, before deciding it was becoming spectacular enough to get up for a better look. She lifted one side of the mosquito net canopy and stepped down from the bed. It was still stifling hot. The open French doors led straight out onto the verandah, and the smooth, polished concrete floor felt cool under her bare feet.

Walking to where there was an unrestricted view of the garden, between the pillars and creepers; Angie was just in time to see a spectacular fork of lightning run between two thunderheads, and then strike down towards the earth in the distance. It lit the whole sky and garden for what seemed like a long minute. Despite expecting it, she was shaken when the thunder crashed almost immediately afterwards, and her heart was left palpitating; a sharp reminder of what was meant by the expression 'jumping out of your skin'.

There were more flashes and cracks of thunder, until at last the rain came. Preceded by a rush of wind that shook the trees and shrubs violently, the drops were heavy and soon poured off the edge of the roof in sheets of water, flowing down into the shallow concrete drainage ditch that ran round the edge of the verandah. The rain would wash away the dust, making everything clean and fresh in the morning sun.

If only life was that simple. Angie felt a chill in the air and turned back towards her bedroom. New Year just around the corner; it was time she started doing something about her marriage. She wasn't happy and no doubt Ron wasn't either. She got back into bed; it had to be possible to change things for the better...

* * *

Gadziwa and his men reached the top of the escarpment in the early hours of the morning, and he moved away from his group. He stood on a rock to give himself a view from the re-entry, out over the Valley below. Although it was dark, flashes of lightning illuminated the whole arena from time to time. He flared his broad, flat nostrils; the sweet rain scent was accompanied by a powerful chemical odour – rather like cordite, which he knew was caused by lightning burning the air. The flashes were getting closer and increasing in both number and intensity.

Slowly, the smell of coming rain overwhelmed the dry, dust-laden air. Perversely, this made the scent of the normal, dry bush more powerful and noticeable – just as the rain was about to eliminate it. He filled his lungs.

Gadziwa revelled in the sheer physical power of his rippling black body, and was proud of his distinctly Negroid features. Indeed, he was proud to be a black man.

He hated the blacks who sought to ape the ways of the white men. He detested the whites who fawned before the great black race. Especially the white missionaries who were sellouts against their own race, kissing the feet of black men and saying they did it all for their God, who was also confused with someone called Jesus Christ. If that was true, it was a strange God indeed. Yes, these Christians and socialists – 'anti apartheid', they called themselves – were like snakes, and beneath contempt.

He laughed out loud as he recalled the time in the early days when he had been captured. The police had taken confessions from two of his comrades, who had admitted their own guilt and named him as their leader. But a missionary church paid for lawyers to defend them. Gadziwa lied easily, and the missionaries told more lies to support his claims and denials. Yet the white Rhodesian judge believed him against his own police, saying that the officers had used force to obtain confessions. Who did the judge think had killed the sellouts if it wasn't Gadziwa and his boys? These people went out of their way to help their enemies.

Gadziwa recalled the briefing he had received from the supreme military command before leaving their Mozambican base. This incursion was to be different from all the ones before.

"Many of our leaders have been released by the rebel regime on the orders of an English Lord," the colonel had said. "Now our comrade leaders have ordered that we should begin the real fighting." Gadziwa had tensed with anticipation.

"We have enough recruits and arms. It is time to take our Chimurenga to the white settlers." The colonel paused for effect. "You will attack the white invaders themselves." Gadziwa relished the prospect. He had found pleasure in subduing the African sellouts, but he yearned to take the war of freedom to the whites who occupied his land.

* * *

It was time to move on from their resting place at the top of the escarpment. Gadziwa roused his boys from their sleep, and bullied them into preparing themselves to complete their journey to safety. He felt the cool relief of the wind that blew ahead of the storm. His boys rolled their eyes in terror in the light of a flash of savage and prolonged fork lightning, as it played between the thunderheads and the hills. The immediate crash of thunder was deafening and caused the very air to vibrate.

As they began the trek inland from the top of the escarpment, solid drops of rain hit them. Great dollops of water, which stung as they landed on heads and bodies. The torrential rain would obliterate all signs of their passing. His ancestors had not failed him.

Chapter 6

Ron's frustration reached a peak when heavy rain started falling in the Valley during the early hours. Despite the heavy cloud build-up all afternoon, he'd harboured a faint hope that the rain might hold off. The irony of that wish, coming as it did from a farmer's son in this water-starved country, took the edge off his disappointment.

They'd lost Gadziwa's trail and the heavy rainfall made any chance of finding it again virtually impossible. They resigned themselves to a miserable night; water seeping through, and under the rough shelters that he and his men had made among the jesse bushes. Their only realistic hope of catching up with Gadziwa now lay in the bastard making some sort of show among the locals up above the escarpment. Or some careless mistake in covering his tracks – but there was small chance of this particular terrorist being careless…

* * *

Gadziwa pushed his men mercilessly. It was no use just reaching the safety of the tribal lands; a group of 20 comrades was too big to be hidden from the soldiers. Soon it would be dawn, he had to split the boys into five sections and give the leaders their orders. He would take one group himself, another would go to Lieutenant Makaranga. The remaining three had their own pre-selected commanders.

"We'll head for that kopje and split up from there," he told the section commander following him. They stumbled noisily among the rocks in the dark, before coming to a fairly level area halfway up the hill. "Form your group and sit down," he told each commander in turn, as they passed him. "There… there… there…" He indicated a place for each unit, so they were arranged around him. As soon as they settled, he called the commanders to his side, and quietly talked them through their group tasks again. He didn't want newly trained comrades to hear details of the plans, not trusting them to keep their mouths shut if they were captured.

Each section was to head for a different 'safe' kraal in the district.

They would work with the kraal-head to find and punish any sellouts, Judases as some called them. His own Mission – the beginning of a new, more active phase of the Chimurenga struggle for freedom – he kept secret. Comrade Chitepo, ZANU's supreme political commander himself had ordered it, after he'd been released from the Rhodesian prison.

"Remember that you must all head back to Chifombo base in Mozambique after three days. So do your work quickly, and get out fast." Gadziwa ended his briefing. "It will be dawn in less than an hour, and we have many kilometres to walk before we get to our assigned kraals – except for you, Sebukwe."

He instructed Sebukwe to create a cache on the kopje, burying all the arms and ammunition, including land mines, which the whole group had helped to carry across the border. Comrades on later incursions would use these. They had to hide the arms carefully, before they moved down to their host kraal at the foot of the hill.

Together with Gadziwa's special Mission, the transport and stockpiling of weapons was a major objective. Not much else could be expected from inexperienced sons of the soil. "You have the furthest to go, Makaranga, so get moving. I'll see you all back at Chifombo." Three of the five groups left.

"I will accompany you, Comrade Captain." Weiner surprised Gadziwa with this choice. Weiner had previously refused to commit himself, and the decision as to where he would go when the main group split up, had been left open. He was the only person besides Gadziwa himself who knew what his secret Mission was.

"You wish to join me in the raid against the settlers?" Gadziwa asked incredulously. "It will be dangerous."

"No." Weiner responded quickly, "I won't be with you for that attack. I am heading for a mission station not far from where you are going tonight. It is known that the mukiwa who work there are supporters of our struggle." Gadziwa noted that the mixed-race commissar used the African name for whites.

"I will do my work from there after you have gone. Mutasa's kraal is on the way, and I need to find out from him who the dissidents are."

Gadziwa had his suspicions that Weiner was a coward, afraid to accompany him on a raid against whites. However, he couldn't fault his logic, so remained silent on the matter. He took Sebukwe on a brief recce of the kopje, to select the exact location of the cache, and left them to it.

"Wake up, wake up." Gadziwa gathered his exhausted three-man section. "We must get to Mutasa's kraal before the sun is too high, and before the soldiers start looking for us with their helicopters." He spurred them into a rapid march; they still had 15 kilometres to travel.

* * *

Dawn came slowly for Ron and his tired, wet team the morning after they'd lost Big Feet and his gang, but at least the rain had stopped. It was surprising how cold the immediate pre-dawn hour could be, even down here in the Valley. Especially if your clothing and other kit was wet through. None of the stop groups had made contact during the night, and it was now almost certain that the terrorists had escaped into the safety of the tribal lands above the escarpment. Predictably, all the terrorists' tracks had been washed away.

Ron made his scheduled early morning report, and Major Swain came to the radio. "You and your men fit, Ronnie?"

"We're wet... and pretty pissed off with having lost that bastard last night, sir, but we're ready to get after him again," Ron assured him. "Bravo Three and I have agreed that they'll come down on our position first and I expect them any minute now." Bravo Three was a stick of four men from Ron's own platoon, under the independent command of a corporal.

"Right, I'll call for choppers to pick you all up, then." The CO went off the air. Thank fuck for that; helicopters would get them to the top of the escarpment in less than an hour. Ron grinned at Njube who was listening in... shit hot.

"It's been organised, Ronnie," Swain came back after a few minutes. "Only one chopper available I'm afraid, so he'll have to make three trips." Ron gritted his teeth in frustration, but Swain continued "...it's better than waiting for wheels, or footing it up the escarpment. He'll be on his way in the next ten minutes."

There was a momentary pause before Swain gave orders for deployment. "I'll be assigning Bravo Two and Bravo Three, to sweep the areas to your left and right. I'm also moving in two callsigns from Simon's platoon. They'll sweep in the opposite direction, away from you, along the escarpment." Hell, this was developing into a big operation. "Make sure you don't deviate from your search patterns without clearance. No need to tell you that the most dangerous time will be at the start of the sweep, when you're closest together. We don't want our own chaps shooting each other up."

The sun was rising quickly now, and they soon heard the chopping sound of the approaching Alouette. Like all helicopters, Cyclone Seven would be its callsign. The pilot swooped low onto the landing zone Ron had selected; a clear patch of ground, with just a few small, low bushes having had to be cut away. The loose vegetation flew in the violent rotor wind, but they were spared the usual dust storm, thanks to the overnight rain.

Even though the chopper had been stripped of all excess weight, it was still not safe to carry more than four fully armed men, in addition to the pilot and gunner-technician. Ron and three of his men were taking the first flight. Mike Njube would lead Ron's remaining men in the second lift. Bravo Three would wait for the third and last flight out – they were going to a separate dropping off point.

Ron considered himself very lucky to have Mike and Herbie with him again on this call-up. Both were on 'temporary assignment' from the Rhodesia African Rifles, and it was very unusual for professional soldiers to work with Territorials. Ron's arrangement with Mike and Herbie was a miracle of organisation – quite outside the normal Army capability and style.

He climbed into the chopper first and agreed the plans with the pilot as his men were clambering aboard. To overcome the racket of the jet engine and rotors, they used a mixture of shouted speech and sign language, and the pilot gave the 'thumbs up' to show he'd understood and agreed.

Ron turned, and quickly checked to make sure his three men were settled, then tapped the pilot on the shoulder, and signalled that they were ready for take off. All pilots hate being on the ground in hot operational areas, where their machines are vulnerable to attack, and he gunned the motor so that they swooped off violently, leaving their bellies on the ground. They banked so sharply, Ron had only to turn his head to the right to look straight down onto the ground through the open doorway. All fighting helicopters flew without doors – another weight reducing measure.

They climbed steeply out of the Valley, the chopper frame shuddering with the lifting thrust of the rotor blades. Rolling Highveld hills, stretching far inland, quickly came into view beyond the escarpment. The land between the hills, and even some of the hills themselves, were covered with a patchwork of fields and numerous African settlements. The kraals were small by any standards. Most comprised about a dozen circular living huts, plus one or two smaller grain storage huts on stilts – to try to prevent termites and other vermin from getting into them.

The chopper headed towards a gravel road, about 15 kilometres inland from the escarpment. The landing zone was distinguished by being close to a low narrow concrete bridge, crossing a dry riverbed. Several days of steady rain would be needed to get the rivers running.

They'd deliberately selected a relatively unpopulated area to drop into, but even so, the nearest kraal was only a few kilometres away. The chopper hovered a metre above the ground as Ron and his stick jumped out, crouching low to avoid the blades. Holding their weapons at the ready, they took up all round defensive positions while the chopper pulled away for its second lift; there'd be a wait of 40 minutes or so before the second stick joined them to commence the assigned search pattern.

"Say, I didn't realise how many people are out there," Bill Polanski called quietly from his position nearby. Bill had come to Rhodesia as a volunteer because he'd finished his tour of duty in Vietnam, and they wouldn't let him go back. Of course, as a trained soldier with combat experience, he'd been welcomed with open arms by the hard pressed Rhodesian military. But Ron's men had wondered if the Army was paying extra for mercenaries.

"Shoot... I earn less here in a week than I got in a day in 'Nam." Bill had answered the question himself, grumbling cheerfully. "I sure as hell don't do it for the money." He got paid the same pittance as everyone else, and Bill volunteered to go back into the bush again almost as soon as he completed each four-week call-up. Of course, Bill was a bachelor and able to do as he pleased. Ron sometimes wondered...

Ron turned to respond to Bill. "This part of the country is very fertile, and well populated. It's one of the areas reserved for traditional African communities, called 'Tribal Trust Lands'; we call them TTLs," Ron told him. "Sort of protected lands set aside years ago for the sole use of the African peasants. And to stop white people from buying up all the land, leaving the tribesmen with nothing. Probably similar to your Indian Reservations?"

Ron checked his watch. The chopper would be picking up the other half of his callsign about now. "I'll be back shortly," he said, and walked across the bridge to the position he'd assigned Herbie and Blikkie, bracketing the landing zone to keep it secure; a terrorist hit on a Rhodesian helicopter would make big news.

"No signs of any terrs or locals yet, sir," Blignaut spoke for both of them. Ron stayed with them for a few moments, before returning to Bill where he answered more questions from the American about life in rural Africa.

Their discussion ended abruptly with the clatter of the approaching helicopter, bringing the other half of Ron's callsign and as soon as the chopper left, Ron called his group together for a briefing.

"OK, men, we're 15 kilometres in from the top of the escarpment." Giving them a point of reference was crucial. "Callsign Bravo Three will be to our left or north of us. That is, nearest to the escarpment over there," Ron indicated, knowing that some people became disoriented after a helicopter ride. "Callsign Bravo Two is already in position inland to our south. So we're at the centre, and we're all going to sweep along in an easterly direction, parallel to the escarpment." He paused, "Any questions so far?"

"Any stop groups ahead?" Mike Njube asked.

"Negative. We wouldn't know where to place them, sarge. And we need a free path ahead of us, so we don't come up against our own guys." He paused to let that information sink in. "The only other troops are behind us, moving away from us." Ron indicated the danger area with a sweeping motion of his left hand. "Major Swain has alerted combined operations up at Mount Darwin as to what we're doing, and he'll keep them informed as we progress our patrol. ComOps will chopper in stop groups when we flush the terrs out." There were no more questions, so Ron organised the order of march, made radio contact with the other callsigns, and everyone moved out. He knew it was a long shot, especially after the night rainfall, but that crafty bastard Gadziwa had to be up here somewhere and Ron wanted to be the one to get him.

* * *

"In two days, it will be what the mukiwa call New Year," Gadziwa spoke to kraal-head Mutasa while they sat enjoying the late morning sun. On arrival at the kraal, a few hours after dawn that morning, Gadziwa had arranged for his three remaining comrades to be hidden in nearby scrub, close to a dry riverbed. None of them were from this part of the country, but that was good. It meant they would not be tempted to run away. As a further deterrent, he told them that the local population was fully indoctrinated; they would be afraid the locals would report any attempt by them to desert. He and the coloured commissar were staying in the relative comfort of the kraal. He arranged for food and drink to be carried to his group by Mutasa's women.

Gadziwa took a deep, cool draft from his pot of millet beer and wiped the foam from his upper lip, before he continued. "The whites will have big celebrations the night before their New Year, and that will be a good time to attack." He spoke very openly with this man. Mutasa was one of the few traditional black leaders in the country who had been completely supportive of the struggle from the beginning. "All we need to do is select a target." He paused and looked at the old kraal-head, giving him an opportunity to make a suggestion.

"There are many, some only half a day's drive from here, in the white men's Umvukwes district, Comrade Captain," he agreed readily. "I know of one where the labourers are very loyal to their white master, so they need punishment as sellouts." Mutasa paused while he shook snuff into the palm of his hand. Closing one broad nostril at a time, he snuffed tobacco into each in turn. It was strong tobacco and he sneezed violently, wiping the mucus away with an upward motion of his wrist. Tears oozed from the corners of his eyes.

He settled back comfortably onto his haunches with a grunt of satisfaction. "But first, I wish to report some Judases who are nearby. These traitors might cause danger for you... and your sons of the soil, if they are not dealt with."

Gadziwa considered. He knew Mutasa would use him for his own ends, even though he was a renowned supporter of the struggle. It mattered not though, Gadziwa felt the need for a little pleasure while his men rested, and they all waited the few remaining days until the night of the main attack.

"They must be brought to me for a trial first," Commissar Weiner interjected.

These politicals were always jealous of their perceived roles in deciding on the guilt and punishment of traitors. Gadziwa ignored him. He recalled Mutasa's hate for a neighbour called Zongoro, which was not unreasonable in view of his crimes. From his previous visits to this area, Gadziwa knew this man to be an Uncle Tom; when the land conservation officers told him to plough his fields along hillside contours, he did it; even worse, in blatant collaboration with the mukiwa, he dipped his cattle against ticks and other parasites. Perversely, this Zongoro met with success, and had become a rich man. Meanwhile others suffered poor grazing, diseased cattle and failed crops.

"These sellouts are not at Zongoro's kraal by any chance?" Though he'd already made up his mind to agree to the request, and was looking forward to carrying out the punishment, Gadziwa enjoyed Mutasa's discomfort at being so easily caught out. He had no intention of allowing the old man to think he could expect a fighting comrade to do whatever he asked.

"Hau!" The old man expressed astonishment at Gadziwa's perception, and he rolled his eyes in fear, clearly viewing Gadziwa with even greater respect. His eyes were yellow and streaked by the thin red blood veins of the regular dagga user. "Yes, Comrade Captain, they are." He bowed his head. "You are wise in all things, Gumbarishumba."

"How long ago is it since we took Zongoro's sons and daughters to Mozambique?" Gadziwa asked. "We also burned his grain storage huts at that time."

"It was before the last rains. Yet he has not learned to reject the white men and support our struggle, comrade," Mutasa emphasised.

Now Gadziwa remembered that Zongoro also ran a trading store that attracted the surrounding population. "You mean his trading store is well stocked, and takes your people's money?"

The old man bridled. "Zongoro stands accused of being a wizard; he is responsible for this drought that is causing all of us trouble." His voice rose. "He has crops, while we have lost ours." The kraal-head became animated, waving his arms about and spitting in the dust. "...Zongoro does it to force people to buy food from his store."

Mutasa's eyes gleamed wildly as he adopted the air of a man who had solved a mystery, backed by irrefutable logic. "Our swikwiro has smelled him out. We would have punished him already, but the white men's laws prevent us." The injustice of it caused the old man to wrinkle his face in disgust, but his passion had burnt itself out; he settled down, reached into his pouch and commenced rolling a dagga joint across his knee in a square of old newspaper.

"I will take my men to see Zongoro tonight." Gadziwa did not believe or trust the spirit medium who had 'smelled out' Zongoro. But it would be a good thing to show the whole district again that the law that ruled was ZANLA law and not the white man's law. "Weiner, you can come with us."

"I have said I will come, Comrade Captain," Weiner replied, "but why wasn't this sellout punished properly last time?"

Gadziwa sucked his teeth in anger at the presumption of this little man, asking such a question of him. Everyone knew that he was the most ruthless of all commanders. "We will see what we will see." He turned his back on Weiner and lifted the beer pot to his lips again.

Chapter 7

Mark drew up behind the Grevilles' car. The trip from the city had been leisurely and he'd enjoyed his mother's cheerful chatter. The girls tumbled out of their grandparent's car and rushed up the steps to greet Angie and their grandmother. His mother waited with him while he unloaded their luggage, and they joined the group on the verandah.

"Thank you for having me for the weekend, Mrs Cartwright," he smiled when she greeted him.

"You're very welcome, Mark. We do like to have a crowd for New Year, and we're so short of men this time." She had an air of homely hospitality about her. "Angie... will you show everyone to their rooms, while I see to the girls please? I hope you won't mind sharing your room with Danie and Martin Venter on Sunday night, Mark?"

A large, cheerful African woman they called Miriam appeared from the passage behind them. She took the children's luggage, and followed Mrs Cartwright as she led the three girls away to their room.

Mark turned his attention to Angie and was rewarded with a smile. Damn pretty woman – but now he saw another side to her; organised, quietly competent. Nice... He tagged along while she showed her parents and his mother to their rooms. "Sorry you've had to wait 'till last, Mark," she turned to him at last, "but you're a little further down the passage."

"No problem." He followed her into a large room... "This looks fine, thanks Angie." Mark found himself feeling slightly awkward in her presence again. What the hell was the matter with him? He'd been with many attractive women before and none had ever affected him like this. He took a grip on himself, and dumped his luggage onto the double bed. He noted two single beds, already made up to accommodate the Venter brothers later. They would all be comfortable.

"I'll show you the nearest bathroom... then the rest of the house, so you don't get lost." She led the way out of the room. "It's been altered several times since it was originally built, so the layout is a bit unusual."

Mark soon realised that the Cartwright place was one of those exceptionally prosperous Rhodesian farms. The rather rustic external appearance of the place, with its thatched roof and old-fashioned wide colonial verandahs, belied the professional quality of the construction, and the superb interior finish. He guessed the Cartwrights had made their money in tobacco, like most other farmers in these parts.

They eventually reached the long family sitting room with its African landscapes and thick oriental rugs, tastefully blending in with the solid furniture and general ambience of the place.

"You're right about it being a bit of a maze, but I think I'll be able find my way around. It's very nice."

"Yes, so spacious... and yet quite homely, isn't it?" She smiled back at him. Despite its size, the house had an appealing, comfortable and lived in feeling. They walked across the beautiful wooden floor, and through the open French doors onto the patio. From there, they had an elevated view of the small valley that this side of the house overlooked.

"Isn't it lovely?" Angie stood beside him. Their outlook over the carefully maintained lawns and gardens was indeed splendid. The sun was low in the sky, and its strong yellow rays shone on the underside of heavy black clouds above a range of blue hills, far in the distance to the north-west.

"It sure is. In fact, I like everything about the place that I've seen so far." There was a small stream flowing through the garden below on the left. The coloured lights, linked from tree to tree, were not switched on. It was still an hour to dusk.

"My father-in-law will be back from the fields soon." Angie looked up at him. "We'll have sundowners here from six-thirty, and dinner through there at about eight." She turned to indicate closed panelled doors that obviously led from the sitting room behind them, into the dining room. "I suppose you might want to get settled in before then? I think I'd better go and get changed too."

"Of course," Mark answered. "See you here later?"

Angie nodded and half turned, then stopped. "Did my Dad warn you that we have a VIP for dinner tonight?"

"Yes, a Lord Hallingbury I believe. Your father told me that he and Mr Cartwright agreed to have him over, but I'm not quite sure why he's here."

"Apparently he's on an unofficial visit to Rhodesia, and the Government wanted him to meet a farmer with no political connections... So, with my father being at the Land Bank, they asked him to make suggestions. Of course 'his Lordship', or whatever we're supposed to call him, will be staying here overnight; but he wants to leave early tomorrow morning. Should be an interesting evening though."

"Obviously, my work has to be kept from him," Mark said, probably unnecessarily, but he was determined to keep things safely under wraps.

"Naturally... Oh, I think I can hear the girls." Angie turned to listen. "I'd better go now, please excuse me."

Mark watched her walk away, enjoying her graceful, unaffected movement. His decision to delay his return to South Africa had been a good one, and he really looked forward to the next few days. His old self-confidence was returning.

* * *

"I see that sanctions are not preventing the essentials from getting through, then," Lord Hallingbury observed dryly.

Mark smiled inwardly; the man was standing next to him on the patio, with a glass tumbler containing a well-known brand of single malt.

"What a pleasant home and farm you have here, Mr Cartwright. How much land do you have?" Hallingbury continued.

"The farm covers just under 4,000 acres; about 60 percent is arable. We run a small dairy herd and a few pigs... also grow some timber, and allow grazing on the rest." Peter spoke from just inside the French doors.

"Your usual, John?" He stood with a decanter poised, and poured when Greville nodded. "But I'm afraid that sanctions are affecting quite a lot of things, including our cash crops. Until four years ago, most of my land was under tobacco. Now it's mainly maize, with lucerne and alfalfa – that's for cattle feed, of course." Peter handed the whisky to John, who helped himself from a soda-siphon, while Mark also opted for the scotch blend.

Peter continued "Fortunately the neighbouring African countries have had to import ever more maize from Rhodesia since their independence, so that's one export that seems to get past sanctions without difficulty... Ah, ladies." He stopped to greet the four women who'd contrived to arrive together. Peter was busy pouring sundowners for the next few minutes, and the women joined the men on the patio. Mark was impressed; what a difference evening wear made. The women added a touch of glamour to the occasion while Angie's petite figure, complemented by her long evening dress, took his breath away. Better and better.

"A wonderful sunset over your beautiful gardens, Mrs Cartwright," Hallingbury greeted her as she joined them.

"Aren't English sunsets also beautiful, Lord Hallingbury?" Angie asked.

"Indeed they are, but different. So much softer, with pastel colours rather than primary, is the best way I can make the comparison. And of course your sunsets are more reliable than ours."

"We had a terrific storm here last night. Lots of thunder and lightning."

"Quite a decent bit of rain too," Kate added.

"But we really need the rains proper to start." Having served everyone with drinks, Peter finally joined them on the patio. "Our dams are near empty and many farmers are already contemplating the loss of their crops this year."

"Do *you* have a farm in England, Lord Hallingbury?" Harriet asked. Mark edged closer to Angie, planning to draw her into a separate conversation. But he saw that she was interested in the general discussion, so decided to join in. He waited while Hallingbury explained that he had never been a farmer, but took an interest as part of his wider concern with former colonies and other members of the British Commonwealth.

"What is your interest in Rhodesia, Lord Hallingbury?" Mark asked, mischievously raising the issue of Rhodesia's suspension from the Commonwealth. But before Hallingbury could answer, Angie's children came running through the sitting room towards the patio and distracted them.

"Ah, the grandchildren." John turned and held his arms open to greet them; the two youngest raced across the room with the eldest following more sedately. The stout maid remained partly hidden by the door – probably too shy of the visiting English Lord to accompany her charges.

"Don't run, girls," Angie admonished. "And Daddy, please don't encourage them. Sorry they're not on their best behaviour, Lord Hallingbury. They're overexcited, but they've come to say goodnight before going to bed."

Mark watched with amusement as Granddad John knelt down to receive their kisses, and everyone focused on the ritual for the next few minutes, including the surprised, but obviously delighted Lord Hallingbury, who received a solemn kiss goodnight on his cheek from each of the three girls.

"What delightful children." Hallingbury turned to Peter as Angie steered the girls towards Miriam, whose curiosity had overcome her shyness to the extent that she was now visible in the doorway. "Do guests always benefit from goodnight kisses?"

"We're rather old-fashioned here," Peter responded, "but I like it that way and fortunately, so does my daughter-in-law. You'll probably find that we have lots of old-fashioned ways here in Rhodesia. Even *after* UDI we still had "God Save the Queen" played in our cinemas – and stood to attention for it."

"What do you think about UDI, Mr Cartwright?"

"Unnecessary, and of little use to either Rhodesia or Great Britain." It seemed that Peter had not agreed with the Rhodesian Government's unilateral declaration of independence at the time, and still thought it was a foolish move. The man's got a good head on his shoulders, Mark decided.

Lord Hallingbury raised his eyebrows. "So you support the concept of 'one-man-one-vote' for the African citizens of Rhodesia?"

"Most definitely not." Cartwright was emphatic. "I'm opposed to anyone, of any colour, being given the vote without understanding and accepting the responsibility that goes with it," he said. "No one who lacks basic education should be allowed to vote, nor should even the most highly educated people, if they don't have a permanent stake in the country." He was obviously passionate about it. "I believe that voting should be recognised as a privilege that comes with responsibility, not a right."

"What about the people who can't get an education – like the vast majority of the Africans here in Rhodesia?"

"You've been misled, Hallingbury." Greville joined the conversation. "Many urban and some rural Africans here already have the basic education requirements for voting by the time they reach our minimum voting age – which is 21." Mark hadn't known that. "The main stumbling block at the moment is lack of interest among Africans, who are generally apolitical." Greville took a sip from his glass.

"Another problem is property ownership – what Peter means when he says people must have a stake in the country. Many native people can qualify through communal – by that I mean tribal – ownership." Mark thought this sounded like a good solution; he wished South Africa had that approach instead of the crazy apartheid system. "But there are some who have lost their tribal affiliations, and have to achieve the property qualification through conventional land ownership," Greville continued.

"One way or the other, don't the black citizens of Rhodesia see themselves as disenfranchised?" Hallingbury obviously wasn't impressed. "Surely that means the current situation of war and sanctions will continue, until the voting issue can be resolved?"

Cartwright rejoined the discussion. "That's a bit of a red herring," he said. "There's more to it than voting, which as John said earlier, few Rhodesian Africans care about. The problem is with the two revolutionary political parties, Nkomo's ZAPU and Chitepo's ZANU – both from the same stable as South Africa's ANC incidentally – plus their respective Russian and Chinese Communist sponsors, who want to add Rhodesia – and the rest of Africa for that matter – to their spheres of influence."

"Aren't we getting into rather complex subjects too early in the evening?" Kate interrupted. "I see Moses signalling that dinner is ready anyway." They all drained their glasses, and she led the way across the sitting room, through the heavy sliding doors, into a wood panelled dining room. Candelabras illuminated the long mahogany table, which was comfortably set for eight.

Mark was pleased to find himself seated directly opposite Angie again. She looked stunning in her pale blue dress. It perfectly complemented her blond hair and bright blue eyes. Her delicate gold necklace caught the candlelight. She positively glowed, and was the focal point of the room. He could see that Hallingbury, who was seated next to her, was charmed. She sat naturally graceful and poised, seemingly unaware of her own appeal. Mark was captivated.

Realising that he was staring at her, he diverted his attention and looked around the table. The men were also dressed for dinner, and Mark was conscious that he cut a rather decent figure himself in his modern black-tie gear. Luckily he'd brought it up from Cape Town, to attend a military function in Salisbury last Wednesday.

"Cartwright's cellar is well regarded by those of us who are privileged to enjoy it, Hallingbury," John commented as Moses served a white; Mark noticed it was from the Paarl region. "Another of his secrets, as it's imported of course. No decent wines are produced in Rhodesia."

"It's South African," Peter added by way of explanation, "which I think is as good as most European. Mind you, I don't know much about European wines any more."

"I can promise you that wine and spirits are the only imported sustenance you will receive tonight, Lord Hallingbury," Kate remarked. "Everything else is home grown or made, much of it on this farm." Mark suspected she thought that Hallingbury might be embarrassed by the rather obvious failure of at least some of the sanctions imposed by the United Nations.

"I look forward very much to enjoying home grown cuisine, Mrs Cartwright," Hallingbury said. Cartwright quickly raised his glass and formally welcomed Hallingbury to the homestead, to which he responded with practised finesse.

"Would you care for some shooting tomorrow, Lord Hallingbury?" Peter changed the subject, obviously taking the cue from his wife. "There's no large game on the farm, but we do have guinea fowl and small antelope – impala, duiker... that sort of thing. There's plenty of waterfowl down by the dams too."

"You could swim or play tennis if you prefer," Mary suggested. "It might be uncomfortably hot trudging around the bush all day, and Angie is a very good player."

"Reasonable, not good, Mum," Angie said.

"Thank you all for your kind invitations, but sadly I have to return to Salisbury quite early tomorrow, so I hope you'll forgive me for not joining you." Mark wasn't sorry to hear that, as far as he knew it was part of the original plan anyway. "There are a few things I must do before I fly back to London tomorrow evening." Hallingbury turned the wine gently in his glass before taking another sip. "But I am sorry to miss out on the shooting Mr Cartwright; what sort of waterfowl do you have on the farm, and what effect does the drought have on them?" Mark suspected that Hallingbury would have liked to stay and play tennis with Angie. He'd do his best to take up the tennis offer himself, though.

* * *

While the conversation flowed smoothly on about hunting, Moses and his assistant brought in the main course, and Angie took the opportunity to study the dinner guests more closely. Lord Hallingbury was quite distinguished looking, in an English sort of way. He wore his black tie and dinner jacket easily, unlike her father-in-law who looked uncomfortable; Peter looked, and obviously felt better in casual clothing.

She decided that Hallingbury was probably not much older than Mark, but looked more elegant – or was it urbane? She was intrigued. She'd thought Mark worldly and experienced, but next to Hallingbury, there was no mistaking that despite his obvious acumen, Mark was less refined. That made her feel a little less intimidated by him. She could imagine Hallingbury describing him as a 'settler' or 'colonial' type. But Mark was definitely better looking... and he was big. Not wiry like Ronnie, but a powerful man in his prime, with hauntingly beautiful, deep-set blue eyes, and a tanned face. Although Lord Hallingbury was almost as big as Mark, he was pale, rather soft looking and had a slight paunch, like an older man.

"I understand that you know your Prime Minister quite well, Greville?" Hallingbury asked.

"I came out to Rhodesia to train as a pilot in 1942 and ended up in the same training outfit as Smith... although we served in different squadrons afterwards," her father replied. "But Cartwright was at school with him at Chaplin near Gwelo, as well as serving in the same RAF number 237 squadron, so he should know him better. As you probably know, that was one of the all-Rhodesian squadrons during the War."

"People change and I haven't seen much of Smithy since the War either." Peter dismissed the connection.

"So you were both on the Empire Air Training Scheme during the War?" Lord Hallingbury demonstrated his knowledge of the role the country had played in training British and Commonwealth aircrews. "I read up on it, and was surprised to discover that nearly 10,000 aircrew trained in Rhodesia – mostly pilots, I believe; I also saw that the RAF continued to operate the scheme here until the mid-1950s."

"Oh yes, a lot of young men came over from England on that scheme," Harriet enthused. "It was such fun when we had to entertain them. Poor things were lonely, so far from home and family."

Angie smiled inwardly and caught her mother's eye; they both raised their eyebrows at Harriet's light-hearted comment. She recalled the scandal about the RAF lover. Time had obviously healed the wounds. Even now, Harriet was still an attractive woman, and Angie could well understand how a young airman might have fallen for her all those years ago.

"Of course you must stand by your sister, John," Angie's mother had said to her father at the time. That was before they'd spotted her eavesdropping, and stopped talking. So it must have happened just before the RAF training scheme ended. Mark seemed not to hold any grudge against Harriet, and it looked to Angie as if he'd inherited his mother's cheerful, outgoing ways in addition to his father's swarthy good looks.

"What business are you in, Mr le Roux?" Angie heard Lord Hallingbury ask. The tension following the question was almost palpable. Perhaps it was just polite interest on Hallingbury's part? But since Mark was engaged in breaking sanctions, Hallingbury could potentially cause problems for both Mark and Rhodesia.

"I trade, Lord Hallingbury," Mark answered easily. "I'm based in South Africa, and South Africa has not imposed sanctions against Rhodesia." Angie smiled at that.

"Commodities?" Lord Hallingbury questioned. Angie decided he had a presumptuous and rather arrogant way about him.

But Mark was impassive. "Just about anything. I'm in business to make money and don't mind how – so long as it's legal, of course," he added coolly. "What business are you in, Lord Hallingbury?" Mark smiled innocently, and Angie saw him in a new light. She suspected now that the two men might be equal rivals in this potentially dangerous game of cat and mouse. She sat forward expectantly. Was

Mark going to tease the British Peer? But Moses arrived, and Kate spoiled the moment.

"...Shall we *all* take coffee in the sitting room?" she said firmly, rising from the table; Hallingbury stood immediately to take her chair. Of course, everyone had to follow suit, and Moses went ahead carrying the tray, leaving an assistant to clear the table.

During the move, Mark somehow manoeuvred close to Angie, and asked quietly if she would play tennis with him the next day.

"I'm really not that good at tennis, Mark." She didn't quite know why she whispered her reply, and she wasn't being altogether truthful. She played regularly on a social basis, and frequently for her sports club.

"That's fine with me; I'm out of practice myself. What time?"

"How about eight-thirty, before it gets too hot?" she suggested. His eyes gleamed with pleasure, and she wondered if he was fibbing about his ability; her competitive spirit rose up. This could be fun...

* * *

Angie was in the kitchen next morning, having breakfast with Kate and the children, when he walked in.

"Good morning to you too, Mark," she responded to his cheerful greeting, and seeing that he was already dressed for tennis, got up from the table. "Sit here; you've plenty of time to have breakfast while I go and change."

"Morning, Mrs Cartwright, young ladies," Mark said, smiling at the three girls.

"Good morning... say good morning to Mr le Roux, girls," Kate insisted. "There's coffee on the stove, or would you prefer tea? Did you sleep well?"

"I slept very well, Mrs Cartwright and I'll help myself to coffee, thank you." He poured coffee from the pot on the hob, before settling himself at the table. "You girls can call me Mark if you like; tell me your names, and how old you are, please." Showing no sign of their usual shyness, the girls competed with each other to tell him. They seemed totally at their ease with him.

"I'll be back in ten minutes or so," Angie said, seeing how easily Mark had made himself at home with her children and Kate, who was offering to make toast for him, while telling him to help himself to sausages, bacon and scrambled eggs.

Angie puzzled over Mark as she changed into her tennis gear. He'd surprised her in the kitchen. Everyone got on with Kate – she was a good hostess – but the children hadn't fazed him either. Somehow she hadn't expected that, thought he'd be much more reserved with them. Was there a softer, more human side to her materialistic cousin? Getting to know this enigmatic man could be interesting.

Chapter 8

It was just after midday and Ron and his men were still searching above the escarpment.

They halted, to prepare their approach to the third kraal in as many hours. "We'll check out this place, then move on to the kopje beside it and take a short break, Herbie." Ron spoke quietly to the tracker. "Cut across and tell Sergeant Njube."

"Ishe," Herbie acknowledged, and set off to cover the few hundred metres that separated them, while Ron paused to radio his position, and tell the other two callsigns his plans, aware that Swain would listen in.

Herbie took much longer than Ron expected, and he was about to chew his balls off for the delay, when he noticed that the tracker was very agitated. "The terrs are very near," Herbie said quietly. "I saw the sign on my way over to sarge, and he's waiting for your instructions."

"Show me." Ron signalled his men to follow and they crossed carefully, keeping out of sight of the kraal.

"See the tread of his takkies here." Herbie pointed to the distinctive 'figure-of-eight' impression left by the trainers, which were known to be popular with terrorists. Definitely terrs; in any case, the locals around these parts hardly ever used footwear.

"You're right, Herbie. The tracks are quite recent too." Ron squatted beside the pathway. "Are there any more?"

"Just these, Ishe. The man was careless. They usually keep off the paths, because they know we'll see their tracks."

"I wonder if this is where they came in this morning, or if they've moved more recently?" Ron pondered. "Anyway, they've been here all right. Headed straight towards the kopje."

* * *

"OK, that's the plan." Ron looked at the seven men under his command. He'd already radioed Swain; Bravo Two and Three had been given orders to move forward and act as stop groups. Now they were racing ahead, and would turn in to close a couple of kilometres behind the sighting. While that was going on, Ron and Herbie scouted round the kopje, and spotted three terrorists lying in a group, under the shade of some bushes about halfway up.

"It doesn't look as if we've got all of them here, sir," Ron told Swain, when he spoke to him next. "Pretty small group. At least three, but not many more we think. We need to move in now, or we'll be compromised by the people in the kraal nearby. I'm amazed they haven't seen us already."

Ron waited a few minutes to give Njube and his men a chance to get into position, about 50 metres to one side of the kopje. Flies buzzed in his face. Big, persistent and numerous, they came from the stockade where the villagers kept their cattle and goats overnight. It was empty now, as the animals would have been let out to graze early that morning. But many of the flies remained near, feeding off, and breeding in the animal droppings in and around the kraal.

"Let's get going, boys." They moved towards the terrs' position. All the men had been told that he wanted prisoners. Ron planned to interrogate them immediately after capture, while they were still in shock. Under those conditions, even well trained terrs might crack, and tell where their comrades had gone and what their intentions were. Ron led his stick in extended line towards the three terrorists.

They followed the well-worn paths, made by locals and their livestock, between the rocks and scrub up the slopes of the kopje. It was evident that goats usually roamed here, because the bushes had been stripped of leaves up to two metres in height. The ground patches between the rocky granite outcrops were completely without vegetation.

Suddenly, a shot rang out to their left – the area he had assigned to Njube's group. Ron and his men squatted down in cover for a moment to listen.

A small African boy ran straight in among them. "Let him go," Ron hissed, and the terrified child sprinted away towards the kraal.

Seconds later, an armed man ran past, a few feet away on Ron's left. Bill stretched out a long leg and tripped him, holding him to the ground with the barrel of his machine gun pressed into the terr's back. "Keep still, you bastard," he snapped.

A split second later, Blikkie caught a second terrorist in a superb rugby tackle.

The sharp crackle of an automatic exploded from about 50 paces away. "Christ," Ron muttered. "That's an RPD." But the deeper beat of an MAG drowned out the crackle, and soon there was silence... that was Trooper Naas Terblanche, affectionately known as Naasty, at work.

"Where are you, sarge?" Ron stood up behind the cover of a granite boulder and looked carefully around. "Herbie, help Bill and Blikkie with their captures."

"Here, sir," Ron heard Njube call from about 100 metres away to the left. "We've killed one, but I think another got away."

"Which way did he go?"

"Not sure. Johnny thought he saw someone run off across the far side of the kopje."

"Can you make sure that the one you shot is dead? Do that before you take your stick on a three-sixty, Mike." Better not lose a definite kill or capture, in the rush to try and catch one doubtful – who was already on the run anyway. Ron turned back to his men and their prisoners. "How're you men getting on?"

"All quiet, sir," Bill drawled, sounding disappointed. He carried his weighty MAG easily.

"This one's definitely dead, sir," Njube called back. "I'm taking his RPD with me while we go round the rest of the kopje."

"OK, sarge, we'll be over here with our captures. Join us when you've finished." Ron paused to radio a sitrep to Swain before settling down to interrogate the prisoners. The major was pleased, but worried that only three of the original 22 terrorists had been accounted for. Shit, as if that wasn't driving Ron crazy. He took a deep breath and ground his teeth before making his reply.

"They must have split up last night, sir. Anyway, we've accounted for five if you count the one we killed in the Valley and the one that just got away," Ron answered, sensitive to the implied criticism.

"OK, OK, you're right. Let me know as soon as your three-sixty is over, Ron."

Ron turned to focus his attention on the captures, eager to get something that might help right now. Later, the cops from Special Branch would take them over.

It was necessary to split the two of them apart, so neither could hear what the other was saying. "Bill, Blikkie... take this bastard over there and keep a good watch on him." He quietly told Blikkie that he should tell their prisoner what a terrible and cruel man Ron was, and relieved they weren't going to suffer the fate of being interrogated by him. There was nothing like putting the fear of God into the bastard. The terr might not be fluent in English, but would be sure to get the general drift of the warnings from 'sympathetic' soldiers. Anyway, Blignaut was capable of speaking rudimentary Shona – the language of the locals... and most of the terrorists in this part of the country.

Keeping Herbie with him to interpret, Ron swaggered up to the terrorist and gave him a hefty kick in the buttocks; to demonstrate his supposed ruthlessness.

"Tell him I'll kill him slowly, unless he cooperates, Herbie," Ron snarled. "I'll cut his balls off, one at a time. Then his cock; I'll slice it off, inch by bloody painful inch." He shoved the barrel of his rifle towards the front of the man's trousers to emphasise his intent, but didn't press too hard. He didn't want the man winded and unable to talk...

As he translated, Herbie rolled his eyes in mock terror at the cruelty of his officer; no man wanted his wedding tackle damaged. There was no doubt the man had got the message anyway, and he began to shiver as he interrupted Herbie in reply. Ron had chosen this one first, because it was easy to see he was in a state of shock. Perfect.

"He says that he was forced to join the gandangas, Ishe," Herbie translated. "He says he supports soldiers and will cooperate fully with us. Says he has been waiting for a chance to surrender, and tell us everything anyway. He's very glad we have saved him."

"How many gandangas were with him?" Ron asked.

"You lying dog." Herbie smacked the man's ear with his open hand. Ron could understand enough of the answer to know that he'd said he was part of a gang of four.

"Maai-Whe!" The terrified man exclaimed in shock and pain, before he jabbered a hurried explanation. Herbie told Ron that the terr had meant to explain, that his band of four had split from a large group of about 20, before the sun came up that morning. He said he and his comrades were just resting before returning to Mozambique.

"That's another lie, you bastard!" Ron jammed his rifle barrel right into the man's crotch this time, though still not hard enough to do any lasting damage.

The grilling went on for several minutes, before it was interrupted by the arrival of Njube and his team.

"We found the tracks of the one terr who got away, sir," Sergeant Njube said when he made his report, "but the locals have deliberately covered all the other tracks."

Ron radioed Swain again. "They are part of the original group but; surprise, surprise, Big Feet has got away again – with the rest. Unfortunately their tracks have been covered by locals driving cattle all over the place," he explained bitterly, "but I'm questioning these two, to see if we can get any more info, before we carry on with the follow-up."

Swain agreed, and Ron directed Bravo Two, who were only a couple of kilometres away, to pick up and follow the tracks of the escaped terr. At the same time they were to look out for any other terrorist tracks.

Ron resumed his interrogation, which yielded the information that this group had been instructed to bury arms on the kopje. The terr swore that this had been their only objective. He insisted they were then required to make their way back to Mozambique, for another load of arms to build up the cache.

"You lie," Ron smacked him hard around the head. Blood trickled from his nose… and from a split lip. "I'm going to speak with your comrade now, and get his story. You'd better be telling the truth, or I'll start on your balls when I get back." Njube kicked the terr in the crotch for good measure. They left Mike's team: Johnny Papadopolous, Tom Blair and Naas Terblanche guarding the capture. Mike and Herbie accompanied Ron. Mike spoke Shona well but it wasn't his home language, and Herbie was more fluent.

"Let *me* question this one, sir," Mike asked on the way over.

"No, I'll have a go first, sarge. I don't want him seriously injured yet." They both knew that Njube would be much rougher than Ron.

The two terrorists gave Ron a host of information over the next hour, including the fact that the kraal nearby was to have harboured them for a few days; he and Mike had suspected that anyway. Ron was content to leave the rest of the information… stuff like where they were recruited and trained, and so on, to Special Branch, who would take the prisoners into their 'care' as soon as they arrived.

"Give them hot tea and something to eat." He allowed himself to show a human side at last. After all, these poor buggers were just recruits – cannon fodder, forced into terrorism by bastards like Big Feet. "Give this one a blanket too, or he'll die before the cops get hold of him." The first man was clearly still in shock, shivering where he lay despite the heat of the early afternoon.

Ron moved across with Njube to have a look at the dead terrorist, and they agreed that this one had been the leader of the small group. Not least because he had the RPD light machine gun, whereas the others merely carried AK47s. He was also quite a bit older than the other two – although that was not always a sign of seniority. Apart from the fact that they all wore the same type of eastern-manufactured trainers, they had no uniform of any kind.

They soon found the arms the terr group were meant to have buried. Instead of getting on with the job, they'd simply left them lying in a pile, near where Herbie and Ron had first seen the terrs.

"We've found the arms cache and it's quite a big one. But what worries me is that Big Feet is still on the loose, sir," Ron reported to Swain. "He's got to be somewhere not too far away, and he'll do serious mischief if we don't find him soon. I want to get after him, so can someone take over here, please?"

"You've done a good job, Ron; that arms cache is a major success, coming on top of your kills and captures." Ron sensed his CO was preparing him for bad news. "I'm going to pull you and your team out for a bit of R&R now," Swain told him. "You've been on the go for several days, and your men must need a break."

"No!" Ron tried to interrupt.

But Swain continued, "Anyhow, ComOps want to get the RLI to take over from you, and they'll be going after Big Feet. Meanwhile, you can base up on the kopje until Special Branch arrives to take over your captures, and the arms cache. Make sure you get signatures for them."

Ron was bitterly disappointed. "Shit, sir…" The Rhodesia Light Infantry were the country's only white professional soldiers, apart from the SAS. "Big Feet is my terr, and my lads will be really pissed off if we can't finish the job."

"Sorry, Ron. Orders are orders. There'll be cold beers for your men when you get back here. You've done your jobs." Ron could tell from the sound of his CO's voice that he was also disappointed, and was trying to mask it by suggesting that Ron and his men needed 'rest and recuperation'.

What crap; the RLI were notorious for muscling in on the action, whenever the Territorial soldiers came up against insurgents. But there was nothing either Ron or Major Swain could do about it. But then, maybe there *was* something Ron could do? He didn't know what, but he was fucked if he'd just stand by and let the RLI get away with it.

* * *

Zongoro sat in the shade of his porch, watching the child of his eldest daughter; she was on a visit from his daughter's home in the big city as it was the Christmas school holiday. The child's mother was something of a favourite too – a qualified nurse and married to a successful businessman. Zongoro had reason to be satisfied with his long life, many wives, children and grandchildren. He wished all of them could live here with him at his kraal. But he knew he had to be satisfied with his five wives and only three of his daughters, together with two of the wives of his sons, and their youngest offspring. The others were all away working in the cities. Even most of the children who were at school chose to stay in town with their parents for the holidays.

But not Sekai. She was living up to her name, which meant 'laughter'. Her grandmother, Zongoro's first and senior wife was teaching her how to fry flying ants. Sekai and the other children had gathered a vast supply when they came in masses with the rain that had fallen last night, even beating against the walls and windows of the homes in the kraal in their frenetic quest to establish new nests. Many had been eaten raw, the children plucking the wings from the insects; they crunched crisply between your teeth, so nutritious that their fat dripped from children's mouths. The winged termites were equally delicious fried in their own fat and eaten hot. That was the way Zongoro himself preferred them, and his senior wife and favourite granddaughter were busy preparing a snack for him.

Sekai showed signs of approaching puberty – one moment playing like a child, and the next behaving as a young woman. Zongoro sighed at the thought of her growing up. Life became so complicated, and this pretty young musikana was sure to lose interest in her family home and, like the others, would prefer the bright city lights. He was determined to enjoy this, perhaps the last year of her childhood.

"Baba…" she came up the steps and knelt before him, offering a plateful of the delicious insects, a slice of bread on the side so he could soak up the excess fat.

"*Masikati, mwana wangu* – thank you, my child," he said, taking the plate from her and stroking her head. She settled quietly at his feet and they chatted while he ate. She told him what she was doing at school in the city, but while he listened, his mind wandered. Yes, he had much to be grateful for, but there was a dark side to his life. Just two years ago, the gandangas had come and taken five of his children – three sons and two girls. What could these bad men possibly want with teenage girls? He feared the worst, and he had heard nothing of any of them since. Rumours were that the boys had become gandangas themselves. He could not believe that of his own sons…

Chapter 9

She beat him easily at tennis that morning. Mark had to admit that Angie was a damn good player, but he knew he'd have done a whole lot better if he'd been keeping his eye on the ball, instead of on her. Her white shorts showed off tanned legs, and a cute bottom to the best advantage. When he realised just how good she was, he started clowning a little, emphasising his own poor showing. He had her doubled over with laughter at times and an unintended bonus was that he managed to snatch enough points to win an occasional game.

"You shouldn't make me laugh so much, Mark; that's cheating," she complained, but he could tell she was enjoying herself.

"You certainly gave me a lesson," he chuckled, and casually resting his hand on her shoulder, he pulled her towards him so that her body pressed lightly against his while they walked away from the court.

"I probably get more practice than you do." She didn't respond to his attention but didn't pull away either. "I'm going for a shower; see you around later?" Mark had to think quickly; he wanted to spend more time with her.

"Why don't we have a swim?" he said reasonably. "It's hot enough."

She paused for a moment before answering. "Good idea. I'll just get changed, and meet you by the pool – but I'd better see what my girls are up to first." He was pleased with this small success.

* * *

Angie changed into her swimming costume, but it took her a while to find the children. She began searching indoors, asking the servants, who seemed to be the only people in the house.

Miriam knew where they were. "Gone with Mees Greville... they wanted to swim with baas Mark," she said, shrugging her shoulders to show that she had no responsibility for the decision.

She could hear Ben and Sheba barking from the direction of the pool even before she got there. The children were splashing in the pool with Mark while everyone else sat under the shade of the lapa. The big stone enclosure, with one open side facing the pool, had a thatched roof. Tables were set up for lunch. The only one missing was her father-in-law, who would still be out on the land, probably been there since dawn.

"Come on in, Angie," Mark called. "The water's lovely." The girls added their encouragement. She dropped her towel on a chair and dived in to join them.

* * *

Mary put down her book and watched as her eldest daughter dived into the water. Something of the old Angie had emerged these past couple of days, and she was pleased to see her enjoying herself. They'd always been close and although Angie had said a few things about her problems at home, it was what she didn't say that caused Mary concern. Blast the man, she thought; I want my laughing, happy girl back again. Angie had her faults too, of course. Didn't everyone? But she hated failure and Mary knew she'd been pulling out all the stops to save her marriage and get things back on track.

She glanced across to where Harriet and Kate were chatting. There was no doubt Kate had spoiled Ron; Peter had probably tried to redress the balance, but he hadn't been successful. Hard to blame Kate really, there'd been no more children after Ron. A traumatic birth and emergency hysterectomy had put an end to her dreams of a large family. Although she and Kate got on well, Mary always felt a little constrained, making a real effort not to talk too much about her four girls in front of Kate.

"Hello everyone; making the most of the weather, I see..." Peter's greeting as he arrived interrupted her thoughts. He smiled a personal salutation at Mary before sitting nearby in the shade, while she reflected on his old-fashioned politeness.

* * *

Angie was resting, holding onto the side in the deep end when she saw Peter arrive. It must be about noon. He tossed his hat onto a nearby table, and settled into a chair in the shade.

"Shut up!" he shouted at the two dogs, picking up a small stick and throwing it at them. They dodged with practised ease, so he had to get up and take them by their collars to lead them away from the poolside. They submitted, and slunk off to a shady spot in the garden to pant in the heat. Both dogs were soaking wet from splashes.

"We'll have to lock them up somewhere tomorrow night for the party or they'll make too much din," Angie heard him tell Kate. "Ah, beer time," he remarked cheerily when Moses appeared with an assistant, carrying a zinc metal bathtub filled with ice, Castle beer 'dumpies' and soft drinks.

Her father got up and walked over to the edge of the pool. "Would anyone like something to drink?" he made himself heard over the noise. The three children were too busy playing, but Mark left them and climbed out before helping himself to a beer.

"Why don't you come in, Mum, Kate, Harriet? It's lovely and cool in the water," Angie called, but the other women shook their heads. They probably didn't want the hassle of changing into their swimsuits, or the disruption a dip in the pool would cause to their hair.

Their mother was obviously not as much fun as Mark, and the girls soon left Angie alone in the pool, going to ask for cool drinks.

Angie enjoyed another ten minutes of peace before she too climbed out, and towelled herself dry. Mark fetched a garden chair, and she adjusted it so she could sit with her legs in the sun while he brought her an orange juice. He dragged his own chair over, and sat down beside her at the edge of the shade. He was very attentive. It made a nice change, being 'looked after'. Was he always like this or was he putting on a show? Angie decided to relax and simply enjoy the experience.

"You're very good with children, Mark. I suppose you spend a lot of time with Jack?"

"Not as much as I'd like; he lives with his mother in Constantia."

That was intriguing. Why would he say his son lives with 'his mother'? "Don't you live with them too?" she asked. Then suddenly felt embarrassed and blushed. She'd hardly been very sensitive.

He seemed not to take offence though and smiled. "My wife and I are separated and waiting for our divorce to come through."

"Oh, I'm so sorry." She felt even more flustered. "Harriet hasn't said anything..."

"There's nothing to be sorry about. My mother is uncomfortable about it all, you know what I mean?" He smiled again. "But anyway, it just didn't work out for Anna and me; we're still friends, and have an amicable arrangement regarding maintenance, and all the rest. I get to see Jack quite often." He seemed quite relaxed about it.

Fortunately for Angie's poise, Sam and one of his staff arrived, carrying trays of cold meats and salads. These were placed on the main table, and overlaid with fine mesh cotton netting, to keep the flies out. Decorative glass beads sewn around the edges of the nets prevented them from lifting in the occasional breeze. Everyone got up and helped themselves, and Angie occupied herself with supervising the girls.

"I'll be going down to the lower dam this afternoon, would anyone care to join me?" Peter asked while they were eating.

"Please excuse me, Peter," her father declined the invitation. "We had a late night last night and beer at lunchtime makes me sleepy, so I'll take a rest." He always took a nap on Saturday afternoon if he could.

"I'd like to come along, Mr Cartwright," Mark said, sounding rather formal but at the same time, enthusiastic. Angie wondered how they'd get along.

* * *

Mark felt the heat of the early afternoon beating down on them as they walked the three kilometres to the lower dam. They'd brought two rifles; Peter carried the 303 calibre and Mark the 22. Both had good quality telescopic sights. Not that they were on a serious hunting trip; that would be an early morning, evening or night-time pursuit. But you never knew your luck, and they would be sure to see something if they didn't take guns. They'd debated taking a shotgun, but Cartwright decided against it, saying it was unlikely they'd see any waterfowl during the heat of the day, and the 22 would do for any guinea fowl or pheasant they came across. Fair enough.

On the way, they stopped so he could show Mark his small herd of cattle. "I used to keep Friesians, also known as Holsteins, but Jerseys give much better quality milk," he explained.

"They certainly are pretty creatures." Mark admired the fine light-brown colouring and placid features of the cows. "They look quite small. Are they fully grown?"

"Yes, Blossom there is nearly eight years old." Peter pointed to one of the cows. "They mature quite quickly, and they can give birth and produce milk from about two years through to seven or eight." They all looked much the same to Mark. "See, those are the two young heifers that I've recently bought as replacement stock. They're just over 18 months. The rest are all lactating apart from Beauty over there who's resting."

"I've only ever seen Friesians," Mark said, "why don't more people keep Jerseys?"

"They do give a lower yield," Peter conceded, "but being healthier, they're less trouble to look after; and as I said, the milk quality is much higher. I only keep a small herd anyway." There were about 15 of them resting in the shade around the edge of the field where they lay contentedly chewing the cud. "Apart from a few pigs and the poultry, they're the only livestock we keep here."

"Ah, here's Madala – the old man. He looks after the herd, and loves them as if they were his children." They greeted the old African who appeared from the bush at the side of the field. They had to go through the rather intricate process of discussing the current condition of each of his beloved cows.

Mark could see that in spite of their not being the major activity on the farm, Cartwright himself was more than a little fond of his cattle. The farmer and his herdsman knew all the animals by name, and they paused to look each cow over as they passed it, before leaving Madala with his herd. The cattle seemed very contented and were clearly used to people.

* * *

Madala watched his master and the visitor leaving, before turning back to his beloved mombies. No one understood cattle like he did, except perhaps young master 'Lonnie, the grandson of Madala's old master. He had trained master 'Lonnie himself, but now the boy lived in the city with his young wife and children. So Madala knew he had to stay here and look after the mombies, at least until master 'Lonnie came home. Madala was sure he would come back one day; the city was not a fit place for a man with a family to live.

Some years ago, the old master had tried to persuade him to stop working. They called it 'retirement', whatever that meant. "You are old like me, Madala and it is time for us to hand over to the young men now." They gave him a passbook from the post office and told him he could draw money every month for the rest of his life, wherever he lived. Huh! So they even tried to get rid of him from the farm. His only home, now that he was old...

This made him very unhappy, but he waited until the old master was alone. "What have I done wrong that you are sending me away, Nkosi?" he asked, "I came here with you as a young man and I have worked all my life for you; do you no longer trust me with the mombies?" The old master denied it, telling him he could live on the farm for the rest of his life if he wanted, but should rest like he was... but Madala was not convinced. "Is it that master Peter does not trust me then?"

"Leave it with me, Madala," the old master sighed. When he came back, he told him that master Peter wanted him to stay and look after the mombies as long as he lived. "Master Peter says that there is no one else he trusts so much as you, Madala."

And so he remained, happy and content. He did not want to go back to Mozambique, which he left as a youngster when memories began. Yes, his old friend Joseph was here, and the cattle that he loved. Young master 'Lonnie understood; his home was here with his mombies. Madala wanted to die here near them, but not until the young master came home to take over...

* * *

Mark followed Cartwright across the next field, which was waist high with healthy looking maize. "There can be good guinea fowl shooting around here – francolin and pheasant too," Cartwright remarked. "But of course they're mostly resting up at this time of day, so we may not see any." They passed irrigation equipment at the edge of the field, which looked as if it had been working earlier that day. "We could get lucky and see a buck in the shade down by the river though."

After they'd crossed the open fields, Cartwright led the way through the bush along the banks of the small river that fed his two

70

dams. That made a lot of sense; the river was dry but the bush was green and lush along its course. He confirmed Mark's suspicion that game might be present there; adding that it was unlikely there'd be large predators around during the day.

"We do have several leopard on the farm," he told Mark, "but apart from a very occasional pride, or loner passing through, there are no lion anymore in this part of the country. All shot out during my father's time; and no big antelope or buffalo left for them to prey on anyway."

The farmer led Mark along barely discernible trails in the thick bush bordering the river. It would have been easier to use the riverbed itself, but then they would be out in the open and not likely to come across any game. Animals would be sheltering in the shade at this time of the day, and more difficult to see if Mark and Cartwright were in the sunlit watercourse.

But it required care to walk through the riverine bush without making too much noise, and this slowed their pace. Mark noticed the older man seemed to be able to practically glide through the bush and, to his embarrassment, began to suspect that Peter was actually slowing down to allow him to keep pace.

They paused when they came to the edge of a fairly open section, and Mark was able to catch his breath. After they'd stood for a moment, Cartwright touched his arm and pointed. It took him a while, but then Mark caught sight of a small buck standing in the shade across the clearing. He raised his thumb to show that he'd seen it. Cartwright raised three fingers and indicated fractionally to one side of the first antelope. Mark saw another buck; this one with horns, and somewhat larger than the first one. He couldn't see the third, so raised his hand to show he'd seen only two. Peter passed him the 303, at the same time taking the 22 and pointing at the larger antelope.

Mark didn't want to miss. He was beginning to like Cartwright and did not want him to think poorly of him. Silently slipping a round into the breech, Mark raised the rifle to his shoulder, then steadied himself before taking aim though the telescopic sight. He was grateful for the periodic hunting expeditions he had enjoyed over the years, both in South Africa and Mozambique. They had all been safaris where the game was found for him by professional hunters, so he was not much good at tracking or finding game, but he knew his shooting was good.

Focusing on the buck at a point fractionally below where its neck joined the backbone above the shoulder blade, he squeezed the trigger to its first pressure point before breathing out, and then steadied himself again.

Crack! The antelope jerked with the impact of the bullet before dropping where it stood. The boom of the rifle echoed round the bush, and two animals sped away. Mark saw that the third buck Cartwright had pointed to was a very young one. This had probably been a small family group, though the amount of crashing in the bush told him that there were several more buck around.

"Neat job... well done."

"Thank you, sir. It's an impala isn't it?" They walked up to where the dead buck lay.

"Call me Peter. Yes. Quite a big one too, so it was probably the lead male in this herd." He lifted the buck's head up by one of the horns. "A nice pair; let's lift him up into the fork of this tree here, and collect him on our way back from the dam."

They spent almost an hour at the dam, where a small group of labourers were strengthening the spillway, using stones they'd brought down to the site on a pickup.

"This is the part needing most attention," Peter said.

Mark couldn't see what the problem was. "It looks OK to me. And there's not much water in the dam anyway."

Peter pointed out two small areas where some stones were missing, and others were loose. "Although it's less than half full now; when the rains come, the overflow can destroy an earth dam in a few hours if the spillway's not strong and secure."

They walked back across the dam wall and Peter indicated some good spots among the reeds for duck shooting.

"I haven't been duck shooting since I was a kid," Mark remarked.

"Could get some in tomorrow morning, if you like."

"That would be great." He knew he was committing himself to a pre-dawn start the next day but hell, he was enjoying himself.

"We'll go straight after they start milking at five." Peter finalised the arrangement. "Ask Sam to arrange for one of the houseboys to bring you tea first thing."

They got back to the farmhouse an hour before dusk and gave the 40-kilo impala over into Sam's care.

"Should we have it as part of the braai tomorrow night?" Mark asked. "Is that long enough for you to hang it, Sam?"

"No, baas, it is better to make biltong."

"OK, good idea. Go ahead, please Sam."

"Sam makes good biltong," Peter added, "but it won't be ready before you leave. Still, you can take some of the stuff from our store in compensation."

Dried game meat was particularly tasty and he was tempted, but he decided against Peter's offer. "That's very kind of you, but I can't carry much on the plane with me. I've enjoyed your hospitality and the shooting so much, I'm glad to be able to contribute a little something for the farm."

"Does baas Mark want the head and horns?" Sam asked. With that strange capability of African 'bush telegraph' – which white men knew existed but did not understand – no doubt all the Africans on the farm already knew a fine impala had been shot that afternoon. They would also know that Mark had been the one who killed it, with one clean shot. That would have established him as someone worthy of respect from the servants and other Africans on the farm. This showed in a barely discernible, but definite change in their demeanour towards him. Mark knew that respect would strengthen over time, provided he behaved in the manner expected of him.

"No thanks, Sam. I've nowhere to keep it," Mark excused himself. "You can keep the skin for yourself too if you like." He hunted for pleasure not for trophies. It would be another matter if he killed a leopard one day though. He'd keep a leopard skin.

"I'm off for a shower. Meet up for drinks at about six, Mark?"

"OK, see you there." Mark now felt completely comfortable with the farmer, a really good bloke. He was pleased to have made the beginnings of a friendship with this thoroughly decent and intelligent man.

* * *

Dinner was casual, and with only family being present, the conversation was relaxed and lively. Angie could see that there seemed to be a strong rapport growing between Mark and her father-in-law, and she noticed that even *her* father seemed to be warming to him, especially when Mark made himself the butt of a few jokes he told during dinner. Later, while they had coffee she heard Peter confirming arrangements with Mark for an early-morning expedition the next day.

"I'm off to bed," Peter announced when most of the others had gone. "Will the last one left please turn off the lights?"

Angie found herself alone with Mark, and was about to suggest another coffee to wind up the evening, when he interrupted her plan.

"I'd like to stretch my legs before I go to bed. Will you join me?"

They followed one of the crazy paving paths that led through the trees and flowerbeds. As they moved further away from the house, they kept more or less within the zone of the coloured lights, which stretched from tree to tree, giving just enough light to see by. The moon was bright, and even though it was quite low in the sky, it added illumination to some of the darker spots behind the trees and larger shrubs.

It seemed quite natural for Mark to take her hand when they negotiated the stepping-stones across the stream. But he didn't let go when they reached the other side and Angie wasn't sure how to handle the situation. She thought it would seem a little provincial to pull her hand away and, if she were to be honest, she rather liked the feel of his hand touching hers; his grip was gentle but firm and his barely suppressed physical strength flowed warmly, creating a pleasant, tingling feeling that went further than her hand. With an effort, she shrugged it off mentally; after all, holding someone's hand was hardly an assault on her virtue. She smiled inwardly at the notion.

Eventually they came to a wooden bench under a large spreading tree, and sat down. He sat very close and she could feel his thigh; firm and warm against hers. He still hadn't released her hand, using it to pull her closer to him. Surely he wouldn't make a pass at her? She felt a frisson of excitement. He had an aura of masculinity and barely restrained power about him, which made her feel vulnerable, yet at the same time protected. Silly fool, she thought – 27 years old; a married woman with three children... yet she felt like a teenager out on a first date. This wasn't quite right and she felt a little guilty. She liked being treated so gallantly by Mark, but sensed his changed mood. He was normally such a good conversationalist – now he was quiet.

They sat in companionable silence for a while, and she steadied herself, putting her racing heartbeat down to the wine she'd had with dinner. She would be more careful in future. She and Mark had known each other when they were children, and there was nothing wrong with taking a walk in the garden with your cousin after dinner, was there?

He pressed even closer. "I hope you're enjoying your stay here, Mark," she said, turning and looking up at him to gain space.

"I'm having a great time. How about you?" Mark spoke quietly; his deep voice very attractive.

"Oh, yes," she moved again, "but I mustn't keep you up too late. I heard you're going out very early tomorrow morning with Peter."

"No, Angie; it's only just after eleven." Mark gently tightened his hold on her hand. "I'm used to late nights and early morning starts anyway."

It was so nice, having someone to sit close to in this romantic setting. Ron never held her hand anymore. She relaxed, and then felt him place his arm around her shoulders... he drew her closer towards him. Now, sure he was making a pass, she almost stood up, but didn't. She'd leave it a little longer before calling a halt. But she didn't really want to stop him, not yet. What was she doing, letting her emotions run away like this? She wasn't in as much control of the situation as she ought to be. Was she waiting for him to kiss her? No! She didn't know what she wanted. But just a few more moments...

* * *

Christ, Mark thought, what am I doing? A married woman with three children, no less. He needed his head read. But his feelings for her were very strong; was he actually falling in love? That must be why he lost his poise when he first met her; love at first sight, for goodness sake. He turned carefully so he could look directly at her, and she responded by looking up at him.

Her clear blue eyes studied him guilelessly. While he looked at her, she blushed; from beyond the hollow below her throat upwards. Her lips parted slightly as she smiled up at him, perhaps to cover her confusion? She was impossible to resist, and Mark bent slowly down towards her, releasing her hand so he could touch her face. Her breath was clean and sweet smelling, with just a faint trace of wine.

"Aren't the stars bright?" She turned away from him to look up at the sky. "Even though there's a sort of mist, you can still see them easily." He glanced up and saw that the moon had a hazy circle around it.

"Rain again soon," he replied. A faint breeze gusted, and he took the opportunity to draw her close to him again. There was no resistance this time and she leant back onto his shoulder; her firm, smooth body fitting comfortably as he looked down at her. She seemed lost in her own thoughts so he deliberately didn't break the spell for a while, content just to have her in his arms.

But he knew he couldn't leave it at that; he had to take it further.

"Angie..." he started without knowing what he was going to say. She turned towards him again and he placed his hand on her cheek, carefully cupping her chin and lifting her face as he bent down to her. His lips touched hers and she melted into his arms, her lips soft and pliant. He kissed her passionately, his one hand holding her face and the other softly stroking her shoulder and pulling her even closer. He could feel her small breasts pressed against him, and her heart beating. Time seemed to stand still; he wanted it to last forever. This pure, gentle lovemaking with their lips as she breathed in his arms.

Suddenly he became aware that she was pushing against his chest. It wasn't a hard push but it was firm and steady, so he reluctantly released her.

"Mark," she whispered as she broke away, "this isn't right." She backed away from him on the bench, and he saw that the realisation of what had happened had shocked her. "What about Ronnie and my girls...?"

"I'm sorry. I just couldn't help it, Angie." He touched her arm to keep her seated on the bench. "I didn't mean to upset you and we haven't done any harm to anyone," he said quietly.

"We shouldn't have done that." She looked angry. Probably didn't believe him. "It'll be on my conscience. I've never done anything like this since I was married. Let's go straight back indoors now, please."

He was taken aback at her reaction. "Angie, I'm sorry," he repeated. What could he do to save the situation? "Don't be angry with me." This was not going to plan. Damn. The whole thing could go pear-shaped if he wasn't careful. Teach him for rushing ahead – gauche again. "Please don't go back yet."

She hesitated before settling down – not close enough for their bodies to touch, her arms folded and her head turned away. Oh,

Christ. She was really agitated. He took his arm away from the bench behind her, judging that she might find it threatening in her present state of mind. He touched her arm gently in what he hoped she would interpret as a non-threatening gesture. She ignored his hand but was tense, and he could tell she was struggling to bring her emotions under control. He judged it best to say nothing and it was several minutes before she broke the silence.

"Mark, I don't know what happened to me then... why I let you kiss me like that. I'm not that sort of person and although I like you..." she seemed to be struggling with herself, "I have Ron and my children to think of." She looked at him with those lovely eyes of hers. "Please let's not do that again."

What could be going on in her mind? During their drive up to the farm, his mother had hinted at things not being quite right between Angie and her husband. He cursed himself for not having pursued the subject. Mark paused for careful thought before setting about repairing the relationship for the future. She kept her distance but looked at him steady and unblinking, patiently waiting for his answer. Her apparently serene manner contrasted with her earlier agitation, and placed him under yet more pressure. He knew he had to be careful; this could go either way.

"I'm sorry if I upset you, Angie, but I just can't help feeling the way I do. I don't want to do anything to hurt you or your children." He paused before continuing. "Come, let's go back now." He offered his hand but she stood without his help. Back at the house, their goodnights were subdued and he stayed behind to switch off the lights. He just hoped he'd saved the situation.

Chapter 10

Shortly before sundown, a breathless Mujiba arrived from the kraal near where Gadziwa had left Sebukwe's section early that morning. The message was not good and the child sympathiser rolled his eyes in fear.

"You have done well, boy," Gadziwa encouraged the prospective freedom fighter. But his mind was already concentrating on the changes he'd have to make to his plans.

"It is no longer safe for us to remain here." Weiner panicked; beads of sweat oozing from his pale brown, pockmarked forehead. "The soldiers will find us. This whole trip is turning into a disaster; it's bewitched!"

Gadziwa was surprised that a half-white man believed in bewitching. He had always thought that spirits, which Africans feared, did not affect white people. The revelation was a useful piece of information, and he stored it away in his mind for possible future use. It would give him more power over the crafty little commissar, if ever he needed it. Gadziwa himself did not think their Mission was bewitched, though he respected, and even feared the spirits of his ancestors. Even if the other men he had led across the border were bewitched, he had taken powerful precautionary measures before leaving Mozambique. He was sure that his own Charms, for which he had paid the sangoma well, would protect him – and probably also the section he was leading.

"It was Sebukwe's carelessness that has caused all our troubles, Weiner. Do you not remember he was responsible for the escape of the first one – the fool who ran straight into the soldiers? Now that he is dead, we will be safer." Gadziwa swept his hand in a dismissive gesture. "Anyway, where else do you suggest we go, *Comrade Commissar?*" he sneered. "Do you want to run around the bush to escape the soldiers? You heard the helicopters all afternoon."

He turned aside to tell Mutasa that he would remain at his kraal, posing as a relative returned from working on the South African mines. "I worked there for two years before joining the freedom fighters, so I know enough to speak about it to the soldiers. But we must expect them to come here tomorrow in their search," Gadziwa warned him, "and Weiner must hide in the bush with the others. The white men will think a coloured being here is very suspicious." Mutasa nodded vigorous agreement.

Gadziwa briefed his boys in the nearby bush, telling them about Sebukwe's group. He wanted to make sure they were fully alert to the danger. "Sebukwe is the fool who allowed that sellout to escape in the Valley," he reminded them, "so he deserved to die. But we will not go to Zongoro's kraal tonight as planned. Instead, keep well in hiding, because these settler soldiers seem to know their business better than most." He looked at each of his men in turn, to make sure that his warning had sunk into their frightened heads.

"If you follow my instructions, you will be safe," he assured them. "I will send women with food and drink now. And I'll be back for you tomorrow before sundown; then we will take revenge for our lost comrades." Leaving them, he studied their hiding place from all angles, making sure they were well concealed among the riverine scrub.

He made his way back over the few hundred metres to Mutasa's kraal, thinking how fortunate he had been in placing himself, and his group, 15 kilometres away from where he had left Sebukwe at the kopje. But he cursed silently at the loss of the arms cache. Fortunately, the helicopters they'd heard during the afternoon had been many kilometres away, mainly heading away from his position, and back towards the Mozambique border. Even so, he had to anticipate that the search would extend to Mutasa's kraal at some stage.

"Send food and drink to Weiner and the boys now, before it gets too dark," Gadziwa ordered, and the old man hurried away to do his bidding.

Mutasa came back. "My women fear that the white soldiers will come while they are taking food to the boys, Comrade Captain."

"No, they will not be here before dawn, and they will not expect to find us here, because they think we would run for the border." Gadziwa ran over his plan, more to satisfy himself of its workability, than to answer Mutasa.

* * *

By midday next day, Gadziwa was congratulating himself on his planning. And on his acting ability.

"Yes, baas, no baas..." He had played the cheerful African worker, back from the mines, and the stupid soldiers who had come to search the kraal swallowed his story.

"We heard there were some gandangas over at Nagoya's kraal, baas," Mutasa offered, equally competent at play-acting. "We heard you have killed the bad men, so now we are safe." The crafty old kraal-head slanted his bloodshot eyes as if to see what effect his story was having on the leader of the soldiers. "Gandangas will not try to come here now, baas," he answered obsequiously to the soldiers' questions. The soldiers made a show of searching the huts in the kraal while Mutasa and Gadziwa sat comfortably, drinking beer and smoking. Mutasa even offered dagga and beer to them, which they refused, though Gadziwa could see some of them were tempted by the offer of the drug.

"These are not the same ones who followed us out of the Valley," Gadziwa told Mutasa quietly while the soldiers continued their search. "These ones are very easy to deal with." He was also relieved that they weren't the dreaded professional troopers called the RLI. He could tell these were part-time settler soldiers again.

"I beg you not to kill them here, Comrade Captain," Mutasa whispered; although he supported the Cause, he was still afraid of the consequences.

"Don't worry, I have more important things to do, old man." Gadziwa dismissed his fears.

They were left alone for the rest of the day, and late that afternoon, Gadziwa said his farewells. The old kraal-head was clearly relieved that he was leaving.

"*Fambai zvakanaka* – go well, Comrade Captain. And give Zongoro something to remember." Mutasa nodded, as if to emphasise his words; Gadziwa could see the thick layer of sweat and dust, colouring the white woolly hair on the old man's head.

"*Sarai zvakanaka* – stay well, old man. You have pleased me this time, and I will see you again when I come back. Perhaps sooner than you think." Gadziwa had given himself two hours before sunset to get to Zongoro's place and, as usual, left his host not knowing when next he might call.

* * *

Gadziwa and his men walked silently into Zongoro's kraal at dusk. "You remember me, Zongoro?" The shock on the old man's face gave Gadziwa a hint of the pleasure he was going to have this night.

"Yes... you are Gadziwa. The one the mukiwa call 'Big Feet'." Zongoro recovered his composure, and remained seated to receive the younger man. The women ran wailing to their huts, while Gadziwa's men surrounded the kraal to ensure that no one escaped.

"I want a little indaba, Zongoro. Your women and children must join us." Gadziwa signalled to his three fighters, and they commenced rooting the families out of their huts. They forced them at the end of their AK47s, into a tight group near where Gadziwa and Weiner were seated with Zongoro, outside his senior wife's dwelling.

"What do you bad men want with us?" Zongoro's fat wife emerged of her own accord from the house behind him. "Why do you frighten the young women and children?" Gadziwa remembered her from when he had last been here two summers ago. "There are no more big children here for you to steal," she berated him. She had not been so spirited then, after he had tied her up and taken her children from her. Yet, although he could see the fear in her eyes, she had recovered her dignity and was a fine looking woman. And magnificent, as a rightfully indignant mother.

Gadziwa stood up from his seat, and struck her in the mouth with the barrel of his gun. The big woman staggered, but did not loose her footing. Her mouth was bleeding profusely and she spat some teeth out.

"Shut up, and don't waste my time, woman." Gadziwa swung the barrel of his gun round and forced Zongoro back to his seat as the kraal-head tried to help his wife. "Join the others over there." He indicated the group of now whimpering women and small children, who sat under guard a few feet away.

His eyes followed Zongoro's senior wife, as she stumbled painfully across and settled with the other wives and their families. Then he saw something that made him stop and stare. There, partly hidden by the others, was the most beautiful musikana that he had seen for a long time. He signalled one of his men to guard Zongoro, while he walked over to the family group.

"Why are you hiding, pretty one?" He pulled the girl to her feet. "What are you afraid of?" Like any well bred musikana, she made no answer, merely casting her eyes down so as not to look directly at him, and grasping her hands shyly in front of her body.

"Leave the girl alone," Zongoro called fearfully from his seat. "She has not yet seen her 13th summer. She is the child of my daughter."

Gadziwa shoved the girl back to the ground, where she had been seated with the other women and children. "Watch this one well. I will deal with her later," he warned the two men who were guarding the group.

The senior wife put her arm around the girl in a gesture of protection, and although the girl-child all but disappeared into the huge woman's bosom, he could see she was trying to wipe the blood tenderly from her grandmother's face.

"You do not offer us hospitality, old man?" Gadziwa observed.

The kraal-head told one of his younger wives to bring beer. This was the minimum hospitality tradition prescribed. Gadziwa walked into the solidly built house behind the old man, fully aware that he was breaching etiquette by doing so uninvited.

Unlike the rest of the homes in the village, this one was built in the white man's style. The house was rectangular, rather than round. And it was built over concrete and brick foundations, instead of straight onto the ground. It was clearly built to last. Gadziwa looked into each of the four rooms, which were spotlessly clean and neatly ordered. There was no one there. He looked up at the tidy thatched roof, and smiled to himself before walking back out to the verandah that stretched across the front of the house.

"Come here, Zongoro," Gadziwa called, and the old man shuffled up the stairs to join him. "Where is your money?" he asked casually.

"I keep all my money at the post office in Sipolilo."

"Give me your savings book." The old man hesitated, but then walked past Gadziwa and into his bedroom. Gadziwa followed, and watched while Zongoro tried to hide the fact that he was reaching under the bed to recover the savings book.

"Now I need cash." Gadziwa was amazed at the large sum registered in the book, over $4,000. But he knew it would be difficult for anyone to get at the money, because it was likely that Zongoro would be well known at the Sipolilo post office. He placed the book into one of his pockets anyway.

"I told you I have no cash."

Gadziwa hit the old man across his face with the barrel of his gun, and he fell to the floor at his feet. "You must keep the cash from your store here, before you take it to the post office."

"I have no cash here." The kraal-head was stubborn, so Gadziwa shoved him towards the door with his boot until they reached the verandah. The women cried out when they saw Zongoro's face swollen and bleeding, as he crawled on all fours to the top of the steps. Gadziwa stood over the kneeling man, his legs on either side of the skinny old body. Taking out his knife he grabbed the old man's jaw with his other hand, and jerked his head backwards to expose his scrawny neck.

"This old man says he has no cash here. Where is the cash, big mother?" He directed his question to the senior wife. "He will die if you don't know." Gadziwa leaned over and casually slashed off one of Zongoro's ears, to show he meant business. The women and children began wailing again, and it was some time before he could shut them up. "I will cut off his other ear, to save him from suffering your noise." He placed his knife below the remaining ear and the group fell silent, apart from one of the babies crying.

"The money is under the mattress in the bedroom," the senior wife answered. "It is all we have. Take it and leave us alone."

Gadziwa shoved the injured man down the steps onto the clean swept ground, and went back inside to collect the cash. He opened the bag but didn't bother to count. There was a good bundle of notes, in addition to a heavy load of coins. He shoved all the notes into his pocket, before tying the bag again and carrying it out to hand over to Weiner.

"This will help you after we have left, Comrade Commissar."

"Where is his savings book, Comrade Captain?" Weiner was not a stupid man.

Gadziwa pondered a while before giving the book to the commissar. There was little he could do with it in the time that he would remain in Zimbabwe, and he could think of no way to get at the money anyhow. Besides, it would cause real trouble if he were captured with it in his possession. Better leave that to Weiner.

* * *

When Ron and his men had got back to company headquarters the previous day, they expected to enjoy their R&R in the Zambezi Valley. Instead, they found HQ busy packing up and almost ready to move out.

"The RLI have got one of your escaped group of terrs, Ron; all four of them. And we've been ordered to move up to the TTL where you tracked them," Major Swain quickly appraised him. "Get your stuff onto your vehicles. You can have your R&R tomorrow."

Typical Army fuck-up. Oh well. "What about Big Feet, sir? Did they get him?"

"No, the bastard is still at large. Maybe you'll get another chance at him?" Swain looked at him quizzically. "What's the big deal with this particular terr, Ron? Do you always just want to get the big fish?"

"No, sir. But I've come across Gadziwa – that's his real name – before. He came damn close to killing me and several of my lads. He's fucking evil."

* * *

They'd arrived at their new camp late that night, but had been sent out at dawn, to investigate reported terrorist atrocities in a nearby African purchase area.

"Shit, look at that." Bill followed Ron into the doorway of the still smoking store. It was obvious the place had been ransacked before being burnt down. Discarded merchandise lay scattered all around.

"Any luck with tracks, Herbie?" Ron spotted him return from his three-sixty with two of the other lads in the patrol.

"Nothing, Ishe; their tracks were covered last night when a herd of mombies was driven all round here."

"Obviously that was deliberate," Ron grumbled to no one in particular. "There's no other reason for cattle to be driven all over the place at night. Well, there's nothing we can do here. Better get up to the owner's kraal, and see if everything's all right there."

The devastation at Zongoro's kraal was complete. All the huts, and the main dwelling house, had been fired. And the plight of the villagers themselves was appalling.

"Tom, come over and see what you can do for this poor old chap." Ron called the team's best medic, Tom Blair, to look at the old man who was resting in the arms of a big woman. They were in the shade of the stone wall of a cattle kraal, not far from the main village.

"He's been beaten badly and they've cut off both his ears and lips, sir. We need to get him hospitalised soon, or he could die from shock and infection."

"Who else needs attention?" Ron could see that others had been hurt, including the woman who was holding the old man. Although badly beaten, she waved Ron away towards a young girl who was slumped nearby, her head hanging down onto her chest. The old woman's shoulders shook, as she wept silently.

Ron turned to the girl and gently lifted her face to see what the matter was. He couldn't see any obvious injuries, but she seemed almost lifeless; her eyes glazed.

"She has been raped," the old woman said bitterly. "Many times by the gandangas who came here last night." Ron turned to go, too shocked and horrified to say or do anything. He felt responsible, somehow.

"The gandanga who did this is called Gumbarishumba," the old woman shrieked at him. "He brings his men here every time, and no one protects us."

"She tells the truth, Ishe." Herbie appeared quietly next to Ron. "I've found his tracks and four others."

Ron's stomach churned, and pity turned to cold anger in his heart. The old woman was right – the whole system had failed her. Here was a decent family, living peacefully; working and building for the future just like his own family. They'd played by the rules, trusting in the law. But the law had failed them, and people like them. Ron was in the front line, and he'd failed to stop Gadziwa...

Chapter 11

Guided by Weiner, Gadziwa and his men arrived at the mission station, which lay on the outskirts of the administrative township of Sipolilo, just before dawn. Weiner went in ahead of them, while Gadziwa and his men remained out of sight. Their tense wait in the growing daylight was alleviated when he reviewed the success of their Mission so far. Zongoro's burning kraal and the cries of the villagers were still fresh in his mind, and they were now in possession of the kraal-head's virtually new pick-up... plus his cash.

Finally, a bearded white man dressed in the strange clothing that Gadziwa recognised as the kind used by some Christian leaders, came back with Weiner. He showed them a shed, just beyond the boundaries of the mission, where they could hide the pickup.

"Now, Comrade Gadziwa," the missionary addressed him respectfully, "please will you and your men leave your weapons and other military equipment here in this lockup cupboard? You will see that I have prepared a safe place for them."

"No, we will not be parted from our weapons," Gadziwa replied emphatically.

"But we cannot be sure that all our students are supporters of the Chimurenga war of independence, or that they will keep quiet about what they see here," the churchman pleaded with him. "And we do not know all our lay teachers well enough; some of them have only recently arrived from Europe and America." He peered anxiously at Gadziwa through thick lenses. "Even though they are sympathetic towards the Cause, and say they are here to support the struggle, we do not yet know how much to trust them. Some do not understand that to win, we have to fight."

Gadziwa listened to the long speech but refused to risk their weapons. The missionary was right to be concerned, but there was no way he was going to place himself totally in the hands of these strange people. "We will keep our weapons but hide them well within our clothes." He ended the argument with a firm sweep of his hand.

The missionary conceded reluctantly, and led them to the mission by a back route, ushering them into a room adjoining the staff dining hall. Gadziwa noticed that only a few members of staff were invited to join them there, and assumed they were trusted ones. The room itself looked as if it might be a small classroom or a large office.

"Do you need to get in touch with Chifombo?" the priest asked after they finished the meal. "We have a radio here and can call them if you wish."

"There must be no radio contact." Gadziwa was adamant.

"It's all right, Captain, we know why you are here."

Gadziwa eyed the man suspiciously. What did he know about their Mission? "There will be no radio contact," he warned, fixing the priest with a stare.

Gadziwa saw fear come to the missionary's eyes, and watched him scuttle away like a chastised dog. With that irritation gone, he sent his men to rest in a nearby room that had been assigned for the purpose. He chose to remain awake, and sat outside in the sunshine, keeping his RPD with him – but out of sight.

Commissar Weiner, who had handed his own RPD over to the churchman, sat next to him but said nothing. He would be remaining at the mission after Gadziwa and his men left to attack the white settlers later that day. Gadziwa would be glad to get rid of this man. He just couldn't blend in with African people; he'd always be a curiosity, attracting attention. Yes, people talked about anything out of the ordinary, and that would be a danger to their objective.

He turned his thoughts away from Weiner, and focused his attention on his next moves. For a brief moment, Gadziwa wondered if he should also leave the pickup at the mission station. No; there was still a very long way to go to the target. Near on a truck, but far on foot. He could not trust anyone else to drive them there either. He'd take the pickup, and use it for their getaway too.

He did not know the area very well and was not sure he could remember, or trust the details of the directions given to him by Mutasa. The missionary said he knew why they were there; could it be that he should ask him for more information?

The decision was taken out of his hands when Weiner interrupted his thoughts. "The Comrade Doctor has offered to help with directions for you to find the place you are planning to attack tonight,

Comrade Captain." He had almost forgotten Weiner's presence next to him. Now it seemed as if Weiner had read his thoughts.

Gadziwa was incredulous. "Who told him?" he said, filled with fury.

"I did, comrade; he knows what we are here to do." Weiner backed away in fear at Gadziwa's angry response. "He does not know the exact place you are going to attack, comrade. I have not told him that – but he says he's got maps…"

Gadziwa grabbed the man's throat in his hand and squeezed; Weiner writhed helplessly in his grasp. "I will kill you next time you speak of our plans without my permission, Weiner," he hissed, pressing his thumb into the windpipe and feeling the ineffective struggling increase as Weiner choked. After a while he released him, and the coloured slid to his knees in front of him. "See how easy it is for you to die."

"I thought you would need help, Comrade Captain," Weiner croaked, remaining on his knees.

Now the fool commissar had told the white man, there was no point in trying to hide their destination from him. "Take me to the missionary," Gadziwa commanded. He'd also decided to try and get new transport; by now, the enemy forces would know Zongoro's truck was missing, and it would be better to get something else.

The missionary took them to a small office, which housed a big, modern radio setup. It was also a treasure house of detailed up-to-date maps covering the surrounding country, and he showed Gadziwa the route he thought they should take.

"After you get over the Umvukwes hills, try to take this side road," he said. "Soldiers and the police will be looking for you on the main roads."

Humph, the fool keeps stating the obvious. "It will be safer for us if you give us a different truck so we don't have to take the one we have here." Gadziwa refrained from mentioning that they'd stolen the truck, but he needn't have bothered.

"Yes, it would be safer; they will be looking for the one you confiscated from Zongoro." The missionary studied Gadziwa from behind his spectacles. "But you cannot take one from here or it will implicate the mission with your attack."

Gadziwa was about to say he'd take a vehicle by force; he did not need anyone's permission, but wondered if it would also be reported as stolen and cause more complications…

The priest interrupted his thoughts. "I know where we can get one for you, though."

Hmmm… this white man was truly useful.

"Give me the keys of the truck and I'll get it changed for you."

Gadziwa hesitated only a moment before deciding to trust the missionary with the keys. "Make sure it is a good one," he said, before turning to study the map again.

* * *

Ron and his soldiers spent the next hour that morning searching the area surrounding Zongoro's kraal for clues. A detective from the CID joined them, concentrating on questioning the villagers. It soon emerged that a pickup had gone missing, so they all focused on trying to find vehicle tracks. There were only three rough roadways that could reasonably be used by wheeled transport, but cattle had been driven along these in the early morning, obliterating all traces.

Eventually Ron was called to look at some tyre marks, several kilometres from the store. "OK men, this looks promising. Let's get going." They climbed onto the back of the tough old Bedford RL and Ron took the wheel himself. As a precaution against ambush and land-mines, the truck had no doors. That made it easier for Herbie, riding in the passenger seat next to Ron to stand up and lean out, so he could keep an eye on the suspect tracks. Luckily, no other vehicle had used the road that day.

* * *

When Herbie finally admitted his frustration, Ron radioed Swain. "We've come to the main road that leads north from Sipolilo up into the Valley, sir… but we can't make out which direction the bastards took. It's a major tarred road and the junction itself is covered in vehicle tracks of all kinds; looks like it's used as a regular stopping point."

"Probably gone north towards the Valley, Ron. They've already done their worst, and they'd be unlikely to risk getting caught in town."

"I could put up a roadblock here and ask questions of traffic going in both directions, sir," Ron suggested. "We have a full description of the pickup."

"How about you drive north up to the edge of the Valley instead?" the CO countered. "In fact, looking at the map, you can go down over the escarpment, cross the Hunyani and Angwa Rivers, and get back here to base-camp the long way round. It's only about 200 kilometres overall, and on that road it'll probably be faster than heading straight back across the rough cross-country tracks."

Ron had this uneasy feeling... "There's still a chance the bastards have gone past Sipolilo, and that opens up all sorts of possibilities for them, including the European farming areas, even Salisbury," he pointed out.

"That can never be ruled out, but it's outside our area of operation, so let's stick to my plan."

Ron knew Swain was right but that was no comfort. His parents' farm was only about 100 kilometres beyond Sipolilo... But then, there were plenty of farms and other potential targets for the terrs to go for, in the unlikely event that they were headed south, instead of north. And, he reminded himself, his job was up here in the Valley. He shifted uncomfortably. Yeah, after all there were the police... and other Army units too – all looking after the farms and towns south of Sipolilo.

"OK, let's get moving. We'll stop for lunch at the Angwa River," he snapped and climbed aboard the old Bedford.

* * *

"You know it's New Year's Eve?" the missionary asked.

Gadziwa's patience was being tried again. "Yes, the farmers and the security forces will be celebrating this white man's festival," he responded. "That is why I have chosen to attack tonight."

At that moment, a nun rushed into the room. "The police are coming, Father."

"Quick, we must hide you and your men." The priest hustled Gadziwa towards the room where his men were resting. "You can hide down here." The missionary moved a bed to one side and lifted a hatch in the floor. Steps led down to a space large enough for them all to get into, with their weapons and equipment.

"Get down there," Gadziwa commanded, and followed when they were all safely below. The priest closed the trap door; the room was too low for Gadziwa to stand up, and he shuffled across the cool earthen floor towards a small source of daylight. The floor of the cellar was well below ground level so the air vent, from which the daylight came, was only half a metre above ground level outside.

Gadziwa saw a police Land Rover draw up in a cloud of dust a few metres away from the vent, near the entrance to the building where they were hiding. Good, the missionaries must have been keeping a lookout. A white police officer stepped out of the driver's side, nearest to the cellar, and a black policeman joined him. They were alone, and he could not see any other enemy vehicles. He saw a nun walk from the door of the building towards the police. It was the same nun who had come in to warn them.

"Good morning, officer, good morning, sergeant." She turned smiling from one to the other. "What brings you here?" Gadziwa heard their conversation clearly.

"Good morning, sister," the white policeman answered. "There has been some trouble in a neighbouring TTL, about 60 kilometres from here." The policeman indicated a north-westerly direction. "We're looking for a white Datsun pickup truck that was stolen from the scene of the crime." He read out a registration number.

"We've seen nothing here, officer."

"Do you know kraal-head Zongoro? His family have been badly beaten, and his 12-year-old granddaughter suffered multiple rape." There was a pause. "His store and homestead have been burned down, and the terrorists mutilated the old man." The policeman had his back to Gadziwa, but he could see the nun; she showed shock in her face, but it didn't reach her eyes, which remained unblinking and cold. Gadziwa was impressed; he'd thought these Christians were weak.

She put her hand up to touch the cross at her breast. "I'm sorry to hear that, officer. We do not know kraal-head Zongoro, but we have heard of him." The voice belied the nun's sympathetic look. "We have not seen the truck you are looking for, but we will keep a good lookout for it, and contact you if we do."

"There were five terrorists, including a coloured man. They're all armed and extremely dangerous," the policeman persisted. "Do you mind if we take a look around while we're here, Sister? It is possible that something or someone is here without you knowing."

"Please come in and search wherever you like." The nun opened the door wide and waved the police through, following them into the darkness beyond. Gadziwa lost sight of them, but remained watching. The sun beat down on the clean, swept dirt quadrangle beyond the driveway where the police Land Rover was parked. White painted rocks, and a few hardy cannas bloomed around the edges of the dusty square and along the gravel roadways. There was space for several vehicles to park outside the building where he and his men were hidden. He could see more buildings – long lines of schoolrooms surrounding the quadrangle. The administrative offices and dining halls all seemed to be on this side. Children were in the Chapel, and he could hear snatches of singing and prayer. That reminded him it was a Sunday. Soon they were released and went past, laughing and playing happily.

Suddenly, he heard footsteps in the room above them.

"Here, lie down and pretend you are sick." He could hear a woman's voice speaking to someone in the local dialect. It was not the same voice as the nun who was with the police. He heard more people move across the room above them, and the bedsprings creaked as they lay down. "Stay where you are until I say so; say nothing to the police unless they ask, and then tell them you are sick. Don't answer any other questions. Just look afraid and they will leave you alone." The woman spoke the Shona language fluently.

Gadziwa guessed that the police must have been conducting a search of the administrative rooms in addition to the grounds and outbuildings. He motioned his men to keep silent, and made sure they all had their weapons ready; he would fight his way out if he had to. There were only two policemen, and neither of them appeared to be carrying weapons, although the African sergeant had a set of handcuffs and a truncheon hanging from his belt. Gadziwa and his three freedom fighters could easily take them on if necessary. For that matter, he could deal with both policemen on his own. He knew he could not rely on his boys, who were afraid of soldiers and policemen.

Some ten minutes later, he heard the police come into the room.

"This is our sick room, officer." Gadziwa heard the voice of the first nun. "This is Sister Winifred, who is in charge here."

"Good morning, sir. *Tikukwazisei,* sergeant," the woman they called Sister Winifred greeted the white officer first, and then the black policeman formally in the Shona language, which made Gadziwa certain she must be an African nun. Further polite greetings were exchanged before the African policeman reverted to English.

"What is wrong with these children?" he asked. Gadziwa gripped his weapon in readiness in the dark cellar immediately below.

"This one has an upset *dumbu* – stomach," she translated for the white policeman's benefit. "This one has an earache..." Gadziwa could hear the group move around the room above him until all four children had been spoken to at their bedsides, and the policemen finally moved off.

Half an hour later, they appeared back at the Land Rover, and the nun, who still accompanied them, saw them off.

"I'll contact you if any strangers come," Gadziwa heard her say and he crawled back to the trap door, impatient to get out.

* * *

Gadziwa took the keys of the replacement vehicle from the missionary and looked sceptically at the dirty old wreck in front of him.

"This is a very old car." He went round to the driver's door and opened it. "It will fall apart before we reach our goal."

"One big advantage is that it is not likely to attract the attention of the police; it's the sort of car they will expect an African to be driving," the missionary pointed out reasonably. Gadziwa gave him a sharp look, and he added hurriedly. "If it was too new, they would suspect it had been stolen."

Gadziwa snorted at the fool, who was digging himself ever deeper with his cringing explanations. Then he turned away to hide his amusement and started the motor, listening as it stuttered reluctantly into life.

"Get in the car," he snapped, and the missionary scrambled into the passenger seat as Gadziwa drove off. The white man had to make two attempts before he finally slammed his door closed. Gadziwa grinned mirthlessly, watching him hold on desperately to both the door and the dashboard, not trusting the door to remain closed, while the vehicle rattled along the mission driveway towards the entrance at the main road.

The car proved to be sufficiently robust, and Gadziwa had to agree it was unlikely to attract much attention from anyone. If the police did stop them, it would be to check the brakes or lights to see if it was roadworthy, so when they got back, he made a point of checking the front and rear lights. Everything seemed to be in working order.

"Yes, I will take it," he told the missionary. "What has happened to the pickup that I brought here?"

"We have arranged for it to be disposed of tonight. We dare not keep it here for any length of time."

"How much money did you get for it?"

"We exchanged it for this car." It was obvious the missionary was no fool.

"The tsotsi who made the swap will be a happy man today."

"Remember that he has much work to do with it before he can use it or get rid of it, Captain. He will have to change its identity completely."

Gadziwa had to acknowledge the truth of this to himself, but it still irked him that he had lost an almost new vehicle in exchange for an old wreck.

"We must eat now, and get ready before we leave." Gadziwa dismissed the car from his mind, and they headed towards the room where they had eaten that morning. "I want to get near the target before it is dark." Driving in the dark would be more likely to attract attention from the police or soldiers.

After they had eaten, the missionary asked him to drive round to a shed at the back of the administration building, where he would meet him. Gadziwa loaded his men into the old car with all their equipment, and drove across to the shed.

"Don't point that fucking barrel at me, you stupid bastard," Gadziwa snapped at the man in the passenger seat next to him.

The missionary was waiting there for them, together with the nun who had dealt with the police that morning. "May I suggest that you hide your guns by tying them to the chassis under the car?" he asked. "If the police stop you, they may search the car, including the boot," he added, to convince Gadziwa.

Although Gadziwa was reluctant to release the weapons, he had to accept the missionary's advice was good.

The doors of the shed were partially closed, making it difficult for anyone to look in and see what they were doing. There was just enough light inside for them to be able to work at the car. They jacked up one side and Gadziwa instructed two of the men to tie the guns to the chassis. He dragged himself on the dust floor to get a good view under the car, and showed them exactly where to place them. Where he could, he chose spaces between the chassis frame and the body. There, they would have some protection from stones thrown up by the wheels, and would not be scraped off if they hit bumps or rocks in the road.

Gadziwa emerged from under the car, and the white nun handed him several sacks. "These are for you to put your other equipment into, so that you can tie them under the chassis as well."

Soon all their arms and equipment – anything that could identify them as freedom fighters – were tied securely to the chassis.

"Are there any trains running from Concession to Salisbury?" he asked, after establishing that it was the nearest railway station to Sipolilo, which had no railway and had to rely on bus services; they would need a story to tell the police if they were stopped before they reached their destination.

The missionary shrugged his shoulders, but the clever white nun answered his question. "Yes there's a slow mixed passenger and goods train once a day. It passes through Concession at four in the morning and it runs every day. It stops at every siding on the way and takes many hours to get to Salisbury, so most people take the bus."

"But surely you're not planning to go to Salisbury after you've completed your raid?" The missionary looked incredulous.

Hah… The fool was not able to understand why he'd asked about the train service. He had no intention of telling them what his true plans were. They already knew too much.

They left the mission just after four that afternoon and drove through the township of Sipolilo, heading for the Umvukwes hills and Concession. The road was much better now, with a proper tarred surface. The loaded car ran surprisingly well, although it did struggle up the hills. From Sipolilo the road was busy with traffic including buses, but most of them were heading north. There was a lot of traffic, which gave comfort to Gadziwa, and their old car blended in well with the other vehicles being driven by Africans.

Suddenly, right in the pass over the Umvukwes hills, they came to a police roadblock.

"Keep silent," Gadziwa snarled at his men. The acrid stench of their fear was strong as they sat in the car waiting in the short southbound queue; the police were busy checking the much longer queue coming from the other direction.

"*Manheru madoda* – good evening gentlemen," the African policeman greeted them politely in Shona. Gadziwa made the correct response.

"Your car is very hot," the policeman remarked; it was true that steam was beginning to rise from the radiator. Gadziwa took a risk and switched the engine off... it shook and shuddered to a hissing halt. He worried that it might not start again, and they would be forced to wait among the police until it cooled; or even worse, abandon it with all their weapons and equipment. But leaving the engine running would definitely cause suspicion.

"It is old, officer and we are all hot in the car."

"Where are you going at this late hour?"

"My brother here," Gadziwa indicated Comrade M'butu who was sitting next to him, "is going to take the early morning train from Concession to Salisbury tomorrow. We don't want to miss it, so we will sleep at the Location in Concession tonight."

"Why are you taking the train to Salisbury when the bus is much faster?"

"My brother is taking four bags of mealie meal to our family in Salisbury, and the bus will not allow such a heavy weight for one passenger." Gadziwa had anticipated that question, and the policeman accepted his answer.

"We are looking for a white Datsun pickup truck. It's almost new, with a double blue line painted along the sides; have you seen one like that today?" the policeman asked.

Gadziwa paused for a moment, as if thinking about the matter before he shook his head. "Sorry but we only left Sipolilo this afternoon," he replied, as if to explain their inability to help.

"We are also looking for five men, one is a coloured." The policeman bent down and looked into the car again; Gadziwa could sense the tension among his boys.

"Would you like us to get out of the car?" he offered, but just then there was a shout from inside a bus, which was at the head of the northbound queue at the roadblock.

The policeman straightened up and left them, striding towards the bus. Gadziwa could see the passengers were milling around the side of the bus, having been asked to disembark by the police. Now they all watched as a drunk was forcibly evicted from the vehicle and pushed to the ground, while the two policemen handcuffed him. He was struggling and shouting abuse at the police, provoking much laughter among the onlookers. A short while later, the policeman came back and waved them through the roadblock.

Gadziwa gave silent thanks to his ancestors… and the drunk. But as he tried to get going, the car stubbornly refused to start. The troublesome car provided a new source of attention and amusement for the bus passengers, now that the drunk was restrained and quiet.

"Get out and push," he hissed at his three companions. Eventually, assisted by several of the bus passengers, the car stuttered to life; Gadziwa slowed to allow his three sweating comrades to catch up and jump aboard the moving vehicle. He dared not stop altogether, in case the car stalled. They pulled jerkily away, leaving the police and their roadblock behind.

"We did well, comrades," he encouraged them. "Soon we will be near our objective where we can rest again before we make the attack."

Chapter 12

Mark and Peter got back mid-morning, to find the kitchen a hive of activity.

"Sam's busy with the preparations, but we've saved some breakfast for you," Kate welcomed them. "I see you've had good shooting..." she sighed, "but this is hardly the best day to be adding to our larder; especially with all the work we have to do." Mark could see her point, and felt a bit of a fool, especially with Angie being there.

"Never mind, give them to me and we'll deal with them while you have your breakfast." Kate smiled to soften the rebuke as she and Sam took the ducks and guinea fowl, carrying them through to the scullery. Mark heard her giving instructions to one of the kitchen hands; the guinea fowl merely to be gutted and hung in the cool room until the afternoon, but the duck to be fully prepared and placed in the freezer straight away for use another time. He muttered an apology to Peter, who hunched his shoulders in solidarity, indicating a chair for him to join him at the kitchen table.

Angie seemed too busy to take any notice of him, so after a hurried bite, Mark went and took a shower before wandering outside to see if he could make himself useful. He saw his mother and uncle having tea in the lapa; they were watching Angie's girls, who were playing on a trampoline near the pool; the water looked inviting, but he couldn't skive off like that – not with so much going on.

He decided to go and help Peter, who was supervising the slaughtering of a pig, along with two sheep, and the large ox that had been brought in from a neighbouring farm. He'd been told the pig would be for their braai, the sheep and ox for Cartwright's farm workers' feast. A smaller, younger ox, and a lamb had been butchered for the guests' braai several days before. Those carcasses were hanging in the farm cold room. There was bound to be something he could do to help...

"Mark!" Angie's father called out to him as he was passing the lapa. "Tell me, how's business?" This sounded like an invitation to talk seriously, so he stopped and sat next to the older man.

"It's tough going, Uncle John. You know how difficult it is; South Africa's under a lot of pressure from the UK, and the USA to stop breaking UN sanctions and supplying Rhodesia. I'm relying more and more on obscure sources, such as the Middle Eastern and North African states; that's in addition to the communist bloc, of course." He was aware that his uncle, being a senior executive with the Land Bank, would have close government connections and be well informed on these matters. He would certainly be involved with the export of cotton, beef, maize and tobacco. Could be useful.

"But that's where you come in, isn't it?" the old boy prompted.

Mark saw that his mother and the children were preoccupied, and not paying attention so was about to continue; but a servant passed, wielding a net on the end of a long pole, skimming leaves and insects off the pool surface. "I do what I can, sir," Mark stalled, waiting for the man to move further away.

His uncle looked irritated, and shifted uncomfortably in his seat. "Our foreign currency reserves are being stretched badly now, and I hope you'll try to ensure that we don't pay too much over the odds for what you get for us, Mark." So that was what the earlier tension had been about. It seemed that old Greville suspected him of profiteering. Mark felt a flush of anger; he was damned if he'd take the sort of risks required in his business, without benefiting from the rewards.

But on the other hand, he was his mother's brother *and* Angie's father. There was no point in antagonising the man, and maybe he had sensible motives for questioning him this way. Besides, he wanted to see more of Angie, and didn't want the unnecessary complication of a hostile father.

"I could probably do better with prices on imports if I had the opportunity to help with exports," Mark said reasonably, adopting a placating attitude; there could be an opportunity for business here. "It might be possible to trade, rather than always having to use US currency, for example." Everything went back to US dollars, even when trading with Eastern Europe. "It would also give me better negotiating power with the agents I use."

He was aware that there were forces with powerful political connections in both Rhodesia and South Africa, who had interests in the export of mineral and agricultural produce. If he could break into the export side of the market, he would be doing very well; he was sure he could offer better deals than they were currently getting – and still make handsome profits.

"There's political sensitivity associated with both exports *and* imports."

Mark was not surprised his uncle was aware of that. It was a pretty open secret that certain political figures were feathering their own nests on the back of sanctions busting. He needed to be very careful here.

"Yes, but it doesn't make for the best trading arrangements if they continue as they are now." He didn't want to make too many waves, or he might lose out on the business he already had by crossing powerful people in both countries. "I really don't want to rock the boat too much. But if there is any way you can help without compromising my existing relations in this country, I'll be happy to make the effort and work with you to bring prices down and save foreign currency."

Mark knew his activities were small beer, compared with the trade involving the sale of Rhodesian maize to neighbouring African states, which couldn't grow enough to feed themselves. It was exchanged for vital petroleum based fuels from South Africa. But he knew he could trade other, more contentious Rhodesian commodities such as copper, chromium, tantalite and other strategic mineral ores, in exchange for arms.

"I don't need to know too much about the details of your work Mark, but I do have influence that I might be able to use for the benefit of the country." John Greville brushed the idea of his direct personal involvement aside. "Of course, I realise you need to make your profits, but we simply can't afford to keep paying at the present level; you could end up killing the golden goose."

Mark was fairly confident that what he brought to the table would be hard to replace. "As you may know, at the moment I supply only certain secret materials," he said, carefully avoiding using the word 'arms'. Should he risk the good business he already had for more? The spares, specialist ammunition and weapons he obtained for the Rhodesian military, admittedly at a good profit to himself, could not be sourced easily elsewhere, but nothing was impossible. "But I have other good connections and trading will encourage them to offer better prices."

The pool-cleaning servant came back into listening range, and Mark was pleased to see his uncle hesitate until he moved on.

"You're talking minerals – base metals – and so forth, I presume? Trade in gold, and foodstuffs like maize *et cetera*, is already spoken for."

Mark nodded confirmation.

"Very well... I'll see what I can do," Greville said, looking at him. "When will you next be back up here?"

"I can't be too sure; but if you think I should come up, I'll make a point of it." The two men made arrangements for Mark to be contacted, if and when Greville felt it might be useful. Mark was pleased with himself; nothing might come of it, but he'd established a decent rapport with his uncle, and at least he wouldn't be a negative factor with Angie.

"I'd better get along and see if I can help Peter with the braai arrangements, if you'll excuse me, Uncle John."

* * *

Angie had avoided looking at Mark when he came into the kitchen that morning. Her emotions were still in turmoil. She should never have allowed him to kiss her. After all, she'd handled this sort of thing before, so what was different this time? It was because – and she had trouble admitting it to herself – she'd wanted Mark to touch her, and to kiss her. She squirmed with embarrassment as she remembered her initial response. It must have made her protestations about Ron and the girls sound so feeble.

"Will you do the potato salad please, Angie?" Kate interrupted her thoughts, and she concentrated on removing the new potatoes from the big pot where they'd been boiling. She drained the water from them in the huge colander over one of the sinks, and left them to cool, turning back to washing and slicing tomatoes into salad bowls.

Angie tried to think it through. Had the realisation that she no longer loved Ronnie made her vulnerable? Surely she could sort things out without involving a third party? But Mark had unsettled her; what had he meant when he said 'he couldn't help feeling the way he did'? Well, she'd never know because she'd make sure she was never alone with him again. Once he got back to South Africa he would forget all about her.

After all, his world was so different to hers. All that international travel. A sanctions-buster; it sounded awfully glamorous... and hazardous. She supposed he must make a lot of money, and that he met a lot of exciting – even dangerous – people. There were rumours that while the USA and England rigidly enforced the UN sanctions, the Russians and the Chinese would trade with Rhodesia – at a price. She wondered if Mark actually went into communist countries to do his deals.

"When did you say Ron is back from the bush, Angie?" her mother asked.

"Not until the week after New Year, Mum; he only went away ten days before Christmas, and they have to do four weeks in the bush each time now." She tried to brush loose hair away from her eye with the back of her hand, but only succeeded in making it worse.

"That's a long time, and it's especially unfortunate that he has to be away for *both* Christmas and New Year." Her mother sounded quite offended. "You'd think they could at least let him have one of the holidays at home."

"Well, I suppose they decided that once someone was going to miss one of the holidays, they might as well miss both," Kate said sensibly.

"It still seems unfair to me. How is Charlotte, Angie? Is she coming to the party tonight?"

Charlie Macdonald had been at school with Angie. She remembered how they'd both fantasised about Mark back then, sharing their secret thoughts about him, and other boys. Charlie was never one to ignore a good looking man, and she would enjoy meeting up with Mark again. And Mark? Well, a fling with Charlie and he would soon forget about Angie. Her friend's attitude towards her marriage had always been a little cavalier and Charlie would have no hang-ups about entertaining Mark...

"Angie...?"

"Oops, sorry Mum... miles away," she gathered her thoughts. "Charlie's fine and yes she's coming. Brian's parents are over from Scotland for an extended visit, and they're looking after her children." Angie took a tray of bowls with prepared salad and found places for them in a fridge.

"Is Brian coming to the party too?"

"No, he went into the Army before Ron."

"Goodness. How often do they get called up these days?" Kate asked.

"Not sure anymore. It used to be once a year, but this is Ron's third call up this year, and he's talking about four weeks every three months from now on." Of course, he volunteered for extra service, making it worse. While many people were contemplating moving away... most of them to South Africa, Ron refused to even consider it.

He was determined to defend 'his' country against the terrorists. "My father, and my grandfather before him, helped build this country from nothing," he always said, "and I'm not about to give it up for anyone. There's enough for everyone here... black and white." He could get really worked up about it. "The so-called nationalists are not interested in sharing power. They want it all for themselves. They want Rhodesia to become a Marxist state."

True, Angie also didn't really like the idea of living in South Africa. Holidays and shopping trips were fine; but it felt like they were visiting a police state, and she never felt entirely comfortable there. Neither of them liked the rigidly enforced racism of South Africa's 'apartheid' policy. But surely they had to make contingency plans in case the worst came to the worst? After all, her sister Linda had recently moved down there with her family and they seemed to be settling in.

Something had to be done to look after the long-term interests of their children. Her father was most concerned about it. Only Ronnie seemed to be blind to it all.

"What a shame all this has happened to us," Angie spoke her thoughts aloud. "All our people; black, white and coloured, except for a few activists, are happy. Why can't we just be left in peace?"

"The whole world is against us, Angie," Kate remarked. "I don't know what we can do about it. Come ladies, let's go and organise the tables and chairs for tonight's braai. Then I suppose we'd better think about lunch."

"I couldn't eat anything at the moment," Angie said and the other women wrinkled their noses in agreement.

"But Kate's right," her mother said. "No doubt the men will want something to eat, even if we don't."

* * *

"Well, the meat's all ready now," Peter told Kate when he and Mark reached the poolside. "We've given the ox and the sheep to the boys for their braai, and set our pig up on the spit."

Mark saw Angie was there with the others and smiled at her. She smiled back, but he sensed that she wasn't her usual friendly, confident self. Better not get too close to her though. He had to take things very slowly after last night. But just seeing her again made him all the more determined to get back into her good books.

"Good, we've almost finished the food preparation too," Kate responded. "I suppose you men would like something to eat now?"

"I need a bit of a wash and a few beers first please, dear." Peter looked at his hands. "You really need a scrubbing brush to get rid of the blood from under the nails."

Mark agreed and they both made their way into the house. "I'll grab a few beers for us from the fridge on the way back," he called as Peter left him in the passage on his way to his own bathroom. The servants would probably be too busy with preparations to bring iced beer to them today.

"Great. Get one for John too. I'll join you out there."

With the pool looking so inviting, Mark changed into his swimming trunks after cleaning up. Handing one of the beers to John, he carefully placed the others in a shady spot, and dived into the sparkling water. The three small girls followed him in, squealing with delight.

"Hey, it's great in here. Why don't you join us, Angie?" He swam away from the children with smooth, powerful strokes while the other ladies all encouraged her, and she went off to change.

* * *

Angie almost refused Mark's invitation, but she felt hot and decided that her earlier embarrassment shouldn't prevent her acting normally. By the time she got back, he had stopped swimming and was playing with the girls at the shallow end, so Angie was able to swim a few lengths on her own. The water was lovely. Cool but not too cold. When she'd finished, she rested at the deep end and watched them play.

Mark swam across with Helen clinging to his back. All the girls could swim, but Helen was still unsure of herself in the deeper water.

Joanne was the strongest swimmer, but Angie saw that she also clung to Mark whenever she could. From the way she looked up at him, Angie could see she adored him. Darn it, even her children weren't immune to his charms. Emma came to Angie's side a few seconds behind the others.

"Your beer's getting warm, Mark," her father called from the lapa.

Mark swam past her on his way to the steps and squeezed her hand discreetly before he lifted Helen from the pool and climbed out himself. She was irritated at how much that little gesture affected her; she'd have to make sure her behaviour from now on corrected any impression he had from her indiscretion the previous night – if only she hadn't let him kiss her...

Chapter 13

They arrived at the Angwa river bridge, and Ron sent four men to do the routine patrol. They reported finding a clean, natural rock pool upstream and, although there were a few hippos in occupancy, it was too inviting not to take advantage. Two men were left to guard the Bedford, while the rest took it in turns to strip off and swim in the cool water. The hippos gathered themselves in one half of the pool that the men avoided, and the two species kept a respectful but wary eye on each other.

As soon as he'd had his dip, Ron left the men swimming in the rock pool, and walked back to the Bedford.

"I've told the men to get out of the pool, get back here and start preparing lunch," Mike Njube said as he joined Ron at the RL. "Blikkie and Naasty can go for their swim straight after lunch," he added as he finished drying himself. A big, powerful but clumsy man, Terblanche was universally referred to as Naasty, not only because of his name and initials, but because the nickname fairly well reflected his general character and appearance.

Their companionable silence was shattered by the rattle of automatic gunfire from the direction of the pool.

It was an MAG, so Ron knew it was one of their own. "Stay here with the truck, Blikkie, Naasty," he snapped. "Let's get over there sergeant." He grabbed his weapon and ran towards the pool, while Mike pulled on his camouflage trousers and followed, barefoot.

* * *

"Bastard must have been hiding in these bushes, watching us all the time we were here, sir," Bill Polanski was standing about 20 metres into the bush on the far, south-east side of the pool. "I only saw him because I came over to have a crap." Ron tried not to laugh as he contemplated the big American squatting in the bush with his machine gun in one hand and a piece of toilet paper in the other.

A few feet away the terrorist lay under a bush, his AK beside him. "Don't think there are any others. I've had a look," Bill added.

"We'll have a proper three-sixty all the same. Herbie," Ron looked around as he called.

"Here, Ishe," Herbie's voice came from about 100 metres further away in the bush.

"Herbie and the doc are already doing a three-sixty, sir," Bill explained. "Johnny and I are covering from here while they do it." That accounted for Ron's entire team.

"Well done, Bill. OK, carry on, Herbie," Ron called, and they set about taking a closer look at the site while waiting for Herbie to return. It was a bugger that their earlier recce had stopped at the pool itself and not gone further, but it also had to cover both sides of the road and the river. There were limits as to how far these checks went – just 20 metres further out, and they would have seen the terr much earlier.

"Have you had a look at this guy yet, Bill?" It seemed pretty obvious he was dead. Bill was not one to 'go easy' with ammo but still, someone should check him over. Ron hunkered down and Bill helped him drag the body from under the bush. Placing his fingers against the terrorist's neck just below the jaw, he soon confirmed him dead. Ron then rummaged through the terrs' clothing and equipment. Meanwhile, Johnny Papadopolous helped Mike make a detailed search of the area around the scrub the terrorist had been hiding in.

"Just his weapon and this pack, sir," Njube reported when they'd finished.

"The tracks are from the same man who escaped from that kopje a few days ago," Herbie announced when he and their team medic, Tom Blair arrived back from their recce. "He was alone – there are no others with him."

"OK, take him down to the truck. Johnny, Bill – give Tom a hand, please." Ron and Mike had a look inside the pack before following the others. It contained only a small quantity of food and ammunition. "I think this bloke was heading home to Mozambique, using the river as his route. Poor sod only had another 15 or 20 Ks to go before he reached the border."

"Better we got him now than he comes back with more of his comrades." Mike had no sympathy for terrorists.

Ron recalled that Sergeant Njube was from a family of military men. Apart from having two brothers serving in the forces, his father had fought alongside British forces during the Second World War, and his grandfather had fought for the British during the 1914-1918 'Great War'. He thought about the many first class African soldiers and policemen who stood to lose so much if Rhodesia did not win this war against terrorism.

If things went the wrong way, black Rhodesians would have no chance of 'taking the gap' to South Africa, Australia or the UK. Ron knew they, and their families, had much more to lose in the terrorist war than any white people. And it wasn't just the policemen and soldiers. What about all the other black people who had worked their way up in civilian life; striving to improve their social, economic and educational status, making their contributions to the country in so many different ways? Ron glanced respectfully across at the sturdy sergeant striding smartly next to him, notwithstanding his bare feet. The most switched on guy in the whole platoon – and most others he knew of.

Arriving back at the truck, Ron reported the contact to Major Swain.

"You'd better wait there until we can get the police over to you, Ron; I'll do that as soon as I can." The CO paused and Ron could hear him ordering his 2i/c to get hold of the police at ComOps in Mt Darwin. "Meanwhile, and since you'll now be too late to join our New Year celebrations anyway, I think you should set up an ambush somewhere along the Angwa River; there could be more terrs travelling along it to get back to Mozambique."

"OK, sir," Ron replied. "I'll get four of my men to set up the ambush and the rest of us will stop here at the Bridge to wait for the cops to take the body." He'd expected this. "I'll set the ambush about three Ks upstream so the activity here doesn't scare off any terrs in the vicinity, and get back to you with an exact grid reference as soon as the men are in place."

Would Big Feet himself use this same escape route on his way back to Mozambique? If so, it would be worthwhile taking part in the ambush himself, leaving Mike Njube to deal with the cops and to guard the truck. No, surely not; Big Feet had a vehicle and would be across the border already if he'd come this way. What did the others think?

"Mike… Bill… over here, please." Ron dug his map out from his combat jacket pocket again. By the time they arrived, the map was spread across the bonnet of the RL. "Do you blokes think Big Feet might have dumped his pickup somewhere near here, and be making his way downstream towards Mozambique?"

Mike and Bill looked at each other sceptically.

"Nah," the American dismissed the idea, "the chances of that are pretty small, sir. Anyway he would have been here at least five or six hours ago, so there's no chance of us getting him here now."

Ron looked across at his sergeant. He knew Mike, as with most Africans, would be more circumspect. "Bill's right, sir," Njube agreed. "I don't think we have any chance of catching Big Feet if he's run for the border, but we might get some of the others who were part of the group he led across the border."

"Do you blokes think Big Feet has gapped it? Or has he stayed to make another raid?" Ron persisted.

"It's not the pattern for a terr to hang around after he's made a big hit, sir." Njube hesitated. "But Big Feet is different."

"Yes," Bill agreed, "and there's nothing to say the terrs won't change their tactics anyhow. Maybe this lot will show more balls than the others."

"He could cause havoc if he stayed in one of the Tribal Trust Lands. Even more trouble if he attacked targets in a town or a white-owned farm," Ron mused.

But Njube obviously felt differently. "He's more likely to move to another, more sympathetic TTL and make attacks from there," he said. "He'd be found too quickly if he stayed in a European area."

"Well, we're stuck here and we're going to set an ambush on the river." Ron's two subordinates didn't look very pleased at that. "What a way to celebrate New Year."

"Shit… I'd forgotten." Bill looked amazed.

"It's a big event for you white folk but not such a big deal for us Africans," Mike pointed out. "But we like any excuse for a party."

* * *

As far as Mark could see, everyone seemed to be enjoying themselves at the farm that evening. The women had done a fine job of creating a festive atmosphere. Candles, placed on the tables around the pool, flickered in old wine bottles, enhancing the alfresco setting. The lapa had become the dance floor. He and Uncle John had been given the task of setting up the stereo, and he was pleased to hear that it was standing up to the heavy usage. Smoke from the braais wafted across every so often. It was a perfect night.

Earlier that evening, Angie had introduced him to the Cartwright grandparents, who were sitting on the farmhouse verandah. It was quieter there, but there was still a party atmosphere and the old folk seemed quite happy, watching the guests having a good time. Mark suspected they must have been pretty strict parents in their day, but now their eyes sparkled with merriment; especially grandfather Cartwright, who seemed to have a good sense of humour. He'd sat with them for a while and exchanged a few jokes with the old boy.

He made his way back to the lapa. "You're by far the prettiest woman here," he told Angie when he managed to claim her for a dance. She'd probably heard that a dozen times that night already, but he couldn't help himself.

"It's really nice of you to say so, but don't you think Charlie's beautiful?" Angie indicated a tall girl with dark brown, almost black hair, and high cheekbones; classically attractive with a lithe, tanned body. "We've been good friends since we were at school together... you must remember her? You always paid more attention to her than you did to me."

Did he detect a slight challenge in her voice? "Well, if I did, I don't remember." It was rather pleasing to think that Angie might be jealous.

"Charlie's a great sportswoman, and one of the top ladies' tennis players in the country. She's staying overnight; maybe you should play tennis with her tomorrow?"

Now Mark was sure she was jealous. "She's attractive, but not a patch on you. She's not my type," he lied. Charlie was just the sort of woman he was normally attracted to, but Angie was something special. "Besides, I think I'm beginning to fall in love with you." Christ, what was he getting himself into? But Mark had the pleasure of seeing her slow blush again. Even the lobes of her ears flushed slightly. He wished he could kiss them. Instead he pulled her body closer.

"Don't say that, Mark." She paused and looked directly into his eyes. "I'm married. I'm not available." At least she wasn't angry, but she looked serious.

Jeez, she was more than pretty, she was beautiful – and her eyes… He watched her recover her composure as the dance came to an end.

"Now here's Tony; I promised to dance with him next." She smiled at him with that serene look, which he was coming to recognise as meaning she was completely at ease with herself, and he reluctantly surrendered her to 'Tony'.

Regardless of what he was doing that evening, Mark watched her discreetly all the time, and was pleased to see that no other man seemed able to affect her the way he could. All the guests seemed to know each other, with the exception of a few soldiers, who Peter had invited from a nearby Army camp at Kate's suggestion. But they were soon made to feel at ease among the friendly crowd. Typical Rhodesians – just make friends with anyone.

With Angie being so popular, he settled down to enjoy the party as much as he could without her. Meanwhile, he danced with the other women, including Charlie.

"Do you remember me from school, Mark?" she asked. "I was in the same class as Angie."

"Of course I remember you. Pretty… and cheeky. Are you still cheeky?"

"Maybe," she laughed. "Where have you been all these years? Angie didn't say anything about you being here until I arrived this afternoon." He felt her deliberately press her body close against his as they danced. There was no need to pull her towards him as he had done with Angie.

Hmmm… a willing little mare. "We only met up again a few days ago, when I went to visit my mother. Angie was there at the time, and kindly invited me to come out to this party with her parents and my mother."

"You live down south, don't you?"

"Yes, near Cape Town, but I travel up here on business from time to time."

"I believe you're sleeping over tonight, and leaving early tomorrow morning; how early is early?" she asked.

"I'm sharing a room with a couple of other chaps… I need to catch a flight from Salisbury back to Jo'burg tomorrow evening, so it'll be well before lunch. How about you?" Her body was moving smoothly against his; there was something almost feline about her.

She told him she was sharing with Angie and her children. "My husband is away on Army call-up." Her eyes looked directly into his; they were languid but calculating. He was startled when he noticed that they were distinctly different colours; one blue/grey and the other dark brown. He'd never seen that before. They fascinated him, and it came as a shock when he realised they'd been looking into each other's eyes for far too long. She pressed her body even more firmly against his. He realised this could get out of hand, and wondered how he could extricate himself without causing offence. After all, she was extremely attractive, and Mark always took care not to upset beautiful women. You never knew when you might want their company in the future.

But he was becoming aroused. Damn. Better take care here, he warned himself. It really was his misfortune to be cast between two delightful, but very different women on one night at the same party. With some reluctance, Mark made up his mind not to dance with Charlie again that evening. He suspected she might discuss him with Angie, and he had no wish to appear fickle.

He pulled away slightly from Charlie, trying not to make it obvious, but she looked sharply at him. She made no comment, but turned frostily polite for the remainder of the dance; despite his efforts, he was sure he had made an enemy. He didn't know how he could prevent it. He just tried to be as pleasant as he could, which she didn't make very easy; she remained ice cold. The moment the dance ended, she switched her attention away from him to a bronzed, fit looking man. They seemed to know each other well...

Later that evening, Mark saw her having a lively conversation with Angie. He was reassured that whatever Charlie thought of him, he had made the right choice.

* * *

"Are you enjoying the party, Charlie?" Angie asked her friend, dying to know how she'd got on with Mark, but being careful not to let Charlie know.

"It's great... there are such a lot of good-looking men around. Where did you get them all, with everyone being away in the Army?"

"Mrs Cartwright asked all the local farmers, and she asked a few soldiers to come along too. What do you think of Mark, seeing him for the first time after all these years?"

"He's even better looking than I remember, but still as stuck up as ever. I think I'm beginning to hate that man." Charlie was always prone to exaggeration.

"But why, Charlie? He's been really friendly to me since we met up again."

She frowned. "Dancing with him was like dancing with someone at arm's length. So boring…"

Angie wondered if she had made a play for Mark and been rebuffed. Yes, that must be it. Despite herself, she was pleased that Mark had shown he could reject another woman's advances. Especially one as attractive… and determined, as she knew Charlie could be. But she didn't want her friend to 'hate' Mark. Charlie could be very spiteful when someone crossed her.

"Oh dear. I think that might be my fault," Angie replied, wondering how much she should tell Charlie.

"What do you mean, your fault?"

Damn, Angie knew she'd been careless. "Oh, you know what men are like at parties…"

"He made a pass?"

"Oh no…" there was no way she was going to divulge the kiss. "He just said something."

Charlie raised her eyebrows, all attention. Angie realised she'd trapped herself.

"He just said he thought he might be falling in love… You know the sort of thing."

Charlie's eyes narrowed. Then she gasped in surprise, and clapped her hands together with delight. Angie relaxed; Charlie had obviously decided to find her revelation amusing. That was good.

"Oh how exciting, Angie. If he loves you, I'll forgive him almost anything. You *must* tell me all about it. I just love an illicit romance."

"Shhh. I'm sure there's nothing to it, Charlie. Anyway, even if he does love me, I don't want him to… I've got Ron and the girls." Angie should have known that her friend would take that attitude; she knew Charlotte looked at things rather differently to her. She could be quite outrageous at times, but she was a loyal friend.

"Oh don't be so silly, darling," Charlie said impatiently. "There's nothing wrong with having a bit of fun. Especially with a man as dishy as Mark. You'll just have to be careful. I'll bet he's got loads of money too..." She paused to look at Mark again. She was about to say something else, but John Cunningham, the tennis champion, was walking towards them.

"Oh, here comes John, we'll talk about you and Mark tomorrow. Have fun, Angie," she said, turning to acknowledge his arrival.

* * *

Although he managed to enjoy several more dances with her, Mark had no chance to get Angie on her own during the evening. She was with both her parents and her in-laws when midnight came. Mark watched the happy, smiling faces and joined in when everyone linked arms to sing Auld Lang Syne. Another year... 1973.

Did these good-natured Rhodesians realise just how precarious their lifestyle, if not their very lives were? He could almost hear the march of African Nationalist rule pounding in his ears. He managed to catch Angie's eye across the swaying bodies and mouthed 'I love you'. This time she didn't blush or turn away but looked almost serious, as though she'd picked up on his sombre thoughts.

The sound of barking dogs caught his attention. Peter came over and asked him to help with the animals. A boisterous group of partygoers had decided to celebrate the New Year by jumping, fully clothed, into the pool and their playful splashing had driven the big dogs into a frenzy of excitement. There were just too many distractions, and he needed Mark's help to haul them away. They locked them in an empty storeroom at the rear of the house, on the far side of Kate's kitchen garden.

"We'll let them out again when things quieten down," Peter said, as they made their way back to rejoin the party.

On the way, Mark found Angie in the kitchen and took the opportunity to give her a New Year kiss. Even that was not really satisfactory, because there were other people about. Angie would not... could not relax in his arms, as she had done the previous night. But he made the best he could of it.

Later, he helped Peter coax a few of the rowdier young men to go quietly to bed, before going himself. Angie and some of the other ladies were drinking coffee in the kitchen, so there was no point in approaching her there. He noticed that Charlie wasn't with them, but then he couldn't see the Cunningham chap either...

Reaching his bedroom, Mark saw that one of the two men sharing his room was stretched fully clothed across his bed. He dragged the sleeping man roughly across to his own bed. Finally, he was able to undress, and get into bed himself. Hell, but he wanted Angie. Yet he realised that he'd have little chance to be alone with her again before he left the next day. He'd just have to find an opportunity to tell her that he'd be back to see her again. He needed to let her know he wanted to see her alone next time he came up. He eventually fell asleep to the sound of snoring from both his companions.

Chapter 14

"We'll leave the car by that river we passed just before the entrance," Gadziwa announced as they drove slowly past their target. They recognised it by the name painted on a big white sign, just before the fence and cattle grid that marked the boundary.

There'd been no traffic for some time, so he turned the car round in the road and headed back to the small river. Getting his men to walk ahead, to make sure there were no rocks or stumps in the way, he drove carefully into the bush by the bridge, and stopped in a small clearing. He switched off the engine; it hissed for a while, still overheating, but eventually settled. They listened intently but could hear only bush sounds. The sun was now very low on the horizon and dusk fast approaching.

"Get under the car and bring out the guns and equipment, then wait for me," he ordered, before walking back through the bush onto the road. Pacing a few hundred metres in each direction, he made sure the car was not visible from the road before returning to his men.

"Check all your weapons and make a good note of where the car is hidden, in case you lose me after the attack. We will walk to our objective from here. On the way, we'll lay some land-mines in the road." This was one of the most important elements of the attack. He hoped they would cause chaos among the soldiers or police, long after he and his men had departed from the scene.

"We will not attack the place until two o'clock in the morning, when the white men will be sleeping and still drunk after celebrating." Gadziwa ended his detailed review of the plan. "After the attack, we will come back here and drive on up the road for a few kilometres towards Centenary."

"Why don't we go back the way we came and stay with the missionaries again?"

Gadziwa regarded the questioner with interest. A young, newly trained recruit named Simon M'butu; he was probably the most intelligent among this group of three men. Gadziwa had picked him out as one of the better recruits before. It was possible that with more training and experience, he could become a section leader.

"Have you forgotten the police roadblock we came through on the Umvukwes hills?" he answered, with more patience than usual. "There may also be a roadblock going towards Centenary. But that is a chance we will have to take, and Centenary is much closer than Sipolilo. If we go back, there is the added danger of Umvukwes. You know we would have to pass through that town, before we even get to the Sipolilo turn off. It would be too dangerous." There was no doubt that his plans were good.

"Anyway, from here we will go straight into the Mazimbe TTL where we have many supporters. It is south – this side – of Centenary, so we will not have to go through the town. In the rapidly fading light, he drew a rough map in the sand.

"You are right, Comrade Captain," M'butu commented respectfully, when they'd finished. Gadziwa doubted his other two men had understood the discussion; they would just blindly follow.

After almost six hours rest, during which Gadziwa was able to catnap, they emerged from the bush by the river, and walked carefully and silently back along the main road towards the entrance. It consisted only of the cattle grid, which they crossed with ease. The sign was still visible in the moonlight. Though they had heard several vehicles rattling over the grid earlier that evening, there was no traffic at all on the main road now.

"*Tula*," Gadziwa hissed when he heard someone strike the gatepost with what sounded like an AK carbine. He stopped them all and checked to see that their equipment was properly secured. "We will leave one land-mine here at the entrance."

They dug into the soft, sandy soil right up against the concrete of the grid, on one of the wheel tracks. The weight of any vehicle on the sand would detonate the mine.

"Bring that plastic explosive, I'm going to boost this mine, to give it extra power." Gadziwa also armed the mine himself, so there would be no mistake. They'd carried it on their backs on the long walk from Mozambique. Before that, it had come from somewhere in the Soviet Union by sea; then by rail and road truck through Tanzania and Zambia, all the way to Chifombo in Mozambique. All this work to get it here made it very valuable. He did not want any mistakes… it must do its work for the Cause. For the great Chimurenga he was fighting, so he could inherit the land of his ancestors; free of the white settlers who invaded his country, and took it from them more than 80 years ago.

When they'd finished covering the mine, he checked that there was no sign, and brushed the surface with a leafy branch. The victims would come in the morning and it must be made difficult to see, even in daylight.

They trudged on, stopping when they heard the first sounds of people. "They are celebrating their New Year, comrades," Gadziwa said quietly. "Hear how they shout. They will not be celebrating tomorrow morning." They were walking on the grass by the side of the road, careful not to leave tracks in the sandy road itself. There were tall trees on each side, and beyond them in the light of the moon, he could see good standing crops; just the kind of farm he would take when they won the war.

"Comrade Captain," M'butu called softly, but with fear in his voice. Gadziwa went forward to see what the problem was. "There is an Army truck." He pointed across the second cattle grid, and up the driveway leading to the buildings, while everyone shrank into cover.

Gadziwa studied the vehicle in silence for several minutes. "There is no one inside or outside guarding it, comrades. They are with the other white settlers, enjoying their celebrations." It was a complication he had not foreseen, and he struggled to maintain his poise. He was determined not to abandon the Mission; they had come too far for that, but he needed to change the plan. They dare not attack the farmhouse now; he had no idea how many soldiers would be in there, and at least some of the white civilians would be armed. He needed time to work out another plan. Making their way cautiously back the few hundred metres to the bend in the road, he had them unload a second land-mine, while he selected the precise location for it to be laid. He chose a place where he was sure there would be deep shade in the morning.

"Hisst." M'butu called for his attention again, and he made his way back to the tree at the side of the road where they were hiding. "There is someone in the field over there, Comrade Captain." Gadziwa followed M'butu's line of direction. He recalled noticing some cattle in this field, when they passed it on their way to the farmhouse. At first he saw only cattle resting there and was about to rebuke M'butu for a false alarm. But then he made out a recumbent figure in the moonlight; beyond the cattle on the far side of the field. So, not everyone was celebrating.

The human figure would certainly be an African farm worker, a herdsman sleeping in the open on this warm, dry night. He studied the form more closely, and made out the faint glow of a small fire that had been allowed to all but die down. Gadziwa pictured him, sleeping lightly under his blanket with his kerrie beside him, ready to see off any threat... even a leopard. It might be that the man had been drinking; they'd heard the sound of merriment coming from the labourers' quarters earlier. He hoped so, as that meant the man would be sleeping more heavily.

The cattle were quiet and appeared settled, but it was likely they were aware of Gadziwa and his men. Better not disturb them, or their resultant restlessness would wake the sleeping figure. They would have to wait before laying the mine, but seeing the man and the cattle gave him an idea. He glanced at his watch and saw it was half past midnight. There was still plenty of time to take action, and no need to rush anything. Nevertheless, he did not want to delay too long, for he wished to make his getaway from this place with plenty of darkness still left.

* * *

The police arrived shortly before Mike left with three men to set the ambush upstream. Ron was surprised to see they were carrying FN rifles; it was bloody unusual for ordinary policemen to carry firearms in Rhodesia; that incident at Zongoro's must have rattled them. The cops asked a few questions and Ron told them the dead terrorist was one who'd escaped from his contact with them two days ago.

"Of course, we didn't get our Sipolilo roadblock up and running until an hour or so after the pickup was reported stolen," the section officer in charge told him, "but we think it's pretty unlikely that they would have headed down that way." He sipped at the steaming coffee Ron had given him. "It's more likely that they headed north for the border and dumped their truck before they came to the roadblock you set up. After all, they must have got here before sunrise today, and we didn't know about the stolen vehicle until about ten this morning; they could have been miles away by that time."

"They could also be holed up somewhere near Sipolilo," Ron suggested.

"Not likely with the sort of ground cover we have there," the policeman replied confidently.

OK, Ron accepted they must have undercover agents operating up there; these shadowy people were supposed to inform the police or district officers of anything unusual happening in the area they covered. "Well, I hope your ground cover's on the ball. The terr we're after is a very smart bastard and totally ruthless."

The copper didn't respond to this; probably didn't want to acknowledge any possibility of the police not doing their work properly. "Will you be maintaining this roadblock overnight?" he asked, changing the subject. "It would be a good idea if you did."

"I suppose you chaps want to get back to the bright lights for New Year celebrations?" Ron had a dig at them.

"Well… there's rumoured to be a party on at the Sipolilo hall." The policeman was unabashed. "We could get back just in time to enjoy the main part of it."

* * *

Ron went to his camp bed beside the truck early that night, but couldn't shake off his sense of unease. Big Feet got his notoriety for a fucking good reason; he was aggressive and intelligent. People just didn't take him seriously enough. Information on this character was that after leaving England, where he had been educated, courtesy of the British Government, and various English charities, he'd been trained in China itself; not just Tanzania, where the more ordinary recruits went. He'd been acquitted of a terrorist charge by the Rhodesian High Court some years ago and disappeared. Since then, the man had escaped every military contact, and had shown himself to be extremely resourceful and dangerous.

Ron watched the stars revolve slowly above his head, even spotting a few satellites; they looked like stars at first, but moved faster across the night sky. A jetliner passed overhead. It was surreal; 6,000 metres above them, meals and drinks were being served to passengers on their way to London, Paris, wherever… and he was lying on the ground, FN at his side. Tomorrow he could be chasing terrorists all over the bloody place, danger round just about every corner.

At eleven-thirty he woke to receive Njube's reassuring radio call to say that all was quiet at the ambush site. Then he listened to the routine midnight radio calls being passed from various patrols and observation points, through relay stations on high ground; the calls linked patrols across the Zambezi Valley and escarpment with their headquarters. Many of them included good wishes for the New Year. A few radio reports even went to the military base, faraway to the east, at the township of Mount Darwin. That was the hub for coordinating all military and police actions in the whole north-east of Rhodesia's operational area, known as "Operation Hurricane".

Gradually, things quietened down. There was the sinister whooping call of hyenas, from what sounded like a long way downriver. Ron lay back in his sleeping bag; the night belonged to the bush again.

Chapter 15

Mark woke at sunrise. Something other than the coming of daylight had roused him. He closed his eyes again and lay thinking for a few moments. That was it... There was more activity than he'd expect on the 'morning after the night before'. The two Venter brothers were still sleeping soundly. They'd both enjoyed the free flowing drink at the party, and Mark didn't think his getting up so early would disturb them. He climbed out of bed, quickly washing and dressing, before he made his way to the kitchen.

"Peter's gone down to look for the dairy herd, ten or fifteen minutes ago," Kate told him, as soon as he walked into the big stone floored room. "They've not been brought up to the dairy for milking yet, so we think there may have been some sort of trouble." The atmosphere was subdued. Two servants worked quietly in the background, but the kitchen lacked its usual business-like bustle.

"I'll go straight there," he replied and headed for the door, pausing to take a few sips at the coffee Kate handed him. As soon as he went out the kitchen door, he could just hear the calves mooing plaintively, from down by the dairy stockade where they waited for their mothers; poor beggars would be hungry.

Dew still covered the veldt, although the sun was now above the horizon. Mark's shoes, socks and legs were soon wet from walking through the tall grass. He took short cuts through the farmyard, fields and bush, to reach the place where he'd last seen the cattle. The sun would dry the grass in another hour or so. It was a pleasant time of day and still cool, although there was not a cloud to be seen in the sky. He could hear the call of the bush doves in the trees; it was too early for the monotonous screech of the cicada beetles. Though he was very definitely a city man, he reflected on what a pleasant place the countryside could be. Especially at moments like these.

He headed straight towards a small group of men at the far edge of the field. His route bypassed the cattle, but even from that distance he could see something was wrong. They were lowing, and it looked as if some of them were struggling to stand up. He expected them to be uncomfortable because they had not been milked that morning, but why weren't they standing up?

As he got closer, he could see Peter kneeling down, with two of his farm hands standing close beside him. They were all looking at something on the ground. He hurried forward, and the two African men stood aside to let him get closer to Peter. Mark saw what looked like a bundle of clothes on the ground next to a fire that had died, probably during the night.

"Madala's been killed," Peter said, looking up from the bundle.

"Poor old bloke. What happened?" Mark wondered if he'd heard right when Peter said 'killed', at first thinking the old fellow must have died in his sleep. Surely there was nothing here on the farm that could have killed him? He wondered about the possibility of leopard, but it was highly unlikely that a leopard would attack a fully-grown man; not even an old one like Madala. He also remembered the mean looking knobkerrie Madala carried.

"Murdered, actually; they've slit his throat." Peter pulled the blanket away to show the old man's head lying back from his neck at an unnatural angle, leaving a gaping space. There was a dark stain of blood, spread wide below the head and body. The huge wound was covered with engorged bluebottle flies. Mark felt physically sick but managed to stop himself retching. Peter did his best to wave the flies away before he covered the body again and stood up, looking old and tired. "There's nothing we can do for him now."

"Christ! Who... why would anyone do this?"

"He might have tried to stop them doing that." Peter pointed to the lowing herd.

"What's wrong with them?"

"They've been hamstrung. I think they've all been injured, but I can't be sure how badly because I only had time to look at a few, before we found Madala here. The ones I saw are finished." He made a cutting motion with his hand. The expression on Peter's face changed from sorrow to anger. "There can be no excuse for this, Mark. The bastards who did it deserve to rot in hell."

Mark was shocked into silence, and it took him a few moments before he recovered himself and squared his shoulders. "We'd better send someone up to the farmhouse to ask Kate to phone the police. I'll stay here and help you with the cattle." Mark had wanted to go up and call the police himself, but immediately dismissed the idea; he couldn't leave Peter alone to deal with the mutilated cows.

"Would you go up there for me, please?" Peter seemed to recover his composure with an effort. "You'll also have to bring back a gun for yourself, if you want to help me put the cows out of their misery as quickly as possible. There's a 400-calibre rifle in the gun safe. Meanwhile, I'll take a closer look to see if there are any we can save."

Mark saw that he'd brought his 303 with him. "OK, Peter; I suppose we'd better leave Madala where he is for the moment. Do you think the police will want to have a look before we move him?"

"Yes, but they'd better hurry. It'll get very hot in a few hours, and I think he's been dead for quite a while."

"Shall I bring the Army boys to help too?"

"No!" Peter shouted. He was visibly shaking, probably with a mix of anger and shock. "I don't want anyone who doesn't know what he's doing killing my cattle," he added quietly by way of explanation. "Of course, we'll have to dispose of the carcasses. Not sure exactly what to do with them just yet. I don't think the Cold Storage Commission will be interested, but ask Katie to phone the abattoir manager at Umvukwes, to see if he'll collect them. The CSC will be closed for the holiday, so she'll have to call him at home."

"I'll get back as fast as I can." Mark turned and started jogging towards the farmhouse, relieved to escape the awful scene for a while. The more he thought about this, the more he feared it might have been a terrorist attack. Ordinary murderers wouldn't have mutilated the cattle as well. And what motive would someone have to kill an old man in his sleep? It was unlikely he would have had much money, and he seemed to keep himself to himself most of the time, so was not likely to have any enemies. Shit, yes; it had to be terrorists.

* * *

"What's going on?" Angie asked Kate as she walked into the kitchen, "I heard people moving about."

"Peter has gone down to the dairy herd. Joseph woke us early and told us he could hear them calling, and that Madala hadn't brought them up for milking." Kate poured Angie a mug of coffee from the big pot on the range. "I'm afraid something might have happened to Madala. He will *insist* on sleeping out in the open with his precious mombies." She looked worried. "And it's only at this time of the year that he likes them to graze outdoors overnight…"

"You're right. He's too old to do that sort of thing, but you'll never stop him."

Just then Mark came in. Where on earth had he been so early in the morning? His expression was serious.

"I'm afraid it's bad news." He paused to catch his breath. "Very bad news." You could tell he'd been running.

"Oh, dear. It's Madala, isn't it?" Kate's hand shook as she rested it on the table.

"Yes." He paused again, looking as if he was searching for the right words. Angie's heart contracted with fear, there must be more to this. "I'm sorry, Kate, but he's been murdered… and the cattle have been seriously injured," Mark said simply.

"Oh no! Surely not murdered," Kate gasped.

Angie was so appalled she was unable to speak.

"I'm afraid so. Peter's asked me to call the police immediately; then I must get back to help him deal with the injured cattle." He described the scene to them. "He's also asked us to phone the abattoir manager at his home, to see if the CSC will take the carcasses. If they will, we must get him to send a lorry to collect them today."

Kate said she'd make both calls, and told Mark where to find the key to the gun safe.

* * *

Mark came back carrying a rifle and a box of ammunition.

Angie was waiting for him, sure there was more to this than he was letting on. "Maybe I'd better go and wake the Army boys." Surely they'd have a role to play in this? She watched for his reaction, ready to probe if necessary.

Mark looked grim. No sign of the devil-may-care, international traveller and sanctions buster now. "Thank you yes, Angie, but Peter doesn't want them getting involved with his cattle. Please tell them before they leave here." She could see the concern in his eyes. "But I agree they need to be alerted. We don't know yet who did this, but I think it may be terrorists."

"*Terrorists*?" A sense of foreboding came over her. "Of course, yes… surely no one else would kill Madala *and* injure the cattle?"

Her voice trailed off as the implications sunk in. But Mark was watching her, so she straightened her back and said "Right... The Army – and I'll ask everyone else to stay inside."

"Good, thanks." Mark smiled at her and turned to go.

Kate came back into the room. "I got hold of the police at Umvukwes and they're on their way. Say they should be here within the hour," she told them. "They did ask if our dogs were OK, and wondered why they didn't wake us."

"Oh, hell." Mark looked embarrassed. "Peter and I locked them up in a shed because they were barking so much last night. Of course, that'll be why they didn't hear anything." He turned as if to go and let them out himself.

"Let's wait until you've gone before we let them out, Mark," Kate stopped him.

Angie saw the problem immediately. "Yes, otherwise they'll follow you, and get in the way while you and Peter are trying to deal with the cattle."

"And you can tell Peter that I finally managed to get hold of Mr Van Staden, the abattoir manager," Kate finished her report. "He wasn't very pleased at being disturbed at home, but apologised when he realised what's happened. Said the commission will take the carcasses at disposal rates – that's because they won't be classified fit for human consumption. Says he'll get a truck up here today, even if he has to drive it himself."

"Thanks, Kate. I'll tell Peter, and you're right about the dogs. They'll be added security for you all here." Mark turned to leave.

"Mees! Mees!" Miriam almost collided with him as she came running into the kitchen from the direction of the servant's quarters. "Gandangas have killed Madala and all the master's mombies!"

"Hush, Miriam or you'll wake the children." Kate comforted the hysterical woman.

"Yes, why not go to my room now and make sure the children are safe?" Angie felt she'd be calmer if she had something useful to do. "Try not to wake them, or Mrs Macdonald, when you get there; just stay quietly in the room so you're there when they wake up. Come with me now, I've got to go and wake the soldiers." Angie walked briskly through the bedrooms and left Miriam with the children, her sobbing now muted.

She woke the sergeant and told him what had happened.

Leaving him to get the rest of his men up, she went straight down to the shed and let the dogs out. They must have sensed something and were very edgy. She made them follow her to the kitchen yard where she gave them water, and closed the gate to keep them in, hoping no one would be careless enough to let them out. Just as she was turning to go back inside, she realised that the grandparents had to be told. They'd surely hear the gunfire if the men had to kill any of the cattle. Oh God, she dreaded the responsibility but there was no one else. She slipped out through the gate.

Granddad Cartwright was in his garden, and greeted her cheerfully. Angie took a deep breath and told him what had happened as gently as she could, not leaving out the possibility that it might have been terrorists. They had to be aware.

He took it with the quiet dignity she knew he would. "Madala was one of my first employees, you know. Recruited him from Mozambique, because there was no labour." His eyes seemed to be looking into the distance. "Yes, Madala stayed on. Peter and I tried to get him to retire several times but he didn't want to. This was his home…" He seemed to be thinking back to those old days, probably when he and Madala were young.

Angie waited while he reminisced before she spoke. "Granddad… would you like me to go and tell Granny?" It would be so painful for him, and the old lady would be distressed.

"No. Thank you my dear, but I'd better do that." He smiled sadly at her. "You must get back to give Kate your support."

When Angie returned to the kitchen, Sergeant Steve and his men were already there with Kate. Other guests were drifting in too, and soon there were more than a dozen people crowded into the kitchen. Word of what had happened was passed to each new arrival but although the mood was sombre, it was surprisingly calm.

"I suppose we'll be stuck here for the rest of the morning?" one of the guests surmised. Everyone agreed there would be a long wait until the police had done their work. People helped themselves to hot drinks and talked quietly among themselves.

"We'd better get moving now," Steve said. He checked that all his men had their kit with them, warning that they might not return to the farmhouse once they left. "Can anyone show us the field where Mark and Mr Cartwright are, Angie?"

Before Angie could answer, they heard the crack, and rolling echoes of a heavy rifle shot in the distance; the destruction of those gentle cows had begun.

Kate drew a deep breath and said; "You'll see them on your right if you drive straight down towards the main road."

"Be careful, Steve. Mark thinks it might have been terrorists," Angie reminded him.

"Thanks, ladies, we'll take care. Make sure no one leaves the farm until the police give the all clear, please. We can't be completely sure they've gone away yet." The sergeant drained his coffee and turned to his men. "Right, let's get going. Thanks for your hospitality, Mrs Cartwright. Don't worry, we'll get the swine who killed your herdsman and injured your cattle."

They weren't long gone, when Sam the cook arrived. "Gandangas are here Missus!" His eyes were still bloodshot from too much booze the night before, but Angie could see fear in them as well.

"You mean they *were* here, Sam," Kate said, clearly determined to help Sam gain control of himself, and get the kitchen going properly to cope with the guests. "Come now and I'll help you get breakfast started."

Everyone knew about Sam's weakness for booze, but he was a good cook, and Kate tolerated his periodic lapses. The farm hands and servants would be as shocked by what had happened as the family were, and probably a good deal more afraid.

* * *

Soon after he shot the third injured animal, Mark saw the Army boys drive up and stop their truck at the side of the road next to the field. Peter was checking each cow, to make sure there was nothing they could do before they shot it. That didn't take long because there was no hope, even if just one hamstring was cut.

For the first time, Mark forced himself to look closely at the damage done by the attackers. Whoever did it had used a sharp cutting edge; probably a machete, or one of those primitive native axes. Even so, it looked as if the attackers had used several cuts to sever the tough tendon. The wound was jagged and bloody. Of course, the poor animal must have suffered terrible pain. Not only from the clumsy hacking, but thereafter from the frantic wrenching of muscles and ligaments as she struggled to get up. It was a devastating injury inflicted in cold blood.

But in addition to hamstringing, the bastards had mutilated the udders on some cows too. That could only have been done after the hamstring wound disabled the cow. Otherwise, even these gentle creatures that had known only affection and kindness from humans in the past might have kicked out and possibly inflicted injury on their attackers. Mark was sickened by this unnecessary cruelty. He could understand the terrorists not using the most humane method by shooting them, because gunfire would have alerted the farm. But if all the swine wanted to do was to deprive the farmer of his cattle, a single hamstring per animal would have ensured the ultimate loss of the herd. Skilled use of an axe in the head would have been even quicker and easier, causing instantaneous death. Cutting their udders was gratuitous cruelty, and the people who did it were no better than savages.

The soldiers came over, and Mark directed them across to Madala's body.

"There's not much we can do here," the sergeant said when he got back. "We'll report what we've seen, and start looking around to see if we can find any sign of the bastards who did it. I'm almost certain it was terrorists and that's our business, not just for the police."

Mark watched them spread out around the field looking for tracks, before going back to his grisly task.

Shortly afterwards, the Army boys returned, and told him they'd made radio contact with their headquarters, and were moving down to the farm entrance. The truck roared off in a cloud of dust.

It was Peter who despatched the last of the herd. Mark recognised it as one of the two 'replacement stock' heifers, a beautiful creature barely 18 months old, that he'd enthusiastically shown Mark just a day or so ago. Mark was standing right next to him as he did it, but couldn't bear to watch. He concentrated instead on the small team of farmhands, who were hitching a dead cow to the tractor that had been brought down from the farmyard. They were using it to drag the carcasses across the field to the side of the road.

"That's the last of them. I don't think I'll want to start the herd again after this. I couldn't face it." For the first time since Mark had met him, Peter looked his age; Mark wondered if he himself looked as weary.

The ground shook under their feet, and a dull thud came from the direction of the main road. They turned to see a cloud of dust rise in the bush.

"Oh, shit. That was a very big land-mine. Definitely an anti-tank mine," Mark said. "Probably a Soviet TM46." Jesus, this was escalating, big time. "Now there's no question it was terrorists, Peter. I'd better get down there and see if the Army needs help." This must be one of the first times an AT mine has been used in this conflict. How many more might there be here? Better be very careful now.

"OK, but I'll have to stay here while my boys finish off, or they'll either run away or be too afraid to do any work," Peter decided. "Take the 400 and plenty of ammo with you. And be careful; there could be others."

Too bloody right there could. "We're damn lucky that your tractor didn't set any off on its way down here. I suggest you have your boys check the road carefully before they take the tractor back to the yard."

Peter nodded agreement. He looked as if he was in a state of shock. Only to be expected, poor bugger. Mark left for the direction of the blast on foot. This was getting really ugly, what a lousy start to the New Year. Mark made his way across the field, stepping over the dusty trails left by the carcasses. He did not source land-mines for Rhodesia; they had no need for vehicle mines, because their enemies operated on foot. And the Rhodesians had their own homemade anti-personnel mines, or used the old Second World War 'Claymores'. They couldn't afford the foreign currency to buy modern stuff from him.

But his suppliers, who laid on demonstrations for his benefit, periodically offered him mines of all types; so he knew quite a lot about the bloody things, and kept the security forces appraised of what was on the market. He took special care when he got near the edge of the road; if the terrorists had followed the usual mine-laying methods, anti-personnel mines could be concealed in the verges.

He jogged along the centre of the sandy road, knowing that it would take more than his weight to set off an anti-tank mine. There was a risk of being ambushed, if there were still any terrorists around, but he was sure they would have pissed off long ago. He concentrated on scanning the bush on both sides, as well as checking the roadway itself for signs of buried mines. No point in getting himself killed here through carelessness. Must make sure he was always clearly visible, and making as much noise as possible. Didn't want any dazed survivors of the explosion mistaking him for a terrorist.

He recalled from discussions at the party the previous night that they were not fighting soldiers, just regimental military policemen. That probably meant they were not trained in bush warfare, so could be more dangerous to their own side than the enemy in situations like this. It might also explain why they hadn't found any terrorist tracks in the field. There had to be some tracks, and surely proper soldiers would have found them?

"Hey," he shouted as he approached the area where he expected to find the truck. "Are you men OK?" He saw it lying on its side by the cattle grid as he rounded a corner. A couple of soldiers were kneeling beside the cab.

"Wilson's been injured. He was driving." Their sergeant looked up briefly. "We'd already checked the farm road for tracks, and I called him up here to wait for us by the main road... we were looking for tracks over there." He pointed to the grass edge. Mark saw how close they must have been; their ears must still be ringing. But these blokes would never find a bloody thing.

"There was no one else in the truck, so the rest of us are OK," the sergeant continued. "We didn't see the land mine in the road," he added unnecessarily. Not surprising, but then to be fair, no one was expecting a land-mine.

They pulled the soldier, who was moaning in agony, out of the cab. Mark waited while they eased him around the deep hole in the ground that marked the site of the explosion, and laid him down on a level stretch. Definitely an AT mine, must have been boosted too – there was a huge crater in the road, right next to the cattle grid. Mark reckoned it was big enough for two men to lie down in.

"Aargh! My feet," Wilson cried out in pain again.

"They look broken, sarge," the man who was tending him said. "Shall we give him morphine?" Blood was seeping from Wilson' split boots.

"Yes. Give him this one ampoule for now."

Mark saw Wilson had that grey pallor signifying deep shock. And blood was trickling from his ears. He took the sergeant aside.

"I suggest you watch out for shock too, Steve, or you could lose him altogether." Mark recalled the time he'd been present at a rescue by professionals, when one of his fellow climbers had a similar injury, 'compression fracture' they'd called it, following a nasty fall on the Drakensburg Mountains in Natal a few years ago. "Get him wrapped in blankets, and try to get some hot, sweet tea into him." It didn't look as if Wilson had a stomach wound, so liquid by mouth would be OK, and it would help tackle the shock. "Do you have a saline drip?"

The sergeant looked at him for a moment, before ordering one of the other soldiers to make tea. "We have no medic. Just our field dressing packs, and I carry two ampoules of morphine. No saline drip, and we wouldn't be too confident about what to do with it if we did; it's a long time since I did my first aid training."

"OK, I can't do anything here for you, so I'll get back to the farmhouse if you don't mind. Do you want me to send anything down or make any phone calls?"

"No it's OK, thanks; I've already contacted HQ and called for a casevac. There'll be a chopper here with a follow-up stick fairly soon and they'll take Wilson out."

That was a relief; at least the follow-up stick should be fighting soldiers. "Yeah, I guess the shit will hit the fan over this lot." Mark paused. "In that case, perhaps I'll stay until they get here. Um... I can bring them up to date about what's happened up at the field with old man Cartwright and the cattle." He realised he had to be diplomatic with what he said to the soldier. But the sergeant was too tied up with his own problems to take much notice or offence at any implied criticism.

Mark looked up as the Alouette clattered overhead and landed on the main road at the farm entrance. Four young but efficient looking soldiers got out, and took up all round defence while the injured driver and two of his colleagues, including the sergeant, got aboard. The helicopter took off again in a cloud of dust, not wasting any time on the ground. Three of the regimental police had been left behind to guard the damaged Army truck. Presumably waiting for recovery by the Army's mechanical engineering corps? Mark walked over to the newly arrived soldiers, and one of the remaining RPs introduced him to the corporal in charge.

"I'm just a guest at the farm, but I've been helping Mr Cartwright with his injured cattle this morning." Mark corrected the impression the RP had given that he was a member of the farm family. "What about coming up to where the old herdsman was killed and the cattle maimed as a start? There must be tracks or something up there."

"We'll take a quick look down here first... but you can stick around in case we need you." The corporal rejected Mark's suggestion, but seemed to know what he was doing.

"No, I'll go back and join Mr Cartwright; you'll find us near the road, or up at the farmhouse if you need us. There are a lot of folk up there by the way; there was a party last night, and plenty of visitors." Mark looked at his watch. It was already after eight. "They'll be wanting to get away soon."

"I wouldn't advise it," the corporal replied. "There could be more land-mines on this road, and it will take quite a lot of time to check it out." He looked round at the sound of an approaching vehicle. "Oh, Oh... Here come the cops, late as usual." A police Land Rover sped up to the cattle grid and stopped. Two men got out.

"What's happened here?" the white patrol officer asked, while his African companion went over to look at the crater and the damaged truck.

"Don't you blokes have radio?" the corporal asked. "The redcaps got hammered by a land-mine just here by the grid, and one of their men has been casevaced." Mark realised how bad things were when he saw that the police couldn't communicate direct with the Army by radio. Any comms would have to come via some central point, and obviously there hadn't been time for that yet.

"The wheels of communication between our two forces grind very slowly through our Joint Operations Command centre, corporal. We saw the chopper as we came up; I suppose that was their casevac?"

The corporal nodded confirmation. "We need to get searching for terr sign here, officer. Will you check out the killing up the road?"

"OK. How will we know what you are doing?"

"Let's try to meet up at the farmhouse later. That'll probably be better than relying on JOC to keep us up to date."

Mark hitched a ride with the police vehicle, urging them to drive carefully. Although he'd kept a look out for land-mines on the way down, he might have missed one. But they soon reached the field with the cattle.

Peter was at the side of the road with the farm tractor, and the sorry pile of carcasses. "I've just got back from doing a search for land-mines between here and the farmhouse, he said. "There's one just a few yards up the road there." He pointed to a bend in the road nearby. "The Army and my boys both had very near misses when they drove down this morning." Mark was pleased to see that Peter seemed to be back to his normal switched-on self. "The vehicle tracks seem to show that the tractor and the Army truck both went over it." Mark shuddered at the thought; thank goodness, the wheels must have missed the detonator each time. "It's clearly visible now because the wheels dug it out of the ground."

They walked up to have a look. Mark instantly recognised the sinister, flat drum, dark green in colour; it was tilted partway out of the hole the terrorists had planted it in.

"Christ, those were pretty close calls," the policeman commented. "I wouldn't have believed it if I hadn't seen it for myself. We'll leave the mine for the Army to clear. Are you sure this is the only one?"

"Pretty sure it's the only one between here and the farmhouse, but the Army should check to make sure. I'm no expert," Peter added.

"It's also possible that the terrs will have laid anti-personnel mines in the roadside bush near their anti-tank mines," Mark warned, causing the policeman to look at him quizzically. "That's standard operating practice for mine laying." Mark knew these folk had little or no experience of land-mines before now. He knew more about mines than any ordinary Rhodesian soldier or policeman.

"OK, but let's get back to the field and have a look at your herdsman first." The patrol officer radioed back to his police station in Umvukwes. He asked them to try to get news of the second mine to the Army patrol… and for the Army to send someone to sweep the whole place.

"I suppose I'd better come with you to see Madala." Peter left with the policemen. Mark got onto the tractor and drove very carefully past the land-mine and into the farmyard.

This was going to be a long day, and already going through his mind were the logistics of changing his travel arrangements back to South Africa. Fortunately it was the middle of the summer holiday season, and he had no vital appointments until Monday week. No, to hell with it. There was no way he was going to leave Angie, or the Cartwright family yet – not with all this crap going on. The bustling cities of Cape Town and Johannesburg seemed a long way away.

Chapter 16

"*Mangwanani, mukomana* – good morning, young lad. Where is Mabunu's kraal?" Gadziwa asked the small boy who was opening a stockade to let the cattle out; they had driven into the TTL well before dawn, but now the sun was near the horizon, and people were stirring at the small village near the cattle kraal. They'd waited here for someone to come so they could get directions. The night had been a success, but it was necessary for Gadziwa to find a safe place to hole up for a few days, while things quietened down. His freedom fighters were elated but tired.

"Eh?" the child's eyes rolled with fear, despite Gadziwa and his men having kept their weapons out of sight in the car. He stood mute and shivering on one leg, the other balanced against his bony knee while a swarm of flies buzzed around the snot dribbling down one side of his grubby face.

Gadziwa repeated the question, but the boy remained too terrified to answer. This was no good. He didn't want to go into the village itself. Although the whole of this TTL was said to be properly indoctrinated to the Cause, it was always wise to be cautious. Gadziwa had been a fighter for too long to take unnecessary risks, but it was clear they would get nowhere with the boy.

"Go to the biggest hut in the kraal and find a madoda to answer our questions," Gadziwa told M'butu, the young freedom fighter he was beginning to trust more and more. "Leave your gun and do not tell them anything, just bring a man here."

M'butu was back in a few minutes; he could get things done without fuss – another good mark for him.

"*Mangwanani, marara sei* – good morning, did you sleep well?" The man replied politely to Gadziwa's greeting. A structured conversation followed, covering their personal well-being, the weather, crops and stock. Such manners were required here in the countryside between adult men, before Gadziwa was able to put his question.

"Mabunu is my brother," the African responded with the air of a man who was announcing an important and welcome piece of news, "What do you want with him?" The relationship of 'brother' did not necessarily mean sibling. But here at least was someone who came from the same wide family, or sub-tribe, as the kraal-head Gadziwa was looking for. Someone who was unlikely to be a sellout.

"I have a message for him from Kaguri." Gadziwa used the name of the commissar who had told him Mabunu could be trusted. The 'brother' of Mabunu would now be unable to ask further direct questions, as that would be unseemly. Instead he offered hospitality to Gadziwa and his companions, which Gadziwa politely declined with patient determination, insisting that his message was urgent. In the end he got the directions he wanted, and they drove off.

Their journey was over rough bush trails, which were occasionally used by wheeled transport, but more often by livestock and people on foot. They passed an abandoned cattle dip, which looked as if it had been deliberately smashed up. The land was parched and there was little in the way of grazing. Crops stood dying in the land for lack of rain, while occasional light breezes caused the dust to rise, sweeping across the sparse bush.

This was typical; a few kilometres away the white farmers had good crops and good grazing, but here Gadziwa's people were suffering. The mukiwa kept all the best land for themselves. He felt his anger rising. Things would be different when Africans took power, and he would make sure he got the best there was to be taken from the white settlers. He would commandeer a place that had many large trees to provide firewood; the place they had attacked last night was ideal.

Here, all the trees had already been cut down for firewood and to build huts. There was nothing but a few small, scraggly thorn bushes left, and he could see it was time these people had fresh land. He knew from folklore that in the days before the white man, people moved on to new pastures after they had 'eaten up' the land they lived on. This all stopped when the white man came, and there was no longer enough space.

They had to wait on the dusty roadway while a man steered his sled, pulled by two oxen, off the track to allow them to pass. The runners followed the deep ruts in the road easily enough. Here was another inequity. The white administrators in the TTL, called land conservation officers, kept trying to stop African people from using their traditional sledges. They claimed that the ruts they made would channel the rain, causing good soil to wash away into the rivers.

The conservation officers gave the tribesmen wheeled carts to replace the sleds they confiscated. These were good as far as they went, but wheels required maintenance, including grease or fat for the axle. Wheeled carts tipped over more easily than sleds did, and they were more difficult to set upright once they went over on these rough roads.

No, any fool could see that it was much better to use sleds. The ruts they cut into the soil made good pathways as they went along. In places, there were scores of these tracks running alongside each other; making nice wide, easily visible pathways across the bush. His people had made their way across their land like this since time began, and the mukiwa had no right to interfere with the old ways.

"I bring you greetings from Comrade Kaguri." Gadziwa was glad to arrive at Mabunu's kraal at last. The sun was halfway to noon and he looked forward to enjoying a rest as soon as he was satisfied of their safety.

* * *

"There is no one in this area who will report your presence to the soldiers, comrade," Mabunu said, as they sat in the early afternoon sun, sipping cool beer. Gadziwa had slept for a while after arriving at Mabunu's kraal. His potent sixth sense told him he could trust this man who came so well recommended by Comrade Kaguri. Two of his men were still asleep in their hut. But he chuckled when he saw young M'butu, who had woken first, take the woman that his three boys had been given to share by Mabunu, back into the hut with him. It was right that young men should have sex as a high priority.

A man's priorities changed as he got older, but later that night Gadziwa himself was certainly going to take up Mabunu's offer of a large woman – the pick of the kraal.

"She was the wife of my brother, but he died last year. So now she belongs to me," Mabunu explained how such a comely woman was available.

Gadziwa was no longer quite so fit and slim himself. In particular, his thighs and buttocks, though still muscular, were heavy. But he took delight in the old saying, 'it takes a heavy hammer to drive a long nail.' He was going to enjoy that woman tonight in his own hut. The privileges of age and seniority were almost as good to contemplate as they were to consummate.

"We have comrades here quite often to deal with sellouts." Mabunu interrupted Gadziwa's thoughts. "The last time was my neighbour's son. He came back from the Gwebi Agricultural College, full of white men's ideas about new ways to work the land and raise livestock." He sniffed, hawked and spat to emphasise his disapproval. "The youngster's father even allowed him to send their cattle to be dipped. I had to send four of my kindred to break up the dip when we found out, or we might have had others copying them. Then Comrade Chipoko came and I asked him to deal with them – about two moons ago. He and his comrades beat the father and the son, and slaughtered their cattle. They have seen the error of their ways."

"So, there is no work for me and my comrades to do here?" Gadziwa grunted.

"Not here comrade, but there are plenty of European farms nearby. I can give you information on the ones where the workers are sellouts. There are others, in addition to the place you have already punished."

"My boys need to rest for a few days before I decide what to do. Meanwhile, I will eat and drink… and pleasure the woman you gave me." He watched M'butu come out of the hut where he had taken the woman. "Come here, young man. There is beer now for a rested warrior." M'butu strutted over with the cocky walk of a young man who had just had sex.

"Thank you, Comrade Captain." The young freedom fighter came forward and squatted in the accepted manner. One of Mabunu's wives brought him a pot from the nearby drum filled with home-brewed millet beer. Gadziwa noted with satisfaction that, even after the youngster was praised, he knew enough to maintain respect for his leader. The young man took a long draft and smacked his lips in an approving manner. That would please Mabunu, for although it was his wives who brewed the beer, he would accept the approbation for himself. It recognised that he maintained proper and effective control over the work his women did.

"What is the name of your neighbour who was a sellout?"

"His name is Dabengwa… Wasiya Dabengwa, comrade." Mabunu took another draft from his pot, straining the solids expertly through his teeth. He wiped the creamy residue from his lips. "His son's name is Domiso."

"You're sure he has been properly converted to our Cause?"

"Comrade Chipoko dealt severely with him, but there is no reason why you should not pay a call on him to assure yourself of his loyalty, comrade. He will pay good attention to such a renowned and feared commander as *Gumbarishumba*."

Gadziwa was pleased with this compliment. "We'll go to his kraal in a few days' time."

Chapter 17

Now everyone at the house was awake, and Miriam brought the three girls through for breakfast. She seemed much happier with so many people being about, and Angie felt comfortable leaving the girls in her care. The kitchen was a hive of activity and, once people had breakfasted, she had her job cut out getting them to move into other parts of the house to make room for more.

The only topic of conversation was, of course, the murder of Madala and the mutilation of the dairy herd. Many were speculating that it was an act of terrorism but one or two didn't agree.

Most of the men wanted to go down to help Peter but Kate talked them out of it, saying that Peter had specifically asked that no one else should leave the farmhouse. "Thank goodness; here's Mark," she said.

Angie looked up to see a very dusty, and weary looking Mark walk into the kitchen. She went over, gave him coffee and remained standing close by. Charlie soon joined them, and Angie smiled to herself. Charlie had this uncanny ability to be near the centre of any action.

"Thanks, Angie. Hi, Charlie." He sipped the coffee and cleared his throat before raising his voice.

"Can I have everyone's attention, please?" The murmur of chatter among the guests eased a little. "Peter asked me to tell you the farm has been attacked by terrorists." Now he had their undivided attention, and carried on quietly outlining what had happened. It was remarkable how calmly the men and women took the awful confirmation of their fears. There were a few sensible questions about what action was being taken, especially about the land-mine danger. No one in the house had heard it go off – it was too far away, and the noise in the house from all the guests would have muffled it anyway – so that news had come as an extra shock to everyone.

"There's still a real danger of more mines," Mark confirmed. "There's the one that blew the Army boys up and we've found an unexploded one, quite near to the homestead entrance. It was run over twice without going off – the wheels just missed the detonator each time – but it's still lying in the road... There could be more, so I'm afraid that everyone will just have to wait here until the Army clears the whole road." Mark paused, and had another sip of his coffee before fielding more questions.

When he finished, he turned to Kate. "Would you like me to phone the abattoir manager to see how he's getting along with that truck to collect your cattle, Kate?"

"Oh, would you? The number's next to the phone in the study."

Mark was back shortly. "There's a phone call for you, Angie." He stood by her side. "It's your husband."

That *was* a surprise; she guessed he must have heard about the attack and hurried to take the call. How could Ron have heard about the farm so soon? She wondered if there wasn't something wrong at his end. Perhaps he'd been wounded? She picked up the phone, "Ronnie?"

"Are you all safe?" His voice came over the line with only the slightest crackling.

He must have heard. "Poor Madala is dead – killed by terrorists. And your Dad's dairy herd have had to be put down – all of them, I'm afraid. But the girls and I are OK, and so are your folks." She paused to make sure she'd remembered everything. "And one of the Army boys, who were here for New Year, has been injured by a land-mine – near the farm entrance, but no one else was hurt. What about you? Where are you?"

"I'm fine. I've stopped at a game ranger's house in the Angwa Valley to make this phone call and I'm on my way to the farm." He sounded on edge.

"You needn't worry about us, Ronnie," she reassured him. "We're all shocked and your parents are very upset of course, but there's no danger now. The police and Army are here."

"Good... I should be there mid-afternoon."

There was something in his voice. "Is there anything you're not telling me?"

There was a pause before he answered. "No, it's OK. Just a small matter that'll soon be sorted... I've got to go now. Tell the folks I'll be there later today."

So she'd been right. There was something... "Be careful, Ronnie. There may still be terrorists around here, and the Army haven't cleared the farm road for land-mines yet." 'Small matters' were usually a sign of big trouble with him.

"Yes, I know, Angela. That's why I'm coming. See you later." He hung up.

She put down the phone with a shaking hand. He was on his way. Remembering Mark's kiss and her initial reaction, she wondered how she'd feel when Ron actually arrived. She shook herself, she'd just have to snap out of it and carry on as normal. After all, she rationalised, it was only one kiss…

Angie went straight to Kate and told her that Ron was well and about his plans. "He's somewhere in the Angwa Valley now, and should be here this afternoon."

Kate relaxed visibly.

Mark was listening. "That's good. I'd better go down to see if there's anything else I can do to help Peter now." He turned to Kate. "By the way, Van Staden is still trying to organise a truck for the cattle, and can't give us an expected arrival time yet. Says he'll phone here as soon as he knows." He turned to go, then paused and looked directly at Angie. "Of course, I'll tell Peter the good news about Ron being on his way."

* * *

As soon as he got out the door, Mark paused to reflect. Now there was no point in him staying, not with Angie's husband and the son of the house on his way home. He'd never deliberately kissed another man's wife before, not the way he'd kissed Angie anyway. He felt like a bastard and didn't look forward to meeting the bloke. But was he prepared to give up on Angie? Well, he'd promised to get back and help Peter, so he put his problem on the back burner. To save time, Mark used his car and found Peter still with the police.

They'd just loaded Madala's body into the back of their Land Rover. "There'll have to be a post mortem, but you can have the body back for burial after that," the policeman was saying.

"You'll be pleased to know that Ron's on his way," Mark told Peter.

"Good heavens; how's he managed that?" Peter asked.

"Sorry, Angie didn't tell me."

Peter looked quite concerned before shrugging it off. "The Army have been up and checked the road, and say there are no more land-mines, but we'll have to wait for specialists to come and defuse the one that's exposed."

"Now the road's been cleared, we'll go up and see if anyone at the farmhouse heard anything last night," the police patrol officer said. "Soon as we've done that, they can start going home and we'll get the body back to the mortuary."

"Everyone's pretty anxious to get away now," Mark told them.

"First, can we get something to mark the exposed mine properly?" the policeman asked.

One of the farmhands was told to go with the police vehicle, load two empty 210-litre drums onto the farm pickup, and bring them down to the land-mine. "But don't try to place them yourself," Peter warned. "Baas Mark and I will do that."

The farmhand rolled his eyes, saying he'd rather not ride in the same vehicle as a dead body; he'd prefer to walk.

"Get in, you silly bugger," the policeman chuckled, making room and pulling him onto the front seat.

"The Army and police found some tracks in the field and bush around here, Mark. Come and have a look at them while we wait for the drums."

"Hell... Look at the size of that bugger." Mark pointed to a footprint in a sandy section of the bush near where Madala had been found. "How the bloody hell did the redcaps miss that?" He knelt down to examine it more closely. "Looks like takkies with a sort of figure-of-eight tread on the sole."

"Yes, the policeman said they're standard terrorist issue trainers. But I've never seen such big feet; must be a hell of a big man." They walked back to the place where Madala had been murdered.

"The terrorists sneaked up on him; there was no sign of struggle," Peter pointed out. "They obviously know their business, to be able to get at Madala without waking him."

"Maybe even the dogs wouldn't have heard them?" Mark still felt bad about having left them locked away overnight.

"Probably not. They would have stayed around the farmhouse. And remember it was me who decided to lock them up not you; so stop blaming yourself." They walked back to the road and arranged the empty drums carefully, to shield the unexploded mine from passing traffic.

"Stay here to look after the carcasses until the truck from the abattoir comes, Moffat," Peter told one farmhand. "Make sure no one touches them and see that no animals get at them." He sent the man who had brought the drums back to the yard with the pickup, telling him to get two men to help him, and bring shovels down to the entrance gate.

"Now I want to go and have a look at the Army truck that was blown up."

"OK, but shouldn't you have breakfast or at least coffee before we go?" Mark was beginning to get worried about the tough farmer. The strain was showing in his eyes.

"No. Let's go down to the truck first. I want to have a word with that Army corporal again too. He said he was going back to the main road when his men finished clearing the farm road. Then maybe I can take a break."

The Army recovery team had arrived at the gate and had already winched the damaged truck upright.

"This baby's almost ready to go," the bearded mechanic said, dragging himself from under the vehicle to speak to them. "We've replaced the axle stub, and fitted the spare wheel." Mark never ceased to be amazed at how the years of sanctions had made the Rhodesians masters of make-do-and-mend.

"Good. My farmhands are on their way to fill in the crater. Our guests will need to get past here soon," Peter commented. "Now, let's go find the follow-up squad."

They went across to the regimental policemen, who were waiting in the shade of a tree while their vehicle was being repaired. "They've found more tracks and followed them back down that way," one man told them, pointing towards a bridge.

"That crosses the river coming off my land, Mark. Let's go and see what's happening." Peter set off on foot with Mark following. His energy had returned with a vengeance.

The corporal and his men were having a 'brew' in the bush near the bridge when they found them. "Join us for tea?" the corporal asked, offering his enamelled tin mug to Peter. Mark shared an Army issue mess-tin with one of the other soldiers. Peter took a few draughts, and then passed the half empty mug back to the corporal.

"The terr who led this lot is well known to us. Bastard called 'Big Feet'." The soldier paused to take a few sips himself. "There were four of them and they hid their vehicle in the bush here while they attacked your farm, sir." The corporal diligently wiped the rim against his combat jacket, before handing the mug back to Peter. "Then they came back and pissed off with it. Can't be sure which direction they went, but I'll bet a pound to a pinch of shit that they headed straight for the Mazimbe TTL."

"That's only about ten kilometres up the road towards Centenary," Peter said.

"Yep, but my Ruperts can't make up their minds what they want us to do; we want to get after them, not fuck about here all day. 'Course, it'll be a hell of a job finding the bastards in the TTL. They'll just mingle with the locals, who are either shit scared, or sympathise with them anyway."

"Come up to the farm while you're waiting if you like," Peter offered.

"Thanks but no, sir. We'll finish our tea. Then I'll call HQ again and see if we can get going for the TTL." He took the mug back and drained it. "That's unless we have to hang around here until the engineers come and defuse that live mine you found."

* * *

"Do you have to leave now, Mark?" Angie asked, even though she felt nervous about him still being at the farm when Ronnie arrived. She worried that somehow Ron might sense something; she wasn't sure she could lie to him. But then, Ron wasn't very good at noticing things about her any more. And anyway, what had it amounted to? Apart from that one passionate kiss in the garden there'd been nothing else. As for Mark thinking that he was 'in love with her' her, she wasn't too sure he meant it… it seemed too soon for that. They hardly knew each other.

"You know I planned to leave before lunch anyway. Now things have settled a bit, and Ron will be here soon, there's no need for me to stay. I must try and get back to South Africa tonight, or early tomorrow morning, if I can." He carried on packing while she stood in the doorway.

The house was busy with other people packing and leaving. It was after midday, and the guests all wanted to be home before dark. Some had a long way to go.

Mark had been at her side when they'd seen her parents and the three girls off a few minutes ago. She'd decided that the children would be safer with her folks in Salisbury than at the farm. Harriet had gone off to pack; she was travelling back with Mark.

"I'm sorry your New Year turned out this way." It had been Angie's impulsive invitation that had brought him here in the first place.

Mark smiled at her. "Everything up till this morning was just great. How could you have known there'd be a terrorist attack?"

"Still..." she bit her lip and shook her head.

"Angie; I'll be travelling up to Salisbury from time to time, can we meet up?" Mark had finished packing and was looking at her with those searching blue eyes of his. He moved closer and reached behind to push the door closed.

Angie knew what was coming next, but didn't back away. He bent down, took her into his arms and they kissed passionately. She was deliberately encouraging him... Why was she doing this? What was it leading to?

The implications broke the spell, and she pushed away from him. "Mark, someone could come in at any moment and see us..." she searched for the right words, "Ronnie and the children..." The consequences didn't bear thinking about. She felt angry, but this was her fault – not his.

"Angie, you must know how I feel by now. Is there a chance?" He hesitated.

"Mark, it's too soon... too complicated. There are things I have to sort out."

He kissed her neck gently before releasing her. "So it's not impossible then? Can I phone?"

The anxious look in his eyes softened her answer, and she smiled back at him.

"Please give me your number." Mark took out his pocket diary and wrote it down. She felt weak at the knees as they left the room; what on earth was she doing?

"I'm sorry you have to leave, Mark." Peter shook Mark's hand in farewell. "I'm not sure what I would have done without your help this morning. You'll always be welcome to visit whenever you're up this way again."

"Yes, thank you for everything, Mark." Kate accepted Mark's farewell hug and gave him her cheek to kiss. Oh damn, they were such nice people – Angie hated the thought of ever hurting them…

Mark kissed Angie again just before he left, and she tried not to look around to see if anyone was watching. Harriet was waiting in the car, and Angie realised no one would take any notice. Their kiss would appear innocent, but her conscience twisted her stomach into a knot.

Despite feeling relieved as the car disappeared down the driveway, she missed him as soon as he'd gone. Was she really falling for him? Impossible – she must not allow it to happen. But he did seem to be everything she wanted and needed in a man…

* * *

Ron heard about the attack on the farm and the atrocities over the radio. When they confirmed it as Big Feet's work, he was so enraged he bloody nearly lost control.

Disobeying Major Swain's orders to return to company headquarters via the Valley, he turned the truck round the moment he heard. Not unexpectedly, Swain was incensed when he found out, and threatened all sorts of disciplinary action. But he calmed down eventually, and granted Ron two day's compassionate leave. At the same time he instructed Ron to place the truck and the men under Mike's command on arrival at the farm, so they could return immediately to company HQ. Ron decided to ignore that part of the instruction, and made sure Mike didn't overhear.

"I should have listened to my gut feeling yesterday, Mike," Ron confessed after brooding over the events.

"No one could have guessed Big Feet would attack a farm, sir," Mike had said patiently. "Especially not your father's."

Ron was not comforted; the killing of Madala was a crime too far. Madala had been his closest friend and mentor during his childhood days. A complete contrast to Ron's father, who had been a hard taskmaster, constantly getting on to Ron about discipline and responsibility. Yes, they'd argued for as long as he could remember, his mother trying to keep the peace. It always ended up with his parents being at loggerheads over him.

Back then Ron used to run away to find Madala and his cattle, sometimes even spending the night away, camping under the stars by the old man's fire. No, there was no way he was going to allow Big Feet to get away with this. But he needed his men to help him track and kill the bastard. He had to face it. He wasn't going to let Mike and *his* men piss off back to company headquarters; there were scores to settle.

* * *

It took four hours to get to the farm, including stops at several roadblocks along the way. At the entrance to the farm they drove carefully past a massive hole in the road, which was being repaired. Further in, Ron stopped to talk to a group of half a dozen soldiers. Apart from the infantry, there were a couple of Army engineers, who told him they'd defused another land-mine close to the farmhouse. The four-man team from the RLI had been there all day, and Ron took the opportunity to speak to the corporal in charge.

"Slit the poor old bugger's throat from ear to ear," the man said, telling him about Madala. "…Blood all over the fucking place; this is the bastard who did it." The soldier pointed to tracks in the sandy soil, near where Madala's body had been found.

"I know that one well… name's Gadziwa."

"We call him Big Feet," the corporal responded.

Ron nodded. "Also known as Gumbarishumba, which means 'lion's paw'. The corporal looked at Ron with respect.

Ron went back to look at the carcasses of the dairy herd, which were being loaded onto a CSC lorry. This distressed him far more than he expected. He could see how they'd rubbed their bellies raw, trying to stand up, and dragging themselves along the ground after they'd been hamstrung. He also saw how the gentle creatures' udders had been needlessly mutilated. He thought about what the terrs had done to his friend, Madala.

That fucking bastard terrorist; he knew now that he had to get Big Feet, no matter what. Ron left the scene of Madala's death and those pathetic carcasses, bitterly angry and frustrated.

* * *

Angie heard an Army lorry arrive and rushed to the front door, getting there just in time to hear Ron tell his men to 'debus'. He ignored her while he told his soldiers that they'd be stopping for a short break before they left again. She waited patiently, but was shocked at his appearance. He'd always been lean but now he looked positively scrawny.

Finally, he turned to greet her. "Hello, Angela. Where are the girls?" He sounded angry, but gave her a perfunctory kiss on the cheek.

"I sent them back to Salisbury with Mum and Dad." She wondered if he'd find something wrong with that. "We thought they'd be safer there."

"Quite right too. I'd like my men to have something to eat here, and then we've got to get going again. I've got some terrorists to kill. Come on, let's go see what Sam can cook up for me and the boys."

"Oh, Ronnie. Do *you* have to do it?" Angie had to almost run to keep up with his long strides through the house to the kitchen. "Can't someone else go after them? There are lots of other soldiers around here." Ron's men were trailing behind them.

"That's what everyone keeps trying to tell me. But this bastard has been slipping past me and my men for almost a week; and now he's killed one of my oldest friends..." Ron spoke without slowing. "We're going to get him. I'll make him wish he'd never seen Madala – or Sapphire Blue." He paused to greet his parents in the living room, and asked Kate if Sam could prepare food for eight men including himself.

"It's all arranged, son," she replied, standing to receive his hug and kiss.

Moses offered to bring beers.

"Good idea, thanks Moses. My men and I are fairly clean, Dad; would you mind if we cooled off in the pool?"

Ronnie didn't seem to want her hanging around, so Angie stayed to help Kate and Sam, while the men went for a swim. He really didn't care, not even making the slightest effort after they'd been apart for weeks...

* * *

"Don't worry, Dad," Ron reassured his old man, who was trying to interfere as usual. "I'm going to get after the bastards as soon as my lads have eaten. The follow-up group down the road are convinced the terrs have escaped into Mazimbe, and I agree with them. Big Feet is not the sort to high tail it back into Mozambique; he'll be better off hiding up in a friendly TTL."

"But surely Mazimbe is outside your area?"

"Uh-ha, but I must get after this bastard myself. We've been chasing him for almost a week this time – on our own. We know his ways better than anyone else. We've got to get him or he'll attack again," he explained with a patience he didn't feel. "I can't understand why he didn't hit the farmhouse itself, though. He's a ruthless bastard, and wouldn't be satisfied with just killing Madala and a herd of cows." Ron saw his father flinch; damn, he hadn't meant to sound so unfeeling. He paused to take a swallow from his beer. The men were enjoying themselves in the pool. Even Naasty was in there; he must be feeling the heat. Unusually, Mike and Herbie did not join in. Probably due to their reticence at being the only African visitors among so many Europeans. They sat rather self consciously, watching the others in the pool and sipping at the cold drinks they'd asked for, instead of beer.

"Have you got the necessary permission to go after them, son?"

Jeez... "No." His father's interference was beginning to irritate. "I'll radio my CO when we've had a break."

"You should clear that up now," the old man insisted, and they got into one of their usual arguments, with Ron battling to keep his temper under control.

The arrival of Angela and his mother interrupted what was developing into a major row, and Ron took the opportunity to turn away and carry out the necessary introductions.

* * *

Angie waited while Ron presented his men to Kate. "This is Sergeant Mike Njube; Mike this is my mother..." Angie had met both Mike and Herbie before but, as always, Ronnie seemed to take delight in introducing the other men to her. Almost as if he was displaying her, he leaned back and smiled, watching their reaction. But she was used to the effect she had on soldiers – most men really. After all, they'd been without female company for several weeks now, and they were very physical. She always tried to be friendly, but not too familiar, wanting to put them at their ease.

"You'll have them all eating out of your hand, Angie," Kate murmured to her when no one else was near. "See how proud Ronnie is of you?"

Angie felt another pang of guilt; if Kate knew about Mark, she wouldn't be so complimentary. It was awful. She really liked Kate and Peter, and could hardly bear the thought of what they would think if they ever found out. But she felt angry that Ron just seemed to want to show her off, yet he had no real time for her. She just couldn't understand it. Darn it all, they hadn't seen each other since well before Christmas.

She recalled Charlie telling her about a conversation she'd had with her husband Brian, who was also in the Army over Christmas. He'd phoned her the night before she arrived for the party and told her to 'make sure you spend the next seven days looking at the floor.' Charlie asked why, and he'd said '…because you'll be seeing nothing but the ceiling for a week after I get home.' Charlie was delighted, and told all the other young women at the party about it, causing gales of laughter. She was such fun.

Angie wasn't at all sure she would have liked Ron being so coarse, but it would be better than the cold, rather abrupt telephone calls he made to her these days. Even now, when they hadn't seen each other for several weeks, she thought he could at least have contrived to spend some time alone with her. And when had he last told her he loved her? She couldn't even recall. Her short time with Mark had given her some idea of what was missing from her life. Ron was fine with the children, but his attitude towards her was becoming, well… offhand. Maybe she *would* meet up with Mark next time he was in Rhodesia.

* * *

"OK sarge, get the men to load up. I'll join you in ten minutes, and we leave immediately afterwards for Mazimbe." Ron needed to have the inevitable radio discussion with Swain while he was on his own. He didn't want Mike and the men listening in while he disobeyed orders.

"My God, Ron! I'll have you under close arrest if you go ahead with this," Swain exploded. He sounded furious.

"Sorry, sir; I know what I'm doing. Big Feet has to be stopped and my lads are the ones who can do it. ...And it's my farm they attacked."

"Where's Sergeant Njube?"

"He doesn't know I'm arguing with you, sir. He's already waiting with my men on the truck... Out." Ron switched off the radio, so that no one would be able to hear base trying to get in touch. He went back to say goodbye to Angela and his parents before joining his men at the truck.

"Ronnie, your father's just told me what you're planning to do," Angie said, putting her hand on his arm. "Please don't do it."

He shook his arm free. "You keep out of this, Angela," he warned. How dare she take his father's side and argue with him in front of his parents?

"But you could get into serious trouble for this," she insisted. "And that's my business too... what about the children?" She was looking up at him defiantly. This was a new Angela. Damned cheek.

"This has got nothing do with you, or the children," he snapped, barely controlling his anger. Didn't she realise he was fighting a war?

"If you get into trouble or get killed, it has everything to do with us." Her flushed face belied her quiet manner of speaking. This was developing into something serious and he had no time for it.

"Shut up and let me get on with my business." Her shock and that of his parents showed on their faces. Were they all *completely* blind to what was going on? Unless he could get Gadziwa, he'd keep on killing and terrorising. The whole country could be lost if the key terrs weren't stopped. He thought he detected a look of understanding in his mother's face, but Angela and his father; they were two of a kind...

Ron turned away and headed for the truck, where his men were waiting. "Head straight for Mazimbe, Mike. We'll take the first track off the main road that leads into the TTL and look for sign there." He climbed behind the wheel. "We've got a job to finish."

Chapter 18

"Have an ox slaughtered, Mabunu, and bring out another drum of beer for tonight. Make it your best ox." Gadziwa, having consumed many pots of beer and spent a pleasurable half hour with the comely fat woman, was in the mood for a party. "Do you have any skokiaan to strengthen the beer? We must celebrate the successes we have so far achieved."

"I would like to slaughter an ox, comrade, but we are suffering from the drought, and my herd has wasted away," Mabunu whined, though he rolled his crafty eyes at Gadziwa with fear.

The man was right to be afraid, and Gadziwa felt anger boil up inside. He faced great dangers to liberate people like Mabunu from the scourge of the white settlers. Yet this fool was not even prepared to slaughter a single miserable ox in his honour. Slowly he gained control of his resentment. Yes, it was true that the tribesmen were suffering. And Mabunu was known to be a solid supporter of the Cause.

Gadziwa thought about the hundreds of dollars he carried with him, the cash taken from Zongoro. He was reluctant to part with much, but perhaps he would make a contribution. "How much will help you part with a good ox?"

"Fifty dollars, comrade." Mabunu looked relieved, his eyes greedy.

"I'll give you 25. It better be a good ox, or you'll see what I can do with you, Mabunu." Gadziwa stood up and stretched himself, demonstrating that it was the end of the matter. "I'll come with you to select the beast." He felt the need to clear his head by taking a walk, and this provided the perfect excuse to give beer drinking a break. "You're in charge while I'm away, Comrade M'butu; do you others hear that?"

His three subordinates had been drinking steadily for several hours, but M'butu still seemed more or less in control of his faculties. Gadziwa noticed that he'd been back to take the woman a second time, and he envied the sexual appetite of a young man.

Mabunu whined that the beast Gadziwa selected was his only decent ox, but cheered up when he saw the 25 dollars. He ferreted it away before instructing his senior wife to prepare for a feast and beer drink that night.

"My senior wife says she thinks she can get some skokiaan, O great Gumbarishumba… but it will cost money," the kraal-head came back and said obsequiously.

"You are playing dangerous games, Mabunu. Take it out of the money I gave you for the ox. It is a skinny ox and not worth 25 dollars." He fixed Mabunu with a glare, and the kraal-head winced away from him as if he'd been physically struck. Gadziwa knew his stare was intimidating, and used it to good effect. Someone had once described his eyes as being like those of a "wild, inhuman madman," which had given him much satisfaction.

"Bring the beer to me for tasting when you have added the skokiaan," he commanded. The homemade spirit would greatly increase the alcohol content of the normally mild millet beer.

When they got back to the gathering place at the centre of the kraal, only M'butu was still awake.

"They have gone to our hut to sleep, Comrade Captain," M'butu said, looking somewhat the worse for wear himself. "I waited for you to come back, but I would like to sleep again for a short while myself, baba." He used the word 'father' as a term of respect, rather than to claim any relationship.

"Youngsters do not have the same stamina as we do, Mabunu, but we must look after them or who will take over from us when we've gone?" Gadziwa looked fondly at the young man. "Go and have your sleep, my son. Be ready for a good time later this evening. There will be plenty to eat and drink."

* * *

Herbie was first off the truck in the late afternoon when they stopped at an entrance to Mazimbe. "Here are some tracks, Ishe."

Ron was elated. This was the first turning they'd come to and it was hardly ten kilometres from the entrance to Sapphire Blue. He got off the vehicle with Mike, and they joined Herbie to look at the marks on the dusty trail in the slanting sunlight. The sun would set soon, but this was the very best light in which to see them. Unfortunately the tracks left behind at the riverbank near the farm entrance had not been clear enough for them to identify any individual characteristics.

"It is a small vehicle," Herbie judged. "It was the only one to use the road today, and it was heavily loaded."

That would stack up if it was carrying Big Feet and his terrorists, Ron surmised. They would be heavily loaded with weapons and other gear too.

"All cars and pickups would be heavily loaded around here," Mike observed dryly. He was right, of course; the drought meant that tribesmen would have to buy food, rather than being able to rely on their own early planted maize. And the only other explanation for a motor vehicle using this poor excuse for a road was to carry bags of maize to the villagers.

Ron made his decision. "OK, it's still our best bet. We'll follow them."

They climbed into the Bedford; Mike in the back this time, with Herbie sitting in the passenger seat, leaning out to follow the tracks while the light lasted. Even after the light became too bad for Herbie to see them, Ron kept going. Despite the onset of dusk, he did not switch on the vehicle lights. He knew that all Army and police units would have been ordered to look out for him and his men, and to try and stop him if they could. But he did not expect helicopter involvement until first light next day. That would give him time to hide the Bedford and take up the chase on foot.

It soon became impossible to see which way to go, and when the truck lurched into a particularly bad washout, almost toppling over, Ron was eventually forced to stop. Everyone got out and he engaged four-wheel-drive to claw out of the donga. Mike went ahead on foot with Herbie, to find a suitable place to stop for a few hours until the moon gave them better light. That would not be until later.

Ron ordered ambush mode. No fires, no lights. It would be an uncomfortable night without hot drinks or cooked food, but he didn't want any tribesmen to know they were there. There were no sounds of wild animals here, just the odd owl hooting to keep them company, and small creatures rustling in the sparse dry grass. He was too stressed to sleep, but managed to doze from time to time.

"Hisst." Ron jerked awake. Mike and another body loomed over him. "I've got an intruder, sir. Bloody near shot him; the stupid bastard sneaked up on us." He pushed the figure forward and Ron could see that Bill was there too, holding onto the stranger.

He sat up. "What are you doing here?" he asked the African squatting before him.

"I come to give you information, sir." There was bright starlight and Ron could just make out the features of an intelligent looking young man.

"What can you tell me?"

"There are gandangas in a kraal not far from here."

"How many?" Ron didn't ask him how he knew; people just knew these things in the bush.

"Four, sir. One is called Gumbarishumba. He is a senior commander, and is the one who led the attack on the European farm last night."

"Shit, that's Big Feet, isn't it?" Bill interjected in his excitement.

Ron ignored him. "Where are they?"

"They are at Mabunu's kraal now."

"Can you take us there?"

"Yes, but you must not take your truck. It will warn the terrorists."

"How do I know you're telling the truth?"

The man shrugged, but didn't answer the question. "I cannot tell you my name, and I will not go into Mabunu's kraal with you. As soon as I have shown you where the gandangas are, I will run home to my own kraal. If it is known that I am the one who showed you, my family will suffer and I will be killed."

Ron was impressed with the young African, who sounded sensible and well educated. "Then why are you risking so much to tell us? You could easily have been shot by my men as an intruder."

"I have good reason to hate these bad men. I seek revenge for what they have already done to me and my family. I cannot tell you more." He seemed in earnest.

Ron decided to chance it. "How long will it take us to walk there?"

"If we leave now, you will get there just before the sun rises."

Ron turned to Mike. "Get everyone up. Who do you think we should leave behind with the RL?"

Mike paused before replying, "Leave Papadopolous with Naasty, sir. Johnny is a steady man. Naasty is a good man in a fight, but he's too noisy for this." Ron approved the selection and they got away in less than ten minutes.

* * *

Gadziwa himself went off to his private hut for a rest, and woke refreshed to the sound of drums announcing the beer drink he had ordered. Summoning the fat woman to his bed, he felt ready for strong booze when he left his hut soon afterwards. He made his way through the darkness to the gathering place. The sun must have set some time ago, and he had many hours of drinking to catch up. He saw his boys were already there, squatting by a small fire with Mabunu.

Some distance from the huts, a group of women were at a cooking fire in a long pit. They were tending the gutted ox on a spit, suspended over the flames. More women were in the shadows beyond, stirring beer in several 44-gallon drums over another low fire. He could hear the women were happy, as they shuffled in a slow dance and chanted together while they worked. The beer they were preparing would not be used for some time, but it would eventually replace what they had drunk earlier in the day, and would be drinking tonight. Mabunu must have a good stock put away in some cool place, and Gadziwa was determined to help drink it over the coming days. The kraal-head was a good organiser and kept his women working well, he decided with approval.

"Greetings, Comrade Captain." M'butu saw him first and stood up hastily to vacate the stool he was using. The other two mumbled greetings and shifted to one side, to make room beside the fire for him.

"Greetings, Mabunu... comrades. It looks as if I have some catching up to do!" He sat down on the stool, and a woman came quickly with a pot for him. "Is this the beer with skokiaan?" He sipped, straining it through his teeth as he drank; yes, it had a strong bite. They would have a good time tonight.

"Does it meet with your approval, Gumbarishumba?" Mabunu asked and Gadziwa gave a grunt of confirmation.

Mabunu looked as if he was about to burst. "We have great news, comrade! One of your land-mines blew up an Army truck by the entrance to the farm you attacked last night." He looked at Gadziwa to see how the news had been accepted, but Gadziwa sipped at his beer again as if assessing it further. "It happened this morning. At least one of the soldiers has died and there are more injured. They had to take them away by helicopter. The truck was destroyed." Mabunu aped Gadziwa and took a draft of his beer. He smacked his lips in appreciation, and screwed his eyes tight at the strong taste of the skokiaan.

Gadziwa was more pleased than he showed. "That is good news, but I am disappointed that they must have found the other mine we laid near the settler's dwelling place, before it did its work."

"It is a great victory. But now we must be prepared, because the soldiers will come into our lands, and they will certainly visit my kraal," Mabunu warned. "All my people are supporters and you are safe here," he added hastily, "but I advise you to hide your weapons and equipment in one of our grain storage bins."

"No! We keep our weapons with us at all times." Gadziwa shook his loaded RPD menacingly, and saw two of his subordinates look guiltily round to find their guns. They had carelessly placed them against the wall of the hut behind them. But M'butu had his leaning against his leg, and simply placed his hand on it.

"But what if the soldiers search the huts, comrade?" Mabunu wheezed. "It has happened before."

"If we have good warning from your people that they are coming, we will hide our weapons in our huts. The soldiers will never look in the roof. If we do not have enough warning, we will fight." Gadziwa would not part with his weapons, but the equipment was another matter; he decided he would allow Mabunu to show him alternative places to hide it more securely, first thing in the morning.

"We must be ready for them to come from tomorrow onwards, but tonight we can relax and celebrate. Their helicopters cannot fly at night, and they will never dare to bring their trucks here in the dark." He took a hearty swallow from his pot.

The beer-drink and feast were great successes. Only Mabunu, M'butu and Gadziwa remained capable of making their own way back to their accommodation in the early hours of the morning. Gadziwa had to help M'butu rouse, and then steer their two drink-sodden comrades to their hut. Even Gadziwa could feel the onset of a heavy head as he lay down to sleep in his private hut. The fat woman was too drunk to be of much use to him, but in truth he wouldn't have been capable if she had. Nevertheless, he determined to beat her in the morning – to show his displeasure at her drunken state. He had to shove her off his blankets before he could get to them himself. He went to sleep, dreaming of the day when Zimbabwe would be free and he claimed his land from a white settler. He would rape the white women. Maybe keep some of them as slaves to use as he saw fit. Yes… that would be a good thing.

* * *

Ron motioned Herbie and Bill to walk on either side of the stranger, while he walked just a step behind him; determined not to lose him during the night march.

Mike came up to Ron and said quietly. "He may be wanting us to settle a score with some old enemy, or he could be leading us away from the terrs, sir."

"You're right of course, but this is the best option we have at the moment, and somehow I think he's telling the truth, sarge." Someone stumbled and cursed behind them. "Stay silent there," he snapped.

"I'll go back and take the tail-end Charlie role again." Ron smiled at the slight misuse of that expression by Njube. Despite the stars, the night was still very dark. The moon had yet to rise and the trail was full of deep ruts and potholes. The last thing they needed was a man down with a twisted ankle, but he knew he could rely on Mike to keep an eye on things from the rear.

It seemed ages before the moon rose and they benefited from the light, which swiftly grew stronger. Now their progress speeded up.

There was just the first hint of dawn in the east when their guide stopped and pointed. "There is Mabunu's kraal."

Ron could just make out the cluster of huts, outlined against the brightening horizon. "Do you know which hut the gandangas are in?"

"No, but the hut that is normally used by visitors is the one furthest from the stockade – see the one over there." He pointed again.

"Where is Mabunu's hut?" Mike asked as he came up to them. The stranger pointed to a large hut on the far, eastern side of the village. "We should check both out, sir. The terrorists could be split up."

It was quite a large kraal, and Ron counted at least 14 huts, excluding the smaller grain storage huts. "I think we should have three groups of two men each, sarge." Ron would have preferred to have three men in each section, but he wanted to form as many stop groups as possible. Going down to one man each would give better coverage. But he wasn't comfortable with men being alone against what could potentially be all four terrorists.

Mike nodded agreement.

"You and I will take one each and we'll put Bill in charge of the other group," Ron decided. "I'll take Herbie, you take Tom. Bill and Blikkie will make a strong team together." He purposely put the two best men on their own together, Herbie was probably the weakest in a fight, and Tom would be fine with Mike.

"I will go now, sir," the young African said.

Good, Ron didn't want the stranger knowing his full disposition and then disappearing. "OK, and thank you. Are you sure you don't want to tell me your name in confidence? You could get a very big reward if there are terrorists here, and only the authorities who administer the payments will know who you are."

But the man shook his head and slipped off – back along the way they had come. Ron turned to prepare for the attack. At last; now was his chance to stop the bastard and to avenge Madala's death – and all the other poor souls who Big Feet had mutilated and murdered.

* * *

Gadziwa woke suddenly, immediately aware of danger. There was something wrong… something bad. He reacted instantly, springing from his blankets and grabbing his RPD and clothes. As he finished dressing, there was a shattering burst of gunfire outside, followed by a brief, shocking spell of silence.

Someone shouted in fluent Shona. "Stay in your huts and you will be safe. Do not move until I tell you!"

Women began wailing all over the kraal. Gadziwa shoved his woman, who was now awake and fumbling in the dark, towards the doorway ahead of him, and kept her there. She started to scream, but he slapped her hard on the side of the head with his open hand. That stopped her screaming, and she just stood there; quivering and weeping quietly while he twisted her arm high up against her shoulder blades, pressing his machine gun into her back. She was naked, but sweating with fear. He felt her squirm, but although she was heavy, she was no match for his overwhelming strength.

Another burst of gunfire. This time he recognised an AK, and a firefight developed. The soldiers had found his boys but they were fighting back, or at least one of them was! He decided to take advantage of the distraction and shoved the woman violently out the door into the pale morning light. She began screaming again but that was what he wanted her to do. He knew the soldiers would not want to kill a woman, so they would hold their fire and concentrate on the fight with his boys. He wrenched the woman's arm, so that she fell to the ground just beyond the entrance to the hut and Gadziwa rolled out, taking cover between her and the side of the hut. The woman was so fat; he hoped the soldiers would not see him sheltering behind her.

He crouched and watched. Two soldiers were engaging his boys. Another two ran in from the darker, western side of the village and joined them. Here was his opportunity; crouching low, he ran into the west and reached the shelter of the stone and wattle walls of the cattle kraal. He paused to look around, making sure he wasn't running into a trap. Then he spotted two more soldiers, a split second before they saw him. They were coming round the far side of the stockade; so there must be at least three groups of two soldiers each. Knowing he'd been seen, he fired at them and saw one go down, followed closely by the second one. He had no idea if he had hit them, or if they'd just dived for cover. Enough. Gadziwa sprinted for the bush from his side of the kraal without looking back.

* * *

"One dead, two captures sir," Mike reported when the firing died down. They finished checking the huts and were fairly sure there were no more terrorists in the kraal. "I heard shots from the cattle kraal area too. That's where Bill and Blikkie were."

"I can't see anyone here who answers the description of Big Feet." Ron walked briskly from the dead terrorist to the two captures. Jesus – surely the bastard hadn't escaped again? But the captures were both built in the usual, relatively small stature common among the Shona people. Christ, he hoped to hell that Bill and Blikkie had got Gadziwa. He'd be in deep shit if they hadn't. Only success would justify his actions.

He turned impatiently. "Mike, you and Tom stay here and cover the two captures, while Herbie and I go find the others. They should have reported back here by now."

Ron and Herbie moved cautiously towards where they'd heard the firing by the stockade. There was a sinister silence. "Bill… Blikkie! Where the hell are you?" Ron called out, his voice harsh in the still aftermath.

"Blikkie's been hit and I can't stop the blood!" Bill shouted from behind the rough stone-built wall. "We need a medic – fast."

"Go get Tom and then stay with Njube," Ron ordered Herbie, who streaked back to the kraal.

Tom went about the task with efficiency. "He's taken one in the upper thigh. I've managed to stem the bleeding, but he's lost a lot of blood. Call for an urgent casevac now, sir. Help me get this drip into him, Bill."

"Contact… Contact… Contact… This is Bravo One." That would grab their attention, and cut into the usual early morning routine radio traffic; everyone would clear the air, giving his call for help priority.

"I got you, Bravo One. Where are you?" The operator at Mount Darwin responded within moments.

"We're at Mabunu's kraal in the Mazimbe TTL, between Umvukwes and Centenary." Ron gave a much broader description than would normally be required. He was well over 100 kilometres outside his authorised area, and even the company's designated area. "I'll give you a grid reference shortly, but we have a seriously wounded man here – Blikkie Blignaut – and we need an emergency casevac. He's lost a lot of blood. Our medic says his life is in danger."

The chopper arrived 40 minutes later from Mount Darwin, and Blikkie was barely alive when they left. It dropped off an RLI fireforce under the command of a lance corporal, who immediately began following up on Big Feet's tracks.

"You stay where you are Lieutenant Cartwright," the order came over the radio from a Major Whitehead at Mount Darwin, whose area they were in. "Captain Venter and two regimental policemen are on their way to you by chopper. You are to surrender to close arrest under him as soon as he arrives. He will hand over command of your men to Sergeant Njube and escort you back to Mount Darwin."

"Yes, sir," Ron replied. He walked over to where Mike was standing and gave him the radio. "I want you to look after this for a while, Mike. I've got the runs, so I'm going for a crap. Take charge while I'm away." Mike gave him a perplexed look, but took the radio from him.

Ron walked into the nearest maize field, instinctively following the route that Big Feet and the RLI fireforce had taken. He stopped and looked at his watch; oh-seven-hundred and the sun was well up, but despite its warming rays, Ron felt a chill.

There were a few alternatives. He had failed in his risky, self-imposed Mission. He still believed passionately that he was the right man to find and kill Big Feet. No thoughts of capture now. But he was responsible for leading an attack that had resulted in the wounding and possible death of one of his men, and the notorious terrorist commander they were after had escaped yet again. A double failure.

Now the Army were going to throw the book at him. Insubordination would be the least of it. He was going to suffer the indignity of being placed under 'close arrest' – right here at the scene of his latest failure… and in front of his own men.

He had brought this shame on himself – and his family – by disobeying a legitimate order from his commanding officer. And he'd ignored his father's advice. What would the Army do? Court-martial, followed by imprisonment? Military imprisonment was notoriously harsh at Brady Barracks. He could tough out the punishment, and reckoned he could take hardship as well as anyone, but he recoiled at the idea of humiliation by those bastard military provosts – 'redcaps' – who ran the show. They would just love to get their hands on an officer, an ex-officer as he would be. He would be at their mercy.

He was clearly no longer fit to lead. Was he even fit to live? It would be very easy for him to take his own life now. Just place the barrel of his FN into his mouth and pull the trigger – that was how it was done, wasn't it? So easy. What about Angela and the children? They'd be well looked after. Both their parents were well off and loved Angela and the girls.

By the time he got out of detention barracks, his career would be destroyed. For sure, Angela would not want to be associated with him anymore. No, she'd probably stand by him; but would he want her pity and sympathy? Things would not be the same between them. He believed his parents would stand by him too. But he'd be forever under an obligation to them, and would have to suffer his father's reproach for the rest of his life. With no career to go back to, he'd be forced to work on the farm. Would he be worthy of taking over the farm when his father got too old to manage it? Would the old man trust him to run the farm, after he had shown such lack of judgement? Whichever way he looked, he was deep in shit.

He was undecided whether to head into the bush to carry on his own follow-up of Gadziwa, or to place the barrel of his gun into his mouth and pull the trigger. He swayed a little and used his rifle to stop himself falling over. His knees almost buckled. Ron had never felt so tired in his life. He heard the approaching helicopter as it swooped low overhead and feathered its blades. It sounded a long way away to his dazed mind. Steadying himself, he walked slowly towards the place where it landed. Damned if he'd let them come and arrest him. He'd hand himself over and face the consequences.

"Take off your belt, remove your boot laces, and hand them all over to Corporal Smith." The captain indicated one of the redcaps who was already standing beside Ron. "That is to prevent your committing suicide while you are in my custody, Lieutenant Cartwright." The humiliation had begun.

Chapter 19

At a small kopje, about a kilometre from the cattle kraal where he'd shot at the soldiers, Gadziwa paused to listen. There had been no more firing since his own discharges. That could only mean one thing. The enemy must have overcome his sons of the soil. He listened for another minute, but the shooting had definitely stopped, so he carried on running.

Many things went through his mind; someone must have betrayed him to the soldiers. He would seek them out and punish them later, but his first priority was to get away. There was no point in trying to fight the soldiers on his own; he knew from experience that there'd soon be many more arriving by helicopter. They would contaminate the whole of the area in a matter of hours. Mabunu and his kraal were now thoroughly compromised. The enemy would find their equipment and the car. He would have to escape on foot.

Staying in Zimbabwe would be too hot for him now, and he needed comrades and equipment to be fully effective anyway. But he was more than 100 kilometres, maybe 150 kilometres from the Mozambique border. Even across that border the Rhodesians were active. Real safety lay more than 200 kilometres away, and a direct line of escape would not provide the cover he needed – he would have to cross many roads and by-pass white occupied areas.

He decided to find the Ruya River and follow it down into Mozambique. That should take him through areas mainly populated by black people, and some comparatively empty country. He knew he could not trust many Africans, but it was better than taking the direct route, which would be cultivated and more open. Eventually he would have to cross the main road that ran from Umvukwes through Concession to Mount Darwin. He racked his brain in an effort to remember exactly where the road crossed the Ruya. He had no map with him. But he knew there was danger everywhere along the road. It might turn out to be better to leave the Ruya, before the road crossed it near Mount Darwin, and head straight for the Mavuradonha

Mountains, and the Zambezi Escarpment. Well, there was a full day's march before he had to decide.

Having made up his mind to head for the Ruya, he altered course immediately to a north-easterly direction. He settled into a steady lope, which would carry him a great distance each day, without tiring too much. Fortunately he was rested, fit and well fed. Any sign of heavy drinking the night before had gone with the adrenaline of his escape. But he would need water, another reason to get to the Ruya as quickly as possible.

There was the sudden clatter of a helicopter close by, and Gadziwa dived for cover under a scrawny thorn tree growing by the edge of a big donga. He pressed his body against the dusty side of the gully. There was a slight overhang, formed by the roots of the tree binding the soil, which at least until now, had prevented it from washing away when the donga filled with rushing water. Gadziwa was sure the helicopter was looking for him. It flew slowly across the bush only a few metres above the scrub, and then hovered above the wash-away itself. It seemed like a full minute, but was probably no more than a few seconds. They did not see him, but he waited several minutes after it had passed, because it flew along just above the donga in the same direction as his intended path. That was good, and he hoped they might report his intended direction of travel as being clear.

By midday, he had a raging thirst, and started casting about for signs of habitation. The bush was parched and the small riverbed that the donga had led him into was completely dry. He feared that even the Ruya might be dry when he got there but, as it was a major river, it should have water beneath the surface.

He came to signs of goats. This was where they'd drunk last time the river had water in it. There was a trough worn into the side of the riverbank, caused by them scrambling to regain the level ground above. Their owner's kraal would be nearby, so when he got to the top, he followed the spoor. Although the trail was old, he soon came to a field of this season's failed maize. Not long after, he saw a few dilapidated huts. There was very little cover, but he paused among the dry maize stalks to look for signs of soldiers. There were none, so he began moving cautiously towards the huts. Some scrawny looking chickens scratched unconcernedly in the dust a few metres from the grain store by the huts – the kraal must be inhabited. His reliable sixth sense told him he was being watched, so he stood stock-still and scanned the surrounding area. At last he caught movement behind a few thorn bushes just beyond the perimeter of the settlement, which quickly resolved itself into an old woman, trying to hide with several small children. Something about her demeanour told him that there were no soldiers in the vicinity.

He went to the largest of the huts and peered into the gloomy interior. This was a poor man's kraal. Slowly his eyes adjusted from the bright sunlight to the darkness inside, and he saw a large earthenware pot standing on one side of the entrance. That looked hopeful. He went in, carefully lifted the heavy pot to his lips and drank some of its cool liquid. The muddy water spilled onto his shirt. Although it smelled foul, it tasted like nectar. He paused, and then drank again before he looked around, to find a container he could use to carry water.

Ah... now his eyes fully penetrated the gloom, and he could make out a drinking ladle. It was propped against the wall, near where the big water pot had stood. He picked the ladle up, and examined it to see if there was any way he could prevent water spilling from its open spoon-like shape. Not very satisfactory, but he soon found another gourd that had been made from the same type of hard skinned vegetable – a marrow. This one had been carefully hollowed out, instead of being fashioned into an open ladle. If he could put a stopper into the long, narrow open neck of this drinking vessel, it would carry water safely. He found an item of old clothing, lying on the bedding by the side of the hut furthest from the entrance, and tore a piece from it. Then he filled the gourd and made an effective stopper with the cloth. He also fashioned a sling, which he tied to it so it could be hung from his shoulder. He would have to make sure that the closed neck did not slope down, or the water would leak out through the cloth.

A further search of the hut revealed a woven basket filled with mealie meal, and a small bag containing hard-dried red beans. Gadziwa commandeered the food to form the basis of his provisions. He scooped the ground maize from the basket into the bag with the beans, and placed the empty basket carefully on the bedding.

There was a small quantity of ready-cooked mealie meal, which he scraped out from the cream-coloured, enamelled interior of a heavy black metal cooking pot. He ate it all. As it was a very poor kraal, he was not too disappointed when he found there was no meat. He had no time to stalk and kill a chicken, and only the inhabitants would know where to look for eggs. He was about to leave when he paused, then took five single dollar notes from his bankroll, and left them in the empty basket. That would be a small fortune to the old woman, and would pay for what he'd taken several times over. These people had very little, and he wanted them to welcome comrades in future – at least to give them food and shelter.

Less than half an hour after he arrived, Gadziwa took a last draft of water from the earthenware pot. He was ready to head back to the river, carrying the small supply of food and water with him. He felt rested, strong and more confident. He peered cautiously from the shadow of the hut. He was a veteran, and would not leave without making sure that nothing had changed out there since he went in.

He immediately spotted the old woman. She and the small children had left their place of hiding. Now they were standing deferentially and silently just six or seven metres away, by the side of their grain storage hut.

He knew they would not be standing like that if there was danger nearby, so he straightened up and said softly "I have left money for your family in the food basket, old woman. *Sarai zvakanaka amai –* stay well mother."

She acknowledged his generosity by respectfully clapping her withered hands together, bowing her head to him as a woman should. The small children hid their shyness behind her ragged dress. He set off towards the river without looking back.

* * *

Throughout the journey, there was danger wherever Gadziwa went. Despite deploying his very best anti-tracking techniques, he knew soldiers would be on his trail; the best he could hope for was to make their progress difficult and therefore slow. His route along the Ruya River took him from the friendly Mazimbe TTL into a white farming area. He could not risk being seen by the African farm labourers, for he knew that most of them were sympathetic to their employers and did not support the Cause. He would get back at these sellouts when the ZANLA – liberation army – had won the Chimurenga, and their political wing, ZANU, was in power. Their political leaders, both Chitepo and Mugabe, promised retribution for all who sided with

Smith's hated settler regime during the war.

He had left the Ruya during the night, having made his way in darkness through a white farming area, and carefully avoiding habitation in case dogs heard him. Negotiating several fences, he reached the main Concession to Mount Darwin road before dawn, and found a place of thick bush near the roadside. By great good fortune, he came across a bundle of firewood, which had been cut to size and tied neatly together, ready to be carried away. Someone had placed the bundle there, and would be certain to come back for it. Gadziwa hid nearby and waited.

As day broke, an old man in a ragged overcoat came and seated himself comfortably on the bundle. He looked as if he was waiting for transport, and Gadziwa guessed this might be a bus stop. The old man and the bundle of wood were on the north side of the road, so the bus he was waiting for would be travelling in the direction Gadziwa wanted to go. He had no choice; he crept up and knocked the old man unconscious with a single blow to the head.

Dragging him into the bushes and removing his greatcoat, Gadziwa slit his throat. Fortunately, the coat had been many sizes too big for the old man, and it more-or-less fitted him, though it was a bit too short. It was a filthy old thing, but Gadziwa rolled in the dust and grass by the side of the road, to make it even dirtier. Unbundling the sticks, he hid the RPD and ammunition in the centre, tying it tightly and using the same strips of bark again.

There was a rich haul of tobacco, paper and even a few coins in the old man's coat, which was made of khaki-coloured, heavy, coarse material. Gadziwa recognised it as being an old Army issue coat, and was glad that he'd killed the old man. Huh... probably an Army pensioner, the sellout. He went back and took the old man's shirt off his body. Tearing it into strips, he wrapped the stinking things around his head like a scarf, to partly hide his face and make him look older. Better throw away the bloodied pieces though, because they'd attract flies. After three weeks' use, his jeans were already filthy, but he rubbed more dust into them, making them look older by cutting them and working the fresh cuts to ragged edges. Last of all, he removed his takkies. He'd have to go barefoot from now on. The old man whose identity he'd taken would not have worn shoes, and going without shoes was no hardship for Gadziwa. The soles of his feet were as thick and hard as any other African's.

It was still early morning, though the sun was now up. Several vehicles passed, including an Army convoy of three vehicles, full of soldiers. No one took any notice of him as they passed. It was as if he didn't exist at all, just a dirty old kaffir sitting in the sun on a bundle of sticks by the side of the road. An hour later, a bus came into view and stopped when he waved it down. It was almost full. All African passengers of course.

The conductor looked warily at him, but Gadziwa pulled his way onto the bus. He ignored the conductor's plea to give him the bundle of wood to place on the roof carrier. The passengers were mainly well-dressed, prosperous looking women accompanied by small, spotlessly clean pre-school children. As he shuffled down the aisle, he sensed that they wanted him to pass them by and not sit too close. The situation amused him, despite the danger he was in. No one wanted a dirty old man to sit near them or their children.

Forcing his way to the back of the bus, he bumped and scraped the seats on each side with his bundle as he passed. Near the back, he found a seat and placed his sticks in the gangway next to him. The two small shiny black children already sitting on the seat pressed against the side of the bus, trying to avoid contact with him. There were two smart women in the seat opposite, and they looked reproachfully at him. They called their children, and he moved his legs into the aisle to let them pass. Scrambling past him, they went to sit on their mothers' ample laps, peeping shyly with big brown eyes.

He must stink, and he had pieces of long grass sticking out from all over the place, suggesting that he'd slept in the bush – which he had. Perfect. They and everyone else would keep their distance. He lifted his bundle up off the floor, and placed it on the seat next to him.

"Where are you going to, old man?" The youthful conductor stood insolently in the aisle chewing on something, but taking care not to stand too close to Gadziwa.

"Where does the bus go to, youngster? Gadziwa mumbled through his ragged scarf.

"We terminate at Mkumbura." The youth was beginning to look anxious – perhaps worried about whether this old man could pay his fare. Gadziwa's heart sang, for Mkumbura was a village right on the border between Rhodesia and Mozambique. He handed over a battered five-dollar note, and the youth counted out three dollars and 50 cents in change, before retreating hastily to the front of the bus.

Soon afterwards they dropped and loaded several passengers at an intersection, before turning off the main tarred road onto a well-maintained gravel road. This led northwards, over the Mavuradonha Mountains. Gadziwa allowed himself to relax, but decided it would probably be dangerous for him to go all the way on the bus to Mkumbura. There would surely be police or Army there, and they would be interested in any male passengers on the bus. He resolved to get off before they arrived at the village itself.

Thick clouds of dust billowed behind the bus as they raced along the road. They stopped at Chimimba and Karoi, and then the bus commenced its laborious haul up the steep sides of the Mountains. The road was precarious in places, and the bus pitched and rolled violently, its passengers clinging to their seats in consternation. But the driver and conductor appeared totally unconcerned, so Gadziwa allowed his head to droop as he caught up with some much needed sleep.

He woke when the bus stopped at a store outside the Mavuradonha Mission, on what appeared to be a major road, though this one was not tarred like other major roads. But it was wide, and had recently been graded smooth. Gadziwa judged they had probably only covered about 100 kilometres, but including stops it had taken them almost four hours. Loading and off-loading passengers, and luggage, from the roof rack took time. The road was very steep in parts, but they were now at the top of the mountain range.

Everyone got out, and Gadziwa took the opportunity to take a piss by the side of the bus. There were only two other men among the passengers.

One stood next to him, and tried to engage in conversation. "I've been hanging onto this for the last 20 kilometres." But Gadziwa just grunted back, shook his mboro, shouldered the sticks with his hidden weapon, and climbed back onto the bus to reclaim his old seat. Several passengers left, and many more joined the bus here.

With the bus now being very full, the conductor again tried to persuade Gadziwa to give up his bundle to be placed on the roof rack. But he played dumb successfully, and the conductor gave up, cursing him for being a '*very* stupid and obstinate old man'. He had to allow a fellow male passenger to sit on the seat next to him, which meant placing his bundle on the floor in the aisle again. No matter, he was able to keep his hand on it protectively, and they eventually got going.

Gadziwa dozed off again…

Suddenly he was slammed to the roof by a mighty explosion from the front of the bus. He was thrown wildly round as the vehicle careered off the road and landed on its side. People were screaming, and thick smoke combined with dust made it hard for him to see. He kept his grip on his bundle, and scrambled over the twisted seats and screaming people to the rear window, which he smashed open by kicking.

"Maai-Whe…" he gasped when the bus rocked precariously as he clambered out; that was a close call. He clawed his way up the steep incline.

The bus lay partly in a deep ditch and was in danger of going right over onto its roof. Gadziwa saw one of the mothers struggling, with her legs trapped under the side of the bus. There was a toddler lying, crushed and silent at her side. Another child – a small girl, was screaming as she struggled ineffectively to pull the woman's legs out from under the bus. There were other passengers who had been flung clear, and were lying injured in the ditch.

They'll be killed for sure when the bus rolls down onto them, he decided. But there was no time for him to do anything for them, he must escape into the bush, and make his way to the border. The mukiwa would be here soon, and the place would be crawling with soldiers. He knew the bus had hit a land-mine laid by his comrades from ZANLA.

Just before he left, he saw the surviving passengers congregate on the roadside, and paused; to save himself tramping through the bush for the border, Gadziwa took a bold decision. Instead of melting into the bush, which had been his first reaction, he waited with the others, sitting innocently by the side of the road near the damaged bus and its stricken passengers. It wasn't long before the soldiers came to investigate the explosion and help the injured. He joined the uninjured passengers, and begged a lift on one of the Army lorries to Mukumbura. The soldiers brought him right to the camp entrance and, of course, no one questioned him. After all, they'd arrived as part of a military convoy. What a joke on the useless white men. This success gave him many ideas for the future.

Getting off the lorry, he walked some distance into the bush on the far side of the road from the camp, until he found a disused ant-bear hole. He squatted down and removed his RPD and ammunition from the bundle of firewood, then carefully wrapped them in a large piece of cloth, together with the bulk of his cash. Finally, he hid the precious bundle carefully down the hole, brushing away all signs of disturbance.

This was the first time he'd let his beloved weapon out of sight since entering Zimbabwe, and he felt uncomfortable without it. But... besides wanting to reconnoitre the Army camp, he needed supplies of food. He planned to sell the wood, to give him cover for the money he was going to use at the Mukumbura store. He hated leaving his cash in the hole, but there was a danger that the soldiers might search him. If they searched him now, they would find only a few dollars – and his bundle of firewood.

* * *

"Mukumbura by the Sea" proclaimed the rustic, hand painted sign at the entrance to the Rhodesian Army Camp on the Mozambique border. A filthy old vagrant peered up at the sign with a sardonic smile; the nearest sea was 600 kilometres away – down where the mighty Zambezi River emptied into the Indian Ocean.

Gadziwa adjusted the bundle of wood he carried over his shoulder, and shuffled on towards the camp. Being broad daylight the soldiers were relaxed, and he wanted to have a good look inside. It could make a perfect target for a mortar attack in the future. In order not to attract attention, he walked in through the main gate, rather than approaching from the bush.

The soldier at the entrance ignored the old kaffir, who paused to offer an obsequious salute as he passed through. The soldier was too busy negotiating with another African, who had a basket of fresh eggs, and several baskets containing live chickens.

He'd expected to be searched; this dirty old man masquerade was a great trick, and he enjoyed the role, making fools of the mukiwa. He shuffled towards the cookhouse, noting the layout of the camp as he went. Especially where they parked their vehicles, in an area together with a petrol bowser, which was topping up an overhead fuel storage tank. He squatted in the dust at the edge of the canvas covering of the kitchen zone, and waited patiently. The sides were open, so he was able to watch everything that went on inside the kitchen, and in the surrounding camp.

"What do you want, you old skellum?" A fat white man with red hair and a khaki apron tied around his waist eventually acknowledged him. Badges marked him as a colour-sergeant. Gadziwa shuffled over and placed his bundle of wood on the ground at the soldier's feet. He knew he looked like a rogue, but trusted his disguise made him look harmless. He squatted ingratiatingly beside the wood.

"We don't need wood here; look – we use gas." The colour-sergeant pointed. Gadziwa pretended not to understand and looked blankly at the cylinders and pipes. "Hey, you. Come and tell this old fool that we don't want his wood." He called a black man over to speak with him.

The African came over and addressed him in the local dialect. Gadziwa mumbled his reply, to disguise the fact that his speech did not have the regional accent.

"You are not from these parts." The man immediately recognised him as a foreigner.

"I have travelled far and I am looking for my grandchildren." Gadziwa had prepared himself to pose as a grandfather whose children had been kidnapped and taken to Mozambique by freedom fighters.

"You will not find them around here, madala."

"I think they have been taken across the Zambezi."

"That is very far away. You will die looking for them. Go home, old man."

"I must find them... and I need money for food."

The African lost patience with him and turned to speak to the colour-sergeant. "He says he needs money for food, baas."

"Give him some of the scraps from over here." The white man indicated a bucket below the big wooden table, which was standing under the canvas shelter. The African tipped the contents of the bucket, which included bread, meat and vegetable scraps, into a paper bag, which he shoved towards Gadziwa.

"*Maita zvenyu*, thank you." Gadziwa clapped his hands politely to the African, and to the white man. He took the food bag and stuffed it into his greatcoat pocket. "But I still need money, so I can buy more food on my journey. This wood is good. I collected it myself."

"He says thank you, but he still wants you to buy his firewood. Says he has far to travel, and will need to buy more food on the way."

"Oh for Christ's sake." The soldier dug into his pockets and took out a note. "Here's a dollar. Leave the wood over there. I suppose we can use it for the boiler."

"Thank you, baas. Thank you, baas." Gadziwa grabbed the money and reverently folded it into another pocket. Then he picked up his bundle of wood, and carried it across to the place the sergeant had indicated. That gave him an opportunity to see more of the camp. From there, he wandered around the perimeter, careful not to get too close to the edge, where he knew the soldiers would be more sensitive.

He came across a group outside a brown tent marked with a red cross. They were standing around someone who was lying on a blanket in the dust. One of the white men, not uniformed, was sitting on a stool next to him, holding a stick. Gadziwa shuffled as close as he dared, then stiffened with shock; he recognised the man lying on the blanket. It was Comrade Captain Musati, a detachment commander he knew from Chifombo. Musati was injured high in his right thigh – there was a bloody, gaping hole in his leg visible through torn trousers.

"One last chance, you bastard. Or I'll give you some of this again," the civilian said, waving the stick towards Musati's injury. Musati made no reply.

"Christ, this is a stubborn one." The white man shoved the stick into Musati's wound and turned it. Gadziwa could swear he heard bone scraping against the stick. Musati's body and limbs twisted involuntarily away from the pain, but he made no sound. "You've given him too much morphine, medic," the civilian said, turning to a soldier in the watching group. The soldier knelt next to Musati and checked his pulse.

"I'll have to give him more or we'll lose him," he said. "His pulse is weak and erratic."

"Let him die," the civilian said. He stood up and beckoned the medic away from Musati, who tried to sit up, but only succeeded in propping himself on his elbow. Another soldier gave him water, which he drank thirstily. Gadziwa was unable to hear what the civilian and medic were saying to each other, but he could see they were arguing. Eventually the civilian turned away in disgust, and the medic hurried back to Musati and gave him an injection. Then he covered him with a blanket, despite the heat. Shortly afterwards, Musati sank into sleep – or was it death?

"Hey, what are you looking at, you old kaffir?" A soldier from the group approached Gadziwa menacingly. "Get out of here."

Gadziwa hobbled away and headed for the gate. It would be bad for him if he were searched. Although he was carrying nothing to identify him, they were sure to uncover his body. They would see that he was not as old as he made out to be. That would be dangerous, and he decided his recce was over.

At least he knew what had happened to Comrade Musati; and he knew the layout of the camp. His time had not been wasted...

Chapter 20

Kate came back from answering the phone and stood at the door. Angie waited for her to say something. She looked strained.

"That was Ronnie." She swallowed hard. "He's under close arrest in Salisbury, and is being court-martialled tomorrow."

There was stunned silence. A knot of anxiety tightened Angie's heart, and she saw the lines on Peter's face deepen into a frown. As she absorbed the impact of what Kate had said, Angie could feel cold fear seeping through her. She'd been worried about Ron's recklessness, but hadn't expected anything like this. What had he done?

Peter carefully laid his newspaper down, stood and put his arms around Kate. "Do you know what he's being charged with?" he asked quietly.

"Something about disobeying orders, and insubordination. He said one of his soldiers was killed, and that he was being held responsible."

"This has come at a bad time." Peter looked grim. "On top of everything else…" He released Kate, and straightened up. "It must be the consequences of that madcap plan of his. I tried to warn him against it."

Kate seemed to have regained control. "Well, what's done is done," she said, taking Angie's hand in hers. "We must stand by him; he must be feeling pretty wretched."

"Yes, of course." Angie squeezed Kate's hand and tried to remain calm herself, grateful that the children weren't here to see their distress. But Peter was right, and now she'd have to pick up the pieces…

"Where exactly is he in Salisbury, Katie?" Peter asked gently.

"He didn't say, I should have asked."

"Don't worry about that, I'll get on to Army headquarters and find out." Peter went off to the telephone, leaving the women comforting each other.

"I'll make some tea." Angie's mind was in overdrive as she went to the kitchen. At least Ron wasn't injured – or killed. She shuddered at the thought. But one of his soldiers had died. She could still see their faces... Oh, God! Which one was dead – what about *his* family? How awful.

She was sitting in the living room, having tea with Kate, when Peter came back. Angie stood to pour his tea.

"I've managed to speak to the officer who's defending him. Chap called Major Adams. He sounds as if he knows what he's about."

Peter explained the official charges and continued, "The good news is they're not proceeding with a charge of mutiny, but Adams has made it clear how serious the other charges are, and he says that Ron will be pleading guilty."

"So what happens next?" Angie asked. Thank heavens it wasn't mutiny, they hung people for that in the Army didn't they?

"Well, Adams is hoping to use the attack on the farm, and Ron's good service record, especially in action, to mitigate the sentence." Peter paused to sip his tea, but he looked shaken. "But he's afraid the Army might choose to make an example of Ron. They don't want anyone else getting ideas that they can get away with what they called; 'insubordinate disregard of several direct orders from his commanding officer'."

"But what will they do to Ronnie?" Angie dreaded the answer, but had to ask.

"I don't know. Major Adams says he will certainly be cashiered; that means he'll be reduced to the ranks, probably as a private soldier again. He'll probably also be sentenced to serve time in detention barracks... military jail."

"Jail! That's terrible," Kate exclaimed, covering her ears with her hands. "How can they put him in jail, just for disobeying an order?"

What would that do to Ron, his civilian career, to their lives? Angie battled with her emotions. Of course she'd stand by him, but why did he have to get them into this mess? She watched Peter, waiting for his response while he sipped at his tea.

"I'm afraid they can, and they may well do it, my dear." He looked grey under his sun-weathered skin. "Remember, one of Ron's men has been killed. We must be prepared for the worst." He mopped his brow. "We'll have to wait for the result of the court-martial tomorrow. Major Adams has promised to phone me as soon as he knows."

"But can't we go to Salisbury to be there with him?" Kate said.

"I asked, but there's little point. They won't let us see him beforehand, and we won't be allowed into the court. And if he is sentenced, they'll send him straight to detention barracks."

"But he might *not* be put into detention," Angie reminded him.

"Yes, there's a chance that they might not. But it's a *very* small one."

"Then I must go there to be with him when they've finished." Angie paused. "I'm going anyway, even if he is sent to detention," she decided. She'd beg them to let her see him. And even if they wouldn't, she'd hang about to try to catch a glimpse so he could see she was there to support him. It was her duty. In spite of all their problems, she couldn't let him down at a time like this.

Peter looked thoughtful, then nodded. "You're right; we'll all go and be near him. They might even let us see him if we're right there."

Kate stood up, with a familiar look of purpose back in her eyes. "Yes, I couldn't bear just sitting here and waiting. Let's go and pack."

* * *

For Ron it had been unmitigated hell all day, starting with the court-martial... followed by a surprisingly severe sentence. It took the court from just eight until eleven that morning to find him guilty, and he'd been sentenced to 84 days in detention barracks.

Swain had been there, flown specially in from the bush to give evidence for the prosecution. Ron appreciated how Swain had tried not to condemn him, always stressing Ron's good service until now, but it was a lost cause.

As expected, he'd been stripped of his commission. Furthermore, after his sentence was over he was required to undergo the six weeks basic training all over again. He'd have to start Army life from scratch, as if he were a new recruit. 'Rehabilitated' they called it.

Everything seemed to be in slow motion; all through the proceedings his mind had been sluggish, and he couldn't find sensible answers to any of the questions they'd asked him. He had this bad feeling that he'd let his defence counsel, and himself down. Even physically he was no good, feeling tired and listless; must get a grip...

"I'll be down to see you in a few minutes," his counsel, Major Adams said, just before they marched him back to a 'holding area'. Ron sat there in a daze, staring at the bars and waiting, but seeing nothing. Christ, he *had* to get a grip. But right now he needed rest. Maybe tomorrow... He closed his eyes.

He jerked awake when Adams came down, and they had a short discussion about the case – mostly Adams talking; Ron himself had nothing to say. There'd been nothing that Adams hadn't warned him about, but then he dropped a bombshell.

"Your wife and parents are here, Cartwright... I've told them about your sentence, and I managed to get permission for them to see you, for a few minutes before you go back to your cell."

Shit! That was the last thing Ron wanted to hear.

But Adams was rambling on. "You'll be sent straight down to Brady Barracks in Bulawayo on tonight's train, I'm afraid, so this'll be the only chance you'll get to see them for the next 84 days. Your sentence starts on the day of your admission to Brady, so the sooner you get there the better."

"I don't want to see them, sir." He couldn't face it. Why the hell had they come, for Christ's sake?

"Good God man, you must. Can you imagine what this is doing to them?"

It was pure hell. His shame was there for all to see as he was marched at the double between two provosts. He ran under their escort and was ordered to halt at a green door. One redcap knocked before opening the door. Ron was ushered in, still clad in his uniform shirt and trousers; they'd removed his badges of rank and other insignia, and they'd confiscated his belt and hat. He had to hold his trousers up with one hand to prevent them falling down. The two MPs loomed impassively, guarding the door.

The room was bare, except for a small table and three chairs; but these had been moved to a corner. The walls were rough, whitewashed brick with dark green enamel paint covering the lower half. The only window was barred. Angela and his parents were standing there, waiting for him.

The degradation almost broke him. They didn't censure him. Angela and his mother both looked close to tears as they hugged him. His father hugged him too. The first time for many years that he'd shown such emotion. Ron felt awkward and was hampered with having only one hand free.

"We've been told about your sentence, and we'll all be waiting for you when you come out, son."

"Thanks, Dad." He knew he'd let them all down but couldn't trust himself to say any more. His father would be thinking how they'd argued, was it really just a few days ago? The redcaps stood ogling, allowing him no dignity or privacy. He already hated them as his persecutors – representatives of the system that was punishing him in such an inhuman way.

"It's time to go." The MP who'd opened the door stepped into the room and moved to Ron's side. Angela and his mother kissed him again, and his father gripped his hand. Ron turned to face the door – and 84 more days of hell.

"We'll write to you, Ronnie," Angela called out as he doubled away.

* * *

The rest of the day he was locked in a cell. Only someone periodically opening the Judas slot in the door to peer at him broke the isolation. Christ, he was already picking up prisoner slang. A tray with a bowl of watery stew, two slices of bread and a mug of weak, sweet tea was shoved through the hatch at lunchtime. He ate and drank mindlessly. He was still dazed and couldn't concentrate on anything. Even his anger had gone.

They came for him just after five that afternoon, and handcuffed his wrists together. He was given a scantily filled kitbag, which he presumed contained a change of clothing, and a brown paper packet.

"That's tonight's dinner and tomorrow's breakfast. It's off to Brady Barracks for you now, *sir*," the military provost sergeant in charge mocked. Ron ignored him.

"Too snooty to talk to the likes of us, hey? At the double... MARCH!" the bastard yelled. Ron ran awkwardly, the handcuffs making it difficult for him to hold both the kitbag and his brown paper bag. At least he'd been given an old webbing belt to hold his trousers up.

The two MPs ran with him, one on each side, to a military Land Rover. He was bundled into the canopied back with his kitbag. He squatted, very cramped, on the metal side seat, which formed the rear wheel arch. A manacle was removed from his left wrist, and he was locked to a rail in the vehicle. The MPs got into the cab, and drove at speed out of the camp. He had difficulty keeping his seat, but hung on grimly while his kitbag and food packet skidded across the floor.

The provost sergeant left him with the second MP at the station. Ron gathered that his companion was less of a bastard than the driver, when he muttered "fuckhead" under his breath as the vehicle disappeared.

He was afraid he might see someone he knew at the station, but although there was still half an hour to go, the train was already waiting. The MP found the train guard, who allocated a four-berth compartment to them. The MP transferred one manacle from his wrist and locked Ron to the metal frame on one of the two lower bunks.

"Sorry, but I can't take any chances," he said. Digging a cigarette out of his pack, he lit it and stood in the doorway to the compartment. He stood with his back to Ron, leaning across the narrow passage, and looking out through the opposite window. Ron thanked God the train was not full, and no one came to share their compartment.

He lay on his bunk and closed his eyes, trying to blank out the past few days. Soon afterwards the train pulled out of Salisbury station, so he sat up and looked inside the brown paper packet. It contained two thick sliced sandwiches with some sort of meat filling and one boiled egg. The bread was already dry. He presumed the boiled egg, still in its shell, was for breakfast tomorrow.

Despite the fact that the journey was less than 500 kilometres, and the train left on time at six 'o clock, the journey took the full 12 hours through the night to reach Bulawayo. It seemed to stop at every station and siding along the way. Pulled by a single diesel locomotive, Ron guessed the train never exceeded 50 kilometres an hour when it was moving. He remembered hearing that they were returning some of the old coal-fired steam locomotives to service on certain routes, in order to save foreign currency. The country had plenty of coal of its own, but all oil based products had to be imported.

Going for a shit was an embarrassing affair. The MP insisted on attaching himself to Ron's handcuffs, and standing at the door to the toilet while he did what he had to.

"Some smart-arse escaped through a toilet window a few weeks ago," the bloke said by way of explanation.

How the hell could anyone get through such a small window?

The train seemed to spend inordinate amounts of time waiting at each station, sometimes accompanied by shouting, and people walking up and down outside. But then Ron was in no hurry. He wasn't looking forward to his destination. He found it impossible to sleep, but must have dozed from time to time, especially in the early hours as the train rumbled along slowly; Gatooma, Que Que, Gwelo, down to Bulawayo. It stopped at Somabula, Shangani and Heany Junction, and several others along the way. They arrived at Bulawayo station on schedule again, at six in the morning.

His escort handed him over with much signing of forms, just like a parcel, to two waiting MPs. He was manacled into the back of another Land Rover, and they sped off to the infamous Brady Barracks.

* * *

A clatter of tin cans alerted Gadziwa. Someone was heading towards him on this track through the Mozambique bush. He melted into cover by the trailside, but he was curious. What manner of people made such a racket when walking through this dangerous place?

To his amazement, a whole platoon of 30 white and mixed-race soldiers came marching along the trail. He guessed they must be Portuguese. They didn't look at all like the Rhodesians. Those swine would never make such a noise. Come to think of it, he'd never seen so many settler soldiers together before. The enemy he and his comrades fought seldom came in groups of more than four. The most he'd encountered at one time was that lot who'd attacked him at Mabunu's place.

But these were enemy too, so he kept a low profile. Thanks to his visit to the Mukumbura store, he had enough food for his immediate requirements. And he'd had sufficient ammunition with him when he'd escaped from Mabunu's kraal. That still irked him. A sellout must have betrayed them. He shook himself free of the thought. Water would need replenishing soon, but he expected to reach the Zambezi River before he ran out. So there was no need for him to try to get any supplies from these people.

They soon disappeared into the bush... back along the trail that Gadziwa himself had been following. If these had been Rhodesians, Gadziwa knew he'd be in serious trouble, because they'd see his tracks and follow up to kill him. But the Portuguese soldiers obviously weren't looking for tracks, and just marched noisily by.

"Keep still, or die." Gadziwa felt steel touch his back and his blood ran cold. How could he have been so careless? The voice came from the bush immediately behind him. He recognised the language as being of the tribe that straddled the border between Zimbabwe and Mozambique in this area. Gadziwa kept still while the noise of the soldiers faded away.

"Where are you from?" The voice was louder now, and the steel pressed harder against his back.

"I have escaped from the Rhodesian settlers, comrade." Gadziwa was sure that he was among fellow freedom fighters.

"Turn around slowly." Gadziwa turned to face his captor, and recognised him as Frelimo, the freedom fighters of Mozambique. He kept his RPD pointing at the trail in front of him, away from the man.

"We are fighting for the same Cause, comrade." Gadziwa tried to ease the tension while more Frelimo materialised from the surrounding bush. How could he possibly have missed them? They must have come up from behind, while he was busy watching the Portuguese. Otherwise, they would never have surprised him like this.

A small man approached, and took over the questioning from the man who had got the drop on him. "Who are you, and where is your base camp?"

"I am Captain Gadziwa, also known as Gumbarishumba. I have come from the ZANLA base at Chifombo in Mozambique. *Viva Frelimo!*" Gadziwa saw them relax.

"You are lucky to have found *us,* Comrade Captain," the leader said sarcastically.

Gadziwa was embarrassed, but he was invited to stand up. "The soldiers were making a lot of noise, comrade," he offered, to cover his shame at not hearing Frelimo's approach.

"They always do. They don't want to meet up with us by accident. Someone could get killed or injured, so they make a lot of noise when they move through our territory. Usually, we keep hidden so they can pass."

The explanation surprised Gadziwa. "They don't try to kill you?"

"No, they leave us alone in the bush, and we leave them alone in their forts. The only time we clash is when we attack their supply convoys, or the dam your Rhodesians, and the South African Boers are building at Cabora Bassa."

Gadziwa noted with interest the reference to the dam across the Zambezi being built in Portuguese territory by white engineers from the south. "My enemy is very different; they are always trying to attack us."

"We know that, and that's why we don't like you ZANLA people here in Mozambique. Your settlers follow you here, chasing after you. But if they can't find you, they chase and kill us instead." Gadziwa had heard that Frelimo were not as friendly in the bush as they were at base camp. These rumours were now confirmed.

"I am not being followed now," he sought to assure them. "I left the dogs behind days ago, and have travelled many kilometres since then. Some by bus, so there are no tracks for them to follow."

"That is good to know, comrade. Where are you heading for?" The small fighter, who had tortoise shell badges of rank, asked.

"I would prefer to get back to Chifombo."

"The river is wide, and there is no bridge if you follow this route."

"Yes," Gadziwa was aware of that, "can you help me?"

Instead of replying, the commander invited him to share a meal. Gadziwa answered many more questions during that meal. But when they had finished, the commander gave him the name of a boatman, and directions as to how to find him. He also told him of a ZANLA contact on the northern bank of the Zambezi. Now he was getting somewhere. He vowed he'd be back to drive the settlers who were occupying his country away, just as soon as he could raise a new team...

* * *

The encampment looked like any other Army barracks to Ron, until they approached the military prison section. Here they drove through high steel shuttered gates into a dreary compound. Three-metre-high, green-painted corrugated iron walls surrounded the compound itself, as if to hide what went on inside from the rest of the world. Rolls of barbed dannett wire topped the walls, increasing the prison-like air of the place. There was no vegetation; not even a blade of grass to relieve the bleak concrete, tar and gravel.

Well he hadn't expected a fucking holiday camp. No point in trying to escape. There was nowhere to go. Last night on the train, Ron had become resigned to his situation and decided to make the best of it. He didn't have much choice anyway.

He was taken straight to a guardroom, formally advised that he was now a 'SUS', soldier-under-sentence, and read a harsh statement about behaviour. This included what he could expect if he attempted 'mutiny' while in detention. 'Mutiny' seemed to cover just about every misdemeanour, and Ron wondered if they emphasised it so much for everyone – or was it just for his benefit? At last his handcuffs were removed, and he was frog-marched to an ablution block. Here, they watched while he stripped, and took a cold shower; then his head was shaved, none too gently, in the quadrangle outside.

Next he was marched at the double to the duty provost officer, who read the riot act all over again, before adding sarcastically: "You mustn't expect any special treatment here just because you used to be an officer, Cartwright." The man held the same rank as Ron had himself until the previous day.

"No, sir." Ron didn't think he'd do his cause any good by ignoring that stupid statement. He was allocated a cell and marched at the double to it. He realised he would be doubling everywhere for the next 84 days; all military prisoners had to do everything 'at the double', even going to the shithouse, unless officially recorded as sick.

They stopped at a shed on the way, where he was issued with a thin palliasse mattress and pillow, plus two coarse Army blankets. No sheets. Nothing he couldn't handle yet. He was also issued with an old Army backpack, filled with bricks.

"You'd better not 'lose' any of the bricks," the quartermaster's corporal warned him maliciously. "They'll be checked every day, before *and* after drill."

His cell was bare except for a fold-down bunk, a galvanised latrine bucket and a chipped white enamel bowl. Hardly the Ritz, but Ron had slept in rougher conditions. He was allowed to drop his mattress and other issue with his kitbag in the cell, but told to keep the brick-filled pack on his back.

"You've missed breakfast, Cartwright. You go straight to morning drill from here... so get moving."

"Ah, ha!" the drill-sergeant shouted with spiteful humour. "Detainees... HALT!" The group of about 30 men stopped doubling on the parade square. "We's got a very *special* SUS with us now!" the sergeant yelled, as he strutted up to within an inch of Ron's face, and looked up at him. "It's an ORRFICER. Youse see men, even *orrficers* end up here when they fucks around." His pale blue eyes bored into Ron's.

"Hey, I didn't tell YOU to halt, you piece of dog turd," he screamed. Ron started doubling again, but this time he ran on the spot – marking time – because the sergeant was blocking the way ahead. "You got DB for disobeying orders and youse at it again before youse hardly in here. I'll show you, you bastard!" Flecks of spittle from the berserk sergeant's foaming lips landed on Ron's chin. "Mark time until I tell youse to stop. DO... YOU... HEAR... ME?" he screamed pedantically.

"Yes, sergeant!" Why was it that the most stupid, low-life soldiers were attracted to serve as military policemen? Petty bullies.

"Yes sergeant... yes sergeant. You think youse still an orrficer?" The man's face was red with rage, and the veins bulged from his short neck. "Youse address me... 'n all the others here... as STARFF unless they's orrficers hor warrant orrficers, do you hear me?"

"No, staff... yes, staff!" Ron itched to wipe the bastard's spittle off his chin.

"I fookin' hate orrficers, so youse better look out." The man sounded Glaswegian to Ron, but he couldn't be sure.

The staff sergeant turned away, leaving Ron marking time at the double while he got the rest of the men doing drill again. He seemed to recall his hate of officers every time he turned and caught sight of Ron.

The other detainees told Ron later that they'd had an easy morning of it, thanks to Staff Sergeant Ritchie's loathing of officers. He kept stopping them, and saying that he didn't mind ordinary soldiers, but he hated officers. Meanwhile he would leave them resting, while he came over to scream at Ron.

Ron was at the edge of exhaustion, when the routine PT session came to his rescue. Press-ups and squats gave his feet time to recover, though there were also star jumps and running on the spot exercises. PT was followed by an assault course, which after his punishment at drill, Ron could barely handle. Fortunately, the instructor chose to ignore his feeble efforts. Thank fuck for that.

Lunch gave him the break he needed to recover again, before that first afternoon's labour. They lined up at the kitchen hatch and collected a bowl with a lid, a spoon and mug before moving to the next window, where a stew of potatoes, cabbage and meat were slopped into the bowl; rice was added to the lid and sweet tea to the mug. Then they stopped at the door on the way out to respond to a staff warrant officer standing there, who shouted at each one: "Report your diet!" to which each SUS had to reply: "Diet correct, sir!" Stupid Army regulations. What would they do if someone complained? Again, all this was done at the run, and they doubled to their cells before they could stop to eat.

After lunch, Ritchie appeared again and assigned him and some others to digging holes in the hard, rocky ground. They had to carry the soil and stones to create a pile across the yard. It was probably the most boring, pointless and backbreaking labour in the camp. The other detainees told him that they'd have to carry it all back tomorrow, to fill and pack down the holes that they'd dug today. All done at the run, of course.

More PT, assault course and full pack drill followed labour, with Ritchie screaming abuse at him again. They were dismissed for supper at six. The evening ended with cell and cellblock cleaning, followed by cold showers. Lockup was at eight.

Tired and demoralised, he just lay on his bunk shelf, resting his feet. A whistle blew a warning at five to nine, and he needed no encouragement to 'stand to' his bunk, for lights out. Despite being woken periodically by the shaft of light every time the cell hatch was opened, he slept soundly for the first time in many days.

Chapter 21

Angie tossed and turned, hardly sleeping at all that first night, wondering if the events had affected Ronnie's mind. When they'd seen him immediately after the court-martial sentence, his eyes had looked strangely lifeless and that worried her. But now that he was vulnerable... maybe if he needed her again, perhaps she could repair their marriage? The next morning, she phoned the Army... and every day after that until, four days later she was finally connected to a doctor. He told her he was responsible for the wellbeing of all military prisoners at Brady Barracks, and he'd carried out a routine examination on Ron's arrival, and again, after his third day in detention.

"As you'd expect, a lot of men suffer from depression at times like these, but your husband is surprisingly well, Mrs Cartwright," he said. "He's a tough character. Full of anger, but there's no sign of mental illness... and he's in superb physical shape." That sounded like Ronnie. "I'd say he was in a state of shock when you saw him, but he's recovered."

She had been told that he'd be allowed to send, and receive one letter a week. Angie felt more comfortable after that; she sat down immediately and wrote him a letter, to reassure him that all was well at home, doing her best cheer him up. She agreed with Kate that they'd take it in turns to write the weekly letters.

* * *

"Angie? I've just heard about Ron and I'm, really sorry." Mark's voice startled her. This was not what she needed right now, on top of all her problems...

"Angie..." he sounded anxious, "is there anything I can do?"

"No," she snapped at him. "I don't think so, Mark. Thanks anyway." She tried to soften her response. How had he got to hear about it?

"I've just been speaking with my mother."

Of course... Harriet. It was almost as if he'd heard her thoughts.

"She told me about Ron and I just wanted to know for myself that you were all right."

Angie relaxed a little. She supposed it was natural that he should offer his sympathy. "Well, it was a bit of a shock at first but I'm OK now." She sat down. "The girls obviously don't realise – they just think Ron's in the bush." The words came much easier now – after all, she'd been repeating them all week. Both to herself and the family.

"I'll be up in Salisbury for a few days next week," he sprung another surprise and gave her the date he was arriving, "and I'd really like to see you then... I'll phone as soon as I get to the airport."

"What time does your plane arrive?" Angie stalled, looking up at the calendar. It seemed perfectly innocent, but somehow she didn't feel quite right arranging to see him. Not now, with Ron being away and in so much trouble.

He told her he was taking the early flight from Johannesburg. "It'll probably take me about 20 minutes to get through immigration and customs, but I should be able to phone you at about nine-thirty or so."

She hesitated a moment before replying, "That's OK. I'll have finished taking Emma and Joanne to school, and Helen to play group by then, so I'll be at home to take your call." Where was this leading?

"I'm tied up in meetings all day Monday, but I'll be free from about six, can I take you to dinner in the evening?"

Ummm... her mind raced. "That's a lovely idea, but I can't. What'll I do with the children?" That should put paid to his idea.

"Can't they come with us? I'd like to see them again too."

She hadn't fazed him at all. "No," she said firmly. "It'll be school next day, and I don't like them staying up too late."

"Yes of course... I'll just come round and visit you then, if that's OK?"

There was no polite way out of that one. "Yes sure, have supper here with us if you like." Angie felt obliged to make the offer. "I'm afraid it won't be quite the same as going to a restaurant."

"Yes thank you, I'd love to. I much prefer home cooking anyway." He sounded pleased. "I'm going to see if I can take Tuesday morning off as well. Perhaps we could go somewhere nice together while the children are at school? If not, I'll make sure Wednesday is free, but I've got to get back to Jo'burg on Thursday."

No, this was going too far. "I'm not sure if that's such a good idea. It won't look very good if I'm seen with you. Not with Ronnie just having gone into Brady," she pointed out. Besides, she didn't want Mark taking her for granted – just because Ronnie was away. Bit of a cheek, really.

"The last thing I want to do is embarrass you, Angie." He sounded contrite. "You're right; let's talk about it when we meet."

In spite of her earlier misgivings, Angie had to admit that she was now actually looking forward to seeing Mark again. But the feeling of disloyalty spoilt it for her. Still, she wondered if he'd had second thoughts about 'loving' her. Would he want to kiss her again? Should she let him? Not in her own home, she decided firmly. They'd just have to enjoy the evening together, and not do anything they shouldn't. She wondered what to give him for dinner. How little she knew about him…

The following day there was another call from Cape Town. "Hello, is that Mrs Cartwright?" a woman's voice asked and Angie confirmed she was.

"I'm Mrs Wyndham, Margaret Wyndham, Mr le Roux's secretary." She sounded like one of those very efficient, older secretaries. "He wanted me to ask if there's anything you'd like him to bring from South Africa when he comes up, next week? Said he forgot to ask you yesterday, and he's sure there must be something because of the sanctions."

"Oh, how nice of him." Did she really want anything? "Ummm… I can't think of anything at the moment." Could she afford it anyway? She didn't want to take advantage of her parents' generosity, now that Ronnie's income was uncertain.

"He especially mentioned your children."

"That's a good idea." They discussed small gifts, but eventually just settled on some sweets she remembered the girls liked last time they were in South Africa on holiday, but weren't available in Rhodesia. His secretary sounded very nice but Mark had surprised Angie again. That was thoughtful and non-threatening… offering to get things for the children. Was she worrying over nothing? Maybe he had no intention of trying to start things up between them again.

* * *

The plane was on time, and Mark phoned Angie from the car hire desk. He got directions and they arranged for him to be at her home around six that evening.

His meetings planned for the next few days had resulted from the discussion he'd had with Angie's father at the farm. His uncle had phoned him less than a fortnight after he got back to South Africa, to give him a contact name and number.

"Unless you think it's really necessary, Mark," Greville had said, after giving him the confidential contact, "I don't think I need to be involved any further."

His uncle was warning him not to abuse their relationship, and he resolved not to speak to him about business again. The old boy had done his bit anyway, and Mark was glad of more opportunities to see Angie. Nevertheless, he noted that Greville had enough sense not to mention the word 'sanctions' when speaking over the phone.

It was after he'd spoken with old Greville that Mark had chatted to his mother. She'd told him about Cartwright being court-martialled, and stuck in military prison. He thought Angie's husband sounded like a bloody fool, but it wouldn't be tactful for him to say anything.

Until now he had kept his trips up to Salisbury few and far between, not wanting to draw too much attention to his connections there. He maintained several passports, making sure his visits to Rhodesia and his supplier countries were never on the same document. Of course, his South African passport was not welcomed in many parts either, so he used his British Passport for the North African visits, and a Kenyan Passport for Communist Bloc visits.

His meetings that day went well, and Mark was confident he'd come away with some profitable opportunities. He drove out to Angie's house in a positive mood, really looking forward to seeing her again. The last time he'd seen her she'd been standing on the farmhouse steps, waving goodbye to him and his mother, looking very small, and a little lost as she disappeared from sight in the rear-view mirror. As they drove back to Salisbury, he recalled Angie having said she had things to sort out. What 'things'? That comment of hers added to the earlier impression he had that her marriage was not running completely smoothly. He needed to know.

"Such a nice girl, Angie," his mother remarked, as she settled down for the drive back to the city.

This created an opportunity to quiz his mother, without it sounding too obvious. "Yes," he said. "What's her husband like?"

She hesitated, and Mark waited patiently for a reply. His mother's seemingly frivolous disposition belied a shrewd mind and he knew she'd give a considered reply.

"He's been a bit of a disappointment," she finally said diplomatically. "At first he and Angie seemed the perfect couple. They both seemed intelligent, level-headed... and very much in love." She paused, as if looking for the right words. "But... he's developed into a bit of a loner, which must be hard for Angie and the girls."

Mark wanted to find out more. "But Peter and Kate seem such nice folk. Very sociable..."

His mother was quick to react. "Oh yes, they are... and with that sort of background you'd have thought Ron would have charm in spades. But it doesn't seem to have worked out that way," she sighed. "Mary thinks he's very spoilt. The 'only child' syndrome, of course."

Mark chuckled inwardly at that. His mother seemed to have forgotten that he was also an 'only child'. Perhaps being separated from his mother at a fairly early age, he'd escaped the 'syndrome'? "But Ron can't be that bad, surely?"

"Oh no. In fact, when Angie first brought him home to meet the family, we rather liked his quiet ways. Mary and John were worried about them getting married so young, but they seemed well suited and Angie was always very strong-willed."

Yes, he'd sensed her strength of character, and liked it.

His mother paused again before she continued. "But over the years Ron's quietness turned to surliness and he can be very prickly. We always feel as though we're walking on broken glass when he's around. Mary's very worried about the whole situation... Look out!" Her hand hit the dashboard.

Mark slowed the car down as he waited for a safe opportunity to overtake a donkey cart, which was taking up more than its fair share of the road; his mother was always a bit of a back-seat driver.

"Is she very strong-willed? I mean Angie." Mark wanted to know more. He tapped the hooter lightly and the startled driver steered the cart off the road.

"Actually, strong willed is probably the wrong expression – a strong character more like." His mother dismissed the difference with a wave of her hand. "Well anyway, it's hard to say now... she was as a child and young girl, but since she married and had the children she seems to have changed."

They left the cart behind and she continued. "She lets that husband of hers get away with murder." His mother sniffed her disapproval. "But you must have seen how Angie sparkles in good company, and she hasn't had a lot of that lately."

Hmmm... much food for thought there. They relaxed into a companionable silence. He had to think this through. He admitted to himself that he was smitten with Angie. Certainly, she was bloody attractive but it wasn't just that. He'd sensed hidden depths and the need to know her better was painfully strong. He didn't want her to slip through his fingers. Not yet. Not without seeing her again.

Ruthless in his business dealings, Mark had always drawn a line between that and his personal life. He baulked at the idea of being labelled a marriage wrecker. But the strength of his feelings for Angie had turned that on its head. He normally avoided married women like the plague. Too much baggage... too much angst. And there were plenty of unattached, willing women around. But... if Angie's marriage was in trouble?

* * *

Mark brought himself back to the present, and glanced at the directions he'd jotted down. The suburb was fairly downmarket, but looked decent enough. The house, a plain bungalow, was set in a neat garden about a quarter of an acre, maybe less. Small by Rhodesian standards. He got out of the car to open the gates, drove a few metres up the short driveway, and parked immediately behind her old Morris Minor. After closing the gates, he knocked on the door. Hearing children in the background, he guessed Angie hadn't heard his knock, so opened the front door and peered in.

There they were, through another door, and seated at a table. "Hello; Angie, girls – it's me," he called and stepped in. Angie appeared, looking a little dishevelled. A wisp of hair had escaped and hung down by her slightly flushed cheek. She smiled up at him and his heart leapt. Nothing had changed. Any doubts were gone in an instant; he was certain now that he loved this woman.

* * *

Angie couldn't stop smiling as she tidied up after Mark left. They had talked non-stop, and it was after midnight before he finally said goodbye. They had so much in common it was almost uncanny. Perhaps family genes had something to do with it. Kissing cousins? She laughed aloud at the corny phrase.

He'd brought the sweets for the girls and they'd been delighted with this unexpected treat. Poor man, he'd been subjected to sticky kisses and shown all their favourite toys. But he'd handled it with aplomb, and had seemed genuinely interested in all they had to say.

Apart from a hug when he'd arrived and a tender kiss as he left, he hadn't touched her. She'd appreciated that. Anything more just wouldn't have been appropriate.

Later, she lay in bed and thought how good it had been to have someone to laugh with, and tease her about her tomboy antics as a child. And to think that all the time she'd thought she was so tough, he'd tolerated her as quite amusing, at best.

She fell asleep, happier than she'd been for a long time, looking forward to the next day when they'd arranged to spend the morning together at a nearby pleasure resort.

* * *

When Mark pulled up outside her house next morning, Angie told him she'd just got back from dropping off the children. She helped him load the car, and he drove the 50 kilometres to a small resort she called 'Mermaid's Pool'. Angie had suggested it when he said he'd like a quiet place nearby for them to enjoy a few hours together.

There was hardly any traffic, so the journey only took about 45 minutes. It really was in a pleasant setting, with a natural waterfall running into a rock pool at the foot of a high, sloping granite hill. The 'waterfall' was not much more than a stream, running down the gently sloping rock face, but the pool at the bottom was full of clean, clear water. Trees round the edge provided dappled shade.

He stopped the car. "It's beautiful, Angie. I've never been here before... I wonder why my folks didn't bring me here when I was a kid?"

She smiled back at him and shrugged. "My family have been coming here for years. It's hardly changed, except they've recently improved the facilities."

They got out to look around. The sun was shining brilliantly, but it was still relatively cool, even in the sunshine. Last night had been a good one. Once they'd got past the 'polite' stage, they'd both relaxed and by the end of the evening, Mark felt they'd established a strong affinity.

"It's not too hot. Looks like you've had rains here?" he remarked.

"Yes, we had good rains last week. That's why the pool is so nice," she smiled up at him. "You can slide down the rock into the pool. It's quite deep, especially at the foot of the waterfall."

He was so attracted to her that he struggled to maintain his poise. He steadied himself. "It's nice and quiet too." The only people he could see were a few cleaners and a maintenance worker. "I suppose it's too early for there to be any other visitors here?"

"Well, it is school term; it'll be busier this afternoon, and it's very popular at weekends. Look over there." She pointed towards a wooden bridge, which crossed the small river. "See how those old railway carriages have been made into changing rooms? One carriage for men and one for women." They were partly hidden by trees. "Shall we take a spot near the cafe and tearoom, there by the edge of the pool?" she asked.

"No, let's find something on the other side," Mark said hastily. They walked round the edge of the pool, and selected a shaded spot next to a brick-built braai, which they could use as a makeshift picnic table. He set up the folding chairs, and went back to drive the car over.

When he got back, he started to unload but Angie stopped him.

"Better leave it in the car until we're ready to eat," she said, "or the ants will get into everything. Let's get changed."

He made his first, cautious move when he took her hand as they walked to the railway carriages. She didn't object. He was keen to re-establish a less platonic relationship today. He knew he'd have to take things slowly, but time was against him. He had to get back to South Africa on Thursday, and he wouldn't be back in Salisbury again for weeks.

* * *

Angie emerged from the ladies' changing room and heard Mark whisper, "Wow, you look smashing in that bikini."

196

She felt herself blush, feeling small and vulnerable with him looming so close. "Thank you," she said awkwardly, and they walked slowly back to the car and picnic area. He took her hand again as they crossed the bridge.

This was a different Mark to the one she'd had dinner with last night. More difficult to talk to and deal with. With any other man, she'd have no problem. Just gently take her hand away and laugh lightly, to spare his embarrassment. She'd had to do that many times in the past and was usually successful. And she'd not hesitated to be very firm with the few who hadn't taken the hint.

But Mark... well, she liked him holding her hand. But she knew she shouldn't be doing this and felt guilty... even looked around to see if anyone could see them. Ridiculous – there wasn't likely to be anyone she knew here at this time of the day. Here he was, making a pass at her again, and she was doing nothing to stop him. Just like at New Year. The whole business was fraught with risk.

She chucked her beach bag into the car and pulled her hand away from his. "Last one in is a sissy." She ran for the pool, and dived straight in. Mark hadn't expected that of course, but he gained on her and dived in moments later. He stayed underwater for a long time, but just as she was beginning to get worried, he burst out of the water inches in front of her. They raced from one end of the pool to the other, reaching and then standing together on a submerged rock by the edge of the waterfall.

"You said people slide down the waterfall?" He looked up at it.

"Yes," Angie nodded, "it's fun. Some people use big truck inner tubes or 'lilos' to slide down on, but you can manage perfectly well without."

"How do you get up there?"

"Come, I'll show you." She led the way up the steep path that ran alongside the waterfall.

About three quarters of the way up, she stopped. "This is where it's safe to get across." She picked her way carefully over and around some small boulders before looking back at him. "Now watch how I go down. You must stick to the main water stream or you could get hurt." She sat down holding onto a nearby rock, then wriggled across to the middle of the stream where the water piled up behind her before she let go.

She sped down, leaning from one side to the other as the water-stream, which was only a few inches deep, altered its course. She controlled the speed and direction of the descent with her feet and hands, but still went fast enough to feel the wind blowing her hair. She hit the pool with a splash, a split second before Mark. He must have followed immediately behind her. They came up splashing and laughing together.

"That was fun. Let's go again." Mark was obviously enjoying himself. They did the slide twice more before Angie called for a break.

"I'll go make some tea, would you like a cup too?"

"Yes, please. I'll come with you."

While they dried themselves, she glanced across at him. Although a big man, he looked as if he kept himself fit. But he was not too heavily muscled, thank goodness. Dropping his towel over the back of a deck chair, he went off and gathered loose dry wood from under the nearby trees, then started a fire in the braai place.

She spread the blanket, and lay down. Propping herself on her elbow, she watched him nurturing the fire. What was it about boys, men and fire she wondered? Despite being very much a city man, he seemed competent in country skills. No wonder he and Peter Cartwright had got along so well.

"That shouldn't take long," he said, sitting close beside her. He began stroking her shoulder absent-mindedly; she ought to stop him now.

But she hesitated, looking at his profile instead. He was gazing into the distance and she could just make out his eyes from the side. Strikingly blue and deep set, they were at their most devastating when he looked directly at her. He kept stroking her gently and she began to relax, just lying there in silence.

The pot suddenly boiled over, and she jumped up to make tea. Mark followed, lifted the pot off the fire and poured the hot water for her. She took her cup and sat in one of the chairs, pulling it close to the blanket, so she could rest her bare feet on it. Mark placed his tea on a small rock within reach and lay on the blanket at her feet, which he stroked.

Then, taking her completely by surprise, he started kissing her feet. She was so startled; no one had ever done that to her before.

"Mark, you shouldn't do that." But she didn't move and predictably, he continued. She leaned back in the chair and he moved closer, kissing her ankles, then her calves. Knowing she'd have to stop him soon, she put it off for just a few moments more. He got to his knees, took her teacup from her hand, put it on the rock next to his, and leant forward to kiss her lightly on her lips before he sat back on his heels.

"Come off the chair, Angie, it might tip over."

"Let's have our tea." She needed time to recover her composure. They drank their tea in silence. When they finished, he gently pulled her down to the blanket.

She didn't resist, but said quietly. "Please don't, Mark. What about Ron...?" Why was she so reluctant to stop him? She wanted him to love her that's why. But only so much – not too much.

He said nothing, just lay beside her and kissed her mouth passionately, his hands moving lightly over her stomach and up towards her breasts. She trembled, but found the strength to take his hand and move it firmly away. There was no knowing if she would be able to stop herself, if she let him do that. He kissed her neck, then her stomach; inching slowly down towards her hips, but she moved again so he couldn't carry on. *That* was too much.

"Angie..." his voice was deep and husky.

She had to be firm. "I can't go that far, Mark. I really shouldn't even let you kiss me like this. It's very hard for me too, you know." She knew she ought not to have admitted that, but the words were out of her mouth before she could stop them.

"I'm sorry, but I can't help myself. You're stronger than I am." Mark eased back and gave her breathing space. He took her face in his hands and looked into her eyes. "Angie, there's no question about it now." He paused, resting on his knees in front of her and holding both her hands in his. "I really am in love with you." She couldn't speak. He looked and sounded sincere.

He got up, pulling her to her feet. "Would you like help with the lunch – or should we be calling it 'brunch'?" he said.

"Oh goodness yes. We have to eat now so I can get back in time to fetch the children." She hurried to the car, relieved that he seemed to understand her reluctance. She felt ridiculously elated, like she'd won a major victory or something.

What was the matter with her? She'd never let anything get this far before. She was strongly attracted to Mark, and falling in love with him could be the next step, if she wasn't careful. Then it would be too easy to give way to her feelings.

She thought fleetingly of Ronnie. He'd treated her badly for a long time now, but he was still her husband... and the girls? Her emotions were just too mixed up right now. She'd think about it later.

* * *

They arrived home in good time for her to be able to fetch the children. When they finished unloading his car they stood awkwardly at the front door.

"I'll not have a chance to see my mother before I go back to South Africa, darling, so it might not be a good idea to tell anyone that I've been here to see you." He eventually broke their silence.

Darling? – He made it sound so natural. "I won't tell anyone," she replied. She'd wondered if he was planning to see Harriet. In fact it suited her not to tell anyone that she'd seen Mark. There'd be too much explaining to do if she did.

"I can't come tonight, but I'll phone you."

"OK." She had mixed feelings but it was mainly relief.

"But I want to see you again, please," he asked. "I'll be back in Salisbury in a few weeks' time."

"I'm not sure we should." She wanted to see him again too, but this was starting to get too serious. "If anyone should get to know..."

"We'll be very discreet."

"It's not just that..." He didn't seem to understand. "I'm being unfaithful and I feel really bad about it," she said miserably.

He took her in his arms. "I love you, Angie. I have to see you again. Please."

"Oh, Mark," this was so hard, "I'll have to think about it."

He looked down at her. "I know it isn't easy for you, Angie – but please tell me you feel something; I can't believe it's all one-sided."

She turned her head away, not wanting him to see her confusion, or to commit herself. He stood there silently, waiting... "It's too soon, Mark," she whispered, desperately seeking the right words. But she *knew* she loved him already.

"OK. I'll wait." He kissed her gently. "I'll phone tonight," he added and she closed the door. She wanted to be with him again too, but it was impossible. Everything would have to come to an end when Ronnie came home, so why prolong the agony? Next time they spoke, she'd have to tell Mark that she couldn't see him any more. She'd explain to him...

Chapter 22

Ron wondered if the provost sergeant's resentment against him would last throughout his sentence. But after the first few days it became simmering hate, rather than active hostility from this man who could, and did make his life even more unpleasant in detention. The other screws made a show of extra harsh discipline against Ron whenever Ritchie was around, but generally left him alone at other times. Most of his fellow detainees were sympathetic, and he sensed that one or two even tried to help when they could – which wasn't often. But Ron wasn't looking for help from anyone. He'd made up his mind to take anything they could throw at him.

There was one notable exception among the detainees – a big, flabby soldier with shifty eyes who toadied up to the staff, and constantly sought opportunities to taunt Ron. Ritchie encouraged him. It seemed the wanker also had a hatred of former officers. He presumably thought Ron couldn't, or wouldn't fight back.

"Do you want me to fuck up that fat arse for you, Cartwright?" a tough looking Afrikaner, who was doing five years for manslaughter, asked one day after a particularly trying session.

Ron had just wanted to keep himself out of trouble, and get his sentence over with, but this was getting out of hand. "I'll deal with him myself," he replied, deciding reluctantly that he'd have to do something about it. After all, it was the job of the screws to make prisoners lives hell, but this was bullshit he didn't need.

The opportunity came in the washrooms that evening after supper. As Ron walked in with his towel and soap ready, his tormentor blocked his way,

"Hey, everyone better stand to attention, here comes the officer."

"You're in my way…"

"Oooh… so *sorry,* SIR." He didn't move. "What you gonna to do about it?"

Ron shoved him aside expecting a straight fight, but just in time he spotted a flashing blade aimed straight at his guts and avoided it by throwing himself backwards. Thank Christ the bloke was slow, but

Ron had no intention of matching his bare fists against a knife. Using the momentum of his fall, he recovered his standing position by swinging sideways off the floor, fully intending to retreat. But there was no escape. A crowd formed instantly to surround them and the fat man had him cornered.

An unseen supporter threw Ron a small iron bar, which he caught and used to break his opponent's wrist, causing the bastard to drop his knife. Ron immediately released the bar, and set about thrashing the man with his fists, giving vent to all his pent up frustration and rage. He beat the bastard senseless while a staff corporal, who was supposed to be monitoring the ablution block, conveniently looked the other way. Ron was amazed that anyone should have a flick-knife in this place; everyone was supposed to be searched on arrival. He took it as a warning that he still had many lessons to learn about life in detention barracks.

"You should have finished him with this, man," the big Afrikaner said, picking up his iron bar.

Before breakfast, at muster parade next morning, Ron was arrested and taken to be charged before the provost officer who'd signed him into Brady a week ago. "You've been accused of assaulting a fellow prisoner, Cartwright. Broken his arm, his jaw... and his nose too, you savage."

Silly bugger couldn't even get the injury list right. "Not guilty, sir." Ron denied it with a straight face.

There was nothing they could do to make the charge stick; it was one detainee's word against another's; of course, no one else had seen anything. But Ritchie got him on another trumped up charge that same afternoon, and Ron was sentenced to seven days in 'the dark cell'.

This meant solitary confinement in a cell without natural lighting or furniture. He was not allowed any clothes other than his underpants and there was no bed, mattress, pillows or blankets. There was a shelf to sit and sleep on and a hole in the floor, which served as a latrine. An 'en-suite' toilet, no less. But of course, it was there to prevent him seeing other people when emptying a shit bucket. The sleeping shelf had to be folded upright, from 'stand to' at six in the morning until 'lights out' at twenty-one hundred.

He was declared fit to go on punishment diet number two for two days. PD2 meant nothing but bread and water, three times a day.

But the visiting doctor refused to sanction that degree of harshness after the initial two days, so Ron was put on PD1 for the remaining five. Accordingly, he luxuriated in porridge for breakfast; watery meat and cabbage stew for lunch, followed by a two-inch bread cube and a cheese-ball for supper. Still no tea, coffee, sugar or jam ration – just water. But once he got onto PD1, Ron found the dark cell no hardship at all. At least Ritchie couldn't torment him here, and he was toughening up. He deliberately maintained a routine of hard physical exercise within the cell, aiming to come out much fitter and tougher, both mentally and physically, than he'd gone in. There was nothing else to do. During those seven days, no letters were delivered and no writing materials were permitted.

But solitary gave him an opportunity to recover from the bruised feet he'd acquired on the first day. It also gave him time for reflection. Facing up to the death of a soldier under his command was the most difficult. They'd held him responsible for Blignaut's death at the court-martial, because he was acting against orders. How could he possibly have prevented Blikkie being killed? It was enemy action, and that was how they'd record it. But still, he'd been held responsible. His actions and the consequences went through his mind for hours at a time, day and night. It had the effect of intensifying his hatred of the bastard Big Feet. Now he needed to avenge Blikkie as well as Madala.

Following on from that he faced, properly for the first time, the question of what to do when he got out. What of his children and Angela? Both his mother and Angela had written to him since his arrival, but he had not replied to either of them. Why? While still in ordinary detention, there'd been enough time to do it, in the evenings before lights out. He knew that most of the other detainees wrote regularly to their wives, girlfriends or mothers. But he couldn't face writing to the people he had let down so badly.

Angela had written to say that he shouldn't worry about money, saying her folks were helping out, seeing her and the children through while he was away. Well, he hadn't been worried anyway. Her parents were well off and could probably look after them better than he could, even after he got out. How could he explain that he didn't want to work in civilian life again? They might be sympathetic employers at the Farmer's Co-op, but by the time he got out of Brady, and then basic training camp, they would have had to cover his job for more than half a year. Surely no employer would take someone back after that length of time?

Meanwhile, his mother's letter carried strong hints about the old man needing help on the farm, perhaps guessing that he would no longer have a job in town when he got out. Christ, that would be the ultimate disgrace... having to rely on his folks for a home and income. He would never submit to that.

When he got out, he would tell Angela and his parents that he needed a new career, and a new life. Family life would be too restrictive.

The answer hit him like a thunderbolt one night, there in the dark cell. And the idea gnawed away at him when he was released back into normal detention barracks. Gadziwa was responsible for giving him the run-around in the bush, killing one of his soldiers, leading to his military disgrace and detention. The swine had attacked the family farm, killed Madala in cold blood and mutilated his father's cattle. In fact, he was responsible for wrecking his life. Gadziwa seemed to be taunting him.

Hunting down and killing Gadziwa filled his head. Nothing and nobody would be allowed to get in his way. He wasn't sure exactly how to go about this, but he had plenty of time to work on it. Meanwhile, in preparation for what had now become his Mission, he would use the harsh detention regime at Brady to toughen up, and treat his time at Llewellin as a refresher course in weapons and fighting training.

* * *

Six weeks into his sentence, some fool calling himself a 'liaison officer' came to tell him that Angela was complaining about him not writing to her. Fucking cheek, the thought of it still caused him to clench his fists. What the hell did Angela think she was up to? She knew very well that he didn't write letters, just fitted in the odd phone call when he had the time. Well, that was impossible here – phone calls were not permitted. Then the idiot officer had gone on about marriage guidance or whatever. Ron had to hold back from punching him, but it would have meant another week or two in the dark cell, so he'd refrained. He told the silly bugger to tell Angela not to bother to write anymore. That'd stop her nagging.

He had something much more important to think about.
Gadziwa…

Chapter 23

A mixture of anger and humiliation washed over Angie as she put the phone down. She looked out of the window into the garden – not really seeing anything.

The liaison officer's voice still rang in her ears. "I'm really sorry, Mrs Cartwright but the truth is that your husband refuses to write to you."

Angie put her hands up to her face and rocked in the chair. God, the humiliation. She could hear the man was embarrassed, having to pass on that sort of message, and almost felt sorry for him. What the hell was Ron playing at? Was it just Ron doing what he did best? Putting up a wall and not letting anyone or anything near him? She despaired.

Why had she even bothered to contact the barracks in the first place? Her stupid, old-fashioned sense of responsibility, she admitted to herself. Ron was her husband, for better or worse. She'd been worried that she'd heard nothing from him since he'd been sent to Brady, despite her writing regularly. She got up and went through to the kitchen to make herself coffee.

Yesterday, she had decided to phone the prison's family liaison officer; he sounded very kind and sympathetic, no doubt used to this sort of thing. He checked and confirmed that Ron had been receiving mail, including her letters but couldn't explain why neither she nor Kate had heard from him.

"Detainees have regular opportunities to write Mrs Cartwright," he'd said. "Would you like me to go and see him tomorrow?"

Naturally Angie said yes. Why? She should have known… and spared herself the indignity of having to discuss their problems with a stranger. The kettle boiled and she sat at the kitchen table with the mug in front of her.

So when the man had phoned back a few minutes ago, besides having to tell her that Ron was refusing to write, he paused before adding awkwardly, "Your husband has asked me to tell you not to write to him again."

Reading between the lines, she surmised that Ron had refused to give him any reasons for his attitude. At that point Angie felt quite desperate, and when the officer suggested that she and Ron go for marriage guidance counselling, after he got out of detention, she'd almost slammed the receiver down. But she stopped herself. Ron's attitude wasn't the officer's fault, and he was just doing his best. But the degrading conversation kept going round and round in her head. She couldn't keep all this to herself any more; her mother would know what to do. She drained her cup, grabbed her bag and took the car keys from the wall hook.

* * *

Angie got back home feeling a little better. Her mother advised patience, but she had seen the dismay in her face at Ron's attitude. The more Angie thought about it, the angrier she became. This was the last straw; she always had to 'understand', and be 'patient'. And he just didn't give a damn...

She realised the phone was ringing. It was Mark, saying that he was coming up to Salisbury again the following week.

"I'll be up there over a weekend this time. Can you arrange for the girls to stay with your folks or someone?" he asked.

It was so good to hear his voice. In the three weeks since Mermaid's Pool he'd phoned often. Even called once from somewhere in Czechoslovakia, which Angie knew was behind the 'Iron Curtain'. And Ronnie couldn't even get a letter to her in the same country...?

"Angie?" Mark was still on the line. "I'd like to spend a weekend with you, please." She was so angry and hurt by Ron that she felt almost inclined to accept. "So we can spend some time together," he continued. "I thought we could go up to the Inyanga Mountains, or Kariba Dam, or wherever you like, so you can have a break. I need a break too."

She hesitated. "I can't do that, Mark. I'm married, remember."

"What if we went with another couple?"

That sounded less problematic. "Who do you have in mind?"

"What about your pal Charlie, or some other friend you can trust? Why don't you suggest it to her? I'll phone back tomorrow to see what she says."

Angie needed time to think. "I'll give her a call, but she might be busy that weekend."

"I love you, Angie."

"Mark…" Why couldn't Ronnie be more like this?

"Ah," there was a pause and Angie could hear a phone ringing in the background, "… I've got to go now, but we'll talk about it again tomorrow. Bye, my darling."

"Bye." She hung up and stood at the phone for a few moments, trying to gather her thoughts. Despite her distress at Ronnie, she was reluctant to take this next step. A defiant little fling; a few illicit hours with Mark might be just what she needed. But a whole weekend, with the one man she could easily love… already *did* love?

But he would phone again tomorrow and she must do something. She knew her mother would almost certainly advise against any further contact with Mark, and Angie didn't want to hear that – not just yet. But Charlie might have some ideas…

Charlie's husky voice came on the line. "Hi, Angie. I was just thinking about you… and Ron. How's he doing? When's he due to come out?"

"He's already been away for six weeks, so he's halfway through his sentence… I still haven't heard from him yet, you know," Angie said bitterly. "I've written regularly, but he just doesn't write back, and they won't let me speak to him." She couldn't bring herself to tell even her best friend what the liaison officer had told her. It was still too new, too raw. It had been difficult enough telling her mother.

"He's a bastard, and he doesn't deserve you," Charlie sympathised. They went on to talk about other things, and they were about to hang up before Angie finally decided to broach the subject.

"Mark phoned me just now."

"Uh…oh. What does *he* want?" Angie had this vision of Charlie sitting up and paying more attention.

"Actually, he's phoned me quite often since New Year." She still hadn't told anyone, not even Charlie, that she'd seen him since then too. Luckily, the children hadn't mentioned it to her mother or father.

"*And?*"

"He wants to know if we can go away for a weekend… you know, you and Brian and me with him to Kariba or Inyanga."

"Ha! Bloody smart Alec. Hmmm… when does he want to go?" Charlie sounded as if she was scheming. Angie gave her the dates.

"He wants to get you into bed, you know." Charlie never minced her words.

"I guessed that, and I don't think I can bring myself to do it, Charlie."

"A weekend with him could be a lot of fun you know." Charlie wasn't put off. "He's good company, he's really nice looking. I'll bet he's got loads of money too. That's a pretty good start," there was a pause, "and Ron's still away for ages, so you'll be safe." She'd obviously forgotten her description of him as being "boring" when he upset her on the dance floor at New Year.

"But it's a very big step, Charlie... you know I've never done anything like this before." Angie chose her words carefully. She didn't want to upset Charlie, who she knew had had at least one extramarital affair.

"Oh, you don't *have* to sleep with him, you know," Charlie dismissed her objections. "Let's see... I can make that weekend. I think Brian's away, but I'm sure I can find someone to go with us. Come on, Angie, you need some fun in your life. I know a really nice place at Inyanga. Very private. No one will see you there."

"Well," Angie demurred. Ronnie had hurt her very much, and she enjoyed Mark's company. Trouble was, could she keep it to just one weekend, or would she find herself getting deeper and deeper into a full blown affair? There were the children to think of.

"Now... let me get hold of Sylvia and see if she can come with us. I'll call you back." She hung up.

Angie didn't like control slipping away from her, and came close to phoning Charlie back to call it off. But she really wanted to see Mark again. Darn it, Charlie was right. She didn't *have* to sleep with him.

But she knew she was kidding herself. Her mind strayed to thoughts of what it might be like to make love with him, and a long forgotten sensation stirred in her body.

* * *

The children were home from school when Charlie phoned back that afternoon.

"I've just met up with Sylvia, and she'd *love* to come with us. I've phoned and booked the cottage in Inyanga too." She had it all arranged.

Well, that was it. Still, she couldn't help a last tweak of conscience. "What if Ronnie or someone else gets to hear that I've been to Inyanga with Mark?" After all, Charlie was experienced in this sort of thing.

"Hell, Angie, that's almost impossible. And even if someone does hear about it, all they'll know is that the four of us went together." Charlie made it sound so plausible. "And don't worry about Sylvia. She's a good friend, and she's never let me down before. It'll be great fun; we'll probably drive up to the Inyanga Mountains Hotel every day. They've got a super golf course there." This was Charlie at her persuasive best. "Meanwhile, you and Mark can stay behind at the cottage if you're afraid someone will see you together. There're plenty of nice walks, it's got a lovely pool and there's even a tennis court."

"I'll have to see if my folks can look after the girls first." That might be a last obstacle in the way of her planned adultery. Putting a name to it, even in her own mind, brought home the enormity of what she was doing.

"And try to see if we can make it a long weekend, Angie. Sylvia and I can take a day or two off, either side of the weekend and we get a reduced rate for four nights." Charlie obviously thought it was a done deal.

"If my folks are OK, I'll ask Mark," Angie said, emphasising that it rested on her folks being available and willing.

She put her worries aside, and when she phoned her mother the die was cast. Her mother thought it was a marvellous idea that Angie should take a long weekend break, and said she'd be delighted to have the children. Of course, Angie hadn't told her about Mark being with them.

"You've been having such a hard time lately, darling. What with Ronnie's problems and everything." As well as emotional support, her parents were helping out financially. Ron's pay from the Army had stopped, and his employer was no longer sending make-up pay. There'd been no income at all for weeks now, and Angie's savings were almost gone. "I'll be able to take them to school and playgroup, unless you'll let me keep them at home?" Her mother was still talking.

"No, Mum they really mustn't miss any school. Are you sure it isn't too far for you to have to drive every day?" Her folks lived seven or eight kilometres away.

"I'll love taking them to school, no problem at all. But what about Helen? Surely she can miss playgroup?"

"Well, OK. I'll tell Alison. I think it'll be her turn that week. But she might want to go, Mum. She loves playing with all her friends."

"I'll let her decide then," her mother said. "The children will be fine with us. You know we love having them to stay."

It was all going so smoothly. Mark, Charlie and now her mother. Angie still felt uncomfortable about her mother's unwitting part in the conspiracy. But she had no intention of backing out of it, not now that she'd made her mind up.

* * *

Mark collected Angie early on Thursday morning and loaded her luggage and a box of provisions into the car boot. He'd brought wine and spirits that weren't readily available up here; also remembered her mentioning the lack of imported foods, so he'd collected a selection from his local delicatessen.

They went back indoors for a last check. "I thought you might like these," he handed her a small parcel.

"Oh Mark," she said, lifting out one of the silk and lace negligees he'd brought. The shop assistant had described them as 'exquisite'. "They're beautiful, but I can't afford these anymore." She closed the parcel and pushed it back at him.

But he refused to take them back. "They're a gift, Angie. You don't have to pay for them." Then he realised what she'd said. "Why can't you 'afford' things anymore?" he asked.

She hesitated before replying. "Ronnie's not being paid at the moment."

"Oh, sweetheart. I didn't know. How are you managing?"

"My folks are helping us, so we're fine for now. And I'm thinking of starting work soon."

"How long before he comes out?"

"He's over halfway through his 12 weeks at Brady," she explained, "but then he has to do another six weeks basic at Llewellin... So it's ages."

He thought he detected a note of resignation in her voice; in fact it verged on indifference. He tried to look sympathetic but his heart skipped a beat. Was there a chance? The extra time was a godsend. Seeing and touching Angie again reinforced his desire to have her for himself. Baggage and all.

They drove across town to collect Charlie and Sylvia just after six-thirty. Sylvia had slept over at Charlie's house to make their early morning pickup easier. It was a bit of a struggle, fitting in two sets of golf clubs as well as everything else, but he'd hired a long-wheel-base Land Rover and it coped.

"I know what sort of man you are, Mark," Charlie said when they found themselves alone together for a few moments. "You'd better not hurt Angie; she's my best friend, and she's pretty vulnerable right now."

"I have no intention of hurting her, but thanks for organising this trip." Stroppy woman should know that he knew she'd set everything up for them.

Charlie touched his arm and looked straight into his eyes. "I didn't do it for you, big boy. I did it for her; she needs some fun in her life. But you'd better be good to her, and don't be rough, or leave her in trouble." Sylvia came up just then and their little contretemps ended. But Charlie had impressed Mark with her loyalty to Angie, and he hoped he'd made his own intentions clear.

Sylvia seemed a decent enough woman, small with a tendency to plumpness. She had short hair with blond highlights; her sparkling hazel eyes appraised him frankly, and he guessed that she was in on the secret. She looked as if she knew a thing or two and could be a lot of fun.

They left just after seven, and he drove the 160 kilometres to Rusape, where they planned to stop for breakfast. The three women chattered away happily while Mark concentrated on driving, taking in the strange countryside. Angie sat in front with him but, wanting to be part of the discussion, spent most of the time with her body angled sideways, her arm resting on the back of the seat. He took pleasure watching her from the corner of his eye as she talked animatedly.

He drove past long stretches of cultivated land, interspersed with granite kopjes, the huge granite boulders balanced precariously on top of each other. Then, after the first 100 kilometres or so, the land changed to more open savannah, with much larger and more extensive granite outcrops; and he could sense the ground rising higher as they approached Rusape. They arrived just after nine and everyone piled out at the hotel. The women disappeared to freshen up while Mark selected a table in the dining room, asking the waiter to bring coffee.

Leaving just after ten, it took nearly three hours to drive the remaining 100 kilometres. The road twisted and turned as they climbed through the foothills of the Inyanga Mountains. Here, the scenery was more classically beautiful. It had changed to deep valleys and rushing streams, with forested sections instead of the open bush they'd passed through before turning off the main Umtali road at Rusape.

Charlie suggested they stop at a local beauty spot called Inyangombi Falls. The cold mountain water, cascading down a jumble of boulders into a series of sparkling pools, looked so inviting that they decided to have a swim. The women changed in the bushes, while Mark did a quick change standing behind the open door of the Land Rover. There was hardly any traffic, and it was just a case of waiting for one vehicle to pass before taking the gap. You wouldn't try that in South Africa, he chuckled to himself.

They drove on refreshed, and finally arrived at the cottage, about a kilometre off the main road. Nestling in the middle of one of the pine forests, the thatched, single storey building had a rustic charm.

The girls followed Charlie around while she showed them the outdoor features; Mark unloaded the Land Rover, and took Angie's with his own luggage straight into the bedroom with a double bed. Be positive, he thought; Angie wouldn't have agreed to the weekend if she hadn't made up her mind to sleep with him. He was a sensual man and he'd been surprised at his own restraint over the past two months. Although frustrated at times, he respected her reluctance, her concerns about her husband and children. She wouldn't be doing this lightly – she must feel strongly about him now, surely? He picked up Charlie and Sylvia's bags and carried them through to the second bedroom.

The women were still outside, so he had a quick look around. The cottage was pretty basic, but perfectly adequate; two bedrooms, a lounge/dining room combined, bathroom and kitchen. Hot water was piped from a wood-fired boiler at the back. The kitchen stove and lounge fireplace were both wood burning. Water came from a storage tank on stilts, a dozen metres from the back of the cottage. There was an electric pump to keep it topped up, and he could see pipes running down the hill to what he guessed would probably be a dam in the valley below.

He saw an African approaching the cottage and went outside to see what he wanted.

"*Masikati, Nkosi,*" the man greeted him.

"'Afternoon." Mark didn't know how to speak their lingo.

"Good afternoon, sir." He immediately switched to English. "My name is Dixon, and I look after this place. My master told me you were coming and I've come up to see if everything is all right." Mark could just make out a few huts some 200 metres away, partly hidden by trees.

"Thank you, I think we'd better ask the ladies." They walked over to the girls. "Ladies, this is Dixon. He's here to see if everything is OK."

"*Masikati* Dixon," Charlie greeted him in his own language. "The swimming pool needs skimming... to get rid of those leaves and insects on the surface there," she pointed them out, "but otherwise everything out here looks fine, thank you."

"*Masikati* madams," he said, looking at all three to include everyone in his reply. "I'll clean the pool while you look inside and tell me if you need anything else. I'll bring firewood in the morning, and light the boiler every morning and afternoon. I can bring eggs and vegetables if you need them – very reasonable prices."

Mark smiled at that; Dixon obviously had a business on the side.

"Thanks, Dixon. We'll let you know when I come out to tell you about the cottage." Charlie was in charge.

Back inside, the girls were looking round the cottage. He watched Angie flush slightly when she saw her luggage next to his in the bedroom. Charlie looked directly at him as they left the room, and arched her eyebrows in acknowledgement of his small achievement. Sylvia rolled her naughty eyes in passing.

This was just the first step. He was surprised how much he wanted this weekend to be special. He wanted Angie to think well of him. Man, he actually felt quite nervous. Mark le Roux nervous – no one would ever believe it. No, this was going to be a really good few days. He'd make sure of that.

Chapter 24

Dusk was falling when Charlie drove off in the Land Rover, with Sylvia waving from the passenger seat.

"We'll probably have a few drinks while we're there and may even stay for dinner," Charlie said before they left, "so expect us when you see us."

"I'd better go and see that the boiler's stoked up with plenty of wood to heat more water," Mark said, gently pulling Angie closer to him, as the car disappeared down the rough road. "I don't think those two left much for us."

"I was embarrassed when I saw you'd put my luggage with yours in the bedroom," she pointed out quietly.

"Well, there's only two bedrooms here, and I wouldn't want to share with anyone else," he smiled at her.

"Everyone just seems to take it for granted that I'm going to sleep with you."

He sensed a warning in her voice, better be careful here. "Please don't make me sleep on the sofa." He leant forward and kissed her lips softly, trying to be conciliatory.

"I thought you were going to see if the boiler had enough wood." Angie seemed appeased, and she didn't push away.

"Mmmm... why don't you go back inside," he said kissing her again. "I'll go and check the firewood, then come back to pour you a drink."

He added wood from the ready cut pile. But the boiler actually seemed to have coped very well, and he heard Angie start the bath running.

"There's plenty of hot water, Mark." She appeared at their bedroom door, carrying her towel and a toilet bag. "I'm going to have my bath now. Can I borrow your shampoo, please? I've left mine behind." He dug it out and gave it to her, watching her walk away. Christ, she was so bloody attractive. And things were going to be all right...

* * *

The water was piping hot, and Angie had to open the window to let some of the steam out, so she could see what she was doing. Despite her light-hearted conversation with Mark, she was still apprehensive. She had thought of suggesting that they should all go up to the hotel together, but she got the impression that the girls didn't expect them to. So she'd tried to appear nonchalant instead. It hadn't been easy.

She lay back in the bath, trying to relax... trying to think of something other than the next couple of hours. She had enough difficulties to face when she got home. For one thing, she'd be very short of money; she couldn't just sponge off her parents. Certainly tennis would have to come to a stop after her club subscription ran out. She wasn't even sure if Ron would be able to get his job back. Not after being in jail. She wondered if military jail was as bad as civilian jail for job prospects? His folks wanted him to go to the farm, but Angie knew for sure Ron wouldn't do that. Although, come to think of it, she didn't know what Ron wanted anymore. And now there was this business with the letters... what had she done wrong?

She lay so long in the bath that the water was losing its heat by the time she got out. Being with Mark had brought home to her just how much was missing in her life. But what she was doing was hardly the right way to go about patching things up with Ron. But she'd come this far, and despite the guilt, she knew there'd be no backing off like some coy virgin. She wanted Mark to take her to bed; wanted to be loved, to be held.

She felt a chill. The steam had gone, and the open window was letting in a light, but cool breeze. She wrapped herself in her bath towel and closed the window. Washing her hair was a bit of a trial. Balancing the water flow on the handheld showerhead wasn't easy, so she eventually decided cold was better than scalding and finished quickly. Walking back to the bedroom, she called out to let Mark know the bathroom was free.

He followed her into the bedroom and collected his towel, while she sat at the dressing table opening drawers.

"I don't suppose there's a hair dryer here?" she asked.

"I doubt it, but you look wonderful anyway; what do you want a hair dryer for? Just dry your hair with the towel. I'll get the fire going in the sitting room later, and you can finish off out there if it's still damp." He came over and kissed her bare shoulder.

"No," he said. "On second thoughts, I'll come and dry your hair myself, as soon as I get out of the bath."

She smiled at him in the mirror. "I've left your shampoo on the windowsill." He kissed her shoulder again and left.

Angie struggled with her hair. Mark's shampoo just wasn't designed for women. She was still at the dressing table when he came back. Clean and fresh, with a towel around his waist, his damp hair combed back.

She watched him carry two candles from the bedside cabinets, and carefully place them on the dressing table where he lit them. Then he switched off the single electric light. At once, the room became softer and his romantic gesture enchanted her. He came up behind, and took the brush from her.

"Come and sit on the bed with me," he said, taking her hand. "We'll be more comfortable while I'm brushing your hair." She rearranged the towel; then sat with her back to him. He held her waist, pulling her close against him. He pushed her shoulders forward a little, and began brushing. He was gentle, but very firm. Using long, powerful but smooth strokes. His legs pressed against her thighs and she tensed.

"Keep still, Angie or it'll tangle."

She relaxed again. No one had brushed her hair for her since she was a child. She'd forgotten what a lovely feeling it was. Some time later she could feel that her hair was dry and behaving perfectly, but he didn't stop brushing... and she didn't want him to.

Finally, he put the brush down, moving her towel aside to expose her body. She felt languorous, almost as though she was watching from a distance. He pulled her gently back and around, and kissed her mouth, rolling them both over smoothly so they were lying side by side on the bed together, with his mouth still on hers. She felt his naked body against hers.

His hand caressed her nipple and it swelled, instantly erect in response. She gasped. He moved his hand down and began caressing her inner thighs, moving her legs apart.

His lips travelled down her neck, his tongue playing over her skin all the while, and onto her breast. Her nipple swelled to reach his tongue, and she felt it being pulled firmly as he sucked it into his mouth. She cried out with pleasure. He moved his lips across to her other breast and began sucking there instead. The juices flowed between her legs, and her body arched up to him as he massaged her wetness with his fingers. Threads of ecstasy ran through her. He moved smoothly on top, and eased himself into her. Penetrating so far, she was surprised it didn't hurt.

"Please be gentle, Mark," she whispered. He paused and kissed her again, not moving, just staying deep inside her.

"You're wonderful, so juicy and warm that I'm struggling not to come on immediately, darling Angie." He rested lightly on her for a few seconds, and then started moving again. She could feel every inch as he slid its full length slowly in and out. No longer afraid of being hurt, she opened herself completely. He steadily built up speed, and she lost control altogether, beginning her orgasm long before he did, but peaking when at last he urgently pumped his fluid into her. This was an entirely new and exquisite experience – her rapture came in waves and she pulled him closer, wanting it to last forever.

He thrust in and out of her slowly a more few times before he stopped, resting his weight gently on her. She fell back, spent and utterly contented. Revelling in the warm afterglow.

They lay a while together, recovering. Then, quite out of the blue, she wondered what she must look like, with just her arms and legs stuck out from under his big frame and giggled softly.

"What's amusing you, sweetheart?"

Did he think she was laughing at him? "I'm sorry. I just had this image of what I must look like. Just think, if someone was looking down at us, I'd have to call out and wriggle my fingers and toes to show that I'm here, somewhere underneath you. I must look like a squashed frog." She giggled again.

He laughed. "You're right. I shouldn't be wasting your beautiful naked body by hiding it under my ugly frame. It's time we got up. I'll get us some drinks." He started lifting himself, but she wrapped her legs and arms around him.

"No, I want you to stay inside me. I'm not going to let you go." She held on to him as tight as she could.

"Mmmm… that's OK by me. I'll just lie on top of you forever." He settled back. "We'll just ask Charlie and Sylvia to bring us food and drink when they get back. Sorry, girls, Angie and I are stuck together here in our bed and we just can't get up." They both laughed.

They lay for a little while longer before she said "No, you're right."

Now he wouldn't move. She pushed but couldn't get him off; he'd made himself so heavy.

"Mark, you're not being fair; you're squashing me." She heaved ineffectively. "The girls will come back and find their friend dead, crushed under her lover." She pushed again but he was immovable, so she surrendered and lay still.

But a few seconds later, he kissed her again and lifted himself off. Rescuing his towel from the tumbled bed, he went off to the bathroom. Angie rolled over and hugged the pillow, reluctant to leave this warm cocoon. Mark's lovemaking had brought her to heights she'd not known before, and she luxuriated in her awakened sensuality.

Mark returned. "Angie, darling." She sat up and moved to the edge of the bed, clutching the sheet around herself. He handed her a towel and she stood up.

He took her hands and looked directly into her eyes. "Thank you for that," he said softly. "You've made me very happy." He pulled her towards him and put his arms around her. Time stood still.

He finally broke the silence. "You'd better go to the bathroom now, or I might just have to take you back to bed again."

She looked up at him and smiled. "Time to catch our breath, I think." He released her and she left the room.

Closing the bathroom door behind her, she caught a glimpse of herself in the mirror. Her body still warm and glowing from their lovemaking. A pang of guilt struck her deep. Against all her instincts, she'd betrayed her husband. As she cleaned herself she could feel her throat closing up. Too late to cry. She'd gone into this with her eyes wide open. There was no going back now.

* * *

Mark dressed and went through to the living room, where he took out the bottle of scotch he'd brought up from South Africa. He reckoned he deserved a double after his heroic efforts. And Angie. She'd wrapped herself around his body – and his heart. He shook his head and knew he no longer had a choice. Come what may, he had to have her. He shuddered, with the uncomfortable feeling that someone was walking over his grave. Must be the cold mountain air.

He left the whisky bottle, went over and knelt by the sitting room grate to light the fire. It caught almost immediately, and the chimney drew well. Then he went through to the kitchen and filled the ice bucket. He checked the champagne, which was nicely chilled. Leaving it in the fridge, he concentrated on pouring his whisky over a few blocks of ice, adding soda to fill the glass.

Back in the sitting room, the fire was blazing, filling the room with flickering shadows. He settled comfortably on the sofa opposite. As he savoured his second sip he heard Angie come into the room. She looked absolutely stunning; the best he'd ever seen her. She seemed to be glowing with health and happiness, and it made her beautiful. She stopped shyly when she saw him looking at her and blushed.

"You're beautiful." He shifted to make space for her. "Come and sit with me." She smiled and joined him on the sofa. He kissed her mouth and fondled her breasts through her shirt, delighted that she was not wearing a bra. "Will you have some champagne, or would you prefer something else? A brandy to warm you up?"

"Oh, yes. A brandy please. It's nice and warm in here, but quite chilly in the bedroom. Can I have it with coke? And please don't make it too strong." Mark got up and poured her a small brandy. They sat in companionable silence for a while before she asked "What shall we do tomorrow? Do you want to play golf with the others?"

"Not really... not unless you want to."

"Oh, no. I'm not much of a golfing fan anyway. I just thought you might want to." She curled up against his body, and he put his hand under her shirt to fondle a nipple while they spoke.

He was totally at ease. Feeling he could trust Angie completely, he began to talk, telling her more than he'd told anyone else before; his inner feelings, his dreams. He spoke about his work, his travels behind the Iron Curtain. It was like a floodgate being opened. Angie listened and asked questions, gently teasing him when he got too serious.

"OK," he said after she teased him again. "We can talk about old times instead. Let's go back to when we were children."

"Oh, no you don't. You'll tease me about being a tomboy. It was Charlie who led the gang, you know." He could only remember that Angie and Charlie were always together, and usually up to no good. "But we both fancied you and you never took any notice of us."

"Remember, I was four years older, and although I sort of noticed you both hung around a bit, I was far too busy doing 'boy' things at that stage of my life." He laughed. "You know; cycling with my friends, swapping comics… and making life as difficult as possible for my pesky girl cousin and her cheeky friend." Angie punched him playfully on his arm.

They spoke about their children. Mark watched Angie's face light up as she talked of her girls. Telling him of their very different personalities, and loveable – and not so loveable – characteristics.

"And Jack?" she asked. "What's he like?"

Mark felt himself smiling. "Well, he's a typical small boy; puppy dogs tails, slugs and snails…" He got up to pour them another drink. "Anna and I were a bit worried that our separation would upset him, but happily he seems to be fine with it all."

Handing her a glass, he sat down again. "I see him as often as I can. Anna's a good mother, and she is as keen as I am to keep things as normal as possible." He sipped his whisky. "I'm a fortunate man I guess, and even more so now." He raised his glass in a tribute to her.

Angie smiled back but he noticed a wary look in her eyes. All this talk of the children had probably reminded her of her husband. Ron cast a shadow between them.

Car lights shone through the sitting room windows as Charlie and Sylvia returned. Angie jumped up. "I'm going to put my bra on, Mark," she whispered as she hurried to the bedroom, her small breasts moving delightfully under her shirt.

* * *

"Christ it's cold out there," Charlie complained as she came through the door. "Hurry Sylvia, and close the damn door behind you. Oooh… look, a beautiful big fire. Good for you, Mark." She went across to warm her hands.

"Drinks, ladies?" Mark got up from the sofa.

"Yes please. Cane 'n coke, and go easy on the coke. Where's Angie?"

"Just popped into the bedroom a moment ago. She's on brandy and coke. How about you, Sylvia?"

It was an enjoyable evening by the fire and they had a light supper just after nine. By ten-thirty they were all yawning. It had been a long day. Mark let the fire die down and they said their goodnights.

222

Angie joined him in bed looking delectable in one of the negligees he'd bought for her. He soon had that off, and they made love again before falling asleep, naked in each other's arms.

* * *

The whole long weekend was idyllic, and Angie came to love Mark deeply as well as passionately. They got to know each other so well, walking and talking alone together during the day, while Charlie and Sylvia were up at the hotel, golfing. Again, she was amazed at how similar their views were.

Until now, her father had been the only man she knew who enjoyed discussing national and world affairs with her. Most men she'd known, especially Ronnie, seemed to think that women should stick to home and children. Even her mother, who she felt very close to, couldn't offer this kind of stimulus. Now she realised just how much she'd been missing that mental cut and thrust. She didn't always agree with everything Mark said, and they'd had some lively debates.

In the evenings, the four of them enjoyed each other's company, with Mark and Charlie ragging each other. Between them, they certainly kept Angie and Sylvia amused.

Sometimes it could be completely different when she and Mark were alone together though. So close and intimate as they walked quietly through the forests or by the dam or the streams; not talking at all, or just chatting about trivial, fun things.

She lost count of how many times they made love, sometimes in the cottage and sometimes outdoors. Once on a smooth boulder in the forest. She moved joyously up and down astride him until they changed places. They'd positioned their clothing under her bottom and back to protect her from the cold stone, but the small of her back ended up scratched and slightly bruised all the same. He rubbed soothing cream onto it in their bedroom that evening and, of course, they'd ended up making love again, with her kneeling on the bed in front of him.

"We don't want to hurt your back again, darling," he explained. She'd thought it a little decadent at first but Mark's accomplished lovemaking gave her so much pleasure that she'd tossed her reservations aside. The strength of her passion over those few days had sometimes shocked her.

* * *

The day they left, Mark asked Angie to come for a last walk alone with him. He took her to their special place, a jumble of flat rocks halfway up a small hill. The valley stretched below them and you could see for miles.

As they sat, comfortable in each other's company, he steeled himself to ask her something that had been puzzling him all weekend. He'd been reluctant to broach the subject earlier, not wanting to spoil the growing bond between them. "Angie?" he began.

"Yes?" she replied, her soft hair blowing in the slight breeze.

"What eventually decided you to spend this weekend with me?"

She bit her lip, and he could see a worry line deepen between her eyes.

"Sweetheart," he touched her arm, "I don't want to upset you. If you'd rather not…"

She took a deep breath. "It's all right, Mark. I want you to know." She drew her knees up to her chest and gazed into the distance.

She spoke quietly, clearly struggling to find the right words. "Ron and I are having problems. I don't really understand why. I don't think I've changed, but he has." She went on to tell him of her months of loneliness and frustration. He stayed quiet. Letting her talk. Getting it all out.

"You asked me about the weekend." Mark saw her hands tighten around her knees. "I'd just spent probably the two most humiliating days of my life – trying to find out why Ron wasn't replying to any of my letters, when you phoned." She shut her eyes and a tear rolled down her cheek.

He couldn't bear all her pain, and took her into his arms while she carried on with her sad story. His heart went out to her. God, he loved this woman.

"I needed to get away from it all, needed to be with someone who loved me, and wanted to be with me." She rubbed her eyes, trying to wipe away the tears and looked up at him. "And that's it really. I just wanted to be loved."

"It's OK, Angie, it's OK." He pulled her close. "I love you, and Ron's a fool. He doesn't deserve you." Mark felt anger at this man who'd made this lovely girl so unhappy.

"But Mark, he wasn't always like that. We were very happy for the first year. It can't be all his fault. I must have done something to make him act this way. But he's so hard to talk to." She was obviously fretting over the whole thing.

"Angie, I can't believe that. Ron sounds bloody selfish. Listen, calm down now. Try to forget about him for the rest of the day. We don't want him to spoil such a wonderful weekend." He kissed her forehead and cheeks, tasting the salt from her tears.

She smiled. "You're right, but I'm glad I've told you. It's been such a relief – I've been bottling it up for so long." She grimaced. "I hate people seeing me cry and I've soaked your shirt."

Mark loved her all the more for that. "I'm a good sponge Angie, and I don't want there to be any secrets between us." He lifted her to her feet. "Time to get back. No more tears, Angie. I promise I'll never hurt you."

* * *

Driving home, everyone was saying that they really must do it again.

"I think you and Mark had the most fun though," Charlie said. "Next time we'll have to bring our lovers too, won't we, Sylvia?" She prodded Mark in his back as she said that. "You've made my best friend very happy, Mark, she's positively blooming."

* * *

Angie looked back on that long weekend with some guilt but a lot of pleasure. She still had feelings for Ron, but they were feelings of sorrow and pity. The anger and hurt still there, but dulled by her new-found love for Mark. She felt sorry for Ron's parents too, who were equally puzzled and hurt by him. At least she had the children – and Mark. But she still felt guilty. Especially when Ron's folks were so nice to her and to the children. The two men in her life couldn't be more different. She was beginning to dread Ron's return.

Chapter 25

There were still two weeks to go at detention barracks, when Ron received his call up papers for basic military training. He'd been issued with a new service number, and his rank was given as 'rifleman'. It was like his past service with the Army had never existed, and they knew nothing about him. But the papers had been sent direct to Brady Barracks, so *someone* out there knew what they were doing.

He was 'required to report to Llewellin barracks at 08h00 on Monday 2nd April 1973'. Great. He was due to be released from detention the Saturday before. Big of them to give him two nights off before it started all over again. Not worthwhile making his way up to Salisbury then; much less the farm.

Recalling the liaison officer incident, he drafted the first letter he'd written for a long time. He addressed it to his mother. Angela could get the information about his call-up from her; that would serve as a reminder not to go running to other people with complaints about him.

"I think it'll be too unsettling for the children to see me for just a day, before I disappear again for another six weeks," he wrote. Truth was, he really didn't feel like facing the family yet. Besides, he had more important things to worry about. "So I'll leave it until after I finish my basic training. It'll be sure to get back to normal after that, and I'll arrange a lift up to Salisbury as soon as it's over." He filled the page, writing that he was fine, and other such reassurances. Then, to close, "I haven't time to write to Angela, so please tell her I won't be home until after the basic training is over. Your son…" But it sounded clumsy and he delayed posting it.

Meanwhile the regime at Brady was making him increasingly fit, delivering the physical and mental toughness he sought. The other detainees now respected him and kept their distance. One day, he caught a look of sheer terror in the eyes of one new detainee, when he challenged the idiot for spilling tea on the floor next to him in the cookhouse. No harm done really, it only splashed his boots. But shit, did he really come across so badly?

Another day, he caught part of a conversation as he walked into the shower room. "… Keep away from that hard old bastard. He'll kill you as soon as look at you; beat one poor bloke half to death…" At 29, Ron was the oldest SUS there by five or six years, and even the staff had begun to show cautious respect.

Well, that was OK by him and he did nothing to encourage idle chatter; Ron just wanted a decent shower. The showerheads hung in an open, straight line from one end of the ablution block to the other, water feeding through a pipe to all the showers from one source. So the pressure weakened down the line, until there was just a feeble trickle from the last few showerheads.

Ron prepared himself to wait until a decent one was available, but when he looked again, the detainee using the best one hastily gave way to him. He shrugged his shoulders, and went across to the favoured shower. This irrational fear of him had its uses, but his hate and revenge were directed at Gadziwa, and everything that he and the other terrorists represented, not at other detainees. He squeezed the lever and a powerful jet of cold water stung his body.

Why the hell was he so determined to kill Gadziwa? After all, the Rhodesian Army had done him no favours; they banged him up like this for trying to do his job, which was to fight terrorists. But Gadziwa represented everything the terrs stood for; everything Ron abhorred. Shit, these so called African Nationalists were destroying his country. Didn't they know it was the Rhodesian pioneers who'd saved this beautiful land from the oppression of warlike Africans? Half the bastards Ron and his Army comrades fought were descendants of slaves. Everyone knew that until they were rescued back in 1890, they'd all been vassals of the legendary savage Matabele, King Lobengula. Yeah, back then the Shona had *welcomed* white settlers.

Ron placed his soap carefully on the windowsill, gripped the lever again and turned slowly in the stream, rinsing off. Sure, there'd been two rebellions; first the Matabele, understandably trying to reinstate their rule. Then, when the settlers were occupied fighting the Matabele, the Shona people rose up and attacked, slaughtering lonely white farmers and miners, and their families. But with the help of a few British troops, those early Rhodesians had fought back, quickly subduing both rebellions, making peace with the Matabele, and punishing the leading Shona troublemakers.

He dried himself vigorously, refreshed but still simmering with anger. For over half a century, the country had enjoyed peace. The colonial administration built hospitals, schools and roads. Settlers like his grandparents created farms on the almost empty land, and built dams and grain stores to prevent famine caused by periodic droughts. In time, they introduced animal husbandry and veterinary controls to prevent the regular devastation of diseases such as foot and mouth, and other, even worse pestilences like anthrax and the deadly rinderpest.

This was the country Ron was prepared to defend with his life; he got on well with most Africans, and knew none who supported these fucking terrs. There was no way he was going to leave his country like so many other white people were doing. And he needed the Army to help him succeed; he knew there was no way he could do it on his own. But not as an ordinary soldier, he needed Army resources. He also needed the freedom to act independently. How the hell could that be arranged? Not easily, yet he was determined to find a way.

In time, Ron's hard labour routine was eased, and he was given improved meal rations as soon as he'd completed the first 42 days. Something to do with regulations covering long-term prisoners. He used the better rations, and increased spare time to toughen up his exercise routines, deliberately driving himself to the edge of exhaustion each day.

He needn't have worried about how to get up to Salisbury. They told him that the seven days he spent in the dark cell, didn't count towards his 84 days' detention. He would be going straight from Brady to Llewellin on the Monday, special permission being granted to allow him to do so... despite his official sentence not being fully completed. The provost officer who gave him this bit of news didn't look up as he spoke but Staff Ritchie, who escorted him there, gawped at Ron to see his reaction.

He was disappointed. Ron showed no sign of emotion, simply answering with the regulation "Yes, sir."

The officer looked up at him sympathetically. "Tough shit, Cartwright." But when he got no reaction threw down the file he was holding and snapped "Dismiss." Ron was marched out again at the double. Even Ritchie said nothing, and Ron was grimly pleased that he'd not shown any sign of weakness in front of the bastards. Next day he redrafted his original letter and sent it off to his mother.

* * *

When he arrived at Llewellin, Ron looked at the youthful faces around him, and wondered if he was the oldest recruit in the entire Rhodesian Army. The RSM came up and called him out of the ragged ranks in their civilian clothes.

"We know about your record, Cartwright but we won't be holding it against you," he said out of hearing from the others. "You've completed your punishment and we'll be fair while you're here."

"Thank you, sir, but I can take it," Ron replied, quietly confident.

The tough looking regimental sergeant major eyed him for a while before saying "Yes, I think you can. Back to your ranks, soldier."

Ron turned smartly and doubled back to join the line of new recruits.

The supposedly harsh induction and training were like a holiday for Ron, but he was determined to take every advantage of what he could learn. No point in wasting the time while he was here. He had to devise extra exercises for himself, in order to maintain the peak condition he'd developed in detention barracks. The physical aspects and weapons training were undemanding, and he could do most things blindfold. But he was surprised by some of the basic soldiering skills he had forgotten. There were some new aspects too, and the training was a lot more focused. When he'd first completed his military training back in 1965, the emphasis had been on conventional warfare. Hard hats, trenches, mass troop movements and all that crap. Now the whole focus was on anti-insurgent warfare. Much better.

He realised he must present a forbidding aspect to the young recruits, who left him to his own devices. So did the training staff. Everyone knew he came from a long term at the notorious Brady Barracks. But despite himself, he soon found he was acting as a sort of role model, with the trainees looking to him for help and guidance. Even the staff seemed to be relying on him to help maintain morale among the trainees. Many of the recruits were only 16 or 17, and they especially needed someone to turn to. The military must be scraping the bottom of the barrel, taking kids straight out of school; they found the harsh discipline and physical training hard to bear.

"There's no such thing as 'human rights' here," the training staff told them at their first parade. "We've taken all your 'rights' away. If you become more useful, we'll give them back to you, one by one, as privileges… which we can take away from you at any time, until you pass out as soldiers." The staff sergeant haranguing them paused. "Just remember – it's all mind over matter – the Army doesn't mind, and you don't matter." That shocked the other trainees, but Ron found the regime soft compared with the last 12 weeks.

Halfway through the six-weeks' basic training, at the end of the 'first phase', the veteran warrant officer who commanded his training platoon told Ron he was going to put him up for promotion.

"You're obvious leadership material, and know your stuff better than some of the training staff here, Cartwright," he said.

"Thanks, sir, but I think you'll find that my record will get in the way." Ron unbent sufficiently to acknowledge the proposal.

Ron was right of course. The WOII's recommendation was later refused at the highest level.

Their company commander, an elderly captain, sent for Ron to tell him. "I'm sorry, Cartwright, but Warrant Officer Gregg's recommendation for your promotion has been rejected, despite my favourable endorsement. It seems that your past sins have not been forgotten."

"That's OK, thank you, sir. I understand." Ron wasn't at all surprised.

"I don't know if the bastards will ever let up, you know. Once they get their claws into you…"

"I can do what's necessary without rank, thank you, sir."

The captain looked at him long and hard. "I think I might have a route that could meet your needs, Cartwright," he said thoughtfully. "I'll contact an old friend of mine, and ask if he'll send someone round to see you before you complete your time here. Meanwhile your conduct here has been exemplary. Thank you."

Ron assumed that was his dismissal. He saluted and began an about turn, preparing to march out.

"Hold on, soldier. Would you like a long weekend pass? I see you didn't even get to go home to see your family before they transferred you here from Brady."

Ron was taken aback by the captain's offer. Was this old bloke for real? He paused, then decided it was a genuine hand of friendship, so replied. "No thank you, sir. My wife and family aren't expecting me until after the training is over, but I'm very grateful for your kindness. It's the first that's been shown to me for a long time."

* * *

On the final Saturday of 'basic training', Ron's intake was at last granted permission to use the troopers' canteen. He was there that afternoon, sitting alone in the garden outside the building, quietly enjoying his first beer for many months, when two soldiers, one carrying the rank of captain, approached his table.

"Can Sergeant Robson and I buy you a beer, Cartwright?" the officer asked. Ron was about to refuse, but something made him change his mind. "Thanks, sir. Castle please." He offered chairs to them and the officer sat down.

The tough looking sergeant went off, and brought three dumpies back to their secluded table. He sported a thick, bushy black beard – Ron had never seen an infantryman with a beard before.

Now the captain ended the small talk and started. "We've been watching you here for the past few days, Cartwright." Yes, Ron thought he'd seen them around. "You've adapted well into the ranks, considering you're a former officer, and an ex-prisoner from Brady."

Ron took a swig from the bottle, raising it to the two soldiers to acknowledge their generosity, before he replied. "I do my best." He placed the bottle carefully on the table.

"No anger?" the sergeant asked.

"Plenty," Ron replied.

"Redcaps?" the sergeant again.

"Well… no, not really. Bunch of arseholes, but just doing their shitty job."

"Who, then?" the captain this time.

Ron thought for some time before he answered. "There's a certain terr I'd like to get. All terrs I suppose, but there's one in particular." He had a feeling that these hard looking men might just serve his purpose.

Ron caught a fleeting exchange of glances between the two before the captain said. "We have a special unit. It's tough, dangerous work, but it would give you all the contact with CTs you want." The captain used the acronym for communist terrorist. "But it wouldn't be an easy life."

"You should know that I was convicted for disobeying orders, by court-martial. They said it was 'bordering on mutiny'."

"Yes, we've looked into all that, and know the circumstances.

Some former subordinates of yours now serve with us. Nevertheless, I would not expect you to disregard orders again." Ron concentrated on a fly that was hovering over the table for a few moments, killed it, and then looked up again.

The captain continued "A fellow soldier could lose his life by any repetition of disobedience; somehow I don't think you'd want that, Cartwright." The captain looked Ron directly in the eye. "But I'd need your word that it'll never happen again."

Ron saw cold grey eyes, staring fixedly, even more questioning than the captain's, from behind the sergeant's bushy beard and long, dark hair. There was something about these men that was completely out of the ordinary. The sergeant's unkempt appearance belied his calm, studied professionalism. Yes, they must be Special Forces; he'd like to be a part of this outfit. He thought for quite a while, saying nothing; this was a tough question. He'd been asking himself the same one for the last four or five months, and he still wasn't sure what the answer was.

Suddenly it came to him. "I might question orders, sir, but I'll never risk another man's life again, not unless I'm under proper orders *and*, like the last time it happened, we're all facing the same risk." The captain might not like that, but it was the truth. Ron picked up his beer from the table.

Robson thought for a moment before visibly relaxing, and the three of them leant back in their chairs.

Chapter 26

Mark now travelled to Rhodesia as often as he could, and he managed to spend two more weekday mornings with Angie. Another visit to Mermaid's Pool, and the second when she came to his suite at Meikle's hotel.

"I really want to spend another long weekend with you, darling," he said while they sat enjoying the lunchtime wine and food, exquisitely presented and served in the privacy of his rooms.

"I'll ask Charlie if she can come again."

"How about you come and stay with me in Cape Town this time?" He wondered how best to persuade her. "We could even go out to the vineyard, and you'll meet my Dad again. How well do you remember him?"

"It's a long time ago, but I do remember him vaguely, a big man with a black beard," she said. "I like the idea," she continued, "but... how can it be arranged?"

"Fly down. South African Airways has a direct flight between Salisbury and Cape Town three days a week. I'll organise your ticket, of course."

"Yes, but what about the children?" She sat up. "And what will I tell the folks? Mine and Ronnie's?"

"Surely we can think of something? We have to. It won't be so easy for us after your husband gets back." Mark had worked out that the man was due back in five weeks; he tried not to think too much about that. But it turned out to be the wrong thing to say...

"I still feel pretty bad about two-timing Ronnie," Angie said. She left the table and went over to sit in an armchair, pulling her legs up against her chest. He'd noticed she always did that when she was under stress. "In fact, I feel awful."

"I can understand that, but he doesn't deserve you; look how he treats you."

"That might be so, but I'm the one in the wrong now." She rocked in the chair, clearly agitated. "It's all right for you, but I'm guilty of adultery," she exclaimed.

"Do you love him?" Mark turned the discussion; he had to get her out of this mood of self-reproach.

"Well… I used to."

"Does he love you?"

"No, not any more. I'm sure he doesn't," she said thoughtfully. "As you know, he hasn't even bothered to write to me; not once. I had to hear from his mother that he wouldn't be coming home until after his basic training." Her mood seemed to change and she sat up straight again.

"Well, *I* love you, for what it's worth," he gently reminded her.

She looked across at him. "Thank you. I love you too, Mark."

"Angie, will you think about leaving him and coming to live with me?" He'd wanted to say that since their trip to Inyanga. "I've got lots of room at home in Cape Town, and I'd love to have you, and your girls down there with me." He committed himself.

He could see he'd surprised her. "Mark, that's wonderful… and generous of you. But I don't think it's come to that yet. I must try to make things work out between Ronnie and me, for the sake of the children at least." She came over and kissed him.

He took her in his arms and pulled her onto his lap. "Well at least come down and spend a long weekend with me."

"Yes, I'll do that." He could see she'd made up her mind. "I just need to think of how to do it without causing problems."

But they couldn't come up with a solution, so left it open that they'd both think about it, and he'd phone her again next week to share ideas.

* * *

Angie phoned Charlie the day after Mark left, and arranged to have lunch with her in town. They discussed the trip to Cape Town and Charlie came up with an answer. But not before she'd squeezed as many details out of Angie as she could about her affair with Mark. Angie had expected that, and rationed her carefully.

"Well, I think there's more to this affair than you're admitting," Charlie had said grumpily.

Angie quietly stuck to her guns, but played the helpless friend. "I need your help, Charlie… please."

Charlie's attitude softened. "Just let the kids stay with your folks again and go down there, darling. He's paying. I can't see what the problem is."

"It's not as simple as that, Charlie. What am I going to tell my folks I'm doing?"

"Going to Cape Town for a long weekend, of course."

"Can't do that. They know how short of money I am, and it wouldn't sound too good if I said, 'it's OK, Mum, Dad. I'll just use your money to pay for it,' or even worse; 'don't worry, Mark is paying.'"

"Ouch. I see what you mean." Charlie sat up straight. Her interest was aroused again; Angie could almost hear her mind working overtime. "I know... Why not tell them that you've been selected to go play tennis for the club in Bulawayo? That's far enough away to be pretty safe."

Angie thought it was a wonderful idea, until she remembered that Llewellin Barracks, where Ron had now moved to, was only about 20 kilometres from Bulawayo.

Then she knew; "But Umtali would be ideal. Charlie, you're a star."

"Hey, you're not such a dumb blonde yourself," Charlie allowed. "Yes, that's your best option. Your folks are hardly likely to know if the club are going there or not, and it's far enough away for them not to find out by accident," she added. "Tell them to phone me in case of need while you're away. Say I'll know how to get in touch with you in an emergency. And you'd better give me Mark's phone number, just in case."

* * *

A few weeks later, it was all arranged. She left the children on the farm with Ron's folks this time, since it was their half-term holiday. Both they and her parents thought it was a good idea for her to take a long weekend, playing tennis with the club in Umtali.

Despite all Charlie's reassurances, it was still nerve-wracking. After all, Charlie wasn't the one taking the risks. Angie steeled herself, and drove to Salisbury airport in a funk, fearful she might run into someone she knew there. She could just imagine them telling her folks... 'Oh, I saw Angie catching the plane to Cape Town – how nice for her.' Then the cat would be among the pigeons... Rhodesia was a small place, with Salisbury's white population not much bigger than that of a medium sized town in South Africa. Once aboard, she relaxed. Mark had booked her first class and she enjoyed the luxury.

He collected her from Cape Town's airport in a red Ferrari.

"Just a Dino 246 GT – for high days and holidays," he explained when she commented on it.

"It's years since I was in Cape Town," she said. "The last time was when I was at University here in the 60s." They chatted happily, while Mark drove through the suburbs towards the slopes of Table Mountain. They skirted past the City and around Signal Hill, passing Green Point and Sea Point... all their apartments and hotels jostling for position along the steep streets leading down to the sea front. They continued towards the pretty area of Bantry Bay. Just before they reached Clifton, under the loom of Lion's Head, he suddenly slowed the car down and took a sharp right into an open garage. It looked as if it was on the very edge of the cliffs, with the sea far below. Mark parked alongside a cream coloured Mercedes-Benz.

He got out, came over to her side and opened the door. A pleasant looking coloured man in uniform appeared and greeted her politely, taking her luggage from the boot. Mark led the way through to the house.

The view was magnificent. The house was built into the side of the cliff, and Angie could look from the patio that stretched beyond the sitting room windows, almost straight down onto the Atlantic Ocean. Big rollers thundered against the glistening black rocks below. Looking to the left, she could see the line of coves with their pure white sands of the Clifton beaches and along Camps Bay. There was another house on the right but it was hardly visible among the rocky cliff-face, and Mark's patio was not overlooked.

"It's lovely." She was stunned. He put his arm around her waist and pulled her back close towards him. She turned her face to kiss him.

He smiled broadly and hugged her. "Let me show you around." The house was built on several levels. His bedroom was directly under the patio and had an equally glorious view of the sea and beaches. There were two smaller bedrooms, and another bathroom on that level. Downstairs was a study and a fourth bedroom.

The study had an outside door leading onto a rocky patio, with a small lawn and a few flowerbeds. Not much more than a few dozen square metres cut into the dark rocks. It had a gate that opened onto a flight of steps, which he told her led down to a small, private tidal beach among the rocks below. She couldn't see it from where they stood because the steps twisted and turned, as they cut their way down between the rocks of the cliff-face. When they got back to the patio, she asked him to hold on to her and, by leaning out over the railings, she could just see the little cove.

"It's not safe for swimming or anything – and the water's much too cold anyway, if you remember." He pulled her back and kept his arm around her waist. "It's also damned dangerous, with slippery rocks, pounding waves and big tides, so please don't go down there alone. Kelp all over the place too."

"That's why you can smell the sea so strongly." Angie drew in a deep breath, savouring it. "I've missed that." She leaned against him, feeling so safe and secure. For a brief moment there was just the two of them together, and nothing to come between them.

* * *

"The old man is really looking forward to seeing you, and I think you'll like Chamdor. We'll pass through Stellenbosch on the way; you'll be pleased to see that the town has managed to keep its old Cape Dutch charm," Mark told Angie, as they drove from Clifton to his father's vineyard between Stellenbosch and Franschoek, the next morning. "Chamdor is a derivative of the French words for 'fields of gold'. The farm was given that name because of the colour of the vineyards in the autumn."

She liked the name, reflecting on its meaning while he negotiated the tight bends in the road.

"Why did you and your Dad move to South Africa, Mark?" she asked. Last night they had re-established their comfortable, intimate relationship, now so much more than just a physical one.

"We moved when he inherited the farm from my grandfather. About the same time as my parents' divorce."

They'd taken the scenic route, away from Cape Town. The road curved along the coast, hard against the steep Twelve Apostles, with a sharp drop down to the sparkling ocean on their right. They passed the pretty settlement of Llandudno, headed round the back of Table Mountain, and were soon driving through the beautiful, leafy suburb of Constantia near the famous Kirstenbosch Gardens. Mark slowed the car as they drove past a set of imposing gates, barring the entrance to a driveway lined with big trees.

"Anna and Jack live up there," he said.

"Must be a nice house."

"Too big really, but she wants to keep it. Everything's settled, and our divorce should go through in the next few weeks." Angie couldn't think of anything to say to that, so kept silent. Charlie was right; he must have a lot of money. He seemed to be very generous with his wife, soon to be ex-wife. Angie wondered if she was lonely, living in such a big place with only her young son for company. Perhaps she also had someone else in her life.

They cut across onto the main road, connecting Cape Town with Somerset West, the Overberg and Eastern Cape. Angie had forgotten how spectacular the mountains were in this part of the world. The Drakenstein – Dragon's Peaks – so bleak looking, yet at the same time, beautiful.

After a long silence, Mark began talking again. "When I finished at Bishops, I went to Stellenbosch; from an English College to an Afrikaans University. My father thought Stellenbosch would give me good contacts here in South Africa, and he was not too keen on Cape Town University, because of its reputation for liberalism and radicalism." He smiled at her.

"That'll be why we never met again after you left Rhodesia, although I suppose you left Uni. before I came down here," she said. They discussed dates and calculated that Mark must have graduated the year after Angie started at CTU. She reflected on how different everything might have been if she'd met Mark again before she married Ronnie.

"Then I joined a bank up in Johannesburg, and was building a career there until sanctions began in earnest against Rhodesia in '67." He turned off the main road, and headed towards Stellenbosch and Franschoek. "I made some interesting contacts, and they invited me to join them in an importing and exporting business. That's how I got into breaking sanctions for Rhodesia. It seemed like a good idea at the time."

"It still seems to be a good idea."

"It certainly pays the bills and leaves some over. But it won't last forever, and I don't think I really want to carry on with the sort of people I'm now dealing with, not after Rhodesia."

"You sound as if you think Rhodesia won't win against the terrorists."

"Well, I hope it will... but I really don't think they have a chance." He looked across at her, as if trying to judge the effect his words were having. "Maybe last another couple of years, but they can't stand up against the whole world for long. Not unless South Africa keeps supporting them, and I wouldn't trust South Africa to do that forever. Rhodesia will run out of money anyway – I have to do all my trading in US dollars."

"Surely it's in South Africa's interests to support Rhodesia? After all, they have their own policemen fighting alongside our soldiers."

"Maybe... for now and until things get worse." Mark grimaced uncertainly; then smiled. "Here we are." He turned onto a gravel road, with long rows of vines on either side.

Angie wondered how much worse things could get, what with sanctions and everything. They passed through wide gates with the name Chamdor above them.

* * *

"Magtig! But you've turned into a pretty little tabby," Uncle Anton chortled. "I haven't seen you since you were a klein meisie – small girl." His heavily accented English brought memories flooding back.

"Thank you," she responded to the big man, who'd risen to greet them after a coloured servant showed them to his study. He seemed much too old to be Mark's father, but he had the same penetrating blue eyes and gracious manners, spiced with a roguish wit. He didn't actually flirt with her, but didn't conceal a candid appreciation of her either. Despite this, she felt at ease with him, somehow knowing that whatever he might have been in his youth, he had mellowed now.

"Here is coffee, or would you prefer tea?" He lifted a bushy eyebrow in question. "You English people always drink tea don't you?"

"Coffee is fine thank you, Uncle Anton." The servant placed a tray next to Angie, it being understood that she was expected to pour for the men. The study was rich with leather chairs and a big partner's desk, but they sat away from the desk at a round meeting table, in between two walls – lined with leather bound books that reached from the dark timber floor to the high, wide ceiling. She wondered how anyone could reach the ones near the top. The other walls carried paintings of mountains and wild animals. There was a ferocious-looking stuffed black Cape buffalo head, with wild staring eyes, and a massive boss and horns above the desk. It was an unequivocally masculine room.

"What is happening with your wife, Markus?" he asked, as Angie handed him his coffee and passed the cream and sugar, which he waved away. That reminded her that his father always called him Markus, and that, as a boy, he'd hated being called by his proper name. She looked across at him, and he made a wry face. But Mark answered his father politely, and the old man turned his attention to Angie.

"You are married?" Mark must have told him.

"Yes, Uncle. And I have three children, all girls." She might as well tell him everything.

"Humph... Where is your husband?"

"He's in the Army at the moment. I don't expect him back until next week." She didn't add anything by way of an explanation for her presence in Cape Town. The old man looked at Mark, but he was peering out the window and didn't look round.

"You are not happy with him?"

Angie blushed, but decided to tell Mark's father the truth. "No... but that's not why I'm here. I'm here because Mark asked me; and I wanted to be with him." Her uncle nodded his head once but said nothing, and looked thoughtful.

"Here's your coffee," she handed Mark his cup and offered a plate of biscuits. Uncle Anton took two rusks from the plate and put one on his saucer, dipping the other into his coffee. He didn't use the side plate she'd set next to him.

"Tell me about Rhodesia."

Mark let Angie do all the talking. It was a lively discussion and her uncle asked a lot of questions. She refilled his coffee cup twice and hers and Mark's once. Despite his brusque manner, she began to like him. He was very open and straightforward.

"Come, and I'll show you the cellars," the old man said when he declined her offer of a fourth cup. He heaved himself out of his chair, collected a walking stick from a leather and brass stand in the doorway, and took Angie's arm in his. Mark followed.

She was persuaded to taste several wines, and felt slightly light-headed by the time lunch came. It was served at a long dining table, with her uncle sitting at the head, and Angie and Mark on either side of him. Servants came and went, but she was careful not to drink too much of the wines on offer. She took her cue from Mark, who declined refills on several occasions. The old man also drank sparingly, but ate well. They all selected fruit for dessert.

"We grow all our own fruit here," he told her. "It keeps everyone on the farm healthy." She readily approved when he asked permission to smoke. He also offered brandy. Neither she nor Mark smoked, but he took a brandy.

"Dad's people produce the best brandy in the country," he said. I normally only drink whisky, but always enjoy a brandy here."

"There's whisky if you want it, my boy. A sweet wine or liqueur for you, Angie? They're made here on the estate." She smiled but shook her head. Uncle Anton leaned back and relaxed in his chair, transferring his attention back to Angie.

"You are pretty, like your Aunty Harriet. It was always said that she had the looks, and your father the brains." The old man now looked intently at her. "Perhaps you have inherited both, and I remember your mother was a fine looking woman too. Yes, you are a mooi meisie, and you have rare intelligence for a woman. Be aware that you might also have inherited some of your aunt's impetuosity, or it will cause heartache." He puffed on his pipe but said no more on the subject. Angie didn't ask him what he meant, because she suspected she knew.

When lunch was over, they went for a walk in the sunshine through the vineyards and orchards, where Angie saw peaches, plums, nectarines and other deciduous fruits. Being early May, much of the fruit was ready for picking and there were many coloured field hands, including women and children, in the orchards. Every few metres, Uncle Anton would stop and send someone to pick a particularly choice specimen. They brought it to him for examination. If he was satisfied with the fruit, he handed it solemnly to Angie for her to take back with her. She soon had her hands full, and he called a bright looking young coloured woman to follow them carrying a basket.

"Thank you so much," Angie said as she offloaded the fruit into the basket, and was rewarded with a smile from the girl.

"The children come to pick the fruit after school," the old man said. Although he was greeted by most of the hands, the smaller children hid behind their mother's skirts when he approached. He was the oubaas, and Angie could see the workers respected their 'old master'. They ran to do his bidding with spirited cheerfulness.

There was a white supervisor in the fields, who also addressed him as oubaas. Angie thought he had a surly attitude, and she didn't like him very much after he was introduced to her and greeted her in an obsequious manner. He seemed insincere and over-eager to please, compared with the coloured farm folk.

"Coloureds are all like children, of course," her uncle commented, "but they'll rob you blind if you let them get away with it. And the adults, men and women alike, are demons for drink. My manager, who is not here today, has to lock anything with alcohol away or we have trouble. Fights and that sort of thing." He seemed to be warning her not to take them at face value. "But they're basically good folk, and can be very loyal." He leaned close to her and said "This supervisor is good at his job and knows all their tricks, but he's no angel and must also be watched." Her uncle must have picked up on her reservations.

They went back to the big 'Cape Dutch' farmhouse for afternoon tea, and sat at a table on the wide, whitewashed verandah while tea was served. There were loads of cakes and biscuits, including the sweet, syrupy koeksisters so loved by Afrikaners. Her uncle insisted on Angie eating one, and she made a brave effort, though she found them far too sweet for her taste.

"It's a lonely life here; my second wife died four years ago and we were not blessed with children, so there's only Markus here." Uncle Anton glanced sideways at him. "*He* spends all his time chasing money." Angie felt sorry for him, in spite of her Aunt Harriet. The old man had cut himself off completely from Harriet and her family ever since their divorce.

"I hope he will come and take over the farm before I die. But a farmer needs a good wife... Ja, and it is possible for cousins to marry," he concluded.

"You're having a go at me at Angie's expense, Dad." Mark laughed, looking at her and raising his eyebrows. He looked at his watch. "I think it's time we were off, anyway." Angie could feel herself blushing deeply.

"When are you going back to Rhodesia?" the old man spoke

directly to her. Angie recovered her composure, while explaining that she had to fly back the day after tomorrow, Sunday.

"You young people, always rushing from one place to another. You must promise to come and see me again next time you're here, mooi meisie, and bring cheer to an old man's heart." Mark stood up.

"I promise, Uncle," Angie replied. "And thank you for a wonderful day." She stood and leaned over to kiss his cheek.

* * *

"Old devil. I do apologise if he embarrassed you. He'll have us married and on the estate before we know what's happened," Mark grumbled good naturedly as they drove away. "Talk about women being match-makers."

Her uncle had surprised her by saying what he did, but he hadn't offended her. Rather the opposite, she was quite flattered that the old man had thought her worthy of marrying his only son.

"Why are you and your wife getting divorced?" Angie asked after a period of silence. The sun was setting over the mountains, throwing long shadows on the dusty driveway. She waited quietly for his reply.

"Well," he paused. "The official documentation cites 'incompatibility', which is exactly what it is." He looked across at her. "We argued a lot about all sorts of things. Our marriage never worked properly from the start. We have very different interests and backgrounds." He switched the headlights on as they reached the main road, and turned towards Cape Town.

"I know it sounds pretty weak, but I was sort of caught up in something that I didn't really want from the beginning. It had to do with my career at the bank and meeting the right people; that sort of thing." He shrugged his shoulders. "She's from a very influential Afrikaner family here. My Dad could be described as a well-connected Afrikaner too, although he's originally of Huguenot stock." Angie had always thought the name le Roux sounded French.

"But as you know I'm mixed; English and Afrikaans, and I find I get on easier with the English. It's difficult to describe, and not the only thing, but my preference for English ways is probably what's behind it."

"I think I can understand."

"Thank you. Anna and I get along much better now we're

separated. And Jack spends quite a lot of time with me when I'm here. I also take him on holiday every year. Despite everything, we have a good relationship."

"I'm glad for you and for him."

"I wish you weren't married, Angie. My Dad might be old but he's no fool." Angie waited for him to continue. "I can't propose to you properly because you're still married, but I do want to marry you."

Her heart leaped. After last night she'd wondered if he might be planning to say something. Not just living with him but marrying him. At once she was both elated and terrified; this brought all sorts of problems to a head. In spite of half expecting him to say something, and reinforced by what his father had said before they left the farm, she was surprised when he said it so unequivocally.

She stared out of the window, watching the lights of the cars as they sped past on the opposite carriageway. They were getting closer to Cape Town now and traffic was increasing. Of course... it was Friday evening. She was acutely aware that Mark was waiting for some sort of response from her. She tried to think carefully, but she was wary and needed more time. She wanted to say the right thing to him. But what was the right thing? She knew she now loved him for sure. More than anything else, she wanted to spend the rest of her life with him, but could she leave Ronnie? And what about the children? It was too confusing.

"Mark, I do love you. Actually too much, and I want you... also too much. But I don't know what to do. There's Ron, the children, Ron's parents." She struggled to find the right words. "It would be hard to leave Ron now, especially when he's in so much trouble." She couldn't look at him, just kept on looking out of the window. She'd given it a lot of thought after he'd asked her to move down to Cape Town with him, and she hadn't been able to come up with a solution then either. It was all very difficult.

Mark filled the silence. "We've got the whole of tomorrow to think and to talk about it. As for your girls, I'd look after them as if they were my own." She could see his profile against the streetlights they passed. "... Jack would soon get to like your girls. He's a gregarious kid and used to ask for a brother or '*even* a sister', as he put it." He took her hand, lifting it to his lips. They took the route through the City on their way to his home at Clifton. It could become her home too…

* * *

The whole weekend was just as wonderful as the first they'd spent together, but bittersweet. On their last night Mark took her out for dinner at one of the area's best seafood restaurants. Their table was angled against the curved windows and the views were spectacular. The waves crashed below them. It was almost like being on the prow of a ship. Mark recommended the Cape speciality, abalone. It was even better than she remembered from the one occasion when she'd enjoyed the seafood during her student days. By now, they were completely at ease in each other's company.

Gradually, marriage had become a reality. He wanted her to move down to Cape Town with the children, and she agreed it would be the right thing to do.

"But I don't know how or when," she said. "I think the children will settle well after a while, but it will upset my folks and it'll devastate Ron's poor parents. I do like them a lot you know, and it's going to hurt them so much." But she accepted Mark's judgment of the long-term future for Rhodesia. After all, it coincided with her own.

"We may even have to leave Africa altogether," he said.

"Where on earth could we go?" Her parents would be really upset if they did that, although she knew her father was already concerned about Africa.

"I'm working on it. Possibly Australia."

"That's so far away, and I've never been there. Not that I've been to many places anyway. Just the UK with my folks when I finished 'A' levels and before I came to Uni."

"When we're together, we'll all go and have a look."

"I don't know when I'll be able to do it, Mark."

"Shall I come up and we do it together?" he offered.

"NO! I mean, I don't know." She was sure Ronnie would be very aggressive if Mark was there, and was afraid the two men might fight. "Please just give me time and I'll think of something." Mark smiled and kissed her. He said he'd wait, but begged her not to leave it too long.

Angie caught her flight and was less nervous of meeting someone this time. She felt quite fatalistic about the whole thing now. There was no question in her mind that she and Mark were soul mates. 'Made for each other', as the old folk would say. It would be so easy, especially if their affair was discovered. She wouldn't fight it – just admit it and endure any consequences that came as a result. But deep inside, she wasn't sure if she could expose her children – and the families – to a broken marriage…

* * *

"How was Umtali, dear?" Kate asked when Angie arrived at the farm that evening. She almost gaffed then, her mind so full of what she and Mark had decided, that she'd forgotten all about Umtali and the tennis.

"Oh, just fine, thank you. Um… we did quite well against them." She ad libbed. She hated lying and knew she was no good at it, but Kate didn't seem to notice.

"We've got some good news for you," she beamed. "Ronnie phoned and confirmed he's coming out on Friday, and he's looking forward to seeing everyone. I told him where you were, and that I'd be able to give you the good news today." Angie's stomach churned into a tight ball and she gasped with shock.

"We knew you'd be delighted," Kate said, wrongly interpreting Angie's reaction.

"How lovely," Angie managed to say feebly, feeling physically sick with what she was facing. Yet she knew he was due home, so should have been prepared. Everything had seemed so pleasant and easy – until now. Ron's imminent return brought home to her the enormity of what she and Mark were planning to do.

She was now more afraid than she'd ever been in her life. Where should she start? She'd need time to think this through. Meanwhile, the children had to be back for school on Monday.

"Don't go home tonight, Angie. It's not safe for you to travel all that way on your own with the girls at night," Kate said.

"I have to, Kate; I don't want them to miss their first day back at school tomorrow."

"Stay overnight and leave early tomorrow," Peter said.

That pleased Kate. "Yes, I'll wake you at five tomorrow, and I'll help you get the girls up and ready. If you leave at half past five, you'll get them to school on time." Angie went along with the plan

* * *

"I had a great time, Charlie but I'd like to meet up with you this week. How're you fixed for lunch tomorrow?" Angie needed to talk, and she knew Charlie wouldn't beat about the bush. She'd be able to look at the situation more clearly, not being emotionally involved.

They met in town the next day.

"He wants to *marry* you? Whew," Charlie made a mock fan with her hand and waved it in front of her face.

"Yes. And I want to marry him, but I'm not sure how to deal with the upheaval. I don't know how Ronnie, or Ronnie's folks will react – or mine for that matter." Angie took a sip of her orange juice. "I'm sure the children will be OK after a while, Mark is very good with them and they like him."

"Is he as rich as we think he is?" Charlie stirred her gin and tonic.

"I don't know, but he's very well off."

Charlie asked about Mark's wife and Angie explained.

"Well, I'd wait until after his divorce, just to make sure," Charlie said. "And I'd try to find out just how much money he has got."

"I can't do that, Charlie... and I don't care anyway. He's got enough to look after the children and me. He said so and I believe him." The waiter brought their food to the table. "But I do think it's a good idea of yours... for me to wait until after his divorce is through before I do anything here." It was all moving so fast...

Chapter 27

"You'll do," Captain Macclesfield said, after glancing at Sergeant Robson. "I'm inviting you to apply for selection as a Selous Scout, Ron. If you volunteer, you'll have to undergo what is probably the toughest selection programme in the Army."

Ron's 'interview', for that's what it had turned out to be, was clearly over. "I'm interested, but what does a Selous Scout do?" he said. "I've never heard of one."

The officer laughed. "I can't tell you much except that it's undercover, working behind enemy lines actually."

This *was* interesting. "You mean like the SAS?"

"Well, in some respects…" Macclesfield contemplated. "But we have a very different role. We're a new and clandestine unit; that's why you've never heard of us. But I suspect that will change as time goes on." The captain paused to sip at his beer. "Some blokes joined us from the SAS – said they were bored there." He looked directly at Ron. "As a married man with children, you should think very carefully before you volunteer. It's a very dangerous role, and I wouldn't normally invite a family man. But your record is… unusual."

Ron was attracted. This could be what he was looking for. "My wife's parents are wealthy and my folks aren't too badly off either. If anything happened to me, my family would be well taken care of."

Macclesfield studied Ron for a few moments. "OK. The selection process is very demanding," he repeated his warning, "but knowing a bit about you and what you've been through, I think you'll pass."

Sergeant Robson interjected. "After that, you'll have a tougher test to get through – convincing your fellow Scouts, both black and white, that they can trust you with their lives. You won't get to go on any Missions, unless *they* accept you."

"I get along with all *good* soldiers, regardless of colour." He knew some African soldiers he'd trust with his life…

"We know that Ron, or we wouldn't be here," the captain said. "Your current commanding officer phoned our boss about you, so we did a bit of checking. Two of your former subordinates are Scouts, and they both recommended you." Ron wondered who they were talking about, but these men seemed to know their business.

"You finish here on Friday and you're from Salisbury?"

"Yes, sir – both correct."

"There's one problem. There's an intake leaving from Salisbury next Monday, and unless you fail, you won't be back in town again for many weeks. The selection programme is indeterminate, and I know you haven't seen your family for a long time."

Macclesfield looked quizzically at Ron. "Do you want to sign up from Monday morning, or do you want to take leave to be with your family? I don't know when the next intake will be."

There was no way he was going to miss out on this. "I'll be there on Monday, sir. Where, what time, and who do I report to?" The family would have to wait. He'd have a weekend with them at least.

"Oh-eight-hundred at Inkomo Barracks. Ask for Sergeant Robson here, and he'll arrange for you to join the others. You'll be travelling together to the training ground." They stood up and said their farewells. "You keep your existing rank as rifleman of course. There's no quick promotion with us." Each man grasped Ron's hand briefly. "Good luck, Ron. I'll see you again when you're through selection."

* * *

Late that Friday afternoon, Ron's lift dropped him off outside the railway station in Salisbury. The station itself was packed with Africans, many waiting to take the long distance train for Ruwa, Marandellas and other stops, terminating at Umtali. Even more waited for the Bulawayo train. There were a few drunks to avoid at the entrance. Plus the ubiquitous vegetable and fruit sellers, their wares spread along the pavement outside. He found a pay phone and called Angela, then bought a banana from an old African woman vendor. Angela sounded strangely subdued, and he wondered if she'd somehow got to hear about him not being able to stay home for more than a few days? Nah – she couldn't have. Must be his imagination...

A separate crowd of African commuters streamed past, making their way down both sides of Railway Avenue, towards the Victoria Street bus station. These would be shop and office workers going home. There was the usual litter; discarded mealie cobs and leaves, banana skins, orange and naartjie peel, mango skins and pips, everywhere.

The big shops in First Street closed at five, but Railway Avenue was still open for business. 'V J Patel General Stores', 'Naidoo Gentlemen's Outfitters', and so on. Advertising "Special Offers" to attract customers... with full wage packets, or able to repay wanela – credit. He was the only white to be seen; all the others would be driving home – or at the bars in the various hotels and sports clubs. Too early for nightclubs.

Angela drove up outside the station, and got out to greet him. Christ, he'd forgotten how pretty she was. He kissed her before throwing his kit into the boot. She tasted good too. Emma and Joanne got out of the back of the car. They seemed a little hesitant. Joanne, always the more boisterous, was the first to smile and give him a kiss. Emma followed suit. They'd both grown. He put his head in the back door but Helen was shy, and although she kissed him at Angela's prompting, he could tell she wasn't too sure about it. Hardly a rapturous welcome, but what else could he expect after such a long time?

"Do you want to drive?" Angela asked.

"No thanks. You go ahead." He climbed into the passenger seat.

"You've lost weight. But you look very well otherwise."

"I'm fine. How about you... and you kids?" He twisted round and looked over the back of the seat at them. He felt strangely detached, as if he wasn't really part of this all-female family group.

"How's school, Emma, Joanne? What classes are you in now?" They told him. "What about you Helen, are you at school yet?"

"She's too young," Emma answered for her. "She still goes to playgroup." Everyone relaxed.

Angela turned into Kingsway. "I thought we'd have the weekend at home together. On Monday, we can leave the children with my folks for a couple of days – that's so they don't miss any school – and we'll go out to the farm. Your parents have missed you."

"What I need right now is a good bath and a few beers. We'll have to go out tomorrow to see the folks." Might as well get this over with, he decided. "I go back into the Army on Monday, I'm afraid." He tensed, waiting for her to start.

She looked at him, clearly taken aback. "Oh, Ronnie. How can they do that to us? You've been away since the middle of December last year!" He saw her colour, the first sign of her annoyance, but she was taking it rather better than he expected. "That's six months, almost to the day, and all you get is a weekend off. It's not fair."

"Sorry, it can't be helped. I'm joining a specialist unit and they've only got this one intake, starting Monday." He had to make it clear this was not negotiable.

Now her blush deepened and spread – he knew she was angry. "Your folks are going to be *very* upset. And so are mine, they're looking forward to having the girls." She turned into Prince Edward Street. The route was busy and she concentrated on her driving before speaking again. "I phoned Mr Smith at Farmer's Co-op to explain." She still seemed to be trying to find a way out. "He said there's no need for you to report for work until Monday week."

Ron had almost forgotten the name of his civilian boss. "There's no way we can do it... Sorry." He thought he'd better sound conciliatory. They drove in silence for a while.

There was a long pause. "So when did this happen?" Angela's neck still showed the telltale flush of anger, and her eyes narrowed as she turned to look at him. "Did you have any say in it?"

"Last Saturday. Um... yes, I could never go back to ordinary civilian life," he admitted. She stared straight ahead as she drove on in silence, but her jaw was fixed in that angry mode of hers. There was no point trying to talk to her when she was like this. In any event, he was determined, no matter what. They pulled into the driveway.

The house looked smaller than he remembered, and felt cramped.

He ran a bath, while Angela disappeared to do something or other. He was in the bath by the time she came back.

"Here's a fresh towel." She hung it on the rail. "Would you like a cup of tea, or a beer? I've stocked up for you." She seemed to have calmed down. That was good. He could do without one of their rows.

"Later," he said, kneeling to wash his hair. That didn't take long. It was short-cropped, Army style. He climbed out of the bath and briskly rubbed his lean frame dry. That felt good.

Throwing the wet towel onto the wash basket, he went through to the bedroom. Angela was there; she was busy emptying his kit bag, piling the dirty clothing to one side, ready for the houseboy to wash. "Where are the girls?"

"They're playing in the garden." Her almost elfin figure had always turned him on. Such a small waist. Must be all that tennis. He walked over and pulled her towards him until her bottom was pressed against his naked body. He moved his hands up inside her shirt, and lifted her bra easily to free her breasts. They too were small, but firm.

"Let me close the door first." She pulled away from him to close and lock the door. He took her in his arms again, and kissed her mouth. She felt very soft and supple, and he began fumbling with her belt and jeans.

"Wait. I'll do it," she said, but he was in a hurry, and pulled them off impatiently. He threw her jeans and panties aside and pressed her onto the bed, spreading her legs apart with his knees as he did so.

"Please be careful, Ronnie. I'm sure I'm still dry inside."

But she wasn't. His cock slipped in easily and he thrust into her. He'd forgotten how warm and accommodating it was inside a woman.

"Aaah... damn," he shot his bolt after just a few thrusts. There was no stopping it. He rested his weight on top of her, keeping still but pushing in as far as he could. Despite being fitter than he'd ever been in his life before, he was breathing heavily. She lay still under him. No reaction. He guessed she needed to get used to having a man in bed with her again. After all, like him, she'd been without sex for six months.

"Did you enjoy that?" she asked quietly. He didn't reply, not wanting to interrupt the sheer pleasure of release.

But then his penis started to shrink. "It was good. But I came on too quickly for my liking. Been hanging onto it for too long, I suppose." Time to get up and clean up. "Never mind... we'll do it again later, and then I'll take my time. I could do with a few of those beers now." He got up, and went through to the bathroom.

* * *

Angie was furious. He didn't give a damn for her or the children. All he cared about was himself and that damned Army of his. Her body was rigid with anger as she tidied the bed. Charlie was right; he was a bastard and he didn't deserve them. She dressed, combed her hair, and went out to the living room to check on the children.

They were still playing in the garden. The outside light was on, and it was not too cold yet. All their running about would be keeping them warm anyway. She looked at her watch.

That whole episode in the bedroom had hardly taken more than a few minutes. She thought about Mark, and their long loving sessions. They couldn't be more different. Now, she felt as if she'd betrayed Mark and shivered at the thought of what she'd just done. Oh, God, she felt awful. She paused to calm herself down, and Ron joined her in the living room, beer in hand.

"What's for supper?" he asked as he sat in his chair. He was wearing a pair of shorts, with a jersey over his shirt, but no shoes or socks.

"I thought you'd like steak and chips, but I haven't cooked them yet."

"That's great. I'm ready to eat any time you are." He looked skinny, and in bed she'd felt his hard unyielding body, as he'd thrust against her. He hadn't even waited for her to take her top off. She felt used and discarded.

"The children need to be bathed and fed first. Why don't you do that while I get started on supper?"

"My fathering skills are a bit rusty, so I'll wait while you do it. I'm thirsty anyway, and it'll give me time for a few more beers."

* * *

In bed that night, Angie thought a lot about what Ron's going into the Army full-time would mean for her and the children. He'd be away most of the time now. She'd have to raise the girls virtually on her own and with very little money. Army pay was notoriously poor. There were married quarters, which would save money as the houses were subsidised. But they were awful, drab places, where your husband's rank counted for everything, and you counted for nothing. His rank would fix her place and that of their children in that closed military society. She remembered they'd 'cashiered' him; that meant he wasn't even a junior officer anymore. But regardless, she knew she couldn't bring herself to move to married quarters.

Any plans she might have had of trying to get their marriage back on track would now be impossible. He'd be away more than ever. She realised she'd be tempted to see more and more of Mark. But would Mark be prepared to keep coming up to see her? After all, he wanted to marry her; she wanted him too. All that bound her to Ronnie now was the children. She could end up losing Mark altogether and living a sort of half-life with the girls until they grew up, leaving her alone with a husband who she hardly ever saw, and who she didn't even like anymore, much less love. Eventually, she fell asleep, her mind in turmoil.

* * *

The conversation became heated in the dining room that evening at the farm.

"I don't think this business of you going straight back into the Army virtually on a full-time basis is a good thing, son," Peter said. "Apart from Angie and the children, there's your civilian career to think about."

"The Farmer's Co-op have already written to say they won't be able to hold my job open for me, Dad. Besides, it's what I want to do."

Angie couldn't believe her ears. "That's not completely true, Ron." She couldn't help intervening, but chose her words carefully. "Your old position has gone, but Mr Smith definitely said they'd find something else for you."

Ron waved his hand dismissively. "Probably some junior role. And anyway, I'm not going back there. I couldn't face the boredom of a civilian job again."

"You're being bloody selfish, thinking only of yourself." Peter Cartwright's anger was evident, and Angie knew that Ron would respond... equally angrily.

"Come and join us on the farm instead," Kate interrupted, obviously trying to prevent the brewing row. "You know your Dad needs help, and Angie being here would be wonderful for us."

"Sorry, Mom, I'm committed. And I don't want to be a farmer, Dad."

Kate turned towards Angie. "Then you and the children must come to live with us, Angie. Ronnie can come here when he's not on duty with the Army," she said. "At least you won't be on your own then."

Angie knew that wouldn't work. She'd be even more isolated and lonely on the farm. "No thank you, Kate. The children must be closer to school, and I have my folks nearby."

"God help us, our son is behaving like a fool." Peter scraped his chair back roughly, and got up to pour himself another whisky. He hardly ever drank after dinner.

"Excuse me. I'm off to bed," Ronnie said and got up from the table. It was only half past eight, and they'd just finished eating.

"Won't you have some coffee first, Ronnie?" Kate tried to keep him with them, but he made for the door.

"Good night, all."

"Leave him be, dear." Peter took Kate's chair, and they went through to the sitting room. Moses followed with the coffee shortly afterwards.

Angie excused herself as soon as she decently could, and went out into the garden. She walked until she found herself by the bench where Mark had first kissed her. She sat down and thought about her next move. She hadn't expected it to come to this quite so soon. Thank goodness they had decided to leave the children with her folks this morning, before they drove out to the farm. She felt a chill in the air and wrapped her arms around herself, wishing Mark was there to take her in his arms instead. Winter was approaching.

Ron was asleep when she got back indoors. She took her nightdress, and moved across to the room the children normally used. She knew what she had to do.

* * *

"Are you determined to go away and join this special unit, Ronnie?" Angie asked next morning. She'd persuaded him to take a walk with her after breakfast.

"Yes."

"I can't live with that."

He kept walking, saying nothing.

Angie walked faster, jogging every so often to keep pace with him. "Ronnie, I *said* I couldn't live with your decision to go away."

"You'll have to learn to."

"No, I'm serious. If you join the Army full-time tomorrow, our marriage will break up."

He stopped and looked down at her. She moved to stand in front of him, looking up to meet his eyes with hers. He showed no emotion, but she could feel her own face burning, hot despite the chill of the morning. Her heart was pounding in her chest, and she felt faint. But she stood her ground. He turned aside to pass her, but she moved again to block his way. She had to take a stand.

"Are you trying to threaten me?"

"No. Just stating a fact." She could feel her nails digging into the palms of her hands and hurting, but she needed to grip onto something to give her strength.

"What do you mean, 'our marriage will break up'?"

Angie gathered all her courage and said "I mean I'll leave you... and I'll take the children with me."

"You want a divorce?"

She couldn't bring herself to actually say it. "If you go away and join this secret unit you're talking about, it will come to that." In spite of everything, it seemed a huge step to take.

"I wondered why you didn't come to bed last night," he said quietly. He paused as if waiting for a reply, but she stayed silent, battling with her emotions. "You've been planning this for some time haven't you?"

"Your decision to go away has forced me into it." She avoided the question, more confidently than she felt.

"What do you want me to say?"

"Do you want me and the children... or do you want the Army?"

"You mean I have to choose?"

She paused before answering. "Yes." What else could she say?

He appeared to relax. "Why can't I have both?" Angie could see a smile flickering across his face. He was mocking her. She struggled to control her anger, but stiffened her resolve.

"Ron, I'm not playing games. I stood by you when you were forced to go into the Army, but I'm not going to if you *choose* to be a full-time soldier." He tried to pass her again, but she moved to stop him. Now she could see he was beginning to get angry.

"Get out of my way," he snapped.

"No ...You must tell me what you want." She could see him struggling with himself.

He started slowly. "You can have your bloody divorce. Now get out of my way..." She hesitated for a moment, wondering if she should ask him to talk to his parents. But her courage failed her, and she looked away while he brushed past.

* * *

"Oh no; surely you can work it out?" Poor Kate was very upset. Ron had been very blunt when telling them at the lunch table.

"Angela is determined, Mum. There's nothing I can do about it."

"No, Ronnie. I asked you not to join the Army full time. You don't have to do it." She knew she was partly responsible, but refused to be the only one taking the blame. Ron's 'affair' with the Army had started long before she'd met Mark.

"What about the children?" Peter asked. Kate looked as if she might cry.

Angie waited for Ron to reply, but he didn't. So she said "I'll look after them of course."

"Where will you be living?"

"I'm not sure yet, Kate. I haven't had time to think anything through," Angie lied.

"You can keep the house," Ron said. "I'll live in Army single quarters.

"Are you sure you two can't work something out?" Kate sounded quite desperate and she looked from Angie to Ron as if seeking some sign of compromise.

"Yes, surely you can come to some agreement?" Peter added. Ron stayed silent, so Angie felt she had to respond again.

"Ronnie says he won't change his mind. I've always given way to Ronnie before, but this is going too far."

Lunch ended gloomily on that note, and Angie went to pack their things. She deliberately left Ron alone with his folks. When she finished, she found them in the sitting room. Kate had been crying.

"Let's go," Ronnie said. "I'll keep in touch, Mum... Dad."

It was very awkward, saying goodbye to Ron's parents. There could be no doubt that Kate blamed Angie for the marriage breaking up. Peter seemed less hostile, and he asked her to bring the children to visit them whenever she could.

"Of course I will, Peter, Kate." Angie responded readily to Peter's request, but she wondered how well she herself would be received – especially when they found out about Mark. She'd probably have to leave the children at the farm and go back home. It was going to be even more difficult trying to explain things to the girls. Well, she'd just have to face these problems as they came. There was no going back now... or was there? Could she really go through with this? It would be so much easier to just go along with Ronnie's plans. No one need ever know about Mark, the girls' lives wouldn't be disrupted. Her relationship with Kate and Peter would soon be mended. But could she spend the rest of her life with Ronnie, when she was in love with Mark? She knew that would never change...

Chapter 28

They drove out to Inkomo barracks on Monday morning, arriving 20 minutes early. Ron was perplexed. True, they'd not been very happy lately. Angela was always complaining about his interest in the Army. However, she eventually seemed to have accepted it. He supposed going full-time would be a bit upsetting for her, but he hadn't expected his marriage to break up over it. Still, he was damned if he'd allow her to upset his plans, or interfere with his decisions.

Their farewell was civilised, but cool. "I'll look after myself from now on, so you won't be hearing much from me," he told her.

On the drive back from the farm yesterday, she had pestered until he agreed with the general terms of their divorce. She'd seemed most concerned about the children. She could have them as far as he was concerned. What would he do with them?

He felt hardly more than a hollow gripe in the pit of his stomach; the children seemed of only background importance. There was something about Angela he couldn't fathom. Now he thought about it, she had seemed distant and more independent when he arrived home on Friday. He'd dismissed this change as being caused by her being on her own for such a long time. He recalled his mother had told him that Angela had been away for the previous weekend – a tennis club event in Umtali. Not typical of her at all. It was little strange. But then, it didn't matter anymore.

She interrupted his thoughts. "I'll take your things out to the farm over the next few weeks."

"Yes." They'd agreed that already.

"I'll leave your car in the garage, so you've got transport when you get back here in Salisbury." They'd agreed that on the drive home yesterday too. This was getting tedious. It was almost as if she didn't want to end it.

"OK. Now I must get going... bye." He turned away and walked into the barracks, glad to escape. Had she been trying to get him to change his mind, even at this late hour? There was no way he was going to pass up this chance. But perhaps she'd come round. She always had before. Having a wife and family to come home to was a nice little bonus after a stint in the bush. Maybe this was just a small setback? He really didn't think she'd want to go through with it.

Sergeant Robson was there, and told him to wait in a long lecture room nearby. Eight others were already there. He immediately felt at home. "Morning," he said. The others nodded their greeting, and they sat quietly talking while more men filed in. At one minute past eight, Captain Macclesfield arrived to address them. Everyone fell silent.

"The boss is with General Walls this morning," he said, "so you'll have to make do with me instead." Walls was the commander of the Rhodesian Army. "This is one of the first organised receptions for volunteers to the Selous Scouts. A few Scouts are already out there, and operational on a small scale. It's proved to be highly successful, and the unit is now scheduled to grow rapidly." Ron watched Macclesfield pause to look around the group. The officer seemed to know several of those present. He nodded recognition at Ron, who returned the compliment.

"You men are the first to undergo our newly developed selection process. It's designed to be tough." He paused. "*Very* tough. For good reason... you'll need to be able to cope with extreme conditions if you become an operational Scout. Even though some of you have been invited here based on your reputation, I don't expect more than five or six of you to pass." He paused again.

Ron recalled his own recent interview with the captain. Now it sounded as if they'd been on the lookout for potential recruits throughout the Army. They must be really serious about this new unit, and there must be powerful backing, for them to be allowed to recruit from other units.

"You can withdraw from the selection process at any time. There'll be no shame in dropping out. If anyone back at your home unit criticises you for not succeeding, I suggest you ask them why they haven't had the guts to try themselves. Finally, and whatever happens, I want to thank you all for volunteering." He answered a few questions and left.

Ron was impressed. No one in the Army had ever thanked him for anything before. But then a quartermaster took over and there was more talk, followed by the usual snail-like military documentation and admin processes.

Later, each man was issued with a single 24-hour ration pack. Ron opened his, and stowed the various supplies separately around his webbing and rucksack. He kept everything, from the packet of mashed potato powder to the tubes of condensed milk, margarine and jam; the tinned ham, even the rock hard 'dog biscuits'. He'd brought several fresh onions from the vegetable rack at home. Uh…uh, not *his* home any longer. Also stowed neatly away in his pack were two half-jacks of brandy.

"Hey, Ron!" Dennis Martins, a soldier he'd known some years ago, greeted him. They renewed their acquaintanceship, and kept together for the rest of the typically slow admin procedure at Inkomo that morning. Dennis was carrying several dozen beers, which filled his rucksack. But he discarded most of his rat pack.

"Want any of this stuff, Ronnie?"

"Yeah, thanks. Sure you aren't going to want it?"

"Nah. You know me, I'm happy to live on beer." Ron helped himself to most of Dennis' rations and stowed them carefully. Only discarding the tin of baked beans and the pilchards – both his least preferred – in consideration of space, and the weight he was carrying. There were sure to be some unpleasant surprises for them by way of route marches and so on, with full packs, during the course.

Two Bedford trucks rolled up, and Robson told them to get on board.

"Hey, sir…" Ron turned and recognised Sergeant Mike Njube.

"Mike." Shit, it was good to see his friendly face. "I'm not 'sir' anymore. But it's good to see you again. How are you?"

"I'm fine thanks. How about you?"

"I see you're a Scout. Congratulations."

"We heard you were coming to join us and we're glad. You'll always be 'sir' to us."

"Who else are you taking about?"

"Corporal Zimunya – Herbie. He knows you're coming, but he's away on a Mission. It's just me that's on instruction and selection duty this time."

"You must leave me to pass selection on my own, sarge."

"Yes. I've already been assigned to work with a different group. Good luck, sir."

Mike climbed into the driving seat of the leading Bedford, and Ron got into the back of the second truck. He'd make bloody sure no one could accuse him of benefiting from favouritism. But this explained the remarks made by Macclesfield during his interview last week. Mike and Herbie must have recommended him.

There were 18 volunteers, so they had plenty of room. Each truck could easily have carried half a dozen more men. Ron noticed with interest that almost half were Africans. It was already after midday, and the morning had been all but wasted. This was not a good omen, and Ron feared this new outfit would be as disorganised as the rest of the Army.

They took the Lomagundi road leading north-west, and headed towards the Great Dyke. He had taken the route many times before. It was a soporific journey. Ron dozed, but he kept waking to see where they were going. He had the soldier's knack of resting when he could, so as to be ready for whatever the Army chose to throw at him. But he also retained his natural instinct – to stay aware of what was going on around him, and where he was, at all times.

About 300 kilometres north-east of Salisbury, they turned off at Makuti and took the main road down towards Kariba Dam. Interesting. This was outside the normal terrorist operating area. They ground down the winding escarpment road until their truck came to a halt at a dirt track leading off the main road.

"Everybody off!" Sergeant Robson, who was driving Ron's truck, shouted. "Camp is by the lake shore, 25 kilometres down this road. Take all your gear with you. Anything left behind on the truck will be dumped here, and anything you drop on the way to camp will be treated as abandoned." He checked the back, jumped into the cab, and followed Mike's empty truck, rattling down the dusty road.

The sun was already low in the western sky, and Ron could see this was wild country. A few kilometres back they'd seen a pair of lions, actually chasing after the leading truck for a brief period. The volunteers laughed and shouted, flapping their hats over the tailgate at them. After a few hundred metres the lions, a magnificent male and a snarling female, tired of the chase, and stopped at the side of the road. There were piles of fresh, steaming elephant dung everywhere.

But it was unlikely there'd be any terrorists in this area. Ron settled his pack and set off at a steady pace, his rifle resting comfortably over his right shoulder. He could easily swing it down to fire if necessary. He started near the middle of a group, but they slowly spread out. It was pitch dark within half an hour. Ron now suspected that the delays at Inkomo had been deliberate, so they'd have to find their way to the camp in the dark. He passed a few men and one passed him, but this was not a race. He soon found himself running alone.

An hour and a half after the start, he caught up with Dennis, who was sitting on the side of the track having a smoke. In the glow of the cigarette, Ron looked closely, and saw that his boots were off. His feet were dark with blood.

"Shit... hard luck, man. Is there anything I can do for you?"

"My feet are buggered," Dennis said unnecessarily. "But I'll be OK, thanks." He raised something to show Ron. "I've got plenty of beers to keep me going."

"Cheers." Ron got moving again. Pity, Dennis was an early failure. Despite being May, and early evening, the sweat trickled down his face. It was more muggy than hot. They were running through very broken country, north-west towards Lake Kariba. He let his legs go faster as he went down each hill, and pushed doggedly uphill, slowing steadily until he reached the top. He deliberately didn't force his pace, preferring to maintain a momentum that took account of the conditions. In the starlight, he could just make out the thick bush on either side. Metre high grass grew between the two wheel tracks that comprised the road; this track was not used often.

His own steady breathing dominated his hearing, but occasionally the whooping call of a hyena intruded. He could not gauge how near, or far it was. Then the sawing snarl of a leopard close by caused his hair to stand on end. The hunting leopard was as much to be feared as any animal. He slapped the magazine on his rifle with each step, trusting the metallic sounds to warn the night killer off. After a while it could be heard no more. Either it was closing in for an attack, or it had moved elsewhere.

"Christ!" he called out involuntarily, when he stumbled over something in the road. He looked back and saw a big black mass on the track behind him. The rich smell of fresh elephant dung assailed his nostrils, and he realised he'd put his foot in a heap. Steady, he warned himself.

At last, he saw lights in the bush ahead, and ran the last few metres.

"Welcome to '*wafa, wafa; wasara, wasara*'." A deep voice greeted him quietly.

"Christ, it's good to see you, Mike." Ron drew deep breaths; in truth he'd recognised Mike's voice, rather than being able to see his ebony face in the dark. "What the hell does all that mean?"

"Wafa means 'I am dead'. And wasara is the shout of fear that people give when lions come marauding into their village. That is the name the Shona people have given to this camp, because of all the wild animals here."

"It's well named then."

"There's your accommodation," Sergeant Njube pointed apologetically.

"Where?" Ron could see nothing but bush.

"Here." Mike walked a few paces and indicated a place where there appeared to be clear ground under some of the surrounding bushes. No beds and no bunks. Not even any blankets. The sound of heavy footfalls approached the camp. "I must leave you now, sir."

He turned away. "Over here, soldier…" Ron heard him greet another volunteer.

Chapter 29

Mark put the phone down and leant back in his chair. There was no question about it, she was fantastic, sorted everything on her own in double quick time. What a woman. He could hardly believe it had happened so quickly. His greatest fear had been that Angie's resolve would fail once she got home. Her family loyalties were very strong, and he was always conscious that would be a major sticking point. Now he hoped she'd not have too many difficulties with her parents. Old Greville himself probably wouldn't be too pleased, but he guessed her mother would take it better. What would *his* mother think?

He got up and stood at the window beside his desk. The view across the city and Table Bay was magnificent. A south-easter was getting up, and white horses were beginning to appear, far out in the bay. He couldn't see the mountain from this side of the building, but knew the 'tablecloth' of cloud would soon come boiling over from the far side of the mountain. A harbinger of contrary weather.

His thoughts returned to Angie... and her children. What was divorce law like in Rhodesia? Probably easier than here in Calvinist South Africa, but Angie would still need all the help and support he could give her. Especially with her having the children to look after and a possibly hostile, or at least unfriendly husband. Mark was impatient to get on with things, but knew he had to be careful. Angie's divorce could be made more difficult if her husband knew about their affair.

There were more 'white horses' on the water, and he knew the wind must be blowing quite strongly now. A squall blotted out his view of Robben Island. A Marxist African leader, Nelson Mandela had been confined there for the last ten or eleven years. Practically forgotten in South Africa, but a rallying point for South Africa's enemies. There were enough of those. In the long run, he knew he would have to take Angie, and her children out of Africa altogether. And Jack of course, but Anna would never leave; he'd have to work on that. It would certainly not be safe in South Africa once the African Nationalists took over.

He moved back to his desk. Angie had said she could manage things on her own for now. But he was worried. The next few weeks were crucial. Angie's spirit was still fragile, and when the realisation of her actions sank in – would she falter? No... he couldn't let this opportunity slip through his fingers. He pressed the intercom, "Margaret..." he'd clear his diary for the next couple of weeks.

"How's Angie?" Margaret asked as she came in, she'd transferred the call.

"She's fine thank you, but I'm going to have to go up there soon. Let's have a look at my diary." They went through his appointments for the next three weeks.

"So, if we get the rest of this week out of the way, I can take the next two weeks off," he concluded. They would move some meetings forward and others back. Margaret would do most of the rearranging. But they reserved two of the most difficult people for him to deal with personally.

"I suppose I'll be able to contact you in an emergency, Mark?"

"Oh, yes. Book me into Meikle's as usual, please." He hesitated before he continued; "I'm hoping Angie and her children will be able to move down here soon." Margaret maintained her most unflappable and discreet demeanour, but he knew her well enough to see through it. "I know it's a bit unexpected, but it's just happened that way."

"Oh, it isn't unexpected. Just a bit quicker than I thought. I'll get you a coffee."

* * *

Angie was encouraged. She could tell that Mark was really pleased things had happened so soon. She could hardly believe it herself.

Now... her mother. She wasn't looking forward to that, but the worry that Kate might contact her first spurred her on. Angie phoned to make sure she would be home, and pre-warned her that she had something serious to talk about.

Angie pulled up outside her parents' house, and took a deep breath. 'One step at a time', she comforted herself.

* * *

Two hours later Angie was heading into the City. Arranging to have lunch with Charlie had been a good idea. She'd been able to excuse herself just as her mother's questions were becoming really tricky. She found parking in Gordon Avenue, right near the corner with First Street. She was late, but then Charlie was normally late herself.

Not this time; she was waiting at her usual table. "Trouble parking?" She sipped her drink, which Angie knew would be a G&T. Charlie summoned a waiter. "I suppose you want your usual orange or Coke?"

"No, I didn't have any trouble parking. Got one nearby. But I've had a tough morning. Mmmm..." She couldn't decide what she wanted...

"Bring another gin and tonic, please," Charlie told the waiter. "You look as if you need something stronger."

"Just the one then. I've got to keep my wits about me for this evening." Angie sat down and leant back in the chair. She closed her eyes, and took several deep breaths. The winter sun was shining through the partly opened glass roof of the restaurant, making it pleasantly warm. Charlie looked at her quizzically.

"My, we're a bit edgy aren't we?"

"I'm leaving Ronnie. Well... actually, we've separated already."

"Wow ...You just keep surprising me, darling. I never thought you'd do it." Charlie leaned forward and put her perfectly manicured hand on Angie's. "Have a drink first – then I must know everything. *All* the details." She looked at her watch. "I'll phone the girls at the office and tell them I'm taking the afternoon off, so there's no hurry."

"I can't stay too long, Charlie. My mother's asked me to spend the night, and I want to see her again before my Dad gets home." Angie's G&T arrived and she drank deep. "Oooh." She coughed, almost choked and grabbed a glass of water. "It's too strong." Gosh, she didn't remember gin burning like this.

"It's a double. You need it."

No wonder. "But I'm thirsty too." She took another gulp of water. "I'll have a lot of explaining to do tonight, so I need to be wide awake. You know what my Dad's like. Even Mum is being difficult."

"What did she think about you and Mark?"

"I haven't told her about him yet. Mum is speaking to Dad now – about the divorce from Ronnie, that is. She's helping in that way, but she's asking a lot of awkward questions."

Angie explained about her discussions with her mother.

"Let's face it, Angie. The damn Army was always going to take first place with Ron," Charlie said. "The timing's perfect, and you've been really smart using that to get away with it. I don't think I could have handled it better myself."

That was high praise, coming from Charlie. Why didn't she feel good about it?

"I suppose his folks weren't too happy?" Angie shook her head in response. "What about Mark?"

Angie took another sip of her drink. It tasted better this time. She felt warm inside. "I phoned him first thing this morning. He wants to come up to help me face the music when Ron gets back." Her cheeks burned from the warmth of the gin, but she didn't care.

"Oh boy… there'll be some fireworks then."

"I've told him not to. I want to handle it myself, and I don't want any violence; you know what Ron's like. But Mark thinks he can deal with it."

"That'll be fun. I'd love to be a fly on the wall when that happens. And I don't fancy Ron's chances against Mark. When's he due back?" Charlie drained her glass and ordered two more doubles. Angie looked down, and was shocked to see that her own glass was empty.

She resolved to be more careful with the second one. "No, Charlie. I really don't want two grown men fighting over me. I don't know when he's due back. Said he didn't know himself, but it'll probably be five or six weeks again."

"Typical of the bastard. I actually don't think you'll have to do anything at all. Just let Ron come back in his own good time, and find out for himself." Their drinks arrived, and the restaurateur Alphonso, who knew Charlie well, came and left menus for them.

"Why aren't you telling your parents about Mark?" Charlie asked.

"Well… it just seems wrong." Angie wasn't sure herself. She took a sip from the new glass and things became clearer; yes of course. "They'll know that it's Mark and me causing the break up, not just Ronnie and the Army. That's why." Oh God; that came out so cold-hearted and scheming. Was she really that bad? Tears came to her eyes.

"Don't cry, Angie. It's good news and Ron never deserved you in the first place." Charlie got up and came round to put her arms around her. She could smell Charlie's perfume, it was lovely; must be very expensive. Tears began to run down her face, and Charlie grabbed a tissue for her. "Here, you're lucky you don't have to contend with mascara." Angie dried her eyes and cheeks.

"Come on and buck up. You mustn't blame yourself. It really is Ron's fault, you know. If he'd been a better husband, you probably wouldn't have got involved with Mark in the first place."

Charlie was a loyal friend. "Yes, but I'm lying about why we're breaking up." Angie dabbed her eyes again.

"Better that way. And it's only your parents and me who need to know. Have another drink to cheer you up."

Charlie lifted her glass. "Here's to your future happiness!"

Angie joined her in the toast and felt better.

"Let the rest find out about Mark later, and they'll never know that your affair with him has been going on for so long."

Angie got up to go to the ladies' to recover her composure, and wash her face. Charlie came with her.

They got back to their table to find two fresh G&Ts waiting. "Alphonso's looking after us, I see," Charlie said. "Let's have a look at the menu. And while we're waiting for the food, why don't you tell me what you're planning to tell your folks?

Angie smiled inwardly, Charlie enjoyed a challenge. She liked to believe she was in charge. It suited Angie to let her get away with it. As usual, she'd listen – but make her own decisions in the end.

* * *

"Mark?" Angie spoke carefully to stop her words slurring. She shouldn't have driven, but she'd felt all right on the way home.

"Hello, darling. How did you get on?"

"I'm a bit unsteady on my feet. Charlie plied me with gin all through lunch."

"I wondered where you'd got to. It's half past three. Have a strong coffee as soon as we've finished talking, sweetheart. Have a lie-down too."

"I've told Mum about Ronnie and me separating, and she'll have told my father by now. I'm going to spend the night there to talk over everything."

"Good. You sure you don't want me to come up?"

"Not yet. Let me see what they say. I'll phone you tomorrow. Will you be at the office again?"

"Yes. I'll bet Charlie enjoyed herself."

"Yes, she had four gins to my three. Doubles too."

"You know what I mean – she'd have loved the scandal."

"Yes, that too."

"Three *double* gins? Goodness, no wonder you're unsteady on your feet. You're not used to it like Charlie. Go have that coffee, and don't forget to set the alarm, or there's no knowing when you'll wake up."

He knew her low capacity for alcohol. "Just now Mark, it's good to hear your voice... I'm missing you." She'd had two coffees at the restaurant with Charlie anyway. Thank goodness they'd refused Alphonso's offer of liqueurs. He'd thought they were celebrating which, in a manner of speaking, they were.

They chatted for a while longer, but she ran out of steam and didn't feel well.

Must get a grip. She went for a shower, to try and clear her head. There was no time to lie down. This was all happening too fast. How would the children react? Would they be very distressed? The next days were going to be very hard. Her problems had hardly begun. Her knees gave way as a black cloud of depression overwhelmed her and she slid down onto the shower floor, sobbing. Resting her head on her knees, she could feel the water pouring down her curved back. It was all too much...

In time, her crying eased and she stood up. Feeling better now, she knew she'd be able to cope. Yes... she was going to go through with it. Otherwise, she'd become a drab Army housewife, shifting from one camp to another for the rest of her life. It was best for the children too. They deserved a better life, and with Mark she could give that to them. Her mind was made up. In the end, it was going to be worth all the heartbreak.

* * *

"How did it go with Dad?" Angie asked, watching while her mother dealt with the children at their supper in the kitchen. Her father would be home soon, and she wanted to find out how the land lay.

"Do be more careful, Joanne. Now look. You've made Helen

spill." Her mother was distracted.

"Joanne," Angie intervened, "what do you say?"

"Sorry, Granny." Joanne didn't look at all contrite, and Angie gave her a warning look.

"I've finished, Granny. Can I go and watch television now?" Emma wanted to know.

"I've finished too." Joanne stuffed the last of her supper into her mouth.

"Go on then, but don't make a mess," her mother cautioned. "Well, he says he's been expecting something for a while now. He knows how unhappy you've been. Thought it might come to a head when Ron went into that jail."

"Brady Barracks," Angie prompted her. "No... I couldn't possibly have done it while he was in prison. That just wouldn't have been right."

"Have you had enough to eat, Helen?" She had, so her mother lifted her off the chair, wiped her face, and the little one ran off happily to join her sisters. In too much of a hurry to have absorbed the conversation.

"No, you're quite right, it wouldn't. Still, your Dad's taken it better than I expected."

"Mum... there's something else I have to tell you." Angie steeled herself.

"What, dear?" She sounded as if she'd been expecting something more.

"I'd rather we spoke in private." Angie didn't want the servants hearing.

They went through to the sewing room. A feeling of déjà vu came over Angie. This was where her mother had disciplined her four children in the old days. She felt apprehensive; how would her mother react?

Her mother sat quietly, hands clasped loosely on her lap, saying nothing. Angie tried twice to come up with the right words. Her rehearsed speech seemed so inadequate now. The silence went on... Angie bit her lip.

"What is it, dear? Whatever it is, it's obviously causing you a lot of distress." Her mother took her hands and held them gently. They were cool, dry and capable. She wished she had her mother's composure.

"I'm in love with someone else," she blurted it out. "It's Mark."

Her mother took a deep breath. "How long has this been going on?"

"It started at the Cartwright's farm; maybe even before that, when he came to dinner here. We were attracted to each other, and things slowly developed after that."

"Those weekends you went away?"

Angie nodded, "Yes, I was with him." It might as well all come out now.

"Who else knows about this?"

"Hello everyone, I'm home." It was her father. He popped his head round the door. "Oops. Sorry. I'll be in the sitting room when you're ready."

He had always been careful not to interrupt when her mother was 'speaking' to Angie, or one of her sisters in the sewing room. What would he think of her? She drew comfort from the fact that he'd stood by her when she got into scrapes before, no matter what. But would he this time? This was in a completely different league.

"Hello, dear. We'll be a while yet," her mother said, and her father's head disappeared. She turned back to Angie. "He'll need time to shower and change anyway. There's no rush. Now..."

"Only you... and Charlie. Oh, and one of her friends knows a little too."

"Mmmm... yes. I might have known she'd have something to do with it."

"No, Mum. That's not fair. It's nothing to do with Charlie. She just helped me when I asked her to," Angie defended her friend.

"So Mark has been here quite a lot and hasn't come to see Harriet?"

"He and I spent *one* weekend here. Remember when I told you I was going to Inyanga? The second weekend, when I said I was going to play tennis in Umtali, I went to his home in Cape Town instead." She didn't want her mother criticising Mark either. "He felt bad about not seeing his mother, but didn't want to cause problems for me."

"Goodness, you've been taking a lot of risks, my girl." She fell silent.

Angie said nothing. She could see her mother was thinking it through.

"...It's probably best we don't tell your father too much at this stage. He'll have to know about Mark of course, but don't say anything about spending weekends with him." Her mother squeezed Angie's hands. "Your father may not be as understanding as me."

Angie nodded. Her father would be very disappointed.

"Come along then."

"I must get the girls off to bed first."

"Of course, yes. And your father will want to say goodnight to them. We'll move into the study when you've settled them down."

"And what about Harriet?"

"Yes, we'll have to tell Harriet too but no more than we tell your father. It wouldn't be fair." Angie nodded her agreement. Her mother was right on both counts.

"She's bound to suspect there's more to it, but we don't need to tell her the details – not yet anyway." Her mother stood up and Angie went to collect the girls.

* * *

The rest of the evening passed off uneasily. Studiously avoiding any mention of Angie's situation, they all made polite conversation at dinner. But Angie could see that Harriet was bursting with curiosity. Her father soon excused himself, retreated to his chair and became engrossed with the evening paper. Harriet fidgeted distractedly over coffee, while Angie and her mother talked about what next had to be done in the garden. Even that subject soon dried up.

"I've had a very tiring few days." Angie stood up nervously. "I'll run a bath, have an early night..." Her father looked up from his paper and seemed about to say something but, after a pause, shrugged his shoulders and wished her goodnight.

Throughout the night, imagined scenes disturbed Angie's dreams and she slept fitfully. Although she was determined to go through with it, she was beginning to dread Ron's reaction when he eventually heard about her relationship with Mark. He'd surely think that he'd been made a fool of, and his pride would be hurt. He was so unpredictable. She feared he might even turn violent under the circumstances.

Chapter 30

Angie phoned Mark the next morning. Despite not sleeping, she felt refreshed and less anxious.

"How did it go last night?" he asked.

"Not too bad. I told Mum everything." There was no point in relating the tense atmosphere during and after dinner. She hoped her father would be over the shock by the time she next saw him. "But my father and your mother only know that we're in love and that we plan to marry as soon as my divorce comes through." Angie didn't mention that she sensed Harriet was secretly pleased.

"Your mother knows *everything*?"

"Well, I told her we spent the two weekends together."

"But my mother and your father don't know that?"

"That's right. Mum didn't think we ought to tell them, and I agreed. But I'm sure your mother suspects there's more to it."

"I think you're wonderful. Doing everything by yourself."

"Thank you…"

"My divorce came through on Friday last week."

"That's good… isn't it?"

"It's very good. Now I can concentrate completely on you – on us, I mean. I've cleared my diary from this weekend, and I'm flying up on Saturday morning to be with you."

Angie had mixed feelings. "That's wonderful." Where would he stay? What would her father say? What about the children? Much as she wanted to see Mark, she realised that his coming up so soon would add complications. But maybe it was best to get it over with…

"I've booked myself into Meikle's – we'd better be careful until you've made some progress with your own divorce." Mark's steady commonsense was comforting. "We need to talk things over face to face before we decide what to do next, don't you think?"

"Yes, I was going to suggest picking you up from the airport, but I think it'll be more discreet for me to meet you at the hotel. It'll be a lot easier all round if as few people as possible know about us."

"I couldn't agree more; it's going to be difficult enough as it is." He was really coming up trumps. "Angie…" She waited. "It's going to be alright you know. It won't be easy, but we'll come through. You're tougher than you think."

She hoped he was right…

* * *

Angie collected the children from school, and spent the whole afternoon at home. It needed a lot of attention, and she got Samson organised while she worked in the garden. Despite being winter, she felt she had to cut the lawn – it was quite straggly. This was the toughest job and she didn't decide to do it lightly.

When they'd first got the house, Ron had kept saying he'd do it, but he just never got round to it. Eventually there'd been an almighty row, and he'd told her to 'get the bloody houseboy to cut the damn lawn'. That was impossible, and he knew it; houseboys just didn't do gardening, and they couldn't afford a gardener. He could make her so angry at times.

So *she* ended up mowing the lawn. The first time she did it, she waited for Ron to come home and admire her effort. Using a hand-push mower was darn hard work.

But he hadn't noticed and she'd had to point it out to him.

"It doesn't look right," he commented.

"What's wrong with it?" she asked, feeling really put down.

"You're supposed to cut in straight lines, so it looks neat. You know, like at the bowling greens."

Angie's blood boiled, but she curbed her anger – she'd been vaguely aware while she was mowing that something was wrong. And he'd put his finger on it darn him; but he could have been nicer about it.

When her father heard that she was doing the mowing, he'd given her a motor mower, and demonstrated how to use it by cutting the lawn for her one day. But now they didn't have enough petrol coupons to operate it, so she was back to using the hand mower.

"Keeps you fit anyway," Ron said. She cut in straight lines now.

It was quite late in the afternoon by the time she finished, and she stopped for a cool drink. Now the roses and flowerbeds, they were in a mess. But she relished the hard physical work and it helped to ease her mental strain; this might be the last, or at least one of the last times she did this. Making everything neat and tidy, almost as if she was working to leave things in good order before she left. She finished raking up all the dead plants and leaves so she could see what still needed doing. Was it the right time to prune back the roses? Too early probably, but she decided to do it anyway. They looked so forlorn, with bare thorny branches. Her heart filled with emotion; this garden was a part of her life...

Angie went inside to get the secateurs. "You're finished, Samson?"

"Yes, madam." He smiled cheerfully. She sighed to herself. Why couldn't he just have got on with the rest of the chores, instead of sitting in the sun on the back step, doing nothing when he'd finished?

"Right, good... now you must clean the bathroom – thoroughly, please." She went through and showed him the parts that needed attention. "And wash the floors with Dettol. Bring the bucket here and I'll mix it for you." It was no good leaving that to him; he'd use the whole bottle if she did. She got him started, had a cup of tea, gave the children Mazoe Orange squash, took the secateurs, and went back out to the garden.

"Get away from those rose cuttings, you silly girl." Angie stopped to comfort Helen, who'd somehow got a branch full of thorns stuck to her.

"Ooowww... it *hurts*, Mummy!" Helen wailed.

"I know, darling, but you must keep still, or Mummy can't get the thorns out."

Angie carefully extricated Helen from the branch, thorn by thorn and took her into the house to apply antiseptic. "Ooowww... sore, Mummy," she wailed again. But she cheered up when Angie stuck a plaster on each of the scratches.

"Now wash the kitchen floor, please Samson." He'd finished the last task and was standing, watching sympathetically as Angie tended to Helen. It was impossible to get angry with him. He was so fond of the children, and Angie could see that he was struggling not to tell her to be more careful dressing Helen's little scratches.

Angie herself was also covered in scratches. She hadn't been able to find her gardening gloves. And the secateurs weren't too sharp either. Still, she'd finished cutting and only needed to rake everything into a heap. She would burn it all in the backyard tomorrow, after she'd taken the children to school.

It was almost dark by the time she finished. She felt tired, dirty and sweaty, but good. She always found gardening therapeutic.

Angie was resting on the rake when the phone rang, and she ran to get the call.

"Hello, darling. I thought you might like to come over tomorrow morning for tea?"

Angie looked at the damage she'd done to her hands and fingernails. "Ummm... thanks, Mum but I've just finished clearing the garden. I want to burn the cuttings and stuff tomorrow morning, after I've dropped the children off." Her mother would fuss about her scratches.

"Can't you get that lazy houseboy of yours – what's his name – to do that?" she pleaded.

"Samson. Mum, you know what he's like... I'll end up with the house, or the neighbours on fire."

"I was just thinking that we need to discuss what to do next, and your father won't be home, so we'll be able to talk."

Well... with Mark arriving on Saturday, perhaps she'd better go and get it over with. "OK, Mum. I'll leave the bonfire until later then."

* * *

Tea with her mother, and an unexpected invitation to play tennis at the club on Thursday, left Angie with no time to burn the garden rubbish as she'd planned. Well, it didn't matter much. It would probably be less smoky if the stuff dried out a bit more before she did it anyway. She'd enjoyed her game at the club. Took her mind off things for a while.

Friday's meeting with Charlie's lawyer, Mr Solomon, went well.

"Charlie Macdonald's a good client of mine and a friend, Mrs Cartwright. Her introduction is good enough for me," he said when she arrived. But Angie was horrified at his fees, and insisted on phoning Mark from Mr Solomon's office, to see if it would be all right. Mark said they weren't too bad, and to go ahead and appoint him. Thank goodness he was picking up the bill. Trust Charlie to know the most expensive – but also probably the best lawyer in town.

Angie dropped the children off at her parents' home on Saturday morning, before going to meet Mark at the hotel.

Although it had only been two weeks since Cape Town, so much had happened that it seemed like an awfully long time since they'd seen each other. Now that Ron had agreed to a divorce and her parents knew about Mark, Angie felt as though a load had been lifted from her shoulders. Mark organised a lovely lunch in his room, and they shared a bottle of champagne to celebrate. Her mother had invited them both for dinner, and they were still on a high when they drove there, just after six.

"So, it's all arranged, then?" her father said to Mark while he poured pre-dinner drinks.

"As far as we can, sir. There's still a lot to go through, and some of it may not be very easy."

"Well, I suppose you'd know about that better than we do," he said, presumably referring to Mark's recent divorce. Mark said nothing. Her father's body language seemed tense and Angie, puzzled at this development, looked across at her mother.

Harriet must also have picked up on her brother's curtness. "You helped me when I needed it, John."

"I think Angie needs our support now, dear," her mother added quietly.

"Humph..." her father cleared his throat. "Well, *I* think you both ought to think again." There was stunned silence. "You're not thinking enough about the children," he added stubbornly.

Angie was shocked. Her father had given no indication before that he was going to do this to her. "Daddy..." she battled to keep calm and stay rational, "we've thought about it an awful lot already."

There was a determined set to his jaw. "The children will suffer. It's not fair on them," he said firmly.

Angie felt anger taking over from shock. "I think we'd better leave now, Mark." She'd pack her things now and go with him.

"Can't we discuss this?" Mark tried to smooth things over.

"Have dinner with us first, before you go," her mother said.

Angie controlled her anger. "Daddy, if Mark and I promise to think it over again when we're alone, will you listen to what we have to say?" She looked directly at her father, she could be every bit as determined as him.

He moved uncomfortably. "I don't know."

Of course, they could just go ahead, whatever her father said, but now she'd calmed down, Angie hoped to avoid a break with her family. She watched her father struggle with his conscience before he nodded agreement.

"There we are then," her mother said hastily. "Now, let's move into the dining room."

* * *

Dinner was a strained affair, and try as he might, Mark failed to lift the gloom. Aunt Mary and his mother tried too, but no one spoke of the divorce again.

As he left that evening he could see that Angie was still angry. She'd even suggested coming back to the hotel with him. But he persuaded her that it wouldn't be appropriate, and would probably harden her father's feelings against them even more.

Their discussion seemed to have calmed her down. "I'm not going to change my mind about us, Mark," she promised him. "Let's see if Mum can talk him round. And if she can't do it, I will."

She sounded confident, but was she? "We did promise your father we'd talk it over though," he reminded her.

Angie looked at him. He'd never seen her so stubborn. "There's nothing more to talk about. We've been over everything a dozen times. No... I'll just have to persuade my father."

He kissed her goodbye and got into the car. It was going to be a long, lonely night. He wanted Angie more than anything else in the world, but he hated the idea of her breaking up with her parents on top of everything else. They were so close and she would need the support of her family to help her to face the divorce and cope with the distress it would cause the children. Would his love be enough for her? Being responsible for her broken marriage was bad enough. It was not a nice feeling...

Chapter 31

"Fool! Must I do everything for you?" Gadziwa snatched the mortar tube from the man's hand, and adjusted it towards the centre of the white men's camp. He carried on round, checking the 50-millimetre mortars that his men had carried from Chifombo. Though commanding a group of well-trained comrades this time, he wanted to be sure of their first attack. It was a wonderful opportunity to heighten his prestige, before they slipped back into the bush again. Military or civilian made no difference to him or to the hierarchy, but he knew they'd be pleased to be able to point to this as a 'legitimate' target, when they boasted of it to the world media. It would please their Christian supporters, and *they* provided the money used for buying arms.

It was quite dark, but he aligned every one of the four mortars they had towards the place where he believed the vehicles would be parked. "Fire when you hear the first mortar go," he told each man. He would aim and fire the first bomb himself.

Shoving the last comrade aside, he knelt beside his mortar, adjusted the aim and dropped the bomb down the tube.

Phoomp! The small missile fired, and soared over the trees towards the white men's camp. A ragged succession of mortars followed as his boys carried out their orders; Gadziwa supervised the man reloading the weapon he'd fired.

Thud! His first bomb detonated, and he could see by the flash that it had landed near or among the lorries. A further three followed, in the same general area.

"Crack... Crack... Bah-bah-bah," the soldiers responded with their rifles, and a machine gun. Their tracers burned uselessly into the bush, far away from where Gadziwa and his men were. He fired his second bomb, and was loading the third when he saw a big flash, which lit up the night sky. There was a heavy explosion – whump! Then the shockwave reached them.

A fuel bowser or storage tank had gone up. There was a brief moment of shocked silence before all hell broke out, the soldiers firing their weapons in all directions. A few tracers came close to where Gadziwa was squatting; their fire was close to the ground. Even though the enemy couldn't see what they were shooting at, this demonstrated their expertise.

He fired one more bomb. "Take this and go to the meeting place, now!" He shoved the mortar to the man working with him. Then he skirted round to each of the other three positions, telling each team to pack up and get going.

This was a huge success; he'd barely entered Zimbabwe, and they had struck at the major military camp of Mukumbura. This showed how good reconnaissance could help. And not one of his team of eight men was hurt.

He'd spent five long months seeking out and training the best; first in Tanzania and then at Chifombo. Already this work was paying off, and he had more confidence in these men than he'd ever had in a group of comrades before. With these sons of the soil, he could wreak havoc among the settlers.

"Maai-Whe," one of his men called softly, and pointed. There, over a kilometre away, Gadziwa saw the flames of a massive grass fire in the direction of Mukumbura camp. The crackling came softly over the night air.

"We have started well, comrades," Gadziwa praised them. "Now we have far to go. First to get away from these soldiers, and then to reach our real target. This one was just for practice." He led his boys away towards the Mavuradonha Mountains. They would head out of the Zambezi Valley, and up towards the fat white farming areas, high on the plateau above.

* * *

"Scoff's up," the Selous Scouts' officer called out, late one afternoon. They'd been in their remote Kariba selection camp for five days, and no rations of any kind had been issued since that first day back in Salisbury. One by one, volunteers had dropped out as hunger, exhaustion and despair defeated them. They'd trained, run and starved. Ron was better off than the others. He had carefully husbanded that first rat pack, supplemented as it was by Dennis' generous offer, but it only lasted until the third day.

On that day, one of the instructors shot a baboon and hung it by its neck, high in a tree above the camp. The dead animal was still in its skin, and in the fierce heat of the Valley, which winter hardly touched, it was soon bloated with gas. By the end of the next day it had lost its gas, and hung limp and stinking from the tree above their heads. Foul liquids dripped from the carcass onto the soil below, and it was host to its own swarms of flies.

During the last five days, they'd all got hungrier and hungrier. They were burning calories rapidly with the rigorous selection and training programme. Everyone gathered berries, wild spinach and roots, with varying degrees of success.

Ron and another volunteer everyone nicknamed 'Congo Bill', had teamed up and succeeded in trapping a few birds and mice to supplement their vegetable gatherings. Old Madala had taught Ron how to set snares when he was a boy on the farm, but he had never guessed how he'd need that skill in the future.

One day, they even managed to catch a snake. Congo Bill, who had seen service as a mercenary nearly ten years ago in the former Belgian Congo, promptly cut its head off. They gutted it before baking it on hot stones near the fire. Ron was surprised at how good it tasted, but it was not nearly enough for two hungry men.

But now, the officer cut the rotten baboon down, and called the volunteers together. "What's the problem with you men?" He chuckled as he called again. "I said... *scoff's up.*" Ron had an unpleasant suspicion of what was going to happen next, but there was no point in delaying it. "You're going to eat it." The officer indicated someone should butcher the rotten baboon.

Ron walked over to join the officer, and slit the belly with his knife, preparing to gut and skin it. An even fouler stench assailed him and he almost gagged. "You don't expect us to eat *that*?" He saw white maggots writhing in the green, slimy flesh and turned his face aside to avoid the worst of the stink.

"There's nothing else on offer, Ron." The officer squatted beside him and began gutting it. Ron forced himself to help. "Someone get a good fire going."

The other volunteers – there were only nine of them left now – gathered wood and built up the fire in the so-called kitchen. Just a jumble of fairly large stones, Ron had cooked the last of his rat pack and tea there two days ago.

The officer continued. "Suppose you're on a Mission, deep in Mozambique, and we can't get a resupply to you." He addressed everyone as the skin came off neatly, and the creature almost took on the appearance of a small human. "We want you to know that you can eat any rotten meat you find in the bush – provided you boil it thoroughly." He separated the limbs of rotten flesh from the baboon's body, and chucked them into the big cooking pot, bones and all. "But when it's cooked, eat it immediately. If you reheat it, you'll die of botulism poisoning." He threw the rest of the carcass, including the skull, whole into the pot, discarding only the skin and intestines.

The baboon flesh bubbled away, exuding the most appalling stench. The officer added a few more pieces of rotting flesh to the stew. Presumably raw waste from earlier meals the instructors themselves had enjoyed. Tentatively at first, Ron and his fellow trainees ate the boiled meat.

"It's both edible and nutritious," the officer said, standing back with the air of a cordon bleu chef. Everyone went back for second helpings. Congo Bill seemed to relish the horrible meal. Somehow, it suited his wild, black beard and unkempt hair.

* * *

Ron was still bloody hungry a few days later as they walked in file along a riverbed. It was late afternoon, and they'd just completed the day's training. He and Congo Bill were together at the rear of the group, foraging for food as usual. Bill stopped off to look more closely at some muddy puddles while Ron carried on, scanning the sand and rocks ahead. Bill would be hoping to find mud crabs, or something similar to add to their cooking pot that night. They were less than a kilometre from camp.

Ron's concentration was interrupted by a deafening scream, which seemed to vibrate every bone in his body. Shit! He spun round and another scream rent the air. A massive elephant towered over him. There was no time to take any evasive action. He dropped onto the sand and rolled instinctively. The elephant's flailing trunk missed him by a fraction. It tried to kneel on top of him, and nearly had him. Ron scrambled closer to the beast, until he was too close for it to get at him with its trunk or tusks. With horrifying speed, it shifted its huge bulk back, trying to crush him. But it was too far over to get him with its massive head. Ron was in the space between its mighty body and front legs. Hot elephant breath and saliva covered him. Ron knew he had no hope. The beast shifted forward, seeking to crush him with its knees. The noise was overwhelming. It was pressing him into the sand. Ron couldn't breathe... the life was being crushed out of him.

It moved again and he was released. He scrambled aside to avoid the huge bulk of the animal as it shifted again and raised itself to a standing position. It was facing away from him. He scurried away bent double, heading for cover in the riverbank. He could hardly believe he was alive. Ron reached the bank and saw the huge animal swing away up the opposite bank, showing no sign of its former fury. It disappeared. Then Ron saw Bill emerge from the riverbed, seemingly from where the elephant had been.

"You OK, Ron?" he called across.

"I'm alive. ...Where the hell did you come from?" he croaked as loud as he could. His ribs were painful, and his chest felt restricted. The other volunteers and the instructor came running back and helped him to his feet.

"Shit, man, but you're lucky," 'Speedy' Gonzales said. "You owe your life to Congo Bill." Two men were in the riverbed, standing by Bill.

Speedy told the tale when they got back to camp. "I saw what happened – this fucking great bull elephant came from the bush by the river bank, and attacked Ron without any warning. ... He had Ronnie, no mistake."

"Didn't you men see it?" the officer asked. "You must have walked right past the bloody thing."

"No sign of it when we went past," the instructor who had been with them answered. It was amazing how such a large animal could be hidden in the bush so close, and how silently elephant can move. This, and their notorious unpredictability, made them the most dangerous of all wild animals as far as Ron was concerned.

"Anyways, it was kneeling down and savaging him, like they do when they get you." Speedy demonstrated to the watching group. "Then Congo Bill came up and started hitting the elephant on its ear with his fucking rifle butt..."

"Now I'm beginning to understand something about your reputation, Bill," the officer said. Everyone looked at Bill with awe.

He was already known as a bit of a character, but this would make him legendary.

"Well, I couldn't shoot in case I hit Ronnie," Bill explained. "He's my friend."

"Thanks, Bill," was all Ron could say. He could feel his body beginning to stiffen.

"So anyway, after Congo Bill hammered this elephant on its ear, it just got up and buggered off," Speedy concluded.

"Unbelievable," the officer shook his head in wonder. "You injured, Bill?"

"Nah. The bugger didn't get me. He got Ron."

"Howzit, Ronnie?"

"I'm OK. Just a bit stiff, and a few bruises."

"Check him out please, sarge." Njube came over and made Ron strip. He checked carefully for broken bones.

He probed at Ron's chest, and then checked his kidneys. "Ouch; go easy, Mike, you bastard."

"There doesn't seem to be any serious damage, but you may have a few cracked ribs. And you've got some impressive bruises." Mike lifted Ron's arms to display his bruises for everyone's interest. "Otherwise, you seem to be OK. You're a tough, wiry bugger – that's why you've got away with it."

Mike gave him four aspirin. "That'll help you sleep." He turned to the officer. "I'll put him on light duties tomorrow, sir."

"Of course. You sure you can carry on, Ronnie?" the officer said.

"Shit. I haven't come this far to not carry on, damn it," Ron said. "Sir," he added as an afterthought.

"Well, you're bloody lucky. There's a major event coming up, but it's not starting until day after tomorrow. Then we'll see if you're fit to do it."

* * *

The next day was pure hell. Every bone and every muscle in his body ached. He guessed the soft sand must have saved him yesterday though. After the rest left at six to go for the usual morning run, he forced himself out of his bag, and sat up with difficulty. He rested after that effort, then crawled out of the basha. Standing up was an even greater effort, but he didn't want anyone to see him crawl. He needed a slash badly and managed to walk, bent over almost double, to the nearest game trail. No desert-lily galvanised urinals here; they pissed on the game trails in the hope that wild animals, recognising the scent of humans, would avoid camp. It didn't always work.

By the time he got back, he managed to stand more or less upright.

"Ah, ha! The elephant's friend is here," an instructor who had remained behind, said with a laugh.

"Fuck off," Ron responded, and went about the painful business of preparing food and tea for himself. Since the day of the baboon, the instructors had issued paltry, but welcome rations of tea, coffee and small quantities of food. The volunteers were still expected to provide for themselves from the bush. He didn't feel much like eating, but was determined to recover in time for the so-called big test tomorrow. They had not been told what it was, but Ron was certain it would be arduous. The instructors seemed to delight in springing surprises on them. The programme was into its second week now, and the volunteers had no idea when it might end.

When the others got back at lunchtime, Ron was feeling much better. The worst of the stiffness had gone from his limbs, and his appetite had returned. Congo Bill squatted down, and dug a small pit near where Ron was sitting. He dragged hot coals from the main fire and spread them over the bottom of the pit, covering them with a thin layer of dirt and leaves. Then he took a large cane rat out of his shirt.

"Where did you get it?" Ron asked, eyeing it hungrily.

"Checked our snare on the way back after assault course." It was bloody, and Ron could see that it had been gutted but not skinned. Bill placed it in the pit before covering it with more leaves and hot coals, topped with earth. It made a small mound.

"Will you be able to keep an eye on it? May need more coals later, just stick them on top. Should be ready for scoff tonight."

"I've got a bit of sadza meal left. I'll get that ready so we can eat it with the rat," Ron replied. "Nice big bugger you got there."

"Yeah," he hesitated. "How're you getting along?"

"I'm fine." Ron handed the scruffy soldier a mug of sweet tea. Congo Bill would never have settled into an ordinary soldier's routine. He was too untidy and got bored quickly. He was dirty, uncommunicative and unruly. But he was top notch when it came to bushcraft. And he had balls, as the elephant incident showed; Ron

286

was sure his actions were more than stupidity or recklessness. A man to be relied on in an emergency.

The men went off for the afternoon's training and exercises, while Ron kept an eye on the cane rat. It made delicious eating that evening.

* * *

Next morning, Ron got up with the rest. Just his ribs were still painful.

"Get over here to collect your loads," Mike Njube called them, and directed each volunteer to a pile of rocks. "They're all painted green, so you can't take any out during the march and replace 'em at the end." Each rucksack was weighed carefully to see that it carried 30 kilograms.

"You OK, sir?" Mike asked Ron quietly, when he collected his pack.

"I'm fine thanks, sarge." He'd given up trying to stop Mike calling him 'sir'.

They were issued with rations, a small tin of meat and 250 grams of mealie meal. They also carried their normal full load of weapons and ammunition. Ron could see it was to be a long exercise, probably a route march. He had no extra food but took a second water bottle. They were now down to eight volunteers, and were split into two groups. One instructor accompanied each group.

The march was hell. They crossed rivers, pushed through thick bush, and climbed steep hills. Near the end of the third day of marching, they stopped on a road where a Bedford was waiting.

"OK, men. Load your packs onto the truck," the instructor who was waiting with the truck said.

Thank fuck... this must be the end of the march, everyone was exhausted.

"And take these sandbags instead."

Shit no; another of their bastard tricks to make them give up in despair. Ron took the filled bag and staggered as he lifted it off the truck. It would definitely be more awkward to carry than the pack. His ribs were aching, but he was determined not to let that stop him.

"You've got to cover the next 12 kilometres in two and a half hours – or fail the selection. Get going, NOW!" There were only three left in Ron's group, including himself and Congo Bill.

"Give me your bag," Congo Bill said to Ron. "I can carry it. It'll help balance me, one bag on each shoulder."

"Fuck off, Bill. I carry my own bag."

They set off at a part-jog/part-march along the road. Was there no end to this? They were all shattered, and Ron's whole body was aching. It was late afternoon, and his breathing became heavier. For the first time in his soldiering career, Ron's mind was not alert. His feet were heavy, plodding down in front of him. There was just no spring left in his step. He was aware of Congo Bill... breathing heavily too, as he marched or jogged, matching Ron's pace.

"Don't wait for me, Bill," Ron gasped.

"I'm not, you bastard. I'm struggling to keep up."

The sun had begun to set, when suddenly an officer appeared in front of him.

Ron tried to avoid him. "Get out of the fucking way." He knew he would struggle to get going again once he stopped.

"No, soldier. It's over; you can stop."

"Piss off, damn you." Ron was sure this was another of their tricks to get him to give up. He felt Bill pull at his shirt; he tried to shake him off, but was forced to stop.

"It's me – Captain Macclesfield. Congratulations, you've passed selection. You're accepted into the Selous Scouts."

Ron walked over to the Bedford and eased the weight off his back. A wave of fatigue suddenly washed over him, and he thought his legs would buckle. Sergeant Robson was there.

"Well done, Ron," he said. "You'll be able to enjoy a week off back in Salisbury, before you start the 'dark phase' week after next."

Ron was bent over, sweat pouring from his forehead and fighting for breath. *Dark phase?* What the fuck was that?

Chapter 32

Angie decided to go to church with her mother the following morning, partly because she knew it would please her, but also because she felt like going herself. The situation was still tense and she'd had a restless night.

Her mother pulled out of the driveway, "I've had no luck with your father... he's being very stubborn. I must say, I feel cut in two over this, my dear." She reached out to touch Angie's hand, and they drove in silence for a while. The traffic was light; they soon arrived and parked in the road round the corner from the church. "He's very worried about the children. He loves them so, you know."

Goodness. Didn't her father think she loved her own children? "Yes, and they love him." She paused deliberately. "And so do I, Mum." Angie thought she'd just make that point. They straightened their dresses and walked slowly to the church entrance.

"I know that, darling. Perhaps you can get him to change his mind when you speak to him." They went in, greeting some of the congregation her mother knew. They had just enough time to settle before the service began.

Mark phoned not long after they got back. He'd had a bad night too. "Angie, I love you with all my heart, but I don't want to cause a rift between you and your parents..."

That made it all the more difficult for her. Was she the only one with resolution? "Are you saying you don't want to go ahead, Mark?"

"No... I want you more than anything I've ever wanted in my life before. What I'm saying is if I have to wait for you, I will. I don't want to, but if you think it's right..." He sounded sincere.

"Mum has had no luck. I'm going to try myself." She arranged to phone him at the hotel when she'd finished speaking with her father.

* * *

Her father was in his study, reading the Sunday paper.

"Come in," he said, folding it and waving her to a chair. "Have you had a chance to speak to Mark yet?"

"Yes. We spoke last night and again this morning… on the phone." She had always been able to twist him round her little finger, but she wasn't sure he'd allow her to get away with it this time. He'd been against her marriage to Ronnie, and she had to admit to herself now that he'd been right.

She might as well get going. "He said he doesn't want our relationship to break up the family."

Her father raised his eyebrows. "Well, perhaps he's got more to him than I thought."

"Daddy, I don't think you understand quite what's been going on between Ron and me these past few years." She told him about how Ron's surly, indifferent ways had grown, and about his sudden plan to make things worse by going full-time into the Army.

"Well, I knew something about all that… although I hadn't appreciated quite how bad it's been for you." Angie waited patiently while he contemplated. He looked up suddenly, "But he hasn't, well, you know. He hasn't hit you or anything like that has he?" Her father looked concerned.

"No, Dad. He's never laid a hand on me, but…" Her throat tightened. She got up and to look out of the window. "Do you know what it's like in those military married quarters?" She explained her fears, and what she thought might happen after the children grew up and left. A tear rolled down her cheek as she spoke.

"There, there, pet." He got up and took her in his arms. "You mustn't cry. I didn't realise quite what this might mean for you." He comforted her and she kept silent.

They sat down again and she dried her eyes.

"Humph," he cleared his throat. "Will Mark be kind to the girls?"

"Oh, Daddy." She could sense his resolve weakening, but knew she had to be very careful. "He's so very good with them. They like him too." She spoke warily, not wanting to rush or pressure him.

There was more silence. Had she managed to convince him? At least he was thinking about it. She judged it was better not to say any more at this stage.

Eventually, he spoke. "Angela," he hardly ever called her that, except when he was cross with her, "you may remember that I was opposed to your marriage to Ron, but I allowed you to talk me round..."

She was about to speak, but he held his hand up. "I was right and should have insisted on you taking more time to think about it."

Oh, God. He was going to dig his heels in. Angie closed her eyes but didn't move. Her father's words hung heavy in the air.

"I'm afraid that I'm going to make a similar mistake again." He sat back and shrugged his shoulders. "But you have my blessing to go ahead."

"Oh, Daddy." Angie jumped up and threw her arms around her father, kissing and hugging him.

"Shush, shush now, my girl. I'm not happy about it. I'm still worried about the children and about you." He patted her back. "Mark will have me to answer to if things go wrong this time."

* * *

Time seemed to fly over the next week. Mark demonstrated his organising and negotiating skills. He established a rapport with her lawyer, and opened a bank account for her to use to cover the costs – and as an emergency fund, if she needed it.

On Friday, they had lunch with Charlie. "How are things going?" she asked, as soon as the greetings and pleasantries were over.

"Mr Solomon said it should take no more than a few months to go through. Says he'll send the paperwork to Ron at his Army address and at the farm," Angie said.

"How long it takes, and the cost, will depend on him keeping to his agreement with Angie not to contest the divorce though," Mark warned.

"The bastard might decide to be difficult." Charlie had never liked Ron.

"Well, we'll just have to fight the case if he is," Mark said, taking Angie's hand. "Let's hope not though. It'll be bad enough for Angie and the children without that."

"Solly's a good lawyer, and he'll get it through in the end for you, no matter what." Charlie was confident.

Her mother had invited Angie and the girls to spend the weekend, suggesting that Mark spend time there as well. "It'll give the girls a chance to get used to Mark being part of the family," she said. Practical as ever.

After dinner on Saturday, Mark said. "We still haven't burnt that garden rubbish of yours, Angie. How about tomorrow?"

Her mother thought that was a good idea, "You can leave the children here if you like."

"I think we'll take them off your hands, Mum. After all, you've had to look after them such a lot lately," Angie replied, looking at Mark for support.

"Yes. I agree, you've been wonderful. I don't know how to thank you."

* * *

Mark got the bonfire going almost as soon as they arrived at Angie's home. The girls 'helped' him light it, but he moved them clear when the flames caught.

"Come and get your cool drinks, girls," Angie called them away to the kitchen. "Shall I bring your coffee out there, Mark?"

"Yes, please." Mark knew he'd have to nurture the fire, as the garden rubbish was still green. It really hadn't had sufficient time to dry out since being cut. He went round lighting the leaves and branches at various places, to make sure the fire caught properly. White smoke curled almost straight up into the cloudless sky. Not even a light breeze. Pity, wind would have helped.

A few minutes later, Angie joined him. "Oh, it's beginning to burn well now," she said. "Here's your coffee."

"Thanks." Mark turned from the fire and took the hot mug into his hands. He took a sip, then set it down on a tree stump and crouched to lift the centre of the bonfire. It needed space for what little air there was to feed the flames.

"Oh, NO!" Angie sounded *very* shocked. Mark looked up from the fire, and followed her gaze.

Standing near the garage and watching them was a tall, wiry looking man. He had medium length, light-brown hair, with a scruffy half-grown beard and scraggly moustache. "What the hell..." Mark stood up and began walking towards the intruder. The man looked like a tramp.

"It's Ron," Angie whispered and Mark stopped. No… not a tramp, a scruffy soldier. The man moved slowly and silently towards them. He stalked rather than walked, his hands seemingly relaxed at his sides – but ready. This man could handle himself. Mark had seen the type before, they looked relaxed and casual but were dangerous opponents. Trained fighting men.

"Hello, Ronnie. Meet my cousin, Mark le Roux."

She was a cool customer. Despite the situation, Mark couldn't help admiring her sang-froid; amazing. He held his hand out. "How do you do?"

Cartwright ignored it. "Where the hell did you come from?" The man had malignant, even mesmerising, pale blue eyes. Staring, unblinking like a snake.

Mark withdrew his hand, aware that Angie had moved to stand beside him. "I'm visiting Angie from South Africa." He was ready, just in case.

"Daddy…" Right on cue, Joanne recognised her father. She came running across the yard towards them.

"We'll speak later." The man turned away to catch his daughter in his arms. The next few minutes were taken up with the children greeting him.

Mark noticed that Emma was less enthusiastic than Joanne, and Helen needed to be coaxed. He took the opportunity to consult quietly with Angie. "What would you like me to do?"

"Nothing; we might as well get it over with today."

"Good." Mark was glad.

"You're back sooner than I expected, Ron," Angie said when the children left them. Emma went to her room, and the two smaller children to play on their jungle gym climbing frame, about ten metres away.

"So it seems." He sounded menacing.

"Your car is where I told you I'd leave it – in the garage." Angie wasn't being intimidated.

"Not even a cup of tea for your husband when he comes back from the bush?"

"Do you want a cup of tea?"

"Yes… please." Angie went off to the kitchen.

"So what brings you here – le Roux isn't it?" Angie's husband studied him, his eyes narrowing.

Mark concentrated on watching the man's entire body language, not just his eyes. "I've come to see Angie."

"How come I've never heard about you before?"

"We hadn't seen each other since we were young schoolchildren." Mark chose his words carefully. "We met again at her parents' place, and I went to the New Year party at your parents' farm." The man seemed to consider this.

"So, you've been seeing a lot of each other."

Mark refrained from answering. Surely his parents must have mentioned that he was there when their farm was attacked?

Angie came back with a mug of tea. She handed to Ron, but moved nearer to Mark.

"I suppose he knows you've asked me for a divorce?" Ron contemplated them both with his cold eyes. "Seems very convenient he's around, now that's happening." Neither Angie nor Mark responded.

He sipped at his tea, "And I come home, unexpectedly, to find the two of you here together." He took a step closer. Mark watched the mug carefully. Hot tea in the eyes for openers?

"Stop this," Angie stepped between them. A small, slight woman between two powerful men. "It's over between us, so why don't you just go, Ronnie?"

He drained his mug and placed it on the ground. "I don't like being made a fool of, that's why." He reached across and grabbed her shoulder roughly. She was still standing between them.

That was too much. "Leave her alone!" Mark tried to get around her.

Ron shoved her to the ground, and used the distraction to send a sudden blow straight at Mark's face. Mark shifted his weight slightly, and the blow grazed his jaw. There'd be a bruise there tomorrow. A second blow followed, immediately behind the first, and he was hard put to avoid its full power. As he'd suspected, he was up against a skilled fighter. The man was fast, like greased lightning. Mark feigned a stumble to the ground at his opponent's feet. Ron followed up, with a kick to Mark's kidneys.

But he was hoping for that. He sideslipped the kick, and caught Ron's heel. Using the heel as a lever, Mark pulled it and swung himself up to his feet. The man tumbled to the ground. Mark swivelled round and dropped his right knee heavily into his opponent's groin. Ron's breath hissed. Mark slammed his fist down into Ron's solar plexus. Another wheeze of breath.

Mark sprang to his feet again, and stepped back to avoid Ron's swinging leg as he tried to trip him. Christ, he was fast... and fit. Few people could have taken that punishment and still come back fighting.

"Stop it!" Angie screamed, trying to get between them again. She got in the way of Mark's finishing blow, and he almost lost his balance avoiding her. "Stop!" she shouted again, standing defiantly, trying to stop the fight.

The two children came running. Mark watched warily as Ron pulled himself to his feet. He'd obviously damaged the man, but he was far too dangerous to write off. Mark stepped back to make room, in case Angie or one of the children got in the way.

"What's the matter Mummy, Daddy, Mark?" Joanne cried.

"Now look what you've done." Angie looked furious. "You started this. I think you'd better go now, Ronnie."

Ron stood for a moment, and then said menacingly. "I'll get you for this, le Roux." He looked searchingly at Angie. "I'll not let any man, or woman, make a fool of me." He dusted down his camouflaged uniform with measured deliberation, turned his back and walked slowly away.

It was unbelievable. Mark knew he'd landed two heavy and well-placed blows, using all his considerable power and weight advantage on this man. Yet he just got up and walked away as if uninjured. He didn't relish having to fight this seemingly indestructible man again.

Mark didn't relax until Ron reversed his car from the garage and drove off. He hoped Angie would understand that he couldn't just stand there to allow her, or himself to be beaten up. He'd expected anger. But the cold fury of the man and the speed of the attack had shocked him.

* * *

Ron barely knew how he got to his parents' farm that afternoon. His rage was all consuming. Twice, he almost turned back to finish that bastard le Roux. On the second occasion, he stopped at Mazoe for a slash. He noticed people staring, and suddenly realised how scruffy he looked. He looked into the bathroom mirror. Filthy and unkempt, his face was covered with hair. Selous Scouts were encouraged to grow full beards – it aided camouflage in the bush. And washing was a no-no; you could smell soap a mile off out there.

He thought about the possible consequences if he did go back and take le Roux out. The cops would have one look at him and he'd be in jail again. A civilian one this time. Shit. Better calm down and take stock. He thought about Angela. Christ but she was an attractive woman. Why the hell was she leaving him, and going off with that bloody Afrikaner cousin of hers? She disliked South Africa as much as he did.

And what about the children? Well, they'd be better off with her, whatever happened. He knew he was no good with kids, and wouldn't have time for them anyway. But with Angela to take care of them, he could enjoy them when he was home – and Angela. He realised he needed her. Soft, pretty, sexual, sensible Angela. Looking after the home and the children. She was good at that. Good at looking after him too.

But she'd become a real nag lately. Well, now that he thought about it, he'd noticed it getting worse for several years. Always complaining about him not talking to her and going off to the Army, especially the Mess. Perhaps he'd overdone it a bit? He'd have to get her up to the farm and have a good talk with her. Persuade her that what he was doing with the Scouts was for the best. He'd compromise; promise to go easy with the Mess in future. Yes, that was it. They'd have a good life and she'd be well looked after, with plenty of company in married quarters. Army wives were renowned for being supportive of each other.

He decided to phone her on the pretence that his parents wanted to talk about the children's future. When she arrived, he'd get her to forget this silly divorce business. That was no way forward. It was upsetting his parents no end too. Ron knew that would weigh heavily with Angela. As soon as she saw sense, he'd go and get rid of that bastard le Roux for good... and then he could get back to fighting this bloody war.

Chapter 33

Gadziwa fretted the whole three days that he kept his men in their mountain hideaway. Nevertheless, he judged it necessary to allow the hue and cry to die down, after their hugely successful attack on the military base at Mukumbura. The missionaries kept him informed about the level of Army activity, and said they would tell him when they thought it was safe for them to move out.

At last the time came. This team was so much better than the last lot; he'd already decided to use the regular bus to take them all to Mazimbe. He split them into four groups of two each, and they waited for the bus at different stops. Their weapons and equipment were hidden in suitcases and sacks. The missionaries gave them all the information they needed about buses and destinations. They'd brought four empty 100-kilogram meal sacks with them from their camp in Mozambique, and each pair of men carried one suitcase and one sack between them. After allowing time for his men to walk to their various stops along the route, he settled with his subordinate comrade at the main mission bus stop and waited.

Gadziwa himself adopted the old tramp disguise again. Some of his boys were young enough to pass as schoolchildren, and they relished the acting roles. It would have been easier if there were only a few of them. But during his last bus ride, the passengers had been mainly women, children and old men. A bus carrying eight fit, mature men would look suspicious to the armed forces. Most young men were normally away in the towns and cities working, so he felt disguises were called for.

He risked allowing the conductor to place most of their luggage on the roof rack. There was no room for it inside. But, acting the stupid old tramp again, he managed to keep his own weapon hidden inside the sack he was carrying onto the bus. At least he would be armed in case something went wrong. His men were delighted at seeing their much-feared commander acting as a dirty, irascible old mampara... a no-good.

Though the bus stopped several times at roadblocks during the journey, no one questioned Gadziwa or his men. They took care to sit apart during the ride, and ignored each other as if they were strangers, not wanting to attract the attention of either the bus driver or the conductor, or indeed the other passengers. You never knew who among them were sellouts. After Gadziwa and the one travelling with him got off the bus, the others knew to disembark at the following two stops. From there, they moved on to their pre-arranged meeting point.

"We will walk from here to the safe kraal," he said when they all arrived. He didn't mention the name of the kraal-head to anyone except his deputy. Splitting his men into two groups of four, he made sure they kept a safe distance apart as they made their way to Mabunu's kraal.

* * *

They arrived at their destination on the afternoon of the next day, and he hid with his companions in the scrub nearby. It looked safe, but they maintained a careful watch from their hiding place, in case the kraal was compromised.

After dusk, Gadziwa himself approached the kraal. He still had his old tramp disguise, but carried his trusty RPD at the ready. "Greetings, Mabunu."

"Uh... Maai Whe!" Mabunu hadn't seen him approach, and jumped with fright.

"It's me, comrade – Captain Gadziwa." He stepped forward into the firelight.

"Welcome, Gumbarishumba." Mabunu clapped his hands respectfully in salutation. "There was much trouble the last time you were here."

"Have things quietened down?"

"Yes, comrade. It has been..." he paused to count, "five moons since you were here." He offered a stool for Gadziwa to sit on, and called one of his wives to bring beer. "The soldiers spent two weeks here, and kept coming back to search. But now they have lost interest." He offered Gadziwa his snuff tin, then trailed a measure onto the back of his hand for himself. "They have not been here for... two moons." Closing one nostril with the side of his hand, he inhaled vigorously into the other, and sneezed violently. Wiping the residue with the heel of his hand, he took another measure, closed the first nostril, and sniffed into the other. More violent sneezing resulted, and his eyes leaked in sympathy with his nostrils.

Gadziwa fixed the kraal-head with a stare. "Who was the sellout that caused the mukiwa to come last time I was here?"

Fear showed in Mabunu's eyes. "I don't know, comrade. It was not someone from my kraal," he added hastily. "I suspect Wasiya Dabengwa or his son, Domiso. But I cannot prove it."

"If it happens again, I will kill you, and burn your kraal."

"I cannot prevent it, Comrade Captain."

"Then I had better kill you now…"

"No… No! Please comrade. I will make sure it does not happen again. I'll send two Mujibas to listen outside the kraal in the dark while you are here. They are both my grandsons, so we will be safe." He summoned two young boys and directed them to keep watch on the outskirts of the kraal.

Gadziwa was satisfied that the youngsters, who as 'Mujibas' were sworn supporters of the Cause, would be on the lookout. "Good. I have seven men waiting outside. They will need food and shelter." He saw the concern in Mabunu's face, so added "We will not be expecting entertainment. We have work to do tomorrow night."

"Any comrades serving Gumbarishumba are always welcome." Mabunu showed his gratitude at not having to accommodate them for too long. "The woman I gave you last time you were here will be disappointed that you cannot stay longer."

"The night is young, Mabunu. Send her to my accommodation while I fetch my men." He walked a few paces into the dark and gave the pre-arranged signal, confirming that all was safe and well. His men materialised, like spirits from the darkness to join him with Mabunu at the fire; his heart swelled with pride at their professionalism. He waited for the kraal-head to settle down from his fright before he made his next demand.

"Of course, I will need to borrow a pickup truck tomorrow night, comrade." Gadziwa stifled a chuckle while Mabunu nearly choked on his beer. "I'll only need it for a few days," he added sympathetically. Watch him squirm. Gadziwa was enjoying himself enormously.

* * *

"It's Ron, dear," Mum warned Angie, before handing her the phone.

"Ah... I've found you at last." Ron sounded belligerent. "I tried home first, of course."

"We're spending the night here with Mum and Dad," Angie explained warily.

"You and le Roux, I suppose?"

"I meant me and the children," she said carefully. Mark was there too, but she wasn't going to ask for trouble.

There was a pause at Ron's end, and Angie said nothing to break the silence. "I've been discussing matters with my folks," he said at last.

She waited for him to continue, but when he didn't, said "Yes?"

"I want them to have some say in what happens to the children."

Angie's heart sank. She'd been afraid of something like this since the incident that morning. "Like what?" she asked.

"It's better if you come here to talk it over."

She supposed it was inevitable that he would use his parents as an excuse to stir things up. "All right," she sighed. "I'll make arrangements to drive up for the day, some time next week." She might as well get it over with, as soon as Mark had gone back to Cape Town.

"That won't be any good... I'm due back in the Army next week. I want you to come up tomorrow, Monday."

But he'd said it was his parents who wanted to talk. After all, she had already agreed with him what to do about their children. "That could be difficult, Ron. I have plans for this week." She'd be much happier meeting his parents on their own. They'd be reasonable, and Angie would be happy to arrange for them to see the children regularly.

"I want to be part of the discussion. But if you're busy, that's OK. We'll wait until I come out again." He paused. "Of course, the divorce will have to go on hold until we've agreed..."

Angie could see where this was leading. "Oh, very well. I'll cancel everything, and drive up tomorrow." Charlie was right; he was a bastard.

"Are you sure, now? I could be back again in a couple of months, and I'd hate to upset your arrangements..."

"You've already upset them. But I want to get this settled once and for all, so I'll be there about ten tomorrow morning." Angie was furious. She wanted to end the conversation so she could think.

"That's OK with me, bye." He hung up.

Angie put the phone down, and held her head in her hands. She composed herself before she went back into the sitting room.

"Ron has started making trouble already," she said simply. "He wants me to go up to the farm tomorrow to talk about the children." She sat down next to Mark. "Says his parents want a say in what happens with them." Her father put his paper down, Mum and Harriet both sat forward.

"I'll come with you," Mark said immediately.

"I don't think that would be helpful," her father intervened.

"I'm sorry, but I don't want Angie going up there on her own," Mark said emphatically. "That man's dangerous."

"No, Mark. He'll be fine with me. He's never laid a hand on me before, just words and threats," Angie persuaded. "And his parents would never let him hurt me. I'll have to deal with it myself. For the children's sake."

"He laid a pretty rough hand on you this morning," Mark pointed out.

Everyone looked shocked – especially her father. They hadn't mentioned that part of the encounter to her parents.

"Oh... he didn't mean to hurt me. Just wanted to get at you," Angie explained hastily. "That's why I must go alone, so he isn't provoked."

"I could come with you," her father offered.

"No, Dad. I really think things will be better if I go alone," she pleaded. "You know the Cartwrights will behave decently. They'll keep Ron and his temper under control."

* * *

Angie left before eight the next morning. "I want to get it over with, and be back here before dark tonight, Mark."

"Please phone so I know you've got there safely."

The journey was not a comfortable one. She worried about her reception from Ron's folks. They'd be sure to blame her for the marriage breaking up now. They would surmise that she'd used Ron's obsession with the Army to ask for the divorce, which she had to admit to herself, was partly true. She still suffered gut-wrenching embarrassment and guilt. It was clouding her thinking. What was she going to say? Suppose they asked her not to go ahead with the divorce? Ron could be very difficult over the children; look what happened to Harriet with Mark. But she took comfort from the fact that Ron was a very different proposition to Uncle Anton.

She stopped at the tiny Mazoe village and went into the tearoom. There was no one to be seen; she had to go behind the counter, and call out before someone finally appeared.

A large lady came through from the dark recesses of the house at the back. "Yes, dear?" Her hair was still in curlers, and she was wearing a housecoat and slippers.

"Could I have a pot of tea, please?"

"Certainly, what about a nice cake to go with it?"

Angie didn't really want anything to eat, but felt obliged to order something. "Can I have a piece of toast instead, please?" This was turning out to be not such a good idea. But she needed to stop and think before she got to the farm, and she couldn't remember anything suitable at Umvukwes.

Well, sitting there in the café cleared her head a little. There was no point in arguing with them about why she was leaving Ron. She'd stick to her guns and face it out. They and Ron could see the children as often as they liked, within reason. If he became difficult, she'd leave him anyway, she decided. With or without a divorce. She'd take the children with her to Cape Town and live with Mark. Ron might try to force her to hand over the children, if he went for a divorce on grounds of her desertion or infidelity.

She'd discussed it with Mark last night. "Never mind, darling," he'd said. "I'll take you and the girls so far away they won't be able to do anything." But that would mean no direct contact with her parents either, and she didn't want that. She also wanted the children to grow up knowing Ron's parents. Yes, she'd tell them that too. Surely Kate and Peter would support an amicable break, for the children's sake and theirs? Angie left the tearoom feeling much better, but still apprehensive.

* * *

There was no one to greet her when she arrived. Joseph must be round the back. She wondered where the dogs were. She hesitated at the door. What a strange feeling; she didn't belong here anymore. Should she knock? Of course not. She walked in as she'd always done, and made her way to the kitchen.

"Angela," Kate greeted her and took her in her arms.

"Kate..." Despite having prepared herself, Angie didn't know what to say. "How are you?" Kate didn't reply, just held her.

"Let's have a cup of tea; Peter and Ron have gone out for a while." That was a relief. At least she could speak with Kate alone. The dogs must have gone with them.

"Yes, thank you." She might as well get straight to the point. "I feel so sad about Ron and me... but it doesn't have to mean the girls lose touch with you and Peter, Kate."

"I was sure you would say that, dear." Kate put the kettle on. There was an awkward pause, while she seemed to be struggling with her own thoughts. Eventually she said "Can't this problem between you and Ronnie be resolved? It would be so much better for the children – and for all of us – if you do." She reached to lift the biscuit tin down from the sideboard.

Angie had expected that approach, and steeled herself to make the reply as planned. "I'm sorry, Kate. I've made up my mind."

* * *

The pickup was a very old one but it ran – just. "You sure you don't have a better one?" Gadziwa challenged Mabunu. It would be especially bad if the vehicle broke down after they made the attack. That would make it very difficult for them to escape. And if his plan went as well as he hoped, there'd be big trouble afterwards.

"It is the only one I have, comrade."

He fixed Mabunu with a stare. "It had better be. If I find out later..." But this time, he seemed to be telling the truth.

"When... how will I get it back, comrade?"

"It would be best if you claim it from the police afterwards." Gadziwa had thought that through. "You can say that we took the truck from you by force. We need the truck to make our escape."

"The police might not give it back to me. Or it might get damaged," Mabunu whined.

It was a good thing that Gadziwa had deliberately left the details of what he was planning until just before they left, leaving no time for Mabunu to whinge further. "You might find that better than getting damaged yourself." He pointed his RPD casually at Mabunu. The man cringed away and said no more. "If you like, we'll burn one of your huts. Then you can point to it as the threat we made to you."

A calculating look came over Mabunu's face. "Yes, comrade. That one over there." He pointed at a derelict grain storage hut, and Gadziwa immediately saw what he was after.

"You crafty old tsotsi. That hut is empty, but you'll claim it was full when the police come."

Mabunu said nothing, but gave a sly smile.

The idea pleased Gadziwa. "Well, that's all to the good. Let the mukiwa pay you for lending me your truck for our attack against them." He knew the white government would pay compensation to anyone who suffered at the hands of 'terrorists'.

"Can you tell me where you are going to attack the mukiwa?" Mabunu pleaded. He'd been trying to get him to divulge that information all last night, and all day today. But Gadziwa judged it not safe to tell anyone in advance. He wanted no possibility of warning for the target. He hinted that it would be a white owned store in one of the settlements nearby, but said no more.

"No. We were betrayed here at your kraal before, Mabunu. I cannot trust you again yet. Next time I come, I might be able to trust you more." There was no harm in keeping the kraal-head on tenterhooks.

The sun was getting low in the sky, and he wanted to reach the main road before dark. "Get on the truck, my sons of the soil. We have work to do." He supervised them climbing on board; the light pickup would be badly overloaded, with eight men and all their equipment, so they'd have to be careful. He drove, with two men squeezed in the cab alongside him. The other five sat, carefully distributed in the open rear.

No matter how carefully he drove, the chassis bottomed every time he went over even the slightest bump in the rough track. "Get out and follow on foot," he told the five in the back. He continued the drive slowly, but kept them running. They reached the main road just after dark. Perfect timing. He stopped 100 metres from the main road, and gathered his boys around him.

He settled down to give full details of his plan to them. Each man had a specific task to complete. A meeting place was arranged in case they got split up. There were many questions.

"We must push the pickup from the main road all the way to near the farmhouse," he told them, "otherwise the dogs will hear it coming and warn the mukiwa." Even though there had been none last time, he had to assume there might be dogs.

Gadziwa wanted to make the attack after midnight. Then they would make good their escape from the enemy; it should all be over by the early hours of the morning.

* * *

Angie was seething with frustration. It was after four, and still she and Ronnie were unable to agree. She was right in her suspicion that his parents were not the problem.

They weren't even taking part in the discussion. "We know we can trust Angie to be fair with the children, Ron," Peter said at lunchtime. "So it's really up to you two, not us."

Now it felt as if Ron was deliberately delaying her, casually throwing something new into the discussion, each time they seemed to have reached agreement. "It'll be too late for me to go home just now, Ronnie," she pleaded.

He looked at his watch. "We're not far from what we want. Let's go and explain everything to my folks now." And about time too, Angie was relieved. They'd reached this point several times through the afternoon.

Ron and Peter hadn't got back to the farmhouse until midday, keeping Angie waiting. Then he'd refused to discuss anything until after lunch. What was he playing at? He'd known she was due to arrive at ten, but he'd chosen to go out with Peter, at half past nine. Did he want her to be stuck at the farm overnight?

"But first, I want to talk about us," he said, completely throwing her.

"I thought we'd said everything there was to say about us – weeks ago."

"Well, I've been thinking…"

Angie felt her shoulders droop with resignation. Here we go again.

"We don't have to go through with it. Divorce I mean." This was a change in tack. He rambled on and on about how important the war in Rhodesia was, and how crucial his part would now be in it. Especially since he'd passed selection for the Scouts.

"Let's compromise," he said eventually. "You stand by me while I'm in the Scouts, and I'll stop going to the Mess so often." He sat back with the air of someone who had made a colossal sacrifice.

But she believed at least he was trying, he really was. "Ronnie, it's much, much more than that. You've become so distant, so strange." How could she explain to him? "You joining the Scouts was just the last straw. You just don't love me anymore," she said in exasperation. Hoping that might make him understand.

He looked surprised. "But I do."

"You do what?"

"Well, you know... I love you."

Good heavens, he'd said it. "Ronnie. I don't know what to say. You haven't said that to me for years." She was flabbergasted.

"Well, there you are then. Now let's forget about all this business and get back to normal."

"I can't do that, Ronnie." She wondered how to put it. "Too much has happened." She felt awful all over again. She loved Mark, but now she felt so sorry for Ronnie; the man she'd married all those years ago. The father of her children... He looked lost and alone. Could she go through with it?

"Well, stay the night here with us, and let me know in the morning. You should spend a few days with my parents too. They've had a nasty shock."

He still didn't understand. "No, I can't stay overnight with you. I'm going back to my parents." Her mind was in turmoil.

"Well, we can't settle this until I get back from the Army again then." He sat back.

Oh, God. "Ronnie, what do you want?"

"I don't want you to take the children away."

She didn't believe that. "Do you want me to leave them with you?" She knew there was absolutely no chance he'd want that.

He looked away before he said. "No, I want you to stay with them – and me."

"There's no way I'll agree to that, Ronnie. I'm really sorry, but I don't want to be married to you anymore." It was painful to be so blunt but she was at the end of her tether, and didn't want to leave him under any illusions.

He was avoiding looking at her. Angie said nothing; just kept looking straight at him. He'd have to say something in the end.

After a long wait, he shrugged his shoulders and finally said "I want something in writing; you know, about the kids and my parents."

"OK, I'll think how to organise that when I get home, and I'm sure there'll be no difficulty in putting together a document that everyone's happy with." She was sure she could get Mr Solomon to do it, and the sooner the better.

Meanwhile, she didn't want there to be any misunderstanding. "But things can never be the same between you and me again, Ronnie…" He sat, saying nothing, so she added "Now, please can I go?"

They went through to see Kate and Peter.

"Angie's said she'll think about things," Ronnie said. They looked very relieved. "But she wants to go back to Salisbury now."

"I'm sure I can come up with something that spells out an amicable arrangement between us over the *children*." She didn't want Kate and Peter getting the wrong impression. "I'll get it across to you and Ronnie before he goes back to the Army next week."

They looked crestfallen; she knew Ron's statement had misled them. She felt awful all over again, but was determined to stick to her guns.

"You won't get home until well after dark, Angie," Kate pleaded. "Please stay the night."

Angie paused, her heart went out to them, but she answered "I've *got* to take the children to school tomorrow, Kate. I can't keep relying on my mother to do it."

"It'll be dark before you even get to Umvukwes, Angie. I really don't want you driving all that way in the dark, please," Peter said quietly. "You can leave at sunrise tomorrow, and be in Salisbury by eight," he added. Ron said nothing.

Angie looked at her watch again; he was right. But she didn't want to sleep in the same house as Ron. In a silly way she felt that would be unfaithful to Mark. "I promised everyone I'd be home tonight…"

"Why not spend the night with Granny and Granddad?" Peter interrupted. Perhaps he suspected her reservations.

"Oh, I don't want to put them to any trouble." Angie was frustrated. Time was moving on, and soon it really would be too late.

Eventually she gave in, and agreed to stay with the grandparents. They were very welcoming, and she phoned Mark and the family from there.

"I'm not happy about you spending the night out there, Angie…" Mark said.

"I'll be quite safe. I'm with Granny and Granddad," Angie replied patiently. "Would you prefer me to drive home in the dark?" she added, feeling drained.

"You know I don't want that; I'll come and fetch you."

"Then we'll have to drive two cars back…"

Eventually she persuaded him. "I'll leave first thing tomorrow morning, and be home by eight," she promised.

Her mother had said she'd take the girls to school again anyway, and that she shouldn't hurry. But Angie wanted to get home as soon as she could. All this was tearing her apart and she was beginning to wonder if it was all worth it.

Chapter 34

Angie woke suddenly... afraid. There were noises outside. Not the ordinary murmur of the night, but sinister, menacing sounds. She heard someone run... then stop. She slid out of bed, pulling on her jeans and shirt over the underwear she'd slept in. She tried to move silently, but her heart pumped so hard that blood rushed noisily in her ears, almost deafening her. Her hands were shaking, and unspeakable fear constricted her throat. There it was again... She moved silently from the side of the bed to behind the bedroom door. It was slightly ajar. Why was she so frightened? There was no logical reason to be. There were always sounds in the night out here. Could it be one of the dogs?

Deep barking in the distance dispelled that theory. Suddenly a strange 'phoomp' sound, then an explosion that seemed to come from right outside the bedroom window, shattered the night. There was the sound of breaking glass. The curtains billowed inwards... then out again.

A cacophony of gunfire, interrupted by the sound of more explosions, came from the vicinity of the farmhouse. Angie dropped to the floor, and scrambled back towards the bed. She just got there, when she heard the door of the cottage crash open. She wriggled as she tried to get further under the bed. A machine gun fired inside the cottage... God help her, it must be terrorists again.

Someone shouted in the Shona language. "They are too old, kill them!" The guns fired again.

Angie cringed under the bed. She tried to squeeze herself into the smallest possible ball. Now there was silence in the cottage, but still intermittent firing from the farmhouse. Someone came into the bedroom... she held her breath.

"There is no one here, except the old people," a voice said from the dining room immediately outside her bedroom. "Turn the lights on." The man in her bedroom stumbled about, but the light eventually snapped on. It was so bright it seemed inevitable they would see her. She froze with terror.

"There is no one here either," the man in her bedroom said from the door. Desperate hope came to her. Oh God, please make them go... the man left the room. She could hear them smashing furniture and scrabbling among the wreckage. Probably looking for money.

"Did you search that room, comrade?"

"There's no one there."

Please let them go away.

"There's no money in here. They might have hidden it in that room." Two men came into Angie's room, smashed the cupboard open, and pulled the bedside drawers out. One fell onto the floor, and its contents spilled all over the place. A man knelt and rifled roughly through the contents. He reached under the bed.

Angie watched in agony as a large black hand fumbled towards her. She squeezed herself into an ever-tightening ball, desperately trying to avoid it. The hand brushed against her and she froze in terror. The hand paused in mid-air, wavered away and then touched again before she felt its powerful grip on her leg. She closed her eyes. God help me, she prayed silently as she was dragged out, helpless. This was it. They'd kill her. She wondered what death would be like. Please let it be quick and painless. But she didn't want to die. She lay curled up on the floor, still gripping her knees.

"Hau!" Angie was pulled roughly to her feet. "Comrades! ...Here is a prisoner for us." Powerful hands forced her arms behind her back, immobilising her.

The second man came over to look. "It is just a youth," he dismissed her. He looked under the bed, then more closely at her again. "No... a female, I think. But she is alone. We must take her to Gumbarishumba." Her arms were twisted behind her back, and she cried out as she was forced roughly into the dining room.

A third man came and lifted her face to look at her; she looked straight back at him, determined to maintain her dignity. He reached for her top, and she tried to shrink away. But she was powerless in the iron grip of her captor. "She is very small, just at puberty." He leered at her, then suddenly grasped and fingered her breasts.

"Let go, you swine!" She screamed, and kicked at him with her bare feet.

"White bitch," the man snarled as he avoided her foot. He slapped her across her face, and she felt the bones in her neck crack as her head whipped to one side with the force of the blow. There was popping in her ears; red and yellow stars exploded before her eyes. If the man behind hadn't been holding her, she would certainly have hit the ground. The hand that struck her was calloused, hard and strong. Swaying, stunned into silence, her arms felt as if they were being twisted out of their sockets. She could taste blood in her mouth, and felt it trickle down her chin.

"Take her outside, but do not let her escape," he told her captor before he turned to the other man. "We'll set fire to this house." Angie was shoved outside. The man had a grip like steel, and his fingers cut into her arms as he pushed her in front of him, his face and sweating body close to hers. He panted over her, his breath hot and stinking. She could barely stand up. There was more firing from the farmhouse and she prayed the Cartwrights were beating off the terrorists. Perhaps they would soon rescue her?

Flames flickered and grew in the thatched roof. The crackling noise reached her, increasing as the flames caught. Sparks swirled up into the night sky. Soon the same sound came from the cottage behind her, and she tried to look round to see what was happening. Her captor turned her around until she could see. It was terrible and she tried to turn away, but the man twisted her painfully back and forced her to keep watching.

Angie found her voice again, and screamed. "There are people in there!" She was horrified at the thought of those dear old folk burning in the cottage a few metres away from her. She hoped they were already dead.

The terrorists came out of the cottage and, hearing her scream, laughed out loud.

"They will die slowly, and painfully, white girl," their leader, the man who'd struck her snarled. "Bring her with us comrades. Gumbarishumba will want her." He turned aside to one of his men and said "Comrade Chibanda is badly wounded." Angie overheard and was glad. "The mortar hit the tree above his head and exploded." They shoved her away from the cottage, towards the farm road.

"Hisst..." They came to a group of men, waiting in the dark. There was an old cream coloured pickup in the road nearby.

"We have a prisoner, Comrade Captain." She was shoved forward to be examined. "She is just a girl, but the others in the house were too old," her captor offered by way of explanation. Maybe they'd leave her alone if they thought she was just a child?

"She's old enough to walk," their huge captain observed. "We were not able to get any from the big house, so she'll have to do." He had a deep, rumbling voice. Her hopes of being dismissed as worthless and left behind were dashed.

"Comrade Chibanda has been injured, Gumbarishumba," the leader of her group confessed to the captain.

"Was he shot?"

"No, comrade… He was hit by the mortar when it struck the tree above him."

"So that's what happened," the captain snarled. "The fool spoiled our surprise attack. It is his fault that the people in the big house have escaped."

"He is badly injured, comrade. The mortar has cut his skull open."

"Is he dead?"

"No, Comrade Captain. But he might not survive."

"I'll make sure he doesn't." He turned to face Angie again. "Tie the girl ready for us to depart," he instructed the man holding her, before turning back to the others.

"The mukiwa at the main house had warning because of Chibanda's foolishness. They killed Comrade Sithole. You! Take me to where Chibanda is." The big man they called captain moved back towards the cottage with the leader of her group. Soon after, Angie heard a machine gun firing. They came running back, and she was forced onto the back of the pickup. The men scrambled around her and she lay among their feet, her hands tied together. The truck started and drove away at speed, bumping roughly along the road. It seemed to have no springs. What she faced in captivity made Angie feel physically ill with fear and her stomach cramped… there were dreadful stories about what terrorists did to women before they killed them. She tried to pray.

* * *

Ron woke the moment he heard the first mortar explode, then all hell broke loose. He grabbed his FN, leapt from his bed, pulled his clothes on and ran for the door. He only had one 20-round magazine of ammunition with him. This sounded like a major attack, and he needed to get one of his father's rifles as back up. He made his way towards the gun safe. A succession of mortar bombs hit the house.

The explosions missed him, but set the thatch alight. Two RPDs and several AKs also opened up, but most of it went high and hit the roof.

"Get down and stay down," he heard his father shout to his mother as he went past their bedroom door.

"I'm heading for the gun safe, Dad," he called, to make sure the old man knew where he was. The key was hidden in a drawer nearby, and he snatched the 303-calibre rifle, and a heavy old 45 revolver. He grabbed a full box of ammunition for each. The enemy fire was becoming more accurate, and bullets shattered windows as well as striking the stone and brick walls around him. He knew his way around the house well enough in the dark. But now the roof was well alight, and the ceiling began to burn through in places.

He ran back to his parents' room. "Come; let's get out of the house, Mum... Dad," he yelled. By the light of the burning roof, he could just make out that his father had a pistol with him. Good. They started making their way back towards the kitchen, away from the attackers, and where the roof was tiled instead of thatch. But the ceiling in the passage was now burning too fiercely, and they were forced back to the bedroom to escape through a window. Ron went first, landing on the polished concrete of the verandah. His father eased his mother out through the window, and Ron helped her to climb over the low verandah wall into the soft flowerbed below. He turned to help his father, but his feet slipped from under him and he fell to the ground. His father tumbled over, landing on top of him. Bloody garden had been watered overnight, making it slippery.

"Keep down, Dad," he hissed and yanked his father back down when he tried to get to his feet. "You stay down too, Mum." Bullets struck the wall above them, and smashed the glass in the window they'd just climbed out of. "Here, Dad. Take this rifle and ammo. He passed him the 303, and turned to fire a double tap with his FN. The target went down. Probably dead by the way he fell, but Ron saw nothing more to fire at, though his father was still blazing away into the base of the shrubs.

"Hold your fire unless you actually see something, Dad." The old man stopped. The terrs continued shooting, but Ron couldn't see the flashes from their weapons.

"We need to get away from the house, Mum... Dad. Wait here."

Ron crawled to the edge of the thick flowerbed, and towards a nearby shrubbery. Desultory firing continued into the house, but the shrubbery was clear. Christ no, there was one of the dogs; it might have been poisoned. Looked like Ben, but Ron couldn't be sure. Where was Sheba? No time to worry about the dogs.

"Can you crawl over here?" he called across. "But keep down and look out for the dog. I think it's Ben and he's dead." Soon they reached the cover of the shrubbery. This was away from the burning house and should be fairly safe.

"What about Angie and the old folk?" his father said. "I'm going across there."

"Stay here with Mum. I'll go to them." Ron stood, and ran across to the nearest tree along the way. He dropped into cover as soon as he got there. The firing had stopped, but he could see flames in the roof of the cottage, just 100 metres away beyond the tennis court. It was open ground, but he gathered himself and ran for a tree near the back of the cottage. Just as he got there, he hit the ground hard, tripping against something soft on the ground. In the flickering light of the blaze, he could make out a body lying under the tree. There were shrapnel wounds in the man's head, but he'd also been shot through and was dead.

"Shit," Ron exclaimed. There, just to one side of the body was a massive footprint. "Gadziwa." There were several 762 short cartridge cases lying across the area. Ron sprinted over to the cottage.

"Granddad... Granny... Angela!" There was no answer, and the cottage was burning fiercely – making a hell of a racket. "...It's Ron. Let me know if you can hear me." He ran right round the burning cottage, going as close as he dared; he felt his beard and eyebrows singe. There was no getting in by the doors or windows. He stopped every few metres, looking and calling out. But he saw no one. Christ they must be all dead. Burning in that raging fire. The sheer horror of it all almost broke him. But anger and determination took over.

He ran back to where his folks were hidden. "It's me." He didn't want his father to shoot him by accident.

"Here, son. We're over here."

"I've got to get after them, Dad. They're being led by Big Feet, the terr I've been after all this time." Ron was almost out of breath when reached them. "He'll get clean away if I don't go after him now."

"What's happened to Angie and the old folk?"

"Bad news, I'm afraid." Ron had his breath back. "The cottage is ablaze, and there's no sign of life. That's another reason for me to get the bastard." His mother sobbed aloud. "I heard a vehicle start up and pull away a few minutes ago," his father said. "It was out there in the road, just beyond those trees."

He had to move fast if he was to have any chance of getting the bastards. "Give me the rifle, Dad. And get hold of the police." Ron took the 303 and ammunition. "I'll be following the terrs in my car." Thank God the folks still had a telephone in the small dairy office; there was no hope of getting back into the house or the cottage now.

"Look out for land-mines," his father called after him.

* * *

Gadziwa was forced to stop in the township of Concession. They broke the lock on a petrol pump and filled the tank, which was almost empty. He'd cursed kraal-head Mabunu for failing to give him enough petrol when he'd taken the pickup. Mabunu's excuse was that he had no petrol coupons left, and there had been no way that Gadziwa could have found fuel before they went in for the attack. So he'd decided to risk being able to collect some on the way out. Fortunately it didn't take long.

While they were stopped, he took the opportunity to have a look at his captive. A small, skinny creature they said was a female. In fact, she looked more like a young boy to him, with skinny legs and hips.

She cringed away from him when he reached over to feel her pale, soft skin. He gripped her arm and ripped her shirt and bra open, revealing small white breasts. She snatched her clothing together, and tried to cover herself, backing away on the floor of the pickup. Hmmm... definitely female though a poor example of one. Unwilling too; he'd enjoy taking his pleasure with her, when he had the time. And she'd make good publicity when he got her back to Tanzania...

They got going again. Despite having lost two men, their attack had been a big success, though having just the one prisoner was a disappointment. He'd have liked at least two. A fully-grown white male, in addition to the female, would have been perfect. This pickup was another problem. It was too small for the load he was carrying. He had to drive much slower than he should have done. Never mind. He had transport, and it was still early. Just a few hours since the attack ended. They turned off onto the gravel road leading towards the Mavuradonha Mountains. It was the same road he'd taken on the bus last time he returned to Mozambique, so he knew it fairly well. They'd have to abandon the truck before they got to Mukumbura. The soldiers would surely be on the look out for them by then.

Thunk! The vehicle hit bottom hard as they crossed onto a bridge, throwing the people in the back all over the place. He stopped and got out onto the concrete bridge.

"Get down and hold on," he snarled. "I can't keep stopping every time we hit a bump."

The men scrambled to find places on the floor, rather than trying to perch on the sides with their feet on the floor.

Now they were crushing the girl. "Hey; leave more space for the woman." The men gave her more room. "You, leave her alone," he threatened. "I need her alive, not crushed to death. She will be my slave." He shoved the last man who was crowding her, away.

"I'll fuck her first, but when I've finished with her, you can all take turns," he promised them. But he shoved her into a corner against the back of the cab, where she would be more or less safe from the men. "Now hold on, we've got to keep going…"

He drove slowly over the ramp at the other side of the bridge. The body of the pickup still hit the chassis, but not so hard this time. The slow climb towards the Mavuradonhas began, and he had to engage a lower gear. The engine was labouring but kept going up the hill. He sped rapidly down the other side, the truck rattling over the corrugations. There would be many of these climbs as they hauled through the foothills.

Chapter 35

Ron saw there were six terrs left. Plus Angela! Her small, barefoot prints stood out clearly among the wide figure-of-eight trainer prints of the terrorists. Thank God she was alive. He called out the good news to his parents.

But she was in Gadziwa's hands... it didn't bear thinking about. She'd been dragged struggling from the direction of the cottage, then loaded onto the back of the vehicle. It had to be a pickup because of the way they'd piled onto the back – and for them to be able to fit seven adults onto one light vehicle.

The truck wouldn't be too difficult to follow – it had one worn tyre, and was crabbing slightly. He got moving, but stopped again at the farm entrance. Getting out, he checked the tracks on the gravel edge to the main tarred road. The trail was clear, especially in the light of the headlamps. As he expected, it turned north-east towards the nearest tribal trust land.

"Just like last time," he muttered. It brought back unpleasant memories, but he was filled with grim determination. This time he wasn't under orders, so he wasn't breaking any. He got back in the car and headed for the first entrance to the TTL.

"Shit..." There were tracks leaving, but no fresh ones going back in. He had to assume that Big Feet was still heading along the main road. He drove on through the village of Centenary. Here, there were many possible exits, but none led to safety for a large group of terrs. He didn't even stop to check for tracks. But he stopped at every other prospective exit, ignoring only white-owned farms.

A few kilometres before Mount Darwin, he got out and checked yet another gravel road, this one turning north off the main road. "Got you, you bastard." He checked his watch. Half past four in the morning. He guessed that the terrs had a 30-minute head start on him, and he'd been going since shortly after three.

He stopped at the bridge over the Ruya River to check the target tracks again. The car headlights shone obliquely and highlighted them well. They looked very fresh. Was there the faintest hint of dust in the air? He might be nearer than he thought. A closer look revealed that the same vehicle had scraped against the leading edge of the concrete bridge. Make no mistake; the vehicle was overloaded. After all, there were half a dozen of the bastards, plus Angela on board. The shock absorbers would be bottoming every time they went over a rough patch. They'd be driving more carefully than they'd like, and he was certain now that he was gaining on them.

* * *

An hour after leaving the bridge, Gadziwa noticed headlights from a car far behind and below them. It was travelling at great speed, and there was no way he could keep the pickup ahead. It might be just any car, but Gadziwa was suspicious and watched it uneasily. It kept gaining on them and didn't turn off or stop.

Bang... Bang... Bang... the boys at the back hammered on the roof of the cab. "I'm not going to stop," he snapped. "You, Tenneka. Lean out and ask them what they want."

"They say there is a car following us, Comrade Captain," Tenneka reported, when he pulled his head and shoulders back inside the window. "And I can see it myself."

"They must all be blind in the back," Gadziwa said. "I have been watching that car myself for the last 20 kilometres." He had to make a choice. "Tell them I know about it and to shut up." Tenneka did his bidding.

One option was to stop and hide at the next village, or any other convenient place. Then he could allow the car to go past. If it stopped, or there was any sign of aggression, they could easily kill the occupants, and perhaps even take the car. Another option was to simply allow the car to catch up and pass them. It was not likely to be hostile and couldn't possibly be full of soldiers, maybe just a lone driver.

They came to a sharp corner, where the road followed the steep contours of the mountainside. He chose to stop here. The mountain rose away on the inner side of the road and fell away steeply on the outside. There was a rocky waterfall, with a trickle of water flowing over the stones, and through a deep-cut culvert under the road. The scrub was thick in the gap between the road and the mountainside. But there was a clear space where vehicles could pull off the road. He turned in and shone the headlights into the bushes. Yes, it looked an ideal place to conceal the pickup.

"Stay where you are!" he yelled. He wanted to check the place out himself, before anyone else got off so they could get going again quickly if it wasn't suitable.

Using the headlights, he soon found a space to drive into, between two rocks surrounded by bushes. "Tenneka! Bring one man with you and come over here." He got them to move some loose rocks out of the way and to cut away a small section of the bush. He considered what to do next. He could set an ambush, kill or capture the occupants and take the car. It was sure to be better than the pickup. But the shooting might attract soldiers... and they wouldn't all fit into one car; that would mean splitting his group. No, he'd let it go past.

"Everyone get off... Comrade Ncube," he called his second-in-command. "I'm making you responsible for the woman; be sure she does not escape." With the help of the others, he got the truck well hidden from the road among the rocks and bushes, hard against the mountainside, but pointing towards the road, so he could drive it away quickly and easily in an emergency.

"The car will probably drive straight past us without stopping." He prepared his men for the next stage. "But it will have to be very slow because of the sharp turn and loose gravel. I have decided not to ambush it, in case the noise attracts soldiers. But if it stops, we will capture the occupants." He placed two men strategically within the area. He moved the prisoner close to where he would be, at the centre, and left Ncube guarding her. He took his last two men and placed them 50 metres along the road, covering both directions of approach. "Get back here as soon as you see or hear anything, but don't leave any tracks," he commanded. Then he walked back, carefully examining the road, and brushing it with a leafy branch to remove signs of their movement.

He settled down to wait. "Come here, woman." He grabbed her arm and pulled her towards him. She kicked at him, but was so weak it was ineffectual. "Keep still, curse you!" But she wouldn't stop fighting, and started screaming when he tried to pull her jeans off.

"We are going to have to hold this one's legs when we fuck her, comrade," he said to Ncube, deliberately speaking English so she would know what was in store for her. The bitch bit him, and he slammed his fist into her face angrily. He lay on top of her, but still she struggled. He was losing his patience and hit her again. Her hands were tied in front of her, so he twisted her onto her belly with her hands underneath, and knelt on her legs to keep them under control. She lay squirming in the dust and he pulled at her jeans again, but it was very awkward. She kept wriggling from under him.

Now he was very angry. He pulled her head back and slapped her face hard. He was about to strike her again, when someone hissed from the dark.

"The car is coming, Comrade Captain!" It was his lookouts.

He shoved the woman back to Ncube. "Cover her mouth, and keep a tight grip comrade. I'm not finished with her." He heard the car as it approached, and saw the headlights flashing as the car took the bends in the road. The whole area they were hiding in was lit up as the car took the hairpin bend. It was going slowly, but didn't stop.

* * *

Ron saw the lights of the pickup far ahead, not long after he crossed the bridge. He increased his speed, reaching 140 kilometres an hour in places; the car practically flew over the corrugations. Driving on a gravel road came easy to him; after all, he'd learnt to drive on the farm, and this road was well maintained. He gained steadily and was soon 'eating' the other vehicle's dust. It would get worse as he got closer. Suddenly he realised that the enemy lights had not been shining ahead for some time. Sure, he expected the lights to disappear every so often on the mountain road... but they should show up periodically. The truck must have stopped somewhere up ahead. Several scenarios went through his head. Gadziwa may have seen him following. Almost certainly had. He could be setting an ambush, or simply trying to hide.

He would have to risk the ambush. There was no backup to wait for. Not yet anyway. Half past five in the morning. Already the sky in the east was lighter. Despite the risk, he kept going. If he didn't, the bastard would escape again. And Angela was with them. Shit. There was just no way he could leave her in their hands.

He swung round a particularly tight bend, taking it slowly. There! He kept going, but now knew exactly where the pickup was; the headlights of his car had briefly illuminated some reflective material on the hidden vehicle. He drove past without pausing, and kept moving for several hundred metres before stopping. He chose his stopping place carefully. He deliberately didn't hide the car, making sure it would be easily visible from the air. He took both rifles and the 45, then headed carefully back along the road.

There was no lookout – clumsy, and out of character for Big Feet, but it made Ron's life easier. He got to the place just as the morning light was becoming a danger. He picked out four, no five men. Four standing in front of the bush, while the fifth drove the pickup from its hiding place. He spotted the sixth man further back in the bush. He was kneeling, holding something on the ground, probably Angela. Good, she'd be out of the way.

Setting the FN to automatic, he stood, partly sheltered by the rocky side of the lay-by, and opened up. He controlled the rate of fire, two rounds at a time, by stroking the trigger very lightly. He didn't have enough ammo to let rip. The first two bursts sent the two nearest terrs down, and the survivors scattered into the bush. He quickly swung his aim to the pickup, guessing that Big Feet would be the driver. But he missed the bastard, who managed to roll out the door onto the ground, and slither away like the snake that he was. The sun came abruptly over the horizon and Ron was silhouetted. An RPD opened up. Stone chips flew around him, mixed with the angry buzzing of bullets. He shrank back against the rock surface.

"That was the easy bit," he muttered to himself. "Now for Gadziwa." He'd got two out of the six enemy. The odds were still not good.

* * *

Angie was suffocating. Panic gripped her. The man who held her was crushing her ribs down into the ground, forcing a dirty cloth into her mouth. Only one thing mattered... the next breath. She heard gunfire and the man shifted his grip, giving her a chance to gulp air into her burning lungs. He pressed down on her again, but this time she managed to maintain a route to air. She sucked short rapid breaths, and began to recover her senses, and the ability to think.

She'd tried struggling, but that just made the man press down harder on her. The rope cut harshly into her wrists, and her hands were numb from lack of circulation. They were trapped awkwardly at the base of her ribs, digging in painfully. She heard more shots.

Surely that meant rescue might be near? A machine gun fired again. It was being fired by the man they called captain. He shouted commands, and the man who held her yanked her to her feet and ran, half dragging her deeper into the bush, away from the road. Her frantic efforts to resist were completely ineffective against the powerful African.

They stopped deep inside a ravine, surrounded by rocks and thick bush. There were four terrorists. Two were missing; but the big, evil leader was still there. Angie tried not to attract his attention.

"I could only see one white man," the leader said, peering out towards the road. "There he is! By the side of the rocks." He fired his gun again. The others fired too but Angie couldn't hear any firing in return.

"Maybe he has been wounded?" one of the others asked.

"Maybe... Has anyone seen more than one?" the leader said.

They shook their heads. "No, Comrade Captain." Two more shots rang out, and bullets crashed in among the bushes next to them. Angie ducked her head even lower, but her heart soared. Help was just out there. She thought of yelling but decided against it. They wouldn't hesitate to kill her, just to keep her quiet.

The captain got up and fired his machine gun again. "There... I've got him!" He jumped up running towards the road, followed by two others. Only the man who held her down stayed in the bush. More heavy shots came, from across the road this time. Angie now recognised them as being friendly fire. The big leader came crashing back into the bushes and fell to the ground. Only one of the two who had gone with him came back.

The man holding her shouted. "Are you all right, Comrade Captain?" There was panic in his voice.

"My leg is injured." The leader rolled over, favouring his left leg. Angie saw a dark stain spreading across his thigh. "But I'm sure I got the white devil."

Surely there was more than one rescuer? She hoped so. There were still three terrorists left. She watched the leader tie a cloth around his leg, and test his ability to stand up. He succeeded.

"We must get away now, or soldiers will come and catch us here."

"What about the one who's still out there?" her captor asked.

"I told you... I'm sure I got him. Do you hear anything?"

"We didn't hear anything last time. Then you went out and got shot, and Tenneka was killed." The man who was holding her spoke again. "We have lost three men to this white devil."

"We'll use the woman as a shield. They will not risk killing one of their own," the leader said. "It will be best if we can take the pickup. Leave the woman here with me, and go to that side to make sure the mukiwa is dead, Ncube." He indicated to the left. "And you, Masuku... go that way." He indicated to the right. "I would go myself if I was not wounded." Angie was passed roughly over to the captain. He grabbed her tied wrists and shoved her to the ground beside him. There was no hope of escape.

Crack... Crack... Two shots rang out and Ncube came rushing back into the bush. "The mukiwa is still alive; he's just got Comrade Masuku."

Chapter 36

"Well. It's quarter past seven, so your mummy will probably be passing Mazoe about now," Mary told the children. "Won't she, Mark?" He was sitting at the kitchen table with them, trying to read the morning paper, but smiled and nodded agreement.

"Now, come along and I'll take you to school," Mary said. He'd offered to do it, but she seemed keen to take them herself. To be truthful, Mark was looking forward to welcoming Angie home, so hadn't pressed his offer too hard.

They'd barely left the front door when the phone rang. "Mr Greville?" the voice asked.

"No. It's Mark le Roux speaking. Mr Greville has left for his office."

"Is Mrs Greville there?"

"No, she's taken her grandchildren to school." Mark didn't like the sound of this. "Can I help?"

"I really need to speak to one of them; can I reach Mr Greville at his office?"

"What's the problem?" Mark was getting really worried now; please God don't let it be Angie. "Is this anything to do with Mrs Cartwright? I'm her cousin... and I'm responsible for her, and her children." He exaggerated his official relationship.

"Well..." The man consulted with someone and came back. "I've been asked to let Mrs Cartwright's family know that she's missing."

Mark's heart sank. "Christ! Angie... Mrs Cartwright is supposed to be home any minute now. What's happened?" It was twenty to eight.

The man on the phone hesitated. "Do you know where she is travelling from?"

"A farm near Umvukwes, called Sapphire Blue."

That seemed to give the man on the phone confidence he was speaking to a family member. "Well, she's not injured as far as we can tell. Just missing."

This was not good. "How come she's missing?"

"There was a terrorist attack on the farm."

"Oh, God. No." Mark's legs almost buckled, but he needed to keep a grip. "When did the attack take place?"

"In the early hours of this morning, we believe. The farmer and his wife, also called Cartwright are OK, but two old people have been killed."

"But what about the young Mrs *Angela* Cartwright." Mark was sorry that the grandparents were dead, but all he cared about right now was Angie. "What do you know about her?"

"They haven't found her yet... think she may have been abducted."

That hit Mark like a physical blow. "What's being done to rescue her?"

"The police and military have it in hand, sir."

Mark put the receiver down and concentrated on keeping his head together. Must get out there... might be able to use his connections to get a helicopter. He ran to grab his diary, and picked up the phone.

* * *

"Get yourself down to New Sarum, Mark and we'll have a chopper on standby for you." Thank God, after a few hurried phone calls Martin Latham was able to help. New Sarum military airport was adjacent to Salisbury's civilian airport.

"Thanks, Martin, I owe you."

Mary arrived home, and Mark briefed both her and his mother before he left. Mary would phone Angie's father, and Mark promised to keep them informed. He also gave them the name and phone number of the police officer who was handling the case. He left the two distraught women, their arms around each other for comfort.

An officer at the base quickly swore Mark into the Air Force, as an 'acting temporary' sergeant; then took him to the armoury, where they issued him with an FN semi-automatic rifle.

"Any chance of a Tokarev 9mm pistol?" Mark asked, chancing his arm.

The sergeant in charge there looked sideways at him. "They're normally reserved for officers."

Mark stood his ground. "It's my weapon of choice, please..."

"Oh very well, then. I take it you don't want the FN?" Mark didn't, and the man took it back. He returned a few minutes later with a modern Tokarev, and got him to sign for it, muttering all the while about it being irregular. By nine-thirty, Mark was airborne and heading for Sapphire Blue in a Rhodesian Air Force Alouette. He really couldn't have asked for more.

When reporting his flight plan, and again when communicating with Mount Darwin, the pilot referred to Mark as a 'VIP'. That was good; it might give him the edge, if he had to ask for anything else.

"That's it," Mark said, pointing to the cluster of buildings; smoke was rising lazily from the roofs of the big farmhouse and the cottage. Police and military vehicles were parked in the driveway near the main house, and people were clustered around the buildings. As they got closer, they could see that water was still being hosed onto the smoking ruins of both homes. Peter Cartwright was directing the operation.

The helicopter landed on a lawn near the main house.

"Hello, Peter." Mark greeted him diffidently. "I'm so sorry about your parents, and the farm." It sounded inadequate.

Peter looked tired, and his face was covered in soot and grime. "Thank you." His clothing was soaked and dirty.

"I've come to see if I can help find Angie," Mark said simply.

"Ron's gone after them, and so have the Army." Peter wiped his brow, smearing more black marks across his haggard face. "The terrorists have definitely taken her with them."

"I'm sure your son will be OK; I understand he's a really crack soldier," Mark offered by way of comfort.

Peter turned back to supervising the farm workers with the fire, and Mark jogged back to the chopper.

The crew were busy talking to a policeman, but the pilot turned to Mark and said "There's some likely action reported up on the Mavuradonha Range."

"Can you get me there?"

"We'll get airborne, and see what we can do." They boarded the Alouette and lifted off.

* * *

The sun was well above the horizon, when Ron heard a chopper approaching. He'd just shot another terr. He struggled to concentrate.

326

That must mean there were only two of the bastards left. Yes... he'd killed or wounded four of the six who'd escaped on the pickup.

"Unnngh..." He shifted gingerly, and refilled the magazine on the 303, slotting one into the chamber. He'd run out of ammunition for the FN long ago. The pain in his guts was unbelievable. That's what they said about belly wounds; they were fucking painful – and potentially fatal. And he wasn't supposed to have anything to drink; not with a stomach wound. He parted his ripped shirt and looked down. The wound was gaping, and his intestines were bulging out. The stomach wall was damaged and leaking; he ignored the pain as he carefully pressed his guts back into the cavity. Probably a fatal, he decided. He was desperate for water. If he was going to die anyway, might as well have water... just a sip to quench his raging thirst. It was getting very hot – perhaps he had a fever?

As the helicopter flew slowly past, Ron waved from his position, in the vain hope that they might spot him. Shit... the pain was appalling. The chopper flew on. There was more activity in the terrs' position against the mountainside. He readied himself to fire again, but no one appeared. He found that resting on his stomach was the most comfortable position, probably because it held his intestines in place. Still no one visible at the terrs' hideaway. Had they made a run for it? They must have heard the chopper and gapped it. Bastards, they still had Angela. He couldn't leave her in their hands.

He sat up. Shit, it hurt. No one shot at him. He was right, they'd fucked off. He pushed his intestines into his belly cavity, and fastened his shirt tight around. Could keep going for hours if it stayed in place. He struggled to his feet and stood, swaying while he got a handle on the pain, and regained his balance. Vision swam back into focus. Better get going; those swine would be off over the border with Angela if he didn't get them. Just two to go, and the bastard Gadziwa one of them. He got across the road and into the riverine bush where the terrs had been holding out. They'd gone all right. He set off after them. The ache in his gut intensified...

* * *

"I'm pretty sure this is the lot you're after." The pilot loosened his headset and shouted to Mark over the clatter of the rotors. "It seems like there's been a fire-fight between a civilian, and quite a large group of terrs up in the Mavuradonha. An RLI fireforce is just going in."

"Can we get there?" Mark was sure the 'civilian' would be Ron Cartwright.

"We can get closer and I'll find out." They flew towards the mountain range.

"Shit, that civilian has shot four of the terrs, three of them dead" he said in amazement.

"Yes, I understand he's a pretty dedicated soldier."

"Oh... I thought he was a civvy."

"Well, yes. But he keeps signing up with the Territorials for more. Just joined some secret outfit, I believe."

"Wait, one..." the pilot listened in to his radio again, "the RLI are reporting that the surviving terrs have gapped it with the hostage. And that civvy has gone in after them." They flew to a sharp bend in the mountain road, where Mark could see another military helicopter lifting off. Presumably having discharged its load of soldiers.

"Can you get me onto the ground here?"

"I doubt the RLI will want you around just now, Mark. There are still two live terrs on the loose."

Christ, he just had to get there. Angie was still in their hands. Mark looked at the area below; the ravine at the apex of the bend in the road was caused by a waterfall and stream, flowing down the mountainside and under the road. A few hundred metres above it there was a level area, before the mountain rose up to its mean height along the range.

"OK, I can understand that," he said more reasonably than he felt, "but can you drop me off on that level piece of ground above the action, please?"

The pilot banked sharply. "We'll take a look." Mark checked his Tokarev for the umpteenth time. Much easier to carry than an FN.

"I could easily land there and drop you off, but I'm not sure the RLI will be too happy with me if I do."

"Please, I'll take full responsibility."

"How will you get back?" The pilot checked his instrument panel. "I've only got an hour's flying time left; I'll have to go up to Mount Darwin in 30 minutes to refuel."

"I'll climb down to the road, and hitch a lift with the Army," Mark said, easing himself towards the open door.

The pilot shook his head, but took the chopper down. "I'll get into deep shit for this, but here goes."

Mark found the top of the waterfall and began to pick his way down. It was thick with bush, and the rocks were treacherous. Some were wet; but the loose ones were the worst, and he lost his footing several times. He slowed down and became more cautious, using the thick vegetation to hold onto, and at the same time keeping his right hand free with the loaded pistol. He suspected the terrorists would be climbing up along the waterfall to escape Cartwright and the RLI below.

Pausing and listening every few metres, he'd been descending the ravine for quarter of an hour, when he heard a noise below. Moving, until he would have a good view of anyone approaching, he eased himself against a large rock and backed into the bush surrounding it. There it was again. Someone slipping on the rocks and crashing among the bushes.

"Owww! My feet are bleeding, I can't go any further," Angie's voice drifted up to Mark.

"Keep moving, Bitch!" He heard a slap and Angie cried out. The fucking bastards. His hands shook with anger as he rechecked his pistol; had to remember there were two of them.

The first terrorist moved into his line of vision, less than 30 metres away. A big bastard who was favouring his left leg. Must be injured, but he was managing to climb slowly up the riverbank. He was carrying an RPD. Now Angie appeared, followed by another African who seemed to be pushing her from behind. It looked as if her hands were tied together. No wonder she was stumbling. The man behind her seemed to be the one responsible for watching her. He was also armed with an RPD. Bad news. A pistol against two machine guns. He'd have to get the drop on them, or this would be a mess.

Must let them get close – very close – to be sure. Twenty metres – in spite of his injury, the big man was extending his lead on Angie and the man behind her. It looked as if she was deliberately slowing their progress. Good for her...

Mark wanted to get the guard first, but the leader was almost certain to see him as he walked past. He'd just have to do his best.

At 15 metres, Mark aimed the pistol at the man behind Angie. His finger tightened on the trigger but the leader stopped again... four or five metres from Mark.

The man turned back and shouted. "Get moving, Ncube. Pick her up and carry her if you have to."

Mark watched as the man called Ncube picked Angie up, and threw her over his shoulder. Angie cried out and kicked but her guard soon had her fast. He saw that her bare feet were in a bad state.

Bugger... It would be much more difficult to shoot the guard now, for fear of hitting Angie. More importantly, he was moving faster now and had taken the lead.

Mark had to focus on saving Angie first. That meant leaving the big terr, while he got her safely out of the way. It was dangerous but the only option. The terrorist carrying her kept his head down, minding his footing. Mark let him come right up, and fired two rounds point blank into the side of the bastard's chest; blood spewed from his mouth. He shoved the dead terrorist and Angie to the ground, and fell on top of them, expecting the big bastard to open up with the RPD. There was a long moment of silence.

"Oh, God, please help me," Angie called from under the dead man.

"Shush." He reached down, and found her hand. "It's me, Mark." Mark turned to look downstream. The terrorist had disappeared. Shit. This was not good; staying where they were was too risky, but he had no intention of leaving Angie alone while he went looking.

He pushed the dead terrorist aside. "Keep down, there's one still alive," he told her as Angie struggled free.

"Thank God you're here," Angie said. He helped her over to the bushes by the side of the ravine.

"Quiet. Get behind me." He shoved her deeper into the bush, behind a boulder. "One of them is still out there..."

"Oh no; please be careful. That's their leader and he's ruthless," she whispered, cringing further down into cover.

* * *

Ron heard a shot. It sounded like a nine-millimetre pistol. He had no idea which side had fired, because both terrorists and security forces used them. There was no answering shot, but he'd heard a chopper fly in above the re-entry earlier; and there was movement behind him. Probably the RLI. They were most likely approaching from above and below... Angela, the terrs and himself in between. Not an ideal position, but that was life, and he didn't have much left of that anyway. His guts were killing him and leaking all over the bloody place.

Shit! There was someone coming down the ravine towards him. He shrank almost gratefully against the bed of the river, the tiny stream trickling soothingly against his belly, cooling it. With the old 303-calibre rifle ready in one hand, he pulled out the heavy 45 revolver, and laid it within easy reach of his right hand.

There it was again; the figure was attempting to conceal itself but not making a very good job of it. Of course, it could be one of the soldiers – possibly even Angela. No, the figure was too bulky. Christ he hoped she was OK. The children would need her, especially when he was gone. He was tired now and his eyes lost focus. Wake up, damn you. He swore at himself and, with an effort, refocused.

A massive boot swung across his vision and kicked the rifle out of his hand. Ron knew it was Gadziwa. He swung aside and an RPD barrel struck against the rock he'd been resting his head on a moment before. The heavy body fell, crushing the wind out of him and he felt his belly split further open. This was the end. After everything, Gadziwa had got the drop on him. He reached out and grabbed the 45. With the last of his strength, he twisted round and fired, with the barrel right up against the massive black form that blocked out the light. He fired again, and again. The revolver was too heavy for him, and he felt his bloodied fingers slipping.

* * *

Mark cut the ropes from Angie's wrists and kept her sheltered behind him, while maintaining a watch from their boulder for what seemed like ages. They heard gunfire from somewhere down the mountainside, back where Angie had come from. He hoped the Army had got that last terrorist, but couldn't take the chance.

They waited another quarter of an hour. At last two soldiers arrived from below.

"Thank God you're here," Mark greeted them.

"Christ, another fucking civvy," one exclaimed. "What the hell are you doing here?" The other one went to look at the terrorist Mark had killed.

Mark was too relieved to get angry. But it was a damn stupid question. "Never mind what I'm doing here. There's a bloody dangerous terrorist around here somewhere, and I've got an injured woman with me." Angie sat up.

"There was. This one here is the last one. Another civvy got the other one down there-aways. Now they're all accounted for." He spoke into his radio. When he completed his report, he turned to Angie.

"You OK, Miss?" he asked politely but appraising. Angie nodded. "Please stay where you are for the moment," he told her.

The soldier took Mark aside. "Who are you to this lady, sir?" he asked deferentially.

Mark thought for a moment. "She's my cousin, why?"

"Is she Mrs Cartwright?"

"Yes." Mark saw apprehension mixed with relief in the soldier's face.

"Her husband. The bloke who got Big Feet is down there." The soldier indicated downstream. "He's very badly wounded, probably a fatal. We don't think he'll last much longer."

Christ, Mark felt sick, but the soldier continued "Bloody brave bastard though, and tough as hell. He followed the terrs up the river here, even with a belly wound. Christ knows how he did it. It must have been fucking painful," he shook his head. "I wouldn't have believed anyone could do that if I hadn't seen it with my own eyes."

Mark had to face Angie, now… "Darling, I've got some bad news for you."

She turned her tired face towards him. "What is it? It can't be all that bad, you've saved my life."

"It's Ron, sweetheart. He's very badly injured."

"Oh, my God." She went pale. "Where is he?"

"He was the one who really saved you. He's not far from here."

"I have to go to him."

"Of course. But I must tell you, the soldier thinks it's fatal."

* * *

Angie followed a soldier back down the waterfall. She slipped and skidded on the wet rocks, her feet didn't hurt anymore. They said Ronnie was dying, and she had to get to him. Mark was trying to help her. Sometimes he was able to stop her falling.

"Please be careful, Miss, you'll injure yourself," the soldier said. But she ignored him. She had to reach Ron as soon as she could.

They got back down to the clearing where there'd been the shootout. Angie looked around in panic. There, a helicopter was landing in the road. A group of soldiers were hunkered down over a stretcher. She wrenched herself from the soldier's grip, and ran up to the group to kneel in the dust beside it. "Ronnie, it's me, Angela," she said, touching his face. He looked dead already, so pallid and so still.

His eyes flickered open. "Angela," he whispered.

Her tears ran, "I'm here, Ronnie." Thank God. He was alive.

"I got Big Feet Gadziwa, Angela," he said, his face contorting. The medic stood up holding a drip, and nodded to the two soldiers to lift the stretcher.

"Wait!" Ron shouted. "Dammit." The soldiers stopped.

"We have to get going, sir," the medic said. "The chopper's waiting and we need to get you to hospital, fast."

Angie reached out and took Ron's hand in hers. "Yes... you got him. You saved my life too, Ronnie. Thank you."

He nodded, saying nothing.

"The medic's right. They have to get you to hospital." She looked up at the man. "Can I go with him?"

He shook his head. "Sorry miss, there's only just enough room for his stretcher and us two medics."

"That's OK," Ronnie spoke again. "Follow in the next chopper if you like."

"I'll follow, and be with you as soon as I can, Ronnie," she said before they took him away; it might have been the morphine, but she could swear there was a smile on his face.

Chapter 37

The three young women walked through the unkempt cemetery, ahead of Angie and Kate. Each carried a single rose. Angie had kept her promise. Every year for the past ten years, Emma, Joanne and Helen came up from their home in Stellenbosch to visit their Cartwright grandparents. Against all the odds, Ronnie had survived until his luck had finally run out. Still obsessed with his personal war against terrorists, he'd been killed on active service in 1979, not long before the end of the war. Angie thought it was probably a blessing that he hadn't lived to see the terrorists win. She still wondered if he'd realised the futility of it all towards the end.

They stopped at the granite headstone. This was the fourth anniversary of his death, and Angie could see that Kate still found it painful.

Emma was first to bend down, pulling the weeds and grass from around the grave. Her sisters soon joined her. When they'd finished, they gently laid down their flowers. Angie stepped back as Kate added a spray of scarlet hibiscus from Sapphire Blue. The girls didn't cry anymore but Angie put her arm around Joanne, who still seemed most affected.

A huge crowd of Africans had gathered some distance away, beyond the headstones. They were singing freedom songs. Most had come by bus, but VIPs arrived in a cavalcade. Prime Minister Robert Mugabe himself followed in a limousine, accompanied by outriders. Everyone had been required to stop as he approached and swept by. She and Kate exchanged glances. They didn't want to attract unwanted attention.

Mugabe's voice came over the loudspeakers. "Comrades. We are gathered here…" the cold wind snatched his voice away, "… honour our fallen comrades…" The murmur of the crowd rose and drowned his voice, "… we salute our brother, Comrade *Gumbarishumba Gadziwa*…" The choreographed voice of the crowd rose to a roar of approval. Gadziwa… Angie lifted her head at the sound of his name.

She tensed, trying to control a shudder at the memory. Another re-interment. Another veteran hero.

They turned and walked slowly towards the car park, but they'd hardly left Ron's headstone when a ragged African man approached them. He was not part of the ceremony in the smartly maintained Heroes' Acre. Here, where Ron was buried, the place had an abandoned feel to it.

"Sakubona Nkosikaas." The man greeted them, but Angie could see he was addressing Kate. He wore an old Army greatcoat, probably dating back to the Second World War, protecting him from the wind. Skinny arms and hands projected from the sleeves and he looked unwell.

"Greetings" Kate said in English. "What can I do for you?"

"You are Mrs Cartwright?"

"Yes."

Now Angie recognised him – he was Sergeant Mike Njube, aged terribly.

"I knew your son, Lieutenant Cartwright. We fought together, side by side... he was a man."

"What is your name?" Kate asked. Angie and the three girls looked on with interest.

The old man glanced over his shoulder before he replied. "I have no name... I am Ndebele, and I fought on the white man's side."

Angie saw Kate's eyes light up in recognition. "You were the sergeant in my son's platoon..."

"Yes, Mrs Cartwright. I was Sergeant Mike Njube." He opened his greatcoat carefully and showed Kate the medals on his chest. "I was later promoted to captain. Before the terrorists took power."

"You must come with me. There is a place for you at the farm if you want it. You will be cared for, and you can send for your family."

"No," he shook his head slowly, "but I thank you. I have come here for the last time to say farewell to my friend before I go to join my ancestors. I will die before the year ends. Mugabe's Fifth Brigade massacred all my family. There is nothing left for me to live for." He saluted them and half turned. "Mrs Cartwright, Miss Angela..." He seemed to be struggling with his thoughts.

"What is it, Captain Njube?"

His eyes were anxious. "You must leave this evil place. Mugabe and his Shona dogs will take your farm and kill you and your family;

and rape the children. Just like they have already done to mine." He spoke quietly; Angie guessed he didn't want the girls to hear. He probably thought they still lived here in Zimbabwe. Now he turned, and she watched him straighten up and stride away. His words lingered in her head. Prophetic? Poor Kate wouldn't want to think about leaving her home, her country. Angie closed her eyes. All those who had already left. All those planning to leave. And... all those who had died. They had become the Scatterlings of Africa.

The End